RaeAnne Thayne finds inspiration in the beautiful northern Utah mountains, where the *New York Times* and *USA TODAY* bestselling author lives with her husband and three children. Her books have won numerous honours, including RITA® Award nominations from Romance Writers of America and a Career Achievement Award from *RT Book Reviews*. RaeAnne loves to hear from readers and can be contacted through her website, www.raeannethayne.com.

Award-winning author **Kate Hardy** lives in Norwich with her husband, two children, one spaniel and too many books to count! She's a fan of the theater, ballroom dancing, posh chocolate and anything Italian. She's a history and science geek, plays the guitar and piano and makes great cookies (which is why she also has to go to the gym five days a week. . .)

Two-time Golden Heart Award finalist **Ami Weaver** has been reading romance since she was a teen and writing for even longer, so it was only natural she would put the two together. Now she can be found drinking gallons of iced tea at her local coffee shop while doing one of her very favourite things—convincing two characters they deserve their happy-ever-after. Ami lives in Michigan with her four kids, three cats and her very supportive husband.

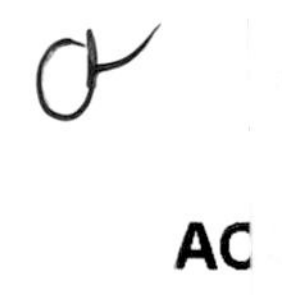

A Mistletoe Vow

RaeAnne THAYNE
KATE HARDY
AMI WEAVER

MILLS & BOON

First Published in Great Britain 2018
by Mills & Boon, an imprint of HarperCollins*Publishers*
1 London Bridge Street, London, SE1 9GF

ISBN: 978-0-263-27468-4

1218

MIX
Paper from responsible sources
FSC™ C007454

This book is produced from independently certified FSC™ paper to ensure responsible forest management.

For more information visit: www.harpercollins.co.uk/green

Printed and bound in Spain
by CPI, Barcelona

A COLD CREEK CHRISTMAS STORY

RAEANNE THAYNE

Chapter One

If she didn't have thirty children showing up in the next half hour, Celeste Nichols would have been tempted to climb into her little SUV, pull out of the Pine Gulch library parking lot and just keep on driving.

She shifted the blasted endlessly ringing cell phone to the crook of her shoulder while she sorted through the books scattered across her cubicle in the offices of the library to find what she would be reading for story hour.

"I told you earlier in the week, I'm not ready to make a decision about this yet."

Joan Manning, her and Hope's long-suffering literary agent, gave a low, frustrated sound of disapproval. "We can't hold them off much longer. We've already stalled for two weeks. They want to start production right after the holidays, and they can't do that without signatures from you and Hope."

Celeste gazed down at a copy of Dr. Seuss's perennial holiday favorite, *How the Grinch Stole Christmas*. She had a feeling she was the one being the Grinch here. Hope was completely on board with the extraordinary offer one of the leading animation companies had made for movie rights to their book, *Sparkle and the Magic Snowball*.

Celeste was the one who couldn't quite be comfortable with the idea of someone else taking control of her words, her creation, and turning *Sparkle* into an animated movie, complete with the attendant merchandising and sublicensing. A fast-food chain was already talking about making a toy for its kids' meals, for crying out loud.

The whole journey of the past twelve months seemed like a bizarre, surreal, completely unbelievable dream.

A year ago she had known exactly who she was—an unassuming children's librarian in the small town of Pine Gulch, Idaho, in the western shadow of the Teton Mountain Range.

Now, to her immense shock, she was a celebrated author about to see the release of her second children's book with several more scheduled in the next few years. Along with that had come things she had never imagined when she'd been writing little stories for her niece and nephew—she had a website, a publicist, a literary agent.

Her quiet, safe world seemed to be spinning out of her control, and this movie deal was the prime example.

"A few more days, Celeste," Joan pushed. "You can't keep stalling. You have to make a decision. Hollywood has a short attention span and an even shorter supply of patience. Do you want your story made into a movie or not?"

She liked Joan very much, as brash and abrupt as the woman could be, but everything with her was an emergency and had to be decided *right now.* Pressure pains stabbed with little forks behind her eyes and her shoulders felt as if someone had jammed them in a vice and was cranking down hard.

"I know. I just need to be sure this is the right choice for Sparkle."

"Sparkle is a fictional character. You need to be sure it's the right choice for *you* and for your sister. We've been going over this for weeks. I don't know what else I can say to convince you this is the best deal you're going to get."

"I know that. You've done a great job with the negotiations. I just need…a little morc time."

"A few days," Joan said, her voice clipped with frustration. "That's all, then I have to give them some kind of an answer."

"I know. Thank you. I'll get back with you tomorrow or the day after."

"Just remember, most people would see this as a dream come true."

Apparently, she wasn't *most people.* After they said their goodbyes, Celeste set her cell phone back on the desk, again fighting the urge to climb into her SUV and keep on driving.

That was her sister Hope's way, to wander from place to place as they had done in their itinerant childhood. Celeste was different. She liked security, consistency. *Normalcy.*

In the past twelve months her life had been anything *but* normal. She had gone from writing only for herself and her niece and nephew to writing for a vast audience she never could have imagined.

It had all started when her sister Hope had come home

the previous Christmas for what was supposed to be a brief stay between overseas teaching jobs. Hope had overheard her reading one of her stories to Louisa and Barrett and had put her considerable artistic skills to work illustrating the story to sell in the gift store of their family's holiday-themed attraction, The Christmas Ranch.

The result had been a sweet, charming Christmas story about a brave little reindeer named Sparkle. Neither Hope nor Celeste had ever imagined the book would be touted by a presenter on one of the national morning news program—or that the resulting sales would explode internationally and end up saving the floundering Christmas Ranch *and* the family's cattle operation, the Star N Ranch.

She was beyond gratified that so many people liked her writing and the story—and especially Hope's delightful illustrations—but some part of her wanted to go back to that peaceful time when her biggest decisions revolved around what to read for her weekly story hour at the Pine Gulch Public Library.

With a sigh, she turned back to the job at hand. She was still sorting through the final choices when the head librarian poked her head into the cubicle.

"Looks as if we're going to have a nice crowd." Frankie Vittori, the head librarian, looked positively gleeful. "I hope we have room for everybody."

"Oh, that's terrific!" she exclaimed, mentally shelving her worries about the movie deal for now.

She meant the words. She loved nothing more than introducing children to the wonder and magic to be found inside the pages of a good book.

Books had saved her. During the chaos of her childhood, they had offered solace and safety and *hope* amid fear. She had no idea how she would have survived without friends such as Anne of Green Gables, Bilbo Baggins, Matilda, Harry Potter and Hermione and Ron Weasley.

"I only hope we've got enough of our craft project to go around. It seems as if the crowd increases every month."

Frankie grinned. "That's because everybody in town wants to come hear our local celebrity author read in hopes of catching a sneak peek at the new Sparkle story coming down the pike."

She managed to conceal her instinctive wince. She really didn't like being a celebrity.

On one level, it was immensely gratifying. Who would have ever dreamed that she—quiet, awkward, introverted Celeste Nichols—would be in this position, having people actually *care* what she had to say?

On another, it was terrifying. At some point the naked emperor was always exposed. She feared the day when somebody would finally ask why all the fuss about her simple little tales.

For now, Frankie was simply thrilled to have a crowd at the library for any kind of reason. Celeste's boss and friend vibrated with energy, as she always did, her toe tapping to unheard music and her fingers fidgeting on the edge of the desk. Frankie was as skinny as a flagpole, probably because she never stopped moving.

Her husband, Lou, on the other hand, was the exact opposite—a deep reservoir of calm serenity.

They made the perfect pair and had two adorable kids who fell somewhere in the middle.

"I know it's more work for you," Frankie went on. "But I have to say, it's a brilliant idea to have two story times, one for the younger kids in the morning and one for early and middle readers after school."

Celeste smiled. "If you do say so yourself?"

Frankie beamed. "What can I say? I'm brilliant sometimes."

"That you are." Since Frankie had come to the library from upstate New York two years earlier, patron usage was way up and support had never been higher.

Frankie was bold and impassioned about the need for libraries, especially in the digital age. Celeste was more than a little envious of her overwhelming confidence, which helped the director fight for every penny of funding from the city council and the community in general.

Celeste would never be as outgoing and vivacious as Frankie, even though she was every bit as passionate about her job as the children's librarian. She liked being behind the scenes—except for the weekly story times, her favorite part of the job.

She checked her watch and quickly stood up. "I guess I'd better get out there."

She picked up the box of craft supplies they would use for the activity she had planned and headed for the large meeting room they had found worked best for story times.

"Oh, I almost forgot," Frankie said with a sly grin. "Make sure you check out the major hottie dad out there at ten o'clock."

Despite her amazing husband, Frankie was always locating hot guys, whether at their weekly lunches at one of the restaurants in town or on the few trips they'd taken into Jackson Hole or Idaho Falls. She always said she was only scouting possible dates for Celeste, which made Celeste roll her eyes. Her last date had been months ago.

"Is he anybody I know?"

"*I've* never seen him before. He's either new in town or a tourist. You can't miss him. He's wearing a Patek Philippe watch and a brown leather jacket that probably costs as much as our annual nonfiction budget. He's definitely not your average Cold Creek cowboy with horse pucky on his boots."

Okay, intriguing. She hadn't heard of anybody new moving into the small town, especially not someone who could afford the kind of attire Frankie was talking about. Sometimes well-to-do people bought second or third homes in the area, looking for a mountain getaway. They built beautiful homes in lovely alpine settings and then proceeded to visit them once or twice a year.

"I'll be sure to check him out while I'm trying to keep the kids entertained."

Frankie was right about one thing—the place was packed. Probably thirty children ranging in age from about six to eleven sat on the floor while roughly that same number of parents sat in chairs around the room.

For just an instant she felt a burst of stage fright at the idea of all those people staring at her. She quickly pushed it down. Normally she didn't like being in front of a crowd, but this was her job and she loved it. How could she be nervous about reading stories to children? She would just pretend their parents weren't there, like she usually did.

When she walked in, she was heartened by the spontaneous round of applause and the anticipation humming in the air.

She spotted a few people she recognized, friends and neighbors. Joey Santiago, nephew to her brother-in-law Rafe, sat beside his father, waving wildly at her.

She grinned and waved back at him. She would have

thought Rafe was the hot dad—all that former navy SEAL mojo he had going on—but Frankie knew him well and he wasn't wearing a leather jacket or an expensive watch anyway.

She loved Rafe dearly, for many reasons—most important because he adored her sister Hope—but also because she wasn't sure she would be standing here, ready to entertain a group of thirty children with the magic of literature if not for his role in their lives so many years ago.

She saw a few other hot dads in the crowd—Justin Hartford, who used to be a well-known movie star but who seemed to fit in better now that he had been a rancher in Cold Creek Canyon for years. Ben Caldwell, the local veterinarian, was definitely hot. Then there was the fire chief, Taft Bowman, and his stepchildren. Taft always looked as though he could be the December cover model on a calendar of yummy firefighters.

All of them were locals of long-standing, though, and Frankie knew them well. They couldn't be the man she was talking about.

Ah, well. She would try to figure out the mystery later, maybe while the children were making the snowman ornaments she had planned for them.

"Thank you so much for coming, everybody. We're going to start off with one of my favorite Christmas stories."

"Is it *Sparkle and the Magic Snowball*?" Alex Bowman, Taft's stepson, asked hopefully.

She blushed a little as everyone laughed. "Not today. Today we're focusing on stories about Christmas, snow and snowmen."

Ben's son raised his hand. "Is Sparkle going to be here today, Ms. Nichols?"

Was that why so many people had turned out? Were they all hoping she'd brought along the *actual* Sparkle, who was the celebrity in residence at The Christmas Ranch?

Last year, Hope had talked her into having their family's beloved reindeer—and the inspiration for her eponymously named series of stories—make a quick appearance in the parking lot of the library.

"I'm afraid not. He's pretty busy at The Christmas Ranch right now."

She tried to ignore the small sounds of disappointment from the children and a few of their parents. "I've got tons of other things in store for you, though. To start out, here's one of everyone's favorite holiday stories, *How the Grinch Stole Christmas.*"

She started reading and, as usual, it only took a few pages before a hush fell over the room. The children were completely enthralled—not by her, she was only the vehicle, but by the power of story.

She became lost, too, savoring every word. When she neared the climax, she looked up for dramatic effect and found the children all watching her with eager expressions, ready for more. Her gaze lifted to the parents and she spotted someone she hadn't seen before, a man sitting on the back row of parents with a young girl beside him.

He had brown hair shot through with lighter streaks, a firm jaw and deep blue eyes.

This had to be the hot dad Frankie had meant.

Her heart began to pound fiercely, so loud in her ears she wondered if the children could hear it over the microphone clipped to her collar.

She knew this man, though she hadn't seen him for years.

Flynn Delaney.

She would recognize him *anywhere*. After all, he had been the subject of her daydreams all through her adolescence.

She hadn't heard he was back in Pine Gulch. Why was he here? Was he staying at his grandmother's house just down the road from the Star N? It made sense. His grandmother, Charlotte, had died several months earlier and her house had been empty ever since.

She suddenly remembered everything else that had happened to this man in the past few months and her gaze shifted to the young girl beside him, blonde and ethereal like a Christmas angel herself.

Celeste's heart seemed to melt.

This must be her. His daughter. Oh, the poor, poor dear.

The girl was gazing back at Celeste with her eyes wide and her hands clasped together at her chest as if she couldn't wait another instant to hear the rest of the story.

Everyone was gazing at her with expectation, and Celeste realized she had stopped in the middle of the story to stare at Flynn and his daughter.

Appalled at herself, she felt heat soak her cheeks. She cleared her throat and forced her attention back to the story, reading the last few pages with rather more heartiness than she had started with.

This was her job, she reminded herself as she closed the book, helping children discover all the delights to be found in good stories.

She wasn't here to ogle Flynn Delaney, for heaven's sake, even when there was plenty about him any woman would consider ogle-worthy.

* * *

Flynn didn't think he had ever felt quite so conspicuously out of place—and that included the times he had walked the red carpet with Elise at some Hollywood premiere or other, when he had invariably wanted to fade into the background.

They all seemed to know each other and he felt like the odd man out. Was everybody staring? He didn't want to think so, but he seemed to feel each curious sidelong glance as the residents of Pine Gulch tried to figure out who he was.

At least one person knew. He was pretty sure he hadn't imagined that flicker of recognition in Celeste Nichols's eyes when she'd spotted him. It surprised him, he had to admit. They had only met a few times, all those years ago.

He only remembered her because she had crashed her bike in front of his grandmother's house during one of his visits. Charlotte hadn't been home, so Flynn had been left to tend her scrapes and bruises and help her get back to the Star N up the road.

Things like that stuck in a guy's memory bank. Otherwise he probably never would have made the connection between the author of his daughter's favorite book, *Sparkle and the Magic Snowball*, and the shy girl with long hair and glasses he had once known in another lifetime.

He wouldn't be here at the library if not for Celeste, actually. He had so much work to do clearing out his grandmother's house and really didn't have time to listen to Dr. Seuss, as great as the story might be, but what other choice did he have? Since leaving the hospital, Olivia had been a pale, frightened shadow of the girl she used to be. Once she had faced the world head-on, daring and curious and funny. Now she was afraid of so many things. Loud noises. Strangers. Crowds.

From the moment she'd found out that the author of her favorite book lived here in Pine Gulch where they were staying for a few weeks—and was the children's librarian, who also hosted a weekly story hour—Olivia had been obsessed with coming. She had written the date of the next event on the calendar and had talked of nothing else.

She was finally going to meet the Sparkle lady, and she couldn't have been more excited about it if Celeste Nichols had been Mrs. Santa Claus in the flesh.

For the first time in weeks she showed enthusiasm for something, and he had jumped at the chance to nurture that.

He glanced down at his daughter. She hadn't shifted her gaze away from Celeste, watching the librarian with clear hero worship on her features. She seemed utterly enchanted by the librarian.

The woman was lovely, he would give her that much, though in a quiet, understated way. She had big green eyes behind her glasses and glossy dark hair that fell in waves around a heart-shaped face.

She was probably about four years younger than his own thirty-two. That didn't seem like much now, but when she had crashed her bike, she had seemed like a little kid, thirteen or so to his seventeen.

As he listened to her read now, he remembered that time, wondering why it seemed so clear to him, especially with everything that had happened to him since.

He'd been out mowing the lawn when she'd fallen and had seen her go down out of the corner of his gaze. Flynn had hurried to help her and found her valiantly trying not to cry even though she had a wide gash in her knee that would definitely need stitches and pebbles imbedded in her palm.

He had helped her into his grandmother's house and called her aunt Mary. While they'd waited for help, he had found first-aid supplies—bandages, ointment, cleansing wipes—and told her lousy jokes to distract her from the pain.

After Mary had taken her to the ER for stitches in her knee and he had finished mowing for his grandmother, he had gone to work fixing her banged-up bike with skills he had picked up from his mother's chauffeur.

Later that day, he had dropped off the bike at the Star N, and she had been almost speechless with gratitude. Or maybe she just had been shy with older guys; he didn't know.

He had stayed with his grandmother for just a few more weeks that summer, but whenever he had seen Celeste in town at the grocery store or the library, she had always blushed fiercely and offered him a shy but sweet smile.

Now he found himself watching her intently, hoping for a sight of that same sweet smile, but she seemed to be focusing with laser-like intensity on the books in front of her.

She read several more holiday stories to the children, then led them all to one side of the large room, where tables had been set up.

"I need all the children to take a seat," she said in a prim voice he found incongruously sexy. "We're going to make snowman ornaments for you to hang on your tree. When you're finished, they'll look like this."

She held up a stuffed white sock with buttons glued on

to it for eyes and a mouth, and a piece of felt tied around the neck for a scarf.

"Oh," Olivia breathed. "That's so cute! Can I make one, Dad?"

Again, how could he refuse? "Sure, if there are enough to go around."

She limped to a seat and he propped up the wall along with a few other parents so the children each could have a spot at a table. Celeste and another woman with a library name badge passed out supplies and began issuing instructions.

Olivia looked a little helpless at first and then set to work. She seemed to forget for the moment that she rarely used her left hand. Right now she was holding the sock with that hand while she shoved in pillow fluff stuffing with the other.

While the children were busy crafting, Celeste made her way around the tables, talking softly to each one of them.

Finally she came to them.

"Nice job," she said to his daughter. Ah, there it was. She gave Olivia that sweet, unguarded smile that seemed to bloom across her face like the first violets of springtime.

That smile turned her from a lovely if average-looking woman into a breathtaking creature with luminous skin and vivid green eyes.

He couldn't seem to stop staring at her, though he told himself he was being ridiculous.

"You're the Sparkle lady, aren't you?" Olivia breathed.

Color rose instantly in her cheeks and she gave a surprised laugh. "I suppose that's one way to put it."

"I love that story. It's my favorite book *ever.*"

"I'm so happy to hear that." She smiled again, though he thought she looked a little uncomfortable. "Sparkle is pretty close to my heart, too."

"My dad bought a brand-new copy for me when I was in the hospital, even though I had one at home."

She said the words in a matter-of-fact tone as if the stay had been nothing more than a minor inconvenience. He knew better. She had spent two weeks clinging to life in intensive care after an infection had ravaged her system, where he had measured his life by each breath the machines took for her.

Most of the time he did a pretty good job of containing his impotent fury at the senseless violence that had touched his baby girl, but every once in a while the rage swept over him like a brushfire on dry tinder. He let out a breath as he felt a muscle flex in his jaw.

"Is that right?" Celeste said with a quick look at him.

"It's my very favorite book," Olivia said again, just in case Celeste didn't hear. "Whenever I had to do something I didn't want to, like have my blood tested or go to physical therapy, I would look at the picture of Sparkle on the last page with all his friends and it would make me feel better."

At Olivia's words, Celeste's big eyes filled with tears and she rocked back on her heels a little. "Oh. That's... lovely. Thank you so much for letting me know. I can't tell you how much that means to me."

"You're welcome," Olivia said with a solemn smile. "My favorite part is when Sparkle helps the animals with their Christmas celebration. The hedgehog is my favorite."

"He's cute, isn't he?"

The two of them gazed at each other in perfect charity

for a moment longer before a boy with blond hair and a prominent widow's peak tried to draw Celeste's attention.

"Ms. Nichols. Hey, Ms. Nichols. How do we glue on the hat?"

"I'll show you. Just a minute." She turned back to Olivia. "It was very nice to meet you. You're doing a great job with your snowman. Thanks for letting me know you enjoy the book."

"You're welcome."

When she left, Olivia turned back to her project with renewed effort. She was busy gluing on the button eyes when the woman beside Flynn finally spoke to him.

"You're new in town. I don't think we've met." She was blonde and pretty in a classic sort of way, with a baby on her hip. "I'm Caroline Dalton. This is my daughter, Lindy. Over there is my son, Cole."

He knew the Daltons. They owned much of the upper portion of Cold Creek Canyon. Which brother was she married to?

"Hello. I'm Flynn Delaney, and this is my daughter, Olivia. We're not really new in town. That is, we're not staying anyway. We're here just for a few weeks, and then we're going back to California."

"I hope you feel welcome here. This is a lovely place to spend the holidays."

"I'm sure it is, but we're not really tourists, either. I'm cleaning out my grandmother's home so I can put it up for sale."

He could have hired someone to come and clean out the house. There were companies that handled exactly that sort of thing, but as he and Olivia were Charlotte's only surviving descendants, he'd felt obligated to go through the house himself.

"Delaney. Oh, Charlotte! She must have been your grandmother."

"That's right."

Her features turned soft and a little sad. "Oh, everyone adored your grandmother. What a firecracker she was! Pine Gulch just doesn't feel the same without her."

His *life* didn't feel the same, either. He hadn't seen her often the past few years, just quick semiannual visits, but she had been a steady source of affection and warmth in his chaotic life.

He had barely had the chance to grieve her passing. That bothered him more than anything else. He hadn't even been ablc to attend the memorial service members of her church congregation had held for her here. He had been too busy in the ICU, praying for his daughter's life.

"I miss her, too," he said quietly.

She looked at him with kindness and warmth. "I'm sure you do. She was an amazing person and I feel blessed to have known her. If you need help sorting through things, please let me know. I'm sure we could find people to give you a hand."

With only a little more than a week to go before Christmas? He doubted that. People were probably too busy to help.

He didn't bother to express his cynicism to Caroline Dalton. "Thanks," he said instead.

"Despite your difficult task, I hope you're able to find a little holiday spirit while you're here."

Yeah, he wasn't a huge Christmas fan for a whole slew of reasons, but he saw no reason to share that with a woman he'd just met.

"Daddy, I can't tie the scarf. Can you help me?" Olivia asked.

She *could* use her left arm and hand. He'd seen her do it at therapy or when she lost herself in an activity, but most of the time she let it hang down uselessly. He didn't know how to force her into using it.

"Try again," he said.

"I can't. It's too hard," she answered plaintively. He sighed, not wanting to push her unnecessarily and ruin her tentative enjoyment of the afternoon.

He leaned down to help her tie the felt scarf just as Celeste made her way back around the table to them.

"I love that snowman!" she exclaimed with a smile. "He looks very friendly."

Olivia's answering smile seemed spontaneous and genuine. Right then Flynn wanted to hug Celeste Nichols on the spot, even though he hadn't talked to her for nearly two decades.

His little girl hadn't had much to smile about over the past few months. He had to hope this was a turning point, a real chance for her to return to his sweet and happy daughter.

At this point, he was willing to bring Olivia to the library every single day if Celeste could help his daughter begin to heal her battered heart.

Chapter Two

She was late.

By the time she helped the last little boy finish his snowman, ushered them all out of the meeting room and then cleaned up the mess of leftover pillow stuffing and fleece remnants, it was forty minutes past the time she had told her sisters to expect her.

They would understand, she was sure. Hope might tease her a little, but Faith probably wouldn't say anything. Their eldest sister saved her energy for the important things like running the cattle ranch and taking care of her children.

She stopped first at the foreman's little cottage, just down the driveway from the main house. It felt strange to be living on her own again after the past year of being back in her own bedroom there. She had moved back after her brother-in-law Travis died the previous summer so she could help Faith—and Aunt Mary, of course—with the children and the housekeeping.

Hope had lived briefly in the foreman's house until she and Rafe married this fall. After she'd moved into the house they purchased together, Faith and Mary had taken Celeste aside and informed her firmly that she needed her own space to create. She was a bestselling author now. While Faith loved and appreciated her dearly, she didn't want Celeste to think she had to live at the ranch house for the rest of her life.

Rather reluctantly, she had moved to the foreman's cottage, a nice compromise. She did like her own space and the quiet she found necessary to write, but she was close enough to pop into the ranch house several times a day.

As she walked inside, her little Yorkie, Linus, rolled over with glee at the sight of her.

She had to smile, despite her exhaustion from a long day, the lingering stress from the phone call with Joan and the complete shock of seeing Flynn Delaney once more.

"How was your day?" she asked the little dog, taking just a moment to sink onto the sofa and give him a little love. "Mine was *crazy*. Thanks for asking. The weirdest I've had in a long time—and that's saying something, since the entire past year has been surreal."

She hugged him for a moment. As she might have predicted, a sleek black cat peeked her head around the corner to see what all the fuss was about.

Lucy, who had been with her since college, strutted in with a haughty air that only lasted long enough for her to leap onto the sofa and bat her head against Celeste's arm for a little of the same attention.

The two pets were the best of friends, which helped

her feel less guilty about leaving them alone during the day. They seemed to have no problem keeping each other company most of the time, but that didn't stop them from exhibiting classic signs of sibling rivalry at random moments.

She felt her tension trickle away as she sat in her quiet living room with her creatures while the Christmas tree lights that came on automatically gleamed in the gathering darkness. Why couldn't she stay here all evening? There were worse ways to spend a December night.

Linus yipped a little, something he didn't do often, but it reminded her of why she had stopped at the house.

"I know. I'm late. I just have to grab Aunt Mary's present. Give me a second."

She found the gift in her bedroom closet, the door firmly shut to keep Lucy from pulling apart the tissue paper inside the gift bag.

"Okay. I'm ready. Let's go."

Linus's tail wagged with excitement, but Lucy curled up on the sofa, making abundantly clear her intent to stay put and not venture out into the cold night.

"Fine. Be that way," she said, opening the door for the dog. The two of them made their way through lightly falling snow to the ranch house, a sprawling log structure with a steep roof and three gables along the front. Linus scampered ahead of her to the front door. When she opened it, the delicious scents of home greeted her—roast beef, potatoes and what smelled very much like cinnamon apple pie.

As she expected, her entire family was there, all the people she loved best in the world. Aunt Mary, the guest of honor, was busy at the stove stirring something that smelled like her heavenly brown gravy. She stepped aside to let Faith pull a pan of rolls out of the oven as Hope helped the children set the table, where her husband, Rafe, sat talking with their neighbor Chase Brannon.

The children spotted Linus first. They all adored each other—in fact, the children helped her out by letting him out when they got home from school and playing with him for a little bit.

"There you are," Faith exclaimed. "I was beginning to worry."

"Sorry. I sent you a text."

Faith made a face. "My phone ran out of juice sometime this afternoon, but I didn't realize it until just now. Is everything okay?"

Not really, though she wasn't sure what bothered her more—the movie decision she would have to make in the next few days or the reappearance of Flynn Delaney in her world. She couldn't seem to shake the weird feeling that her safe, comfortable world was about to change.

"Fine," she said evasively. "I hope you didn't hold dinner for me."

"Not really. I was tied up going over some ranch accounts with Chase this afternoon, and we lost track of time."

"Fine. Blame me. I can take it," Chase said, overhearing.

"We always do," Hope said with a teasing grin.

Chase had been invaluable to their family since Faith's husband died, and Celeste was deeply grateful to him for all his help during the subsequent dark and difficult months.

"I'm happy to blame you, as long as that means I wasn't the cause of any delay in Aunt Mary's birthday celebration," Celeste said with a smile as she headed for her great-aunt.

She kissed the woman's lined cheek as the familiar scent of Mary's favorite White Shoulders perfume washed over her. "Happy birthday, my dear. You are still just as stunning as ever."

Mary's grin lit up her nut-brown eyes. "Ha. Double sevens. That's got to be lucky, right?"

"Absolutely."

"I don't need luck. I've got my family around me, don't I?"

She smiled at them all and Celeste hugged her again, deeply grateful for her great-aunt and her great-uncle Claude, who had opened their hearts to three grieving, traumatized girls and gave them a warm haven and all the love they could need.

"We're the lucky ones," she murmured with another hug before she stepped away.

For all intents and purposes, Mary had been her mother since Celeste turned eleven. She had been a wonderful one. Celeste was all too aware that things could have been much different after their parents died if not for Mary and Claude. She and her sisters probably would have been thrown into the foster care system, likely separated, certainly not nurtured and cared for with such love.

She had a sudden, unexpected wish that their mother could be here, just for a moment, to see how her daughters had turned out—to meet her grandchildren, to see Hope so happily settled with Rafe, to see the completely unexpected success of their Sparkle book.

December always left her a little maudlin. She supposed that wasn't unexpected, considering it had been the month that had changed everything, when she, her sisters and their parents had been hostages of a rebel group in Colombia. Her father had been killed in the rescue effort by a team of US Navy SEALs that had included Rafe Santiago, who was now her brother-in-law.

She wouldn't think about that now. This was a time of celebration, a time to focus on the joy of being with her family, not the past.

She grabbed a black olive out of a bowl on the counter and popped it in her mouth as she carried the bowl to the table.

"I talked to Joan this afternoon," she told Hope.

"I know. She called me, too. I reminded her that any decision about making a movie had to be made jointly between us, and each of us had veto power. Don't worry, CeCe. I told her firmly that I wouldn't pressure you. You created the Sparkle character. He belongs to you."

That wasn't completely true and both of them knew it. She might have written the words, but it was Hope's illustrations that had brought him to life.

"I don't know what to do," she admitted as Faith and Mary joined them at the table carrying bowls and trays of food.

"Your problem has always been that you analyze everything to death," Mary pointed out. "You know someone is going to make a Sparkle movie at some point. It's as inevitable as Christmas coming every year. People love the story and the characters too much. If you like this production company and think they'll do a good job with it based on their reputation, I don't know why you're dragging your feet."

Mary was right, she realized. She was overthinking, probably because she was so concerned with making the right decision.

She hated being afraid all the time. She knew it was a by-product of the trauma she and her sisters had endured at a young age, but neither Hope nor Faith seemed as impacted as she had been.

Hope seemed absolutely fearless, spending years wandering around underdeveloped countries with the Peace Corps, and then on her own teaching English. Faith had plowed all her energy and attention into her family—her marriage, her children, the ranch.

Celeste's life had become her job at the library and the stories she created.

In some ways, she supposed she was still a hostage of Juan Pablo and his crazy group of militants, afraid to take a move and embrace her life.

"Everything's ready and I'm starving," Mary said cheerfully. "What are we waiting for? Let's eat."

Dinner was noisy and chaotic, with several different conversations going at once.

"How did story time go?" Faith asked when there was a lull in the conversation.

She instantly remembered the shock of looking up from Dr. Seuss to see Flynn and his daughter.

"Good." She paused. "Charlotte Delaney's grandson, Flynn, and his daughter were there. I guess he's in town to clean out Charlotte's house."

"Flynn Delaney." Hope made a sound low in her throat. "I used to love it whenever he came to stay with Charlotte. Remember how he used to mow the lawn with his shirt off?"

Celeste dropped her fork with a loud clatter, earning her a curious look from Hope.

"Really?" Rafe said, eyebrow raised. "So all this time I should have been taking my shirt off to mow the lawn?"

Hope grinned at him. "You don't *need* to take your shirt off. You're gorgeous enough even when you're wearing a parka. Anyway, I was a teenage girl. Now that I'm older and wiser I prefer to use my imagination."

He shook his head with an amused look, but Celeste was certain his ears turned a little red.

"You said Flynn came into the library with his daughter," Faith said, her voice filled with compassion. "That poor girl. How is she?"

Considering Flynn's connection to Charlotte, whom they all had loved, everyone in Pine Gulch had followed the news reports. Celeste thought of Olivia's big, haunted eyes, the sad, nervous air about her.

"Hard to say. She limped a little and didn't use her left arm while we were doing the craft project, but other than that she seemed okay."

"Who is Flynn Delaney and what happened to his daughter?" Rafe asked.

"It was all over the news three or four months ago," Chase said. "Around the time Charlotte died, actually."

"You remember," Hope insisted. "We talked about it. He was married to Elise Chandler."

Understanding spread over Rafe's handsome features. "Elise Chandler. The actress." He paused. "Oh. That poor kid."

"Right?" Hope frowned. "What a tragedy. I saw on some tabloid in the supermarket that Flynn never left her side through the whole recovery."

Somehow that didn't seem so surprising, especially considering his devotion to his daughter during story time.

"What happened to her?" Louisa asked. At eleven, she was intensely interested in the world around her.

Her mother was the one who answered. "Elise Chandler was a famous actress," Faith said. "She was in that superhero movie you loved so much and a bunch of other films. Anyway, she was involved with someone who turned out to be a pretty messed-up guy. A few months ago after a big fight, he shot Elise and her daughter before shooting and killing himself. Even though she was injured, Olivia managed to crawl to her mother's phone and call 911."

Celeste had heard that 911 call, which had been made public shortly after the shooting, and the sound of that weak, panic-stricken voice calling for help had broken her heart.

"She seems to be doing well now. She didn't smile much, but she did tell me she loves the Sparkle book and that her dad used to read it to her over and over again in the hospital."

"Oh, how lovely!" Hope exclaimed. "You should take her one of the original Sparkle toys I sewed. I've still got a few left."

"That's a lovely idea," Mary exclaimed. "We definitely should do something for that poor, poor girl. It would have broken Charlotte's heart if she'd still been alive to see Flynn's little girl have to go through such a thing."

"You *have* to take it over there," Hope insisted. "And how about a signed copy of the book and the new one that hasn't come out yet?"

Her heart pounded at just the *idea* of seeing the man again. She couldn't imagine knocking on his door out of the blue. "Why don't *you* take it over? You're the illustrator! And you made the stuffed Sparkle, too."

"I don't even know him or his daughter."

"As if that's ever stopped you before," she muttered.

"It would be a really nice thing to do," Faith said.

"I baked an extra pie," Aunt Mary said. "Why don't you take that, too?"

All day long people had been pushing her to do things she didn't want to. She thought longingly of jumping in her SUV again and taking off somewhere, maybe Southern California where she could find a little sunshine. As tempting as the idea might be sometimes, she knew she couldn't just leave her family. She loved them to bits, even when they did pressure her.

She wanted to tell them all no, but then she thought of Olivia and her sad eyes. This was a small expenditure of effort on her part and would probably thrill the girl. "That's a very good idea," she finally said. "I'll go after dinner. Linus can probably use the walk."

"Perfect." Hope beamed at her as if she had just won the Newbery Medal for children's literature. "I'll look for the stuffed Sparkle. I think there's a handful of them left in a box in my old room."

What would Flynn think when she showed up at his house with a stuffed animal and an armful of books? she wondered as she chewed potatoes that suddenly tasted like chalk.

It didn't matter, she told herself. She was doing this for his daughter, a girl who had been through a terrible ordeal—and who reminded her entirely too much of herself.

Chapter Three

"Are you sure you don't want to help? This tinsel isn't going to jump on the tree by itself."

Flynn held a sparkly handful out to his daughter, who sat in the window seat, alternating between watching him and looking out into the darkness at the falling snowflakes.

She shook her head. "I can't," she said in a matter-of-fact tone. "My arm hurts too much."

He tried to conceal his frustrated sigh behind a cough. The physical therapist he had been taking her to since her injury had given him homework during this break while they were in Idaho. His assignment was to find creative activities that would force her to use her arm more.

He had tried a wide variety of things, like having Olivia push the grocery cart and help him pick out items in the store, and asking her help in the kitchen with slicing vegetables. The inconsistency of it made him crazy. Sometimes she was fine; other times she refused to use her arm at all.

After their trip to the library, he'd realized his grandmother's house was severely lacking in holiday cheer. She had made a snowman ornament and they had nowhere to hang it.

Any hope he might have harbored that she would show a little enthusiasm for the idea of decking their temporary halls was quickly dashed. She showed the same listless apathy toward Christmas decorations as she had for just about everything else except Celeste Nichols and her little reindeer story.

Other than hanging her own snowman ornament, she wasn't interested in helping him hang anything else on the small artificial tree he had unearthed in the basement. As a result, he had done most of the work while she sat and watched, not budging from her claim of being in too much pain.

He knew using her arm caused discomfort. He hadn't yet figured out how to convince an almost-seven-year-old she needed to work through the pain if she ever wanted to regain full mobility in her arm.

"Come on. Just take a handful and help me. It will be fun."

She shook her head and continued staring out at the falling snow.

Since the shooting, these moods had come over her out of nowhere. She would seem to be handling things fine and then a few moments later would become fearful, withdrawn and just want him to leave her alone.

The counselor she had seen regularly assured him it was a natural result of the trauma Olivia had endured.

He hated that each step in her recovery—physical and emotional—had become such a struggle for her.

After hanging a few more strands, he finally gave up. What was the point when she didn't seem inclined to help him, especially since he'd never much liked tinsel on trees anyway?

His father hadn't, either, he remembered. He had a stray memory of one of his parents' epic fights over it one year. Diane had loved tinsel, naturally. Anything with glitz had been right down her alley. Her favorite nights of the year had been red carpet events, either for her own movie premieres or those of her friends.

His father, on the other hand, had thought tinsel was stupid and only made a mess.

One night when he was about seven or eight, a few years before they'd finally divorced, his mother had spent hours hanging pink tinsel on their tree over his father's objections, carefully arranging each piece over a bough.

When they'd woken up, the tinsel had been mysteriously gone. As it turned out, Tom had arisen hours before anyone else and had pulled off every last shiny strand.

After a dramatic screaming fight—all on his mother's side—she had stormed out of their Bel Air house and hadn't been back for several days, as he recalled.

Ah, memories.

He pushed away the bitterness of his past and turned back to his daughter. "If you don't want to hang any more tinsel, I guess we're done. Do you want to do the honors and turn out the lights so we can take a look at it?"

She didn't answer him, her gaze suddenly focused on something through the window.

"Someone's coming," Olivia announced, her voice

tight. She jumped up from the window seat. "I'm going to my room."

He was never sure which she disliked more: large, unruly crowds or unexpected visitors showing up at the door. Nor was he certain she would ever be able to move past either fear.

With effort he forced his voice to be calm and comforting. "There's no reason to go to your room. Everything is fine. I'm right here. You're okay."

She darted longing little glances down the hall to the relative safety of her bedroom, but to her credit she sat down again in the window seat. When the doorbell rang through the house, Flynn didn't miss her instinctive flinch or the tense set of her shoulders.

He hoped whoever it was had a darn good excuse for showing up out of the blue like this and frightening his little girl half to death.

To his shock, the pretty librarian and author stood on the porch with a bag in her hand and a black-and-brown dog at the end of a leash. In the glow from the porch light he could see her nose and cheeks were pink from the cold, and those long, luscious dark curls were tucked under a beanie. She also wasn't wearing her glasses. Without the thick dark frames, her eyes were a lovely green.

"Hello." She gave him a fleeting, tentative smile that appeared and disappeared as quickly as a little bird hunting for berries on a winter-bare shrub.

"Celeste. Ms. Nichols. Hello."

She gave him another of those brief smiles, then tried to look behind him to where Olivia had approached. At least his daughter now looked more surprised and delighted than fearful.

"And hello, Miss Olivia," the librarian said. "How are you tonight?"

Her voice was soft, calm, with a gentleness he couldn't help but appreciate.

"Hi. I'm fine, thank you," she said shyly. "Is that your dog?"

Celeste smiled as the dog sniffed at Olivia's feet. "This is Linus. He's a Yorkshire terrier and his best friend is a black cat named Lucy."

"Like in *Charlie Brown's Christmas*!" She looked delighted at making the connection.

"Just like that, except Linus and Lucy are brother and sister. My Linus and Lucy are just friends."

Olivia slanted her head to look closer at the little dog. "Will he bite?"

Celeste smiled. "He's a very sweet dog and loves everybody, but especially blonde girls with pretty red sweaters."

Olivia giggled at this, and after another moment during which she gathered her courage, she held out her hand. The little furball licked it three times in quick succession, which earned another giggle from his daughter.

"Hi, Linus," she said in a soft voice. "Hi. I'm Olivia."

The dog wagged his tail but didn't bark, which Flynn had to appreciate given how skittish Olivia had been all evening.

She knelt down and started petting the dog—using her injured left arm, he saw with great surprise.

"He likes me!" Olivia exclaimed after a moment, her features alight with a pleasure and excitement he hadn't seen in a long time.

"Of course he does." Celeste smiled down at her with

a soft light in her eyes that touched something deep inside him.

"I'm sorry to just drop in like this, but I couldn't help thinking tonight about what you told me earlier, how the Sparkle book helped you in the hospital."

"It's my favorite book. I still read it all the time."

"I'm so happy to hear that. I told my sister, who drew all the pictures, and she was happy, too. We wanted to give you something."

"Is it for my birthday in three days? I'm going to be seven years old."

"I had no idea it was your birthday in three days!" Celeste exclaimed. "We can certainly consider this an early birthday present. That would be perfect!"

She reached into the bag and pulled out a small stuffed animal.

"That's Sparkle from the book!" Olivia rose to see it more closely.

"That's right. My sister made this while she was drawing the pictures for the first Sparkle book last Christmas. We have just a few of them left over from the original hundred or so she made, and I wondered if you might like one."

Olivia's eyes went huge. "Really? I can *keep* it?"

"If you want to."

"Oh, I do!" Almost warily, she reached for the stuffed animal Celeste held out. When it was in her hands, she hugged it to her chest as if afraid someone would yank it away.

For just a moment she looked like any other young girl, thrilled to be receiving a present. The sheer normalcy made his throat suddenly ache with emotions.

"He's *sooo* cute. I love it! Thank you!"

Olivia threw her arms around Celeste in a quick hug. Flynn wasn't sure if he was more shocked at her use of her injured arm or at the impulsive gesture. Like a puppy that had been kicked one too many times, Olivia shied away from physical touch right now from anyone but him.

Her therapist said it was one more reaction to the trauma she had endured and that eventually she would be able to relax around others and return to the sweet, warm little girl she once had been. He wondered if Dr. Ross ever would have guessed a stuffed reindeer might help speed that process.

Celeste probably had no idea what a rare gift she had just been given as she hugged Olivia back. Still, she looked delighted. "You're very welcome," she said. "You will have to come up to The Christmas Ranch sometime. That's where the real Sparkle lives."

Olivia stepped away, eyes wide. "The real Sparkle lives near here?"

"Just up the road." Celeste gestured vaguely in the direction of her family's place. "We've got a herd of about a dozen reindeer. Sparkle happens to be a favorite of my niece and nephew—of all of us, really. That's where I got the inspiration for the stories."

"Can we go see them, Dad? Can we?"

He shrugged. That was the thing about kids. They dragged you to all kinds of places you didn't necessarily want to go. "Don't know why not. We can probably swing that before the holidays."

Christmas was just around the corner and he was completely unprepared for it. He didn't like celebrating the holidays in the first place. He didn't really feel like hanging out at some cheesy Christmas moneymaking venture aimed at pouring holiday spirit down his throat like cheap bourbon.

But he loved his daughter, and if she wanted to go to the moon right now, he would figure out a way to take her.

"I like your tree," Celeste said, gazing around his grandmother's cluttered living room. "I especially like the tinsel. Did you help your dad put it up?"

A small spasm of guilt crossed her features. "Not really," she admitted. "My dad did most of it. I have a bad arm."

She lifted her shoulder and the arm in question dangled a little as if it were an overcooked lasagna noodle.

To her credit, Celeste didn't question how she could use that same arm to pet the dog or hold a stuffed reindeer.

"Too bad," she only said. "You're probably really good at hanging tinsel."

"Pretty good. I can't reach the high parts of the tree, though."

"Your dad helps you get those, right?"

"I guess."

Celeste picked up the bag of tinsel where Flynn had left it on the console table. "Can I help you put the rest of it up on the side you didn't get to yet? I'm kind of a tinsel expert. Growing up on The Christmas Ranch, I had to be."

Olivia looked at the tree, then her father, then back at Celeste holding the tinsel. "Okay," she said with that same wariness.

"It will be fun. You'll see. Sparkle can help. He's good at tinsel, too."

How she possibly could have guessed from a halftinseled tree that he had been trying to enlist his daughter's help with decorating, he had no idea. But he wasn't about to argue with her insight, especially when Olivia obediently followed her new heroine to the tree and reached for a handful of tinsel.

"Can I take your coat?" he asked.

"Oh. Yes. Thanks." She gave a nervous little laugh as she handed him her coat. At the library, she had been wearing a big, loose sweater that had made him wonder what was beneath it. She had taken that layer off apparently, and now she wore a cheerful red turtleneck that accentuated her luscious curves and made his mouth water.

He had an inkling that she was the sort of woman who had no idea the kind of impact she had on a man. As he went to hang her coat by the front door, he forced himself to set aside the reaction as completely inappropriate under the circumstances, especially when she was only trying to help his kid.

When he returned to the living room, he found her and Olivia standing side by side hanging tinsel around the patches of the tree he had left bare.

Her cute little dog had finished sniffing the corners of the room and planted himself on his haunches in the middle of the floor, where he could watch the proceedings.

Flynn leaned against the doorjamb to do the same thing.

How odd, that Olivia would respond to a quiet children's librarian and author more than she had her counselor, her physical therapist, the caregivers at the hospital. She seemed to bloom in this woman's company, copying her actions on the lower branches she could reach. While she still seemed to be favoring her injured arm, occasionally she seemed to forget it hurt and used it without thinking.

All in all, it wasn't a terrible way to spend a December evening while a gas fire flickered in Grandma Charlotte's fireplace and snowflakes fluttered down outside the window.

After several moments, the two of them used the last of the tinsel and Celeste stepped away to take in the bigger picture.

"That looks perfect!" she exclaimed. "Excellent job."

Olivia's smile was almost back to her normal one. She held up the stuffed animal. "Sparkle helped."

"I told you he would be very good at hanging tinsel."

Whatever worked, he figured. "Let me hit the lights for you," he said. "We can't appreciate the full effects with the lights on."

He turned them off, pitching the room into darkness except for the gleaming tree. The tinsel really did reflect the lights. His mom had been right about that, even if she had gotten so many other things wrong.

"Oh. I love it. It's the prettiest tree *ever*," Olivia declared.

"I have to agree," Flynn said. "Good job, both of you."

"And you," Olivia pointed out. "You did most of it earlier. We only filled in the gaps."

"So I did. We're all apparently excellent at decorating Christmas trees."

Celeste met his gaze and smiled. He gazed back, struck again by how lovely she was with those big green eyes that contrasted so strikingly with her dark hair.

He was staring, he realized, and jerked his gaze away, but not before he thought he saw color climb her high cheekbones. He told himself it must have been a trick of the Christmas lights.

"Oh, I nearly forget," she exclaimed suddenly. "I have another birthday present for you. Two, actually."

"You do?" Olivia lit up.

"Well, it's not actually your birthday yet, so I completely understand if you want to wait. I can just give them to your dad to hold until the big day."

As he might have predicted, Olivia didn't look all that thrilled at the suggestion. "I should open them now while you're here."

"I guess I should have asked your dad first."

He shrugged, figuring it was too late to stop the cart now. "Go ahead."

With a rueful, apologetic smile, she handed the bag to Olivia. "It's not wrapped, since I didn't know it was your birthday when I came over. I'm sorry."

His daughter apparently didn't care. She reached into the bag and pulled out a book with colorful illustrations on the cover.

"Ohhh," she breathed. "It's another *Sparkle and the Magic Snowball* book!"

"This one is signed by both me and my sister, who did the illustrations. I figured since it's your favorite book, you ought to have a signed copy."

"I love it. Thank you!"

"There's something else," Celeste said when his daughter looked as if she were going to settle in right on the spot to reread the story for the hundredth time.

Olivia reached into the bag and pulled out a second book. While it was obvious the artist had been the same, this had different, more muted colors than the original Sparkle book and hearts instead of Christmas ornaments.

"I haven't seen this one! *Sparkle and the Valentine Surprise*."

"That's because it's brand-new. It's not even in stores yet. It's coming out in a few weeks."

"Dad, look!"

She hurried over to him, barely limping, and held out the book.

"Very nice. We can read it tonight at bedtime."

"I can't wait that long! Can I read it now?"

"Sure. First, do you have something to say to Ms. Nichols?"

Olivia gazed at the woman with absolute adoration. "Thank you *so much*! I just love these books and the stuffed Sparkle." Again, she surprised him by hugging Celeste tightly, then hurried to the window seat that she had claimed as her own when they'd first arrived at Charlotte's house.

He gazed after her for a moment, then turned back to Celeste.

"How did you just do that?" he asked, his voice low so that Olivia couldn't hear.

She blinked, confusion on her features. "Do what?"

"That's the first time I've seen her hug anyone but me in months."

"Oh." Her voice was small, sad, telling him without words that she knew what had happened to Elise and Olivia and about Brandon Lowell.

"I guess you probably know my daughter was shot three months ago and her mother was killed."

Her lovely features tightened and her eyes filled with sorrow. "I do. I followed the case, not because I wanted to read about something so terribly tragic, but because I…knew you, once upon a time."

Color rose on her cheeks again, but he had no idea why.

"She's been very withdrawn because of the post-traumatic stress. I haven't seen her warm up to anyone this quickly since it happened."

"Oh." She gazed at Olivia with a soft look in her eyes. "It's not me," she assured him. "Sparkle is a magic little reindeer. He has a comforting way about him."

He was quite certain Celeste was the one with the comforting way, especially as she had created the fictional version of the reindeer, but he didn't say so.

"Whatever the reason, I appreciate it. I had hoped bringing her here to Idaho where we can be away from the spotlight for a few weeks might help her finally begin to heal. It's good to know I might have been right."

The concern and love in his voice came through loud and clear. Flynn obviously was a devoted father trying his best to help his daughter heal.

Celeste's throat felt tight and achy. This poor little girl had watched her mother's life slip away. "She's been through a horrible ordeal. It might be years before the nightmares fade."

"You sound as if you know a little something about nightmares." He studied her closely.

She didn't want to tell him she *still* had nightmares from those terrible weeks in captivity and then their miraculous rescue with its tragic consequences. She had cried herself to sleep just about every night for weeks. In a second rapid-fire blow, just as the overwhelming pain of losing their father had begun to ease a little, their mother had lost her short but intense battle with cancer and they had come here to stay with Uncle Claude and Aunt Mary.

She couldn't tell him that. She barely knew the man,

and he had demons of his own to fight. He didn't need to share hers.

"Everybody has nightmares," she answered. "To paraphrase John Irving, you don't get to pick them. They pick you."

"True enough."

Her dog made a little whiny sound and started looking anxious, which meant he probably needed to go out.

"I need to take Linus home. Sorry again to drop in on you like this out of the blue."

He smiled a little. "Are you kidding? This has been the best thing to happen to us in a long time. She's completely thrilled. And thanks for helping with the Christmas tree. It looks great."

"You're welcome. If you need anything while you're here, my family is just a short walk away. Oh. I nearly forgot. This is for you."

She reached into the bag and pulled out the pie Aunt Mary had boxed up for easier transport.

"What is it?"

"My aunt makes amazing berry pies. She had an extra and wanted you to have it."

He looked stunned at the gesture. "That's very kind. Please give her my thanks."

"I'll do that." She reached for her coat but he beat her to it, tugging it from the rack so he could help her into it.

She was aware of him behind her again, the heat and strength of him, and her insides jumped and twirled like Linus when he was especially happy.

She was being ridiculous, she told herself. She wasn't a thirteen-year-old girl with a crush anymore.

She quickly shoved her arms through the sleeves and stepped away to tie her scarf.

"Are you sure you're okay walking home?" he asked. "Looks as if it's snowing harder. Let me grab my keys and we'll drive you home."

She shook her head, even as she felt a warm little glow at his concern. "Not necessary. It's not far. I like to walk, even in the snow, and Linus still has a little energy to burn off. Thank you, though."

He still looked uncertain, but she didn't give him a chance to press the matter. She returned to the living room doorway and waved at his daughter.

"Goodbye, Olivia. I hope you enjoy the book."

She looked up with that distracted, lost-in-the-story sort of look Celeste knew she wore frequently herself. "I'm already almost done. It's super good."

It was one thing in the abstract to know people enjoyed her work. It was something else entirely to watch someone reading it—surreal and gratifying and a bit uncomfortable at the same time.

"I'm glad you think so."

Olivia finally seemed to register that she had on her coat. "Do you really have to go?"

"I'm afraid so. I have to take Linus home or Lucy will be lonely."

To her surprise, Olivia set aside the book, climbed down from the window seat and approached to give her one last hug.

"Thank you again for the books and for the stuffed animal," she said. "It was the best birthday ever—and I haven't even had it yet!"

"I'm so glad."

"Goodbye, Linus," Olivia said. She knelt down to scratch the Yorkie again and Linus obliged by licking her face, which made her giggle.

When Celeste turned to go, she found Flynn shaking his head with astonishment clear on his handsome features. She remembered what he had said about Olivia not warming to many people since her mother's death, and she was deeply grateful she had made the small effort to come visit the girl.

"I hope we see you again," he said.

Oh, how she wished he meant for *his* sake and not for his daughter's. "I'm sure you will. Pine Gulch is a small place. Good night."

She walked out into the snowy December night. Only when she was halfway back to the Star N did she realize she didn't feel the cold at all.

Chapter Four

Over the weekend she tried not to think about Flynn and his sweet, fragile daughter. It wasn't easy, despite how busy she was working an extra shift at the library and helping out in the gift shop of The Christmas Ranch.

Even the multiple calls she and Hope took from Joan about the movie development deal couldn't completely distract her random thoughts of the two of them that intruded at the oddest times.

She knew the basics of what had happened to Elise Chandler and her daughter at the hands of the actress's boyfriend, but she was compelled to do a few internet searches to read more about the case. The details left her in tears for everyone involved, even the perpetrator and his family.

Brandon Lowell obviously had been mentally ill. He had been under treatment for bipolar disease and, according to evidence after the shooting, had stopped taking his medication a month before, claiming it interfered with his acting abilities and the regular television role he was playing.

He never should have had access to a firearm given his mental health but had stolen one from Elise's bodyguard a few days before the shooting.

She found it a tragic irony that the woman used a bodyguard when she went out in public but had been killed by someone close to her using the very tool intended to protect her.

The whole thing made her so very sad, though she was touched again to read numerous reports about Olivia's dedicated father, how Flynn had put his thriving contracting business in the hands of trusted employees so he could dedicate his time to staying with his daughter every moment through her recovery.

None of that information helped distract her from thinking about him. By Monday afternoon, she had *almost* worked the obsession out of her system—or at least forced herself to focus on work as much as possible, until Frankie came in after a morning of online seminars.

"I figured out who he is!" her friend exclaimed before she even said hello.

"Who?"

"You know! The hot dad who came to story time last week. I spent all weekend trying to figure out why he looked so familiar and then this morning it came to me. I was washing my hair and remembered that shower scene in *Forbidden* when the hero washes the heroine's hair and it came to me. Elise Chandler! Sexy dad is her ex-husband. It has to be! That cute little girl must be the one who was all over the news."

Flynn must hate having his daughter be a household name, even though her mother certainly had been.

"Yes. Flynn Delaney. Charlotte Delaney, his grandmother, lived close to The Christmas Ranch and he used to come spend summers with her."

"You knew all this time and you didn't say anything?"

It wasn't her place to spread gossip about the man. Even now, just talking to her dear friend, she felt extremely protective of him and Olivia.

"I'm sure they would appreciate a little privacy and discretion," she said. "Olivia has been through a terrible ordeal and is still trying to heal from her injuries. I don't think they need everybody in town making a fuss over them."

"Oh, of course. That makes sense. That poor kid."

"I know."

"How is she doing?"

She thought of Olivia's excitement the other day when she had taken the books to her and that spontaneous, sweet embrace. "She's still got a long road but she's improving."

"I'm so glad."

"Olivia is apparently a big Sparkle fan, and that was the reason they came to the story time."

She had been touched several times to remember the girl telling her how much her book had helped during her recovery. Who would have guessed when she had been writing little stories for her niece and nephew that an emotionally and physically damaged girl would one day find such comfort in them?

To her relief, Frankie dropped the subject. Celeste tried once more to return to her work, vowing to put this ridiculous obsession out of her head. An hour later her hopes were dashed when Frankie bustled back to the children's section, her eyes as wide as if she'd just caught somebody trying to deface a book.

"He's here again!"

She looked up from the books she was shelving. "Who's here?"

"Hottie Dad and his cute little girl! Elise Chandler's poor daughter. They just walked in."

"Are you sure?"

"He's a hard man to miss," Frankie said.

Celeste's heartbeat kicked up several notches and her stomach seemed tangled with nerves. She told herself that was ridiculous. He wasn't there to see her anyway. Maybe he wouldn't even come back to the children's section.

"I wonder what they're doing here," Frankie said, her dark eyes huge.

It wasn't to see her, Celeste reminded herself sternly. She was a dowdy, shy librarian, and he couldn't possibly have any interest in her beyond her status as his daughter's favorite author.

"Here's a wild guess," she said, her tone dry. "Maybe they're looking for books."

Frankie made a face. "He doesn't have a library card, does he?"

"Probably not," she acknowledged. "They're only here for a few weeks, then they'll be returning to California."

The thought was more depressing than it should have been.

"Well, ask him if he wants a temporary one while he's here."

Why did *she* have to ask him anything? She wanted to hide here in the children's section and not even have to face him. But a moment later Olivia limped in, Sparkle the stuffed reindeer in her hand along with the new book.

"Hi, Ms. Nichols! Hi!"

Celeste smiled at both of them. "Hello. It's lovely to see you today. Happy birthday!" She suddenly remembered.

"Thank you," Olivia said. "I begged and begged my dad to bring me to the library today."

"Did you?"

She held up Sparkle. "I had to tell you how much I liked the new book, just as much as the first one. Sparkle is *so funny.* I've read it about ten times already."

"Wow. That's terrific. Thanks for letting me know."

"And my dad read it to me twice and he laughed both times. He hardly *ever* laughs."

"Not true," he protested. "Okay, it's true that I laughed at the book. It's hilarious. But it's not true that I hardly ever laugh. I don't know where you came up with that. I laugh all the time. I'm a freaking hyena."

Celeste laughed out loud, which earned her a surprised look from Frankie.

"You're so lucky that you had the chance to read the new book," Frankie informed her. "Half the children in town would willingly forgo all their presents under the tree if they could lay their hands on the next Sparkle book."

Even though she was grossly exaggerating, the library director had the perfect tone with Olivia—friendly and polite, but not overly solicitous. She had a feeling Flynn would hate the latter.

"It's really, really good," Olivia said solemnly. "I still like the first one best, but the second one is almost my favorite."

Frankie smiled, but before she could answer, one of the other library volunteers came over with a question about checking out DVDs, and she reluctantly excused herself to deal with the crisis.

"Is there something I can help you with?" Celeste asked after her friend walked away. "Would you like a temporary card so you can check out materials? I'm sure that wouldn't be a problem, considering I know where to find you."

"No. Actually, we have another reason for being here."

If she wasn't mistaken, Flynn looked a little uncomfortable, which made her even more curious.

"Oh? What is it?"

He didn't answer and Olivia didn't say anything, either. Finally Flynn nudged her. "Go ahead."

"It's my birthday," the girl began.

"I know. I think it's great that you decided the library is the perfect place to celebrate a birthday. I completely agree!"

Olivia giggled a little. "No, we're not celebrating my birthday here. I told my dad the only thing I want for my birthday is to have pizza."

"Ooh, pizza. My favorite," she said, though she was still mystified about why they might be at the library and why Flynn still looked uncomfortable. "Are you looking for a book on how to make pizza?"

The girl shook her head. "We're going to the pizza restaurant down the street."

"I can highly recommend it. It's one of my favorite places."

Olivia gave her a shy look. "That's good. Because I want to have pizza with *you* on my birthday."

She blinked, taken by surprise. "With…me?"

"Yes. That would be the best birthday ever. My favorite thing to eat and my new friend and the lady who writes such good Sparkle books." She beamed as if the matter was settled.

"Don't feel obligated," Flynn said quickly. "If you already have plans, we completely understand. Isn't that right, Olivia?"

"Yes," the girl said.

Dinner. With Olivia and Flynn. She thought of a hundred reasons why she should say no. How could she possibly eat with these nervous butterflies racing around in her stomach? And she probably wouldn't be able to think of anything to say and would look even more stupid than she felt.

All those reasons paled into insignificance. Olivia wanted to have pizza with her for her birthday, and Celeste couldn't let her own social awkwardness stand in the way of making that particular wish come true.

"I would be honored to come help you celebrate your birthday. Thank you for inviting me."

Olivia's smile was sweetly thrilled. "She said yes, Dad!"

The sight of this tough-looking man gazing down at his daughter with such love just about broke Celeste's heart. "So I heard. That's great." He turned to her. "What time are you finished with work?"

"Five-thirty."

"Would seven work for pizza? We can pick you up."

"I can meet you at the restaurant."

"We don't mind. Do you still live at the Star N?"

She knew he probably didn't mean for that to sound pitiful, but she still had to wince. That wasn't exactly true. She had gone off to Boise for her undergraduate work, then Seattle for her master's degree. She wasn't *completely* a homebody, even if she had jumped at the chance to return to her hometown library to work.

If she was living on her family's ranch, it wasn't because of any failure to launch, only because of the tragic circumstances of Travis's death.

"I live on the ranch but not in the main house," she told him. "I'm at the foreman's place, the small log house closest to the entrance."

"Perfect. Plan on us at seven."

She was going out to dinner with Flynn Delaney and his daughter. This certainly wasn't the way to get the man out of her head, but she didn't see how she could refuse.

The truth was she didn't want to anyway. She was both touched and flattered that sweet Olivia wanted to spend time with her for her birthday.

"Sounds good. Meanwhile, are you sure you don't want to check out some books on a temporary library card? We still have a great selection of holiday books available. It's the section there against the wall."

"Can we?" Olivia asked her father.

"Just a few," he said with a reluctant nod. "It might be tough to keep track of more than that while we're clearing out Grandma Charlotte's house."

Olivia headed immediately toward the Christmas storybooks, leaving Flynn alone with Celeste—or at least as alone as they could be in a public library.

A few moms she knew were browsing through the children's section with their toddlers, and she was pretty sure she caught more than one appreciative glance in his direction. As Frankie said, he was a hard man to overlook.

"Thanks for agreeing to come with us," Flynn said.

"It probably wasn't fair to spring that on you out of the blue. I would have called first, but I didn't have a phone number. I guess I could have found the number for the library, but I didn't think about it until we pulled up."

"It's fine."

"Seriously, you made her day. She has been asking me all afternoon if you could come to her birthday celebration. I didn't want to disappoint her. It's still pretty tough for me to deny her anything these days."

She couldn't imagine almost losing a child. The fear must have been overwhelming.

"I'm touched, if you want the truth. I don't believe I've ever been anyone's birthday wish before."

A strange glint appeared in his gaze, an expression she couldn't quite identify. After a moment he smiled. "Face it. You sealed your fate the other day when you showed up in person with a new book *and* a cute stuffed toy. You're now officially the coolest person in town."

She had to laugh at that ridiculous statement. "If that's the case, you both need to get out and meet more people in Pine Gulch."

Amusement crinkled the corners of his eyes. "We won't be here long enough to move in social circles around here. Anyway, I think Olivia and I are both quite happy with those we have already met in Pine Gulch."

Her heartbeat seemed to accelerate all over again at the teasing note in his voice. Her gaze met his and he was smiling at her with a warm look in his eyes that sucked away any ability she might have had to offer a semi-intelligent response.

To her relief, one of the moms came over to ask her a question about the puppet-book packages they lent out—

probably more to get a closer look at Flynn, she suspected, than out of any genuine quest for information.

He moved away to join his daughter while she picked a few other books and the moment was gone.

He had to finish taking care of things at his grandmother's house and get out of Pine Gulch.

As Flynn drove the short distance from Charlotte's house to the Star N Ranch, he was aware of a low, insistent unease. This town was growing on him, sucking him in.

He had always enjoyed coming here as a kid to spend time with his grandmother. The setting was beautiful, nestled against the Tetons, with pine forests and crystal clear streams.

The pace here seemed so very different from his childhood home in Southern California, quieter, gentler somehow. Almost like a foreign country, without convertibles and palm trees and self-absorbed celebrities.

He always felt a sense of peace settle over him the moment he passed through the city limits into town.

He thought he loved it here because of Charlotte, because she was such a steady source of love and support despite the chaos of the rest of his world. When he came to Pine Gulch, there were no raging fights that could go on for days, no slamming doors, no screaming voices. Only his calm, funny, laughing grandmother, with her colorful aprons and her bright smile and her small, tidy house beside the Cold Creek.

She was gone now, but he was aware of that same peace seeping through him, so very welcome after the terrible past few months.

It didn't make sense, he knew. He was only here to

finish taking care of Charlotte's house, not to find some kind of peace.

That was part of the reason he was so drawn to Celeste Nichols, he acknowledged as he neared her family's ranch. She had a calming way about her that drew him to her.

He couldn't imagine any two people more different than Celeste and Elise—the sweet children's librarian and author and the passionate, flamboyant, ambitious actress.

His marriage had been a mistake from the beginning. After growing up with a mother in the entertainment business—and a father who had hated it—and seeing the neuroses and the superficiality of that way of life, he had wanted no part of it.

After high school and college, he had set his business degree aside and obtained a contractor's license instead. After only a few years his construction company had established a reputation for quality and dependability. Then at one of his mother's frequent parties, he had met a stunning—and hungry—young actress.

She had pursued him aggressively, and he—like probably most guys in their early twenties—had been too flattered to use his brain. In his lust-addled state, it had taken him several weeks to realize she was more interested in his connection to his mother and her powerful Hollywood circle than in him.

But by then Elise had become pregnant, despite the precautions they had taken. He had done what he thought was right and married her, but it had been the ultimate exercise in futility. Both of them had known from the beginning it would never last. The two years before she had filed for divorce had been among the toughest of his life, sweetened only by his complete adoration for his baby girl.

Everything he did, then and now, was for Olivia. That was the only reason he was driving to pick up Celeste Nichols right now, not because of this powerful attraction he hadn't been able to shake since that first day in the library.

What was it about her? Yes, she was pretty in a calm, buttoned-down kind of way with those lovely dark-fringed green eyes and dark curls. She had an understated loveliness she seemed to be doing her best to hide from the world.

His entire life he had been surrounded by beautiful women who were empty shells once a guy broke through the surface to the person inside. Despite their short acquaintance, he was certain Celeste wasn't like that.

Her kindness to Olivia touched him. He tried to tell himself that was the reason for this strange reaction to her. It was gratitude; that was all.

Somehow he wasn't buying it as he passed the entrance to The Christmas Ranch on his way to the Star N.

"What is that place?" Olivia asked, gazing out the window at the colorful holiday display they could see from the road.

"It's a place where people pay money to help find the Christmas spirit," he explained. "They have different activities here like sledding, sleigh rides, that kind of thing."

"Look, Dad! That sign says Home of the Real Sparkle," she read. "That must be where he lives! Can we pay the money and see him and maybe do some of the other stuff? The sledding and stuff?"

Her request took him by surprise, especially considering how apathetic she had been about decorating their house for Christmas. She hadn't summoned much energy at all for celebrating this year. He couldn't blame her after what she had endured, but it was one more thing that broke his heart, especially considering how excited she had been about the holiday season in years past.

Maybe Celeste Nichols and her reindeer book were rubbing off on Olivia.

"We'll have to see. I thought you weren't very interested in Christmas this year."

"I guess we could do a *few* Christmas things," she said slowly. "Whether we do them or not, Christmas is coming anyway."

"True enough." For a girl who had just turned seven, she could be remarkably wise sometimes. She was tough and courageous, he told himself. Even if she was struggling now, she would make it through this eventually.

"Is this where Celeste lives?" Olivia asked when he pulled up in front of the little house not far from the bigger Star N ranch house.

"That's what she said. The foreman's house."

"Look. She has a Christmas tree, too."

Since her family ran The Christmas Ranch, he would have been more shocked if she *didn't* have one.

"I wonder if I can see her cute little dog, Linus."

"I wouldn't be a bit surprised," he told her.

Olivia opened the passenger door almost before he had the SUV in Park, and she raced up the driveway without him, only limping a little. While he was still unbuckling his seat belt, she was already at the doorbell, and by the time he reached the door, Celeste had opened it and was greeting his daughter.

"Of course," she was saying. "You can absolutely come in and meet Lucy the cat. She loves new friends."

Apparently his daughter had invited herself inside. He rolled his eyes but followed her when Celeste held open the door for both of them.

The house wasn't large, perhaps only eight or nine hundred square feet. The living room was decorated in a casual, comfortable style, heavy on bright colors, with lots of plump pillows and books. The Christmas tree was about the only holiday decoration, he was surprised to see.

"Nice place," he said.

"Thanks. I just moved over a few months ago from the main house, but so far I've been enjoying it. I'm close enough to help out with my niece and nephew when my sister Faith needs me. At the same time, I'm far enough away from the chaos that I can write. I've even got my own writing space in the second bedroom."

"It's comfortable."

She smiled. "I like it."

Her furry-faced little dog scampered in from the kitchen, followed by an elegant-looking black cat, who watched them carefully from the doorway as if trying to determine whether they were friends or foes.

"Hi, Linus." Olivia sank to the floor to pet the dog. After a moment, the cat sidled over.

"That's Lucy," Celeste said. "She can be a little snooty at first, but once she warms up, she'll be your best friend. Just give her a moment."

Sure enough, while Olivia mostly paid attention to the small dog, the cat moved closer and closer until she rubbed her head against Olivia's leg.

"I think she likes me," she whispered.

"I'm sure of it," Celeste said with a smile.

"Looks as if you need to pick up a pet or two," she said to Flynn in an undertone.

"Don't give her any ideas," he said in the same low voice. Their gaze met and he felt a strange jolt in his gut at the impact of those green eyes behind the glasses.

"You don't want a little dog?"

He shrugged. When he was a kid, the only pets had been his mother's annoying, yippy little purse pooches. He had never really thought seriously about it before, too busy with work and his shared custody of Olivia.

When things settled down for her a little, maybe he would think about it. She did seem to be enjoying Celeste's pets.

Both he and Celeste seemed content to watch her petting the two pets, and he was aware of that elusive sense of peace seeping in again.

"How's the house cleaning going?" she asked him.

He thought of the work still ahead. "I don't think I realized what an undertaking it was to clear out eighty-five years of living. After about three days of work, we got one of the rooms cleared out today."

"Good work." She paused. "If you need help, I'm available most evenings."

She looked embarrassed after she spoke, though he wasn't quite sure why, when he took the offer as nothing but generous and kind, especially in the hustle-bustle of the holidays.

"Thank you," he said sincerely.

She gazed at him for a moment, then shifted her attention back to Olivia, but not before he saw a hint of color climb her cheeks.

"What are you doing with your business in California while you're here?"

"I'm doing as much as I can long-distance, but it hasn't been easy. Since the shooting, I've basically had to trust my second-in-command to take much of the load at the sites. I've been handling the administrative things after Olivia goes to bed. Everyone who works for me has been great. I couldn't ask for better people in my company, but I think we're all ready for things to start getting back to normal after the holidays."

She looked between him and his daughter, her expression soft. "You're a good father, Flynn. Olivia is lucky to have you."

"I don't know about that," he muttered. "A good father would have known what was going on at her mother's house. I should have seen it. It wasn't a stable situation for a young girl. Elise had boyfriend after boyfriend traipsing in and out of their lives, all tabloid fodder. Brandon Lowell at least had stuck around for longer than a few months. I was stupidly grateful for that, but if I had been paying more attention, I would have seen his downward spiral. Maybe I could have stepped in earlier."

"What would you have done?"

"I don't know. Found him the help he needed, at the very least. Maybe filed for an emergency custody order so we could have avoided all this trauma and pain." The nightmare of the shooting was as vivid and stark as if it had happened the day before. "Elise called me right before it all went south."

"She did?"

He checked to be sure Olivia wasn't paying attention to them but to the animals before he continued. "She told me Brandon had been drinking all day and was acting strangely. She was worried about him, but she didn't sound panicked or anything, was just calling to ask my advice. She'd done this before, called me for advice when he was drinking too much or having a manic episode, but something told me this time was different. I was on a job site fifty miles away, so I told her to grab Olivia and take her to my house, and I would deal with the situation when I got back."

He was quiet, regret a harsh companion. "I wish to hell she had listened to me. She was always so stubborn, thinking she knew best. I was about five miles from her place when I got the call from the police. I'll never forget that instant when it felt as if the whole world changed."

Chapter Five

She couldn't imagine what he must have gone through, knowing his daughter had been hurt. She also could tell by the threads of guilt twining through his voice that he blamed himself for not being able to control the situation and keep his daughter safe.

"What happened wasn't your fault," she murmured.

"Wasn't it?" he asked, the words clipped.

Unable to resist the need to offer him comfort, she reached out her hand and rested it softly on his.

She completely understood where he was coming from. She knew all about that crushing weight of responsibility.

In that last panicked rush toward the helicopter and the navy SEALs, she had been terrified as usual. She had hesitated, frozen in fear. Her father had paused to go back for her and shoved her in front of him, pushing her forward with his usual words of encouragement as they had raced to safety.

He had thrust her into the helicopter ahead of him, but her split second of fear had had a terrible cost. Her father had been shot just before he would have been able to make it to safety.

If she hadn't been so afraid, if she had started to run when he had first told her to go, maybe her father would still be with them now.

"Wouldn't it be wonderful if we were all given one do-over in life?" she murmured. "One free pass to go back and change one action, one decision, one thoughtless word?"

He gave her a searching look, as if trying to figure out what moment she would alter. Finally he nodded. "One would be a start, I suppose, though I probably could use about a half dozen free passes."

"Instead, we have to do our best to live with the consequences of our choices."

"Not an easy task, is it?"

No. She had been trying for nearly twenty years.

He flexed his hand and she realized with great chagrin that she was still touching him. She pulled her fingers back quickly, her skin still tingling from the heat of him.

After an awkward moment, he turned to his daughter. "Olivia, we should probably take off or someone else will eat our delicious pizza."

"We haven't ordered it yet," she said with a concerned frown. "Do you think they'll run out?"

"I was just teasing. But we really should go."

"Okay," she said reluctantly. She rubbed noses with Linus and petted Lucy one last time, then stood up.

She might have been mistaken, but Celeste thought she seemed to be moving better, even than a few days before.

Flynn drove a luxury SUV that smelled of expensive leather with hints of his woodsy, intoxicating aftershave. As he drove to the pizza place in town, she and Olivia talked about the books the girl had checked out of the library and about her schoolwork and her home in California.

He seemed content to listen, though once or twice she caught him giving her a sidelong glance, no doubt trying to figure out how he had gotten saddled spending the evening with the boring children's librarian.

Monday night was family night at the Rocky Mountain Pizza Company—The Rock, as they called it in town. From the outside it looked as though the place was hopping.

This was one of the more family-friendly hangouts in Pine Gulch. Though it had a pool table in the back room, it also featured foosball and air hockey tables, as well as a few vintage video games like Ms. PAC-MAN and pinball.

Celeste came here about once a month, either with her sister or with friends. Usually she enjoyed the delicious wood-fired pizza and the comfortable, familiar atmosphere. The scent alone—garlic and yeast and a fabulous red sauce—made her stomach rumble.

On the heels of that first sensory overload, though, Celeste became aware that people were looking with curiosity at her and her companions.

She saw the police chief, Trace Bowman, and his wife, Becca, at one table with their children. In the next booth were Nate Cavazos and his wife, Emery, one of her good friends. Emery and Becca both looked intrigued.

For a wild moment, she wished she had refused the

invitation from Olivia—or that she had persuaded Flynn to take them all the way to Jackson Hole or even Idaho Falls, somewhere far away from Pine Gulch where people didn't know her.

Instead, she squared her shoulders, waved at her friends and did her best to ignore their speculative looks.

"Hi, Celeste," Natalie Dalton, the hostess chirped the greeting while looking at Flynn and Olivia with curiosity.

She used to babysit for Nat and her siblings. "Hi, Natalie. Great to see you. I miss seeing you at the library these days."

"I still come in, though mostly at night for study groups. I just don't have much reason to hit the children's section anymore unless I've got one of the little ones with me."

Her father and stepmother had two children together, in addition to the four Wade Dalton had had with his first wife, who had died tragically in childbirth.

Natalie turned her attention to Olivia and Flynn. "Hi, there. Welcome to The Rock. I don't think we've met. I'm Natalie."

Celeste felt as though she had the manners of a dried-up turnip right now. "Sorry. This is Flynn Delaney and his daughter, Olivia."

She smiled at them both. "Hi, Olivia. Hi, Flynn."

"We're here celebrating a certain young lady's seventh birthday today," Celeste said.

"Happy birthday!" Natalie exclaimed, beaming at her and holding her hand out for a fist bump.

"Thank you," Olivia said. She didn't meet her eye, and though she raised her hand halfheartedly to bump Nat's, she quickly lowered it again and looked at the floor.

What had happened to the animated birthday girl

who had chattered in the car about her favorite Jan Brett Christmas book? Now she seemed nervous and uneasy, as if she wanted to be anywhere else in the world than the best pizza place in the entire region.

Celeste placed a comforting hand on her shoulder. When she'd first arrived in Pine Gulch after their Colombian ordeal, it had taken her a long time before she could completely relax in public places like this. She imagined Olivia was feeling the same way.

"I've got the perfect table for a birthday girl," Natalie said, her cheerfulness undeterred by Olivia's reticence. "Follow me, guys."

Indeed, she led them to an excellent table overlooking the Christmas lights on Main Street. From here, they even could see the fun display in the window of the local toy store.

"Thanks," Flynn murmured. Olivia slid into the booth first and Flynn went in after her. Celeste slid across from them.

"What's good here?" Flynn asked, scanning one of the menus Natalie left them.

"Everything," she answered honestly. "The pizza, the pasta, the sandwiches. You can't go wrong."

"I wanted pizza," Olivia said, her voice still small.

"Pizza it is," Flynn said. "Why don't we order three personal size? Then everybody can choose the toppings they like."

"The personal size is usually huge," she told him. "At least enough for two people."

"That's okay. Pizza leftovers are one of the true joys in life, right?"

When he smiled, she thought *he* should have been the movie star in the family instead of his mother and former wife. He would break hearts all over the world with those completely natural good looks.

Her stomach jumped all over the place again. Oh, this crush was *so embarrassing.* She would be lucky if she could eat any pizza at all.

At least she was able to talk casually when he asked her to help him choose between pizza selections. A few moments later the server, Lucy Boyer—Natalie's cousin—headed over to take their order.

She beamed when she spotted Celeste. "Hey, Ms. N. How are things?"

"Great, Lucy. How are you?"

"Can't complain. I'm working on my college essays and it's such a pain. You probably love that kind of thing, since you're a genius author and all. You might not know this, but for some people writing is *hard.*"

She didn't want to burst that particular fantasy by telling her the truth, that sometimes every single word was a struggle.

"Hey, what's this I hear about a Sparkle movie in the works?"

How on earth did rumors spread like that? She hadn't made her final decision yet, though she knew she couldn't wait much longer.

"A movie?" Olivia exclaimed. "Really?"

For some reason, Flynn's easy expression had tightened, and he was gazing at her with his brow furrowed.

"I don't know yet. Possibly." Probably.

She still wasn't sure she wanted to see her baby on the big screen, but at this point she didn't know how to stop that particular train.

"That's seriously cool. I'll be the first in line to buy tickets. That's such a great story."

"It's my favorite, too," Olivia said.

"Cool! I heard from a little squirrel that you've got a birthday today."

Olivia nodded. She looked as though she was torn between withdrawing into herself to hide from the attention and any kid's natural excitement about being the star of the day.

"We'll make sure your pizza is perfect, then. What kind do you want?"

Olivia ordered cheese, which Lucy assured them would come with a special birthday surprise. Celeste picked her favorite, margherita, which came with fresh basil and the hand-pulled mozzarella The Rock was famous for, and Flynn went for the meat lover's delight.

After she left, Flynn picked up the conversation.

"A movie?" he asked.

"We're in talks," she answered. "It's a terrifying proposition, to be honest."

"Will the real Sparkle be in the movie?" Olivia asked.

Celeste smiled. "It's going to be animated, so no."

She and the little girl started talking about their favorite holiday films—Olivia's was *Elf*, while Celeste still favored *It's A Wonderful Life*.

In no time, their pizza arrived. Olivia's surprise was that her pizza was shaped like a Christmas tree.

The pizza was every bit as good as usual, cooked just right in the wood-fired oven.

Flynn apparently agreed. "Wow," he said after the first bite. "That's a good pie. If I'd known how good, we would have been eating here every night since we came to town."

"Doug and Jacinda DeMarco, the owners, are big on the artisan pizza scene. They make their own mozzarella and burrata and try to use locally sourced produce and meats wherever they can. They have an extensive greenhouse where they grow their own fresh herbs and vegetables year-round. It's quite an operation."

"Who would have thought I could find such a good pizza in the wilds of eastern Idaho?"

She smiled, proud of her little community. While it might be primarily a ranching town, Pine Gulch was gaining a reputation as a foodie destination and a magnet for artists.

"I understand they get customers from as far away as Jackson Hole who read about the pizza online and want to try a slice."

She was finishing her second slice when she spotted her friend Caidy Caldwell coming in with her husband, the local veterinarian, and their children. Caidy had grown up in Cold Creek Canyon and had been a friend for a long time. Celeste loved seeing her so happy with Ben.

When she spotted Celeste, she waved, said something to Ben and the kids, then headed in her direction.

"Hi, Celeste! I'm so glad I bumped into you. Great story time last week. The kids really enjoyed it."

"Thanks. It was great to see you there."

"I don't know how you always manage to find such absolutely charming stories—old favorites and then so many that no one has ever heard before."

"That's my job," she said with a smile. That was one of her favorite parts about it, seeking out the new and unusual along with the classics everybody expected and loved.

"You do it well," Caidy said. "Almost *too* well. We might have to quit coming to the library. Every time you read a new book the kids have to buy it."

"Because they're all so good." Her stepdaughter, Ava, had joined her.

"Right. But now the shelves of our home library are bulging."

"You can never have too many books," Celeste answered.

"That's what I always say," Ava exclaimed. She turned to Olivia. "Hi. I'm Ava Caldwell."

"Sorry. This is Flynn Delaney and his daughter, Olivia. Flynn, this is my friend Caidy Caldwell and her daughter, Ava. Ava also has a brother about your age named Jack and a new baby brother who is the cutest thing around, Liam."

As her friend smiled at the two of them, Celeste didn't miss the flash of recognition or sympathy in her gaze before she smoothly masked her reaction. Caidy obviously had followed the news stories and knew what had happened to the girl.

"I'm happy to meet you both," her friend said with a smile. "Welcome to Pine Gulch. I hope you're staying around for a while."

He shook his head. "I'm afraid not. Only until after the holidays."

"Well, you picked one of the best times of the whole year to be here. You won't find many prettier winter wonderlands than this part of Idaho."

"It's lovely," he agreed.

"I didn't mean to interrupt your dinner. I just needed to ask you again what time practice is tomorrow. I know you've told me a half dozen times but I swear Christmas makes my brain leak out of my ears."

"Four thirty sharp at the St. Nicholas Lodge at the ranch. We should be done by six thirty."

"Perfect. My kids are so excited about it."

Celeste had no idea how Hope had persuaded her to take on one more thing, in this case organizing a small program to be performed at an inaugural Senior Citizens Christmas dinner a few days before the holiday.

Hope's particular skill was getting Celeste to do things she ordinarily never would attempt—like publish her books and then agree to allow one of those books to be made into a movie.

"Olivia, if you're going to be here through Christmas, you should think about being in the play," Ava suggested.

Flynn tensed up at the idea, his jaw taut. To Celeste's surprise, Olivia only looked intrigued.

"I was in a play in school once. It was fun."

"This isn't a huge production," Celeste assured Flynn. "We're just doing a simple Christmas program. Everybody who wants to participate gets a part. We're mostly singing songs everybody already knows."

"Can I do it, Dad?"

He frowned. "We'll have to talk about that. We're pretty busy cleaning out the house. I don't know if we'll have time to go to practices and things."

"There are only three practices," Celeste said. "Tomorrow, Thursday night and Saturday morning, and then the show is Tuesday, the day before Christmas Eve. She would be more than welcome to come. The rehearsals and the show are all at the St. Nicholas Lodge at The Christmas Ranch, just five minutes from your place."

A Christmas program. With an audience, applause. The whole bit. He wanted to tell them all absolutely not, to grab his daughter and drag her out of here.

He'd had enough of performers to last him a lifetime.

His entire life, he had been forced to wait on the sidelines while the important females in his life sought fame and recognition. His mother had made it clear from the time he was old enough to understand that he could never be the most important thing in her life—not when her adoring public already held that honor.

Elise had pretended otherwise, but when it came down to it, he had been even less important to her, only a stepping-stone on her journey to success.

He didn't want Olivia anywhere near a stage or a movie set. So far she hadn't shown any inclination in that direction, much to his relief. He wanted to keep it that way.

He told himself he was being ridiculous. It was only a Christmas program, not a Broadway production. Still, he didn't want to offer her any opportunity to catch the performing bug.

She was still so fragile. While her physical wounds had mostly healed, emotionally and mentally she was still had a long journey.

Was he being too protective? Probably. Her therapist in California told him he needed to relax and let go a little. He didn't need to watch over her every single moment. Right now he had a tendency to want to keep her close, to tuck her up against him and make sure nothing terrifying or tragic ever touched her again.

That wasn't a healthy approach, either. He couldn't protect her from everything, even though he wanted to.

"Can I do it, Dad?" she asked again.

This was the same girl who freaked out in large crowds, who didn't like loud noises and who tended to panic if strangers tried to talk to her.

Did she seriously think she could handle being onstage in front of a bunch of strangers?

"We can talk about it later," he said.

"Absolutely," Caidy said with a cheerful smile, though he thought he saw soft compassion in her gaze.

Did she know about what had happened to Olivia? Probably. Most of the damn world knew. It had led media reports around the world for a week, had been on the cover of all the tabloids and celebrity rags.

When an Oscar-nominated actress is gunned down by her equally famous if mentally ill boyfriend—who then shoots her young child before killing himself—people tended to pay attention.

If he thought he could come to this remote corner of Idaho and escape notice, he was delusional. He doubted he could find anywhere on the planet where the news hadn't reached.

Maybe he could have taken Olivia on an African safari or something, but even then he wouldn't have been surprised if people in the veld knew of Elise Chandler.

"It was nice to meet you," Ava said politely. "I hope we see you at rehearsal tomorrow."

His daughter needed friends, he thought again. They had always been important to her. Before everything happened, she always had been begging to have a friend over to use the pool or watch a movie.

Since her release from the hospital, she hadn't been interested in doing the normal things a seven-year-old girl would do. Ava Caldwell was older than his daughter, maybe eleven or twelve, but she seemed very kind. Maybe Celeste knew of some other likely candidates Olivia could hang out with while they were in town.

If it helped her interact with children around her age, would the Christmas program really be that bad?

Being a parent was a tough enough gig under the best of circumstances. Throw in the kind of trauma his daughter had endured and he felt as though he was foundering, trying to stay afloat in thirty-foot swells.

The Caldwells waved and headed for their table, and Flynn returned to his delicious pizza. The people at the Rocky Mountain Pizza Company knew what they were doing when it came to pie, he had to admit. Olivia, he saw, ate two pieces and even some of the family-style tossed salad, which seemed something of a record for her, given her poor appetite these days.

While they ate, they talked about Christmas and books and a couple of movies they had all seen. Three different times, people who came into the restaurant stopped at their booth to say hello to Celeste.

Olivia seemed to find that of great interest. "Do you know everybody who lives here?" she finally asked.

Celeste laughed, a light, musical sound. "Not even close, though it feels like it sometimes. When you live in a place for a long time you get to know lots of people. I've been in Pine Gulch since I was eleven—except for the years I was away in Boise and Seattle for school."

"Where did you live before that?" he asked, suddenly intensely curious about her.

He was even more curious when her cheerful features seemed to go still and closed. She didn't say anything for several long seconds, so long that he wasn't sure she was going to answer him at all.

"It didn't seem like a tough question," he said mildly.

"For you, maybe," she retorted. "You grew up in California with your mother after your parents divorced, and spent your summers here with Charlotte, right?"

How did she know that? he wondered. He only remembered meeting her a few times back when he would come to visit and didn't remember ever sharing that information with her. Maybe Charlotte had told her.

He gave her a close look but she seemed lost in her own thoughts.

"That's right," he answered. "And you?"

"No one specific place," she finally answered. "I lived all over the globe, if you want the truth. I was born in a hut in Ghana, and before I was eleven, I lived in about two dozen countries. My parents were missionaries who started health clinics in underserved places of the world. Before I came to Pine Gulch, we were living in Colombia."

Some kind of vague, unsettling memory poked at him, a whisper he had once heard about Celeste and her sisters. Something to do with a kidnapping, with her parents.

He couldn't put his finger on the details. What was it? Was that the reason for those secrets in her eyes, for the pain he sensed there?

He opened his mouth to ask her, but before he could a loud clatter echoed through the place as a server busing the table next to them dropped the bin of dishes.

At the sudden, unexpected sound, Olivia gave one terrified gasp and slid from her seat under the table.

Damn, he hated these moments when her PTSD took over. They left him both furious and profoundly sad. He took a breath and leaned down to talk her through it, but Celeste beat him to it. She reached down and gave Olivia's shoulder a comforting squeeze beneath the table.

"It's okay. You're okay. It was only dishes. That's all. I know you were startled, but you're safe, sweetheart."

Olivia was making little whimpering noises that broke his heart all over again.

"I don't like loud noises," she said.

"Especially when you don't expect them and don't have time to prepare. Those are the *worst*, right?"

To his shock, Celeste spoke with a tone of experience. He gazed at her, trying to remember again what he knew about her and her sisters.

"They are," Olivia said. Though she still sounded upset, he could no longer hear the blind panic in her voice.

"Why don't you come up and finish your pizza? If you want, I can ask Lucy about fixing you one of their best desserts. It's a big gooey chocolate-chip cookie they bake in the wood-fired oven and top with hand-churned ice cream. I think you'll love it. I know it's my favorite thing to eat when I've been startled or upset about something."

After another moment, Olivia peeked her head out from under the booth. "They're not going to make that sound again, are they?"

"I don't think so. That was an accident."

"I hope they don't have another accident," she answered in a small voice.

"If they do, your dad and I are right here to make sure nothing hurts you."

That seemed enough to satisfy her. His daughter slid back onto the seat. She still had a wild look in her eyes, and he noticed she edged closer to him and constantly looked toward Celeste for reassurance while they finished their pizza.

He didn't miss the protective expression Celeste wore

in return, an expression that turned *his* insides just as gooey as that chocolate-chip cookie she was talking about.

He couldn't let himself develop feelings for this woman, no matter how amazing she was with his child, he reminded himself.

He had to focus on his daughter right now. She was the only thing that mattered.

Chapter Six

"Is she asleep?" Celeste whispered an hour later, when they made the turn onto Cold Creek Road.

He glanced in the rearview mirror and could see Olivia curled into the corner, her eyes closed and her cheek resting on her hand.

"Looks like it." He pitched his voice low. "She's always been a kid who can sleep anywhere, especially when she's had a long day. Driving in the car has always knocked her right out. When she was going through the terrible twos and used to fight going to bed, I would strap her in her car seat and drive her around the block a few times. She always ran so hard that when she finally stopped, she would drop like a rock by the time we hit the first corner."

"Did she stay asleep?"

"Yeah. That was the amazing part. She never seemed

to mind when I unstrapped her from her car seat and carried her into the house to her bed. I was kind of sorry when she outgrew that phase and started sleeping in her own bed without a fuss."

Beside him, he caught a flash of white in the darkness as Celeste smiled a little. "I imagine she was an adorable toddler."

"Oh, she was. Scary smart and curious about everything."

He felt a sharp pang in his heart when he thought again about how much she had changed, how she had become so fearful and hesitant. Would the old Olivia ever return, or was this their new version of normal?

"I wish you could have known her three months ago. Before."

Celeste reached out to touch his arm briefly, like a little bird landing on a branch for only a moment before fluttering away again.

"She's a wonderful girl, Flynn. A terrible thing happened to her, yes, but she's already demonstrated what a survivor she is. Trust me. She'll get through it in time. She may always have those dark memories—nothing can take them away completely—but eventually she'll learn how to replace them with happier thoughts."

He glanced over at her. "Is that how you coped?"

He could sense her sudden fine-edged tension. "I don't know what you mean."

"What happened to you? I vaguely remember my grandmother saying something about you and your sisters enduring a terrible ordeal, but I've been racking my brain and can't remember what. I should. I'm sorry."

She was silent for a long time and he didn't press, just

continued driving through the quiet night through Cold Creek Canyon.

The creek here wound beside the road and through the trees, silvery in the moonlight. Tall pines and firs grew beside cottonwoods along the banks, at times almost forming a tunnel over the road. It was beautiful and mysterious at night with the snow fluttering gently against the windshield and the occasional house or ranchette decorated with Christmas lights.

She finally spoke when they were almost to the Star N. "It's a time of my life I don't like to think about," she murmured.

"Oh?"

She sighed. "I told you my parents moved us around the globe under sometimes difficult circumstances."

He nodded, wondering what her life must have been like without any kind of stable place to call home. Had she thrived there or had she always felt as if something were missing in her life?

She loved to read. Perhaps books had been her one constant friend through all the chaos and uncertainty.

"When I was eleven, we moved to Colombia to open a clinic in a small, undeveloped region. My parents were assured over and over that it was a safe area to bring their daughters."

"It wasn't?"

"The village where we lived might have been safe, but several in the region were not."

With reluctance he pulled up in front of her house, wishing he could keep driving. He shouldn't have worried. She didn't appear to notice where they were, that he had parked the vehicle and turned to face her. She hardly seemed aware he was there as she spoke, her features tight and her eyes focused on some spot through the windshield that he had a feeling wasn't anywhere close to eastern Idaho.

"We had been living in the village about six weeks when the clinic drew the attention of the local rebel leader in one of those unstable villages who happened to be in need of some extra cash to fund his soldiers. I guess Juan Pablo thought he could get a handsome sum in ransom if he kidnapped the crazy American do-gooders. The only trouble with that plan was that my parents weren't associated with any larger organization with deep pockets. They were free agents, I guess you could say. There was no money to pay a ransom and no one to pay it."

"What happened?"

"Juan Pablo didn't believe my parents when they insisted no one could pay a ransom. He thought if he held us long enough, the US government at least would step in, especially with the lives of three young girls at stake. We were held hostage for several weeks in a squalid prison camp."

What the hell had her parents been thinking, to drag three young girls all over the world into these unstable situations? He was all for helping others and admired those selfless people who only wanted to make a difference in the world, but not when it cost the well-being of their own children.

"Did someone eventually pay the ransom?"

She shook her head. "That was never one of the options. Juan Pablo was just too stupid or too blinded by greed to realize it. Instead, after we had been held for several weeks, a team of US Navy SEALs mounted an early-morning rescue."

She paused, her head bowed and her dark curls hiding

her features. When she spoke, her voice was low, tight with remembered pain.

"The rescue wasn't a complete success. My father was…shot by Juan Pablo's rebels while we were trying to escape. He died instantly."

"Oh, Celeste. I'm so sorry."

"You can see why I feel great empathy for Olivia and what she's going through. Seeing a parent die violently is a trauma no child should have to endure."

"I completely agree," he said. "Again, I'm so sorry."

She lifted one shoulder. "It happened. I can't change it. For a long time, I struggled to deal with the injustice of it all. My parents were only trying to help others and my father paid the ultimate price for his benevolence. I can't say I've ever really found peace with that or ever will, but I've been able to move forward. For what it's worth, I freaked out at loud noises for a long time, too. Probably a good year or two after the accident."

"You seem to handle them fine now."

She gave a small laugh. "I wouldn't be a very good children's librarian if I couldn't handle a little noise, believe me. I would have run screaming into the night after the very first story time."

"So how did you come to live with your aunt and uncle?" he asked.

She shifted her gaze to his for only a moment before she looked out the windshield again, as if she couldn't quite bear to make eye contact while she told the rest of the story.

"In possibly the cruelest twist of all, our mother was diagnosed with cancer shortly after we were rescued from Colombia. She had been sick for a while but hadn't sought the necessary medical care. She'd apparently suspected something was wrong before we were taken and had made an appointment for tests in Bogota in the days right around our kidnapping—an appointment she couldn't make, for obvious reasons. It was…an aggressive and deadly form of cancer. Largely because she didn't get the treatment she needed in a timely manner, she died four months later, after we came back to the States."

Unable to resist, he reached for her hand and held it in his for a moment, wishing he had the words to tell her how much he admired her.

So many people he knew would have pulled inside themselves and let the tragedy and injustice of it turn them bitter and angry at the world. Instead, she had become a strong, compassionate woman who was helping children learn to love words and stories, while she wrote uplifting, heartwarming tales where good always triumphed.

She looked down at their joined hands, and her lips parted just a little before she closed them and swallowed. "After our mother died, Uncle Claude and Aunt Mary opened their home and their hearts to us, and we've been here ever since."

"And thus you entered the world of Christmas extravaganzas."

This time her laugh sounded more natural—a sweet, spontaneous sound that seemed to slide through his chest and tug at his heart. He liked the sound of her laughter. It made him want to sit in this warm car with her all night while soft Christmas music played on the stereo and snow fluttered against the windshield and his daughter slept soundly in the backseat.

"There was no Christmas Ranch before we came here. Uncle Claude had the idea a year later. My sisters and I share the theory that he did it only to distract us because he knew the holidays would be tough for us without our parents, especially that first anniversary."

"You were kidnapped at Christmastime?" That only seemed to add to the tragedy of it, that people could cruelly and viciously use an innocent family for financial gain during a time that was supposed to be about peace on earth and goodwill toward men.

"Yes." She leaned back against the seat and gazed out at the snowflakes dancing against the windshield. "My mother and father would try to keep up our spirits during our captivity by singing carols with us and encouraging us to make up Christmas stories."

"Ah. And you've carried on their storytelling tradition."

"In my feeble way, I guess you're right."

"Not feeble," he protested. "*Sparkle and the Magic Snowball* is a charming story that has captured the hearts of children and parents alike."

She looked embarrassed. "Mostly because of Hope and her beautiful illustrations."

"And because the story is sweet and hopeful at a time when people desperately need that."

She shifted in the seat, her cheeks slightly pink in the low light.

"I never expected any of this. I only wanted to tell stories to my niece and nephew. I don't know if I would ever have found the courage to submit it to a publisher. I didn't, actually. If not for Hope, all the Sparkle stories would still be in a box under my bed."

He released her fingers, not at all sure he liked this soft tenderness seeping through him. "Your parents would be so proud of you. Who would have guessed when you were sharing stories with your parents and sisters while you were all hostages during a dark Christmastime that one day you would be a famous author?"

"Not me, certainly."

"Does writing make you feel closer to your parents?"

She stared at him for a long moment, her eyes wide. "I… Yes. Yes, it does. I never realized that until right this moment when you said it. Sometimes when I'm writing, I feel as if they're with me again, whispering words of comfort to me in the darkness."

It would be easy to fall for her. Something about her combination of vulnerability and strength tugged at him, called to him in a way no other woman ever had.

He didn't have *time* for this, he reminded himself sternly. His daughter needed all his attention right now while she tried to heal. He couldn't dilute that attention by finding himself tangled up with a lovely librarian, no matter how much he might want to be.

"I had better go," she said after a moment. Did she also sense the growing attraction between them? Was that the reason for that sudden unease in her expression? "You should get a certain exhausted birthday girl home to her bed. Besides that, Linus and Lucy are probably wondering what in the world I'm doing out here for so long."

"Of course."

With far more reluctance than he knew he should feel, he opened his door and walked around the vehicle through the lightly falling snow to her door.

The December night smelled of pine and smoke from a fireplace somewhere close. The familiar mingle of scents struck deep into his memories, of the happy times he used to spend here with his grandmother. She had been his rock, the one constant support in the midst of his chaotic family life.

He breathed in deeply as he opened her car door. As they walked to her house, he realized with shock that this was the most peaceful he had felt in weeks, since that horrible day when he'd pulled up to Elise's house to find sirens and flashing lights and ambulances.

"You don't have to walk me to the door, Flynn. This isn't a date."

He suddenly *wished* it had been a date, that the two of them had gone to dinner somewhere and shared secrets and stories and long, delicious kisses.

If it had been a date, he possibly could give into this sudden hunger to kiss her at the doorstep, to finally taste that lush mouth that had been tantalizing him all evening.

"I want to make sure you don't slip," he said. It wasn't exactly a lie, just not the entire truth. "Ice can be dangerous."

She said nothing, though he thought her eyes might have narrowed slightly as if she sensed he had more on his mind than merely her safety.

They both made it up the steps without incident, and it only took her a moment to find a key in her purse.

"Good night," she said after she unlocked her door. "Thank you for including me in Olivia's birthday celebration. It was an honor, truly."

"We were the lucky ones that you agreed to come. It was a dream come true for her, sharing delicious pizza with her favorite author."

"I imagine her dreams will become a little more lofty as she gets older, but I'm happy I could help with this one." She gave him a sidelong look. "I hope I see her at the rehearsal tomorrow for the Christmas program. She really seemed to be interested in participating, and we would love to have her. Don't worry. She'll have fun."

Damn. He had almost forgotten about that. The peace he had been feeling seemed to evaporate like the puffs of air from their breaths.

"Don't plan on her," he warned.

"Why not?" she asked with a frown.

He raked a hand through his hair. "She's been through a brutal experience. Would you have been ready for something like this right after your own trauma?"

"I don't know," she admitted. "But if I expressed any interest at all, my aunt and uncle would have been right in the front row, cheering me on."

"I'm not your aunt and uncle," he said, with more bite in his voice than he intended.

She froze for just a moment, then nodded, her sweet, lovely features turning as wintry as the evening. "I'm sorry. You're right. I overstepped."

Her words and the tight tone made him feel like an ass. She was only trying to help his child.

"I'm sorry," he said. "I just can't see how getting up in front of a bunch of strangers and singing about peace on earth will help a young girl suffering from PTSD."

"I suppose you're right. I will say that my parents firmly believed a person could ease her own troubles while helping others—or at least trying to see them in a different light. Living here with Uncle Claude and Aunt Mary only reinforced that message. They started The Christmas Ranch so my sisters and I could find comfort in the midst of our own pain by bringing the joy of the holidays to others. It worked for us. I guess I was hoping it would do the same for Olivia, but you're her father. It's ultimately your decision."

Talk about backing a guy into a corner. What was he supposed to do?

Olivia *had* expressed a desire to participate, the first time anything had sparked her interest in weeks. He certainly had the right as her father to make decisions about what he thought was best for her, but what if he was wrong? What if she truly did need this? How could he be the one to say no to her?

"Fine," he said reluctantly. "I'll bring her tomorrow. If she enjoys herself, she can come back. But if I believe this is at all stressing her, I'll immediately put an end to it."

She smiled and he was struck again by how lovely she was. Behind her quiet prettiness was a woman of true beauty; she just seemed determined to hide it.

"Oh, that's wonderful. We'll be thrilled to have her. We'll see you tomorrow afternoon, in the main lodge at the ranch. Do you know where it is?"

"I'll figure it out."

"Excellent. I'll see you both tomorrow, then."

He knew that idea shouldn't leave him with this bubbly anticipation.

"Good night. Thanks again for having dinner with us."

"You're welcome. It was truly my pleasure."

He started to leave and then, prompted by the impulse that had been coursing through him all evening, he reached forward and kissed her softly on the cheek, the light sort of kiss people gave to even their casual acquaintances in California.

She smelled delicious—of laundry soap and almonds and some kind of springtime flowers. It took him a moment to place her scent. Violets—sweet and fresh and full of hope.

Instantly, he knew this was a mistake, that he would be dreaming of that scent all night.

Her eyes, wide and shocked behind her glasses, were impossibly green. It would be easy—so very easy—to shift his mouth just a few inches and truly kiss her. For an instant the temptation was overwhelming, but he drew on all his strength and forced himself to step away.

"Good night," he said again. To his dismay, his voice sounded ragged.

"Yes," she answered with a dazed sort of look that he told himself was only surprise.

He didn't give himself the chance to explore if that look in her eyes might have some other source—like a shared attraction, for instance. He just turned around and headed down the steps of her porch and toward his vehicle and his sleeping child.

When she was certain Flynn was in his car, driving back down the lane toward the main road, Celeste moved away from the window and sank into her favorite chair. Lucy—all sleek, sinuous grace—immediately pounced into her lap. She took a moment to pet the cat, her thoughts twirling.

For a moment there she had been almost positive Flynn Delaney had been about to *really* kiss her. That was impossible. Completely irrational. She must have been imagining things, right?

Why on earth would he want to kiss *her*? She was gawky and awkward and shy, more comfortable with books and her fictional characters than she was with men.

They were from completely different worlds, which was probably one of the reasons she'd had such a crush on him when she was a girl. He represented the unattainable. His mother was a famous movie star, and he was certainly gorgeous enough that *he* could have been one, too, if he'd been inclined in that direction.

He had been married to Elise Chandler, for Pete's sake, one of the most beautiful women on earth. How could he possibly be interested in a frumpy, introverted *children's librarian*?

The absurdity of it completely defied reason.

She must be mistaken. That moment when he'd kissed her cheek and their gazes had met—when she'd thought she'd seen that spark of *something* kindling in his gaze—must have been a trick of the low lighting in her entryway.

What would it have been like to kiss him? *Really* kiss him?

The question buzzed around inside her brain like a particularly determined mosquito. She had no doubt it would have been amazing.

She was destined never to know.

She sighed, gazing at the lights of her little Christmas tree sparkling cheerily in the small space. If she weren't careful, she could end up with a heart as shattered as one of the ornaments Lucy liked to bat off the branches.

It would be so frighteningly easy for her to fall for him. She was already fiercely attracted to him and had been since she was barely a teenager. More than that, she liked and admired him. His devotion to Olivia and his concern for her were even more attractive to Celeste than those vivid blue eyes, the broad shoulders, the rugged slant of his jaw.

If he were to kiss her—truly kiss her—her poor, untested heart wouldn't stand a chance.

After a moment she pushed away the unease. This

entire mental side trip was ridiculous and unnecessary. He wasn't interested in her and he wouldn't kiss her, so why spend another moment fretting about it?

Still, she couldn't help wishing she never had encouraged him to allow Olivia to participate in the Christmas program at the ranch. He was only here for a few weeks. The likelihood that she would even *see* the man again would have been very slim if not for Olivia and the program, and then she could have let this hopeless attraction die a natural death.

No worries, she told herself. She would simply do her best to return things to a casual, friendly level for his remaining time in Cold Creek.

How hard could it be?

Chapter Seven

Dealing with thirty jacked-up children a week before Christmas was not exactly the best way to unwind after a busy day at work.

Celeste drew in a deep breath, let it out slowly and ordered herself to chill. The noise level inside the two-story St. Nicholas Lodge was at epic levels. In one corner, a group of third-grade boys tossed around a paper airplane one of them had folded. In another, two girls were singing "Let it Go" at the top of their lungs. Three of the younger boys were chasing each other around, coming dangerously close to the huge Christmas tree that was the focal point of the lodge.

All the children were so excited for Christmas they were putting off enough energy to power the entire holiday light displays of three counties.

How she was supposed to whip this frenzy into organized chaos she had no idea.

"Whose crazy idea was this again?" her sister said, taking in the scene.

She sent Hope an arch look. "Go ahead. Raise your hand."

Hope offered up a rueful smile. "Sorry. It seemed like a fun idea at the time, a way to keep the local kids engaged and involved and give their parents a little break for shopping and baking, with the payoff of a cute show for the senior citizens at the end. I suppose I didn't really think it through."

"How very unlike you," Faith said drily from Celeste's other side.

Faith's presence was far more of a shock to Celeste than the wild energy of the children. Their eldest sister was usually so busy working on the cattle-raising side of the business that she didn't participate in many activities at The Christmas Ranch.

Perhaps she had decided to stop by because Louisa and Barrett were participating. Whatever the reason, Celeste was glad to see her there. The past eighteen months had been so difficult for Faith, losing her childhood sweetheart unexpectedly. It was good to see her sister reaching outside her comfort zone a little.

"I guess I didn't expect them all to be so…jacked up." Hope couldn't seem to take her gaze away from the younger children, who were now hopping around the room like bunny rabbits.

"You obviously don't have children," Faith said.

"Or work in a children's library," Celeste added.

"All kids act as if they're on crack cocaine the whole week before Christmas," Faith continued. "How could you not know that?"

"Okay, okay. Lesson learned. Now we just have to do our best to whip them into shape. We can do this, right?"

At the note of desperation in Hope's voice, Celeste forced a confident smile. "Sure we can."

Though she had her own doubts, she wouldn't voice them to Hope. She was too grateful for her sister for bringing light and joy back to the ranch.

After Travis's death in a ranching accident, Celeste, Mary and Faith had decided to close The Christmas Ranch, which had been losing money steadily for years. It had seemed the logical course of action. The Star N had been all but bankrupt and the Christmas side of things had been steadily losing money for years.

The plan had been to focus on the cattle side of the Star N, until Hope came back from years of traveling. She put her considerable energy and enthusiasm to work and single-handedly brought back the holiday attraction.

Part of that success had come because of the Sparkle books, which still managed to astonish Celeste.

She would always be deeply grateful to Hope for reminding them all of the joy and wonder of the season. Helping her with this Christmas program was a small way to repay her for all her hard work on behalf of the family.

"We've got this," she said to her sisters with a firm smile that contained far more assurance than she really felt.

She stepped forward and started to clap her hands to gather the children around when the door opened and a couple of newcomers came in. She turned with a smile to welcome them and felt an actual physical jolt when she saw Flynn and Olivia.

Despite his agreement the night before, she had been

certain Flynn would end up not bringing Olivia. She had seen the clear reluctance in his eyes and knew he worried the girl wasn't ready for this sort of public appearance.

She was thrilled for Olivia's sake that he had changed his mind, even if it meant she would have to do her best to ignore her own reaction to him—and even though she wouldn't have been nearly as exhausted today if not for him.

Her night had been restless. She couldn't seem to shake the memory of that moment when he had kissed her cheek—the warmth of his mouth, the brush of his evening shadow against her skin, the delicious, outdoorsy scent of him.

She shivered now in remembered reaction.

"Are you cold?" Faith asked in a low voice.

No. Exactly the opposite. "I'm fine." The lie rolled out far more easily than she would have expected. She had never been very good at stretching the truth.

"That must be Flynn," Hope said in an undertone, following her gaze to the newcomers. "Wow. He's really filled out since he was a teenager. Where's a nice lawn to be mowed when we need it?"

Faith laughed aloud, something she did very rarely these days. She had become so much more sober since Travis died.

"Good luck with that, finding a patch of bare lawn in Idaho in December," Faith said. "Too bad you can't talk him into shoveling snow without his shirt."

That was an image Celeste didn't need to add to the others in her head. She felt herself color, then immediately regretted the reaction when her sisters both looked between her and Flynn with renewed interest. Drat. They were both entirely too perceptive. The last thing she needed was for either Hope or Faith to get any matchmaking ideas where Flynn was concerned.

She quickly left her annoying sisters and moved forward to greet the newcomers.

Olivia looked nervous, half hiding behind her father. She visibly relaxed when Celeste approached.

"Hi, Celeste."

"It's my favorite just-turned-seven-year-old. Hi."

"It's noisy in here," Olivia informed her in an accusing sort of voice, as if it was *Celeste's* fault all the children were so wild.

"I know. Sorry about that. We're just about to get started. Once we focus everybody's attention, things will calm down. How are you today?"

Olivia smiled a little. "Okay, I guess. My dad didn't want to bring me, but I asked him and asked him until he finally said yes."

"I'm so glad," she said.

She shifted her gaze finally to Flynn and found him watching her with an unreadable look. She was suddenly aware that she must look tousled and harried. She had come straight from work, stopping at home only long enough to let Linus out and yank her hair up into a messy bun. She wore jeans and her favorite baggy sweater, and she was pretty sure her makeup had worn off hours ago.

For just a moment, she wished she could be beautiful and sophisticated instead of what she was—boring.

"Hi," she said to him. To her dismay, her voice sounded breathless and nervous. "I wasn't sure you would come."

"Apparently my daughter is relentless. Kind of like someone else I know."

She had to smile at the slightly disgruntled note in his voice.

"This will be fun. You'll see. We're going to practice until about six thirty. If you have shopping to do or want to go back to work on your grandmother's house, you're welcome to return for her then. Actually, I could even drop her off. It's not far."

He looked around at the chaos of the jacked-up children and then back at his nervous daughter.

"I believe I'll stay, if you don't mind."

What if she *did* mind? What if the idea of him watching her for the next two hours made her more nervous than a turkey at Thanksgiving?

She didn't know what else she could do but nod. "Sure. Of course. There are sofas over by the fireplace where you can make yourself comfortable. If you'd rather be closer to the action here, feel free to bring over a chair."

"Thanks."

He then proceeded to take neither of those suggestions. Instead, he leaned against the wall, crossed his arms over his chest and turned his full attention in her direction.

"Right." She swallowed and glanced at her watch. They should have started practicing five minutes ago.

She clapped her hands loudly and firmly three times to grab everyone's attention and said in her most firm librarian voice. "By the count of ten, I need everybody to gather around me and freeze in your best Christmas statue pose. Ready? One. Two. Three…"

By the time she hit four, all thirty children—thirty one now, including Olivia—had made their way to her and adopted various positions. Destry Bowman, one of the older girls, was stretched out on the floor pretending to be asleep. Cute little Jolie Wheeler looked as if she was trying to do a figure eight on skates. Her niece, Louisa, appeared to be reaching on tiptoes for something, and it took Celeste a moment before she realized she was trying to put ornaments on an invisible Christmas tree.

Olivia looked uncertain, standing nervously with her hands clasped in front of her.

Celeste gave her a reassuring smile and then turned her attention to the other children.

“Perfect. Statues, you can all relax now and sit down.”

The children complied instantly and she smiled. They might be a wild bunch but she loved them all. Each was someone whose name she knew, either from being neighbors and friends with their parents or from church or her work at the library.

“Thank you! This is going to be great fun, you’ll see. The senior citizens and your families are going to *love* it, trust me, and you’ll have fun, too. Are you all ready to put together a great show for your families?”

“Yes!” they shouted as one.

“Let’s get to it, then.”

He never would have predicted it when he walked into chaos, but somehow the ragtag collection of hyperactive children had calmed down considerably and were working hard together.

Celeste had organized the children into small groups of five or six and assigned one older child to teach them the song or dance they were to perform. She in turn moved between the groups offering words of advice or encouragement, working on a lyric here or a dance move there.

He found it charming to watch, especially seeing her lose her natural reserve with the children.

Was that why she had become a children’s librarian, because she was more comfortable interacting with them?

He was curious—but then he was curious about *everything* that had to do with Celeste Nichols.

Naturally, he kept a careful eye on his daughter, but she seemed to have relaxed considerably since they'd walked in. Just now she was talking and—yes!—even *laughing* with three children he'd heard call Celeste their aunt, a couple of boys about her age and a girl who appeared to be a few years older.

Had Celeste said something to them, somehow encouraged them to be especially welcoming to Olivia? He wouldn't have been surprised, but maybe they were as naturally compassionate and caring as their aunt. Whatever the reason, the children seemed to have gone out of their way to show kindness and help her feel more comfortable, which went a long way toward alleviating his own concerns.

He doubted anything could make him feel totally enthusiastic about Olivia performing in the little production, but it helped considerably to see her enjoying herself so much and interacting with her peers.

He wasn't sure he was ready to admit it, but Celeste might have been right. This little children's performance in a small community in Idaho might be exactly what Olivia needed to help her begin to heal from the horrors she had endured.

He finally relaxed enough to take a seat on one of the sofas by the fireplace and was reading through email messages from his office on his cell phone when one of the women Celeste had been talking with when he and Olivia arrived took a seat on the sofa across from him.

"Hi, Flynn. You probably don't remember me, but I'm Hope Santiago. Used to be Nichols. I'm Celeste's sister."

Ah. No wonder she had looked familiar, though she

only shared green eyes in common with her sister. Instead of Celeste's silky brown hair and quiet, restful loveliness, Hope Santiago was pretty in a Bohemian sort of way, with long, wavy blonde hair and a cluster of exotic-looking bracelets at her wrist.

He had met her before, he thought, back when he used to come here for the summers.

"Hello. Sure, I remember you. You're married now. Congratulations."

She gave a pleased-as-punch smile and gestured through the doorway to what looked like an office where a big, tough-looking dude with a couple of tats was speaking on a cell phone.

"That's my husband, Rafe. He and I run The Christmas Ranch together."

"The two of you must just be overflowing with Christmas spirit."

She chuckled. "We do our best. Thanks for letting your daughter participate in the show. It means a lot to Celeste."

He wasn't sure he had exactly "let" Olivia do anything. He'd been steamrollered into it, when all was said and done, but so far things seemed to be working out.

He shrugged. "It's for a good cause, right? Making some older people happy. That can only be a good thing, right?"

"Exactly." She beamed at him.

"You're the artist," he realized suddenly. "The one who took Celeste's Sparkle story and turned it into a book."

She nodded. "That's me," she answered.

"They're charming illustrations that go perfectly with the story," he told her. "I read the second book again to my daughter last night, for about the twentieth time in just a few days. It's every bit as sweet as the first one. The two of you make a great team."

She looked pleased at his words. "Thanks, but Celeste is the creative genius. I just took her fabulous story and drew little pictures to go with it. Any success the Sparkle book has seen is because of her story."

"That's funny. She said almost exactly the same thing about you and your illustrations."

"She would," she said with a laugh. "Don't make the mistake of thinking we're always adoring sisters, so sweet to each other we'll make your teeth hurt. We're not afraid to have it out. I think I've still got a little bald spot in the back of my head where she yanked out some hair during a fight when we were kids. She might look sweet and all, with that quiet librarian thing she has going, but she can fight dirty, even when you're bigger than she is."

He had to laugh. He glanced over at Celeste, who was holding an upset preschooler on her lap and trying to calm him, her face close to his. Flynn did his best to imagine her in a physical fight with one of her sisters. He couldn't quite make the image fit, but had to admit he enjoyed trying.

She must have felt his gaze. She looked up from the little boy and whatever she was saying to him. He saw her swallow and watched her features turn rosy, much to his secret enjoyment. After a moment, she turned back to the child and he shifted his gaze back to Hope, who was watching him with interest.

"Looks as if we're just about wrapping up here," she said casually. "If you haven't had dinner, why don't you and your daughter come up to the ranch house after practice? Aunt Mary is making lasagna and her famous crusty bread sticks. You can celebrate with us."

"What are you celebrating?"

"We just agreed to let a film studio begin work on an animated Sparkle movie. It's going into production immediately, with hopes that it will be out by next Christmas. And with the money we're getting for the film rights, we're paying off the second mortgage our uncle took on the Star N. We'd love to have you celebrate with us."

His stomach rumbled on cue while he was still trying to take in the surprising invitation. "That's very kind of you, but I don't want to intrude."

"Intrude on what?" Another woman who looked enough like Celeste and Hope to make him certain this was their other sister joined them by the fireplace.

"I invited Flynn and his daughter over for lasagna. Aunt Mary won't mind, will she?"

"Are you kidding? She'll be over the moon to have a few more people to fuss over, and you know she always makes enough to feed half the town."

His first inclination was to say no. He even opened his mouth to refuse the invitation, but then he caught sight of Olivia looking more relaxed and animated than he had seen her in a long time. Right next to her was Celeste, apparently done calming the upset little boy and now smiling at something Olivia had said.

He couldn't seem to look away.

"Sure," he answered before he had a chance to think it through. He had no plans for dinner beyond warming up the pizza they'd had the night before, and he had a feeling Olivia was getting a little tired of his meager culinary abilities. "Thank you for inviting us. Lasagna sounds delicious, and we would be honored to celebrate with you, especially since Olivia is your biggest fan."

"Excellent," Hope said, looking delighted.

"I'd better call Aunt Mary and let her know to set two more places at dinner," Faith said.

The two of them walked away, leaving him wondering what he had just done.

Chapter Eight

This was a mistake.

Flynn sat at the big scarred kitchen table at the Star N wondering what on earth he had been thinking to agree to this.

Since the moment he sat down he had been aware of an itch between his shoulders, a feeling that he didn't belong here.

He couldn't quite put his finger on why.

The food was delicious, he had to admit. The lasagna was perfectly cooked, cheesy and flavorful with a red sauce his late mother's Italian chef would definitely have endorsed. The bread sticks were crispy and flavorful, and even the tossed salad seemed fresh and festive.

He couldn't fault the company. It was more than pleasant. He enjoyed listening to Celeste's family—her aunt Mary, who turned out to be a jolly woman with warm eyes and an ample girth, her two sisters as well as Hope's husband, Rafe Santiago, and Chase Brannon, a neighboring rancher who seemed more like part of the family.

More important, Olivia seemed to be more relaxed and comfortable than he had seen her in a long time. She sat at one end of the table with Celeste's niece, Louisa, her nephew, Barrett, and the other boy he had seen them with at the rehearsal. It turned out the boy was Rafe's nephew. From what Flynn could tell, the boy lived with Rafe and Hope, though Flynn didn't completely understand why.

The children were deep in conversation, and every once in a while he heard laughter coming from that end of the table. Olivia even joined in a few times—a total shocker.

So why did he feel so uneasy? He didn't want to admit that it might have been because he was enjoying himself *too* much. He didn't need to find more things that drew him to Celeste, when he already couldn't seem to get the woman out of his head.

"So what do you do in California?" Chase asked.

The man treated all the Nichols sisters as if he were an older brother. He seemed especially protective of Faith, though she hardly seemed to notice.

"Construction. I've got a fairly good-size operation, with offices in San Diego, Los Angeles and Sacramento."

"Delaney Construction. Is that you?" Rafe piped up.

He nodded, intensely proud of what he had built out of nothing. The company had become a powerhouse over the past decade, even in the midst of a rough economy.

"You do good work," Rafe said. "A buddy of mine is one of your carpentry subs. Kevin O'Brian. I flew out for a few weeks last spring to help him on a job, a new hospital in Fullerton."

"Right. He's a good man."

"That's what he said about you."

"Wow. Small world," Hope said.

He and the men spent a few moments talking about some of the unique challenges of working in the construction industry in Southern California.

"Have you ever thought about moving your operations out to this neck of the woods?" Chase asked. "We don't have a lot of hospitals and the like going up, but there are always construction projects around here, especially in the Jackson area."

The question took him by surprise. Three months ago he would have given an emphatic no to that question. He had a business in Southern California, contacts and subcontractors and jobs he had fought hard to win.

He glanced at Olivia. He had other things to concern himself with now, like what might be best for his daughter.

Small-town life seemed to agree with her, he had to admit. Maybe she would be able to heal better if she were away for longer than just a few weeks from the life they had both known in California.

A change of scenery appeared to have helped the Nichols sisters move beyond the trauma in their past.

"I haven't," he answered truthfully. "It's definitely something to think about."

He glanced across the table to see Celeste listening in, though she was pretending not to.

What would she think if he stuck around town a little longer than a few weeks?

Probably nothing, he told himself. They meant nothing to each other.

"What are you doing with that property of your grandmother's?" Mary asked.

"I'm hoping to put it up for sale in the next few weeks."

"You're not planning to subdivide it, are you?" she asked, her gaze narrowed.

He could probably make more money if he did that, but somehow he didn't think his grandparents would approve.

"That's a nice piece of land there by the Cold Creek," Brannon said. "Somebody could build a beautiful house on it if they were so inclined."

If he were going to stay here—which he most definitely *wasn't*, based on a simple dinner conversation—he probably would take the bones of the house and add on to it, opening up a wall here or there and rebuilding the kitchen and bathrooms.

It was a nice, comfortable house, perfectly situated with a gorgeous view of the mountains, but it was too small and cramped for comfort, with tiny rooms and an odd flow.

All this was theoretical. He planned to sell the property as-is, not take on another project. He had enough to do right now while he was helping his daughter recover the shattered bits of her life and learn to go on without the mother she had adored.

The conversation drifted during the dinner from topic to topic. The Nicholses seemed an eclectic group, with wide-ranging interests and opinions. Even the children joined in the discussion, discussing their projects at school, the upcoming show, the movie deal they were celebrating.

He was astonished to discover he enjoyed every moment of it. This was exactly what a family should be, he thought, noisy and chaotic and wonderful.

He had never known this growing up as an only child whose parents had stayed together much longer than they should have. He had learned to live without a family over the years, but it made his chest ache that his daughter would never have it, either.

Her sisters were matchmaking.

Celeste could tell by the surreptitious glances Faith and Hope sent between her and Flynn, the leading little questions they asked him, the way they not-so-subtly discussed the upcoming movie deal, careful to focus on Celeste's literary success, as if they were trying to sell a prize pig at the market.

It was humiliating, and she could only hope he hadn't noticed.

How could they possibly think Flynn might be interested in her in the first place? If they had bothered to ask her, she would have explained how ludicrous she found the very idea.

They didn't ask her, of course. They'd simply gone ahead and invited the poor man to dinner. Why he agreed to come, she had no idea. By the time dessert rolled around, she still hadn't figured it out—nor did she understand how he and Olivia seemed to fit in so effortlessly with her family.

Hope and Faith and Aunt Mary all liked him, she could tell, and Chase and Rafe treated him with courtesy and respect.

As for her, she liked having the two of them here entirely too much.

She tried to reel herself back, to force herself to remember this was only temporary. They were only at the ranch for the evening. Her sisters' matchmaking intentions were destined to failure. Not only *wasn't* he interested in her, but he had made it abundantly clear he was going back to California as soon as he could.

"Practice went well, don't you think?" Hope asked, distracting her from that depressing thought. "The kids seemed to be into it, and what I heard was wonderful."

"It won't win any Tony Awards, but it should be fun," she answered.

"With all you have going on around here, I still can't figure out why you decided to throw a show for local senior citizens," Flynn said.

Hope took the chance to answer him. "We've always had so much community support over the years here at The Christmas Ranch, from the very moment Uncle Claude opened the doors. The people of Pine Gulch have been great to us, and we wanted to give back a little. I guess we picked senior citizens because so many of them feel alone during the holiday season."

"Many of these people have been friends with me and my late husband for years," Mary added. "This seemed a good chance to offer them a little holiday spirit."

"I think it's nice," Louisa declared. "So do my friends. That's why they agreed to do it."

Celeste smiled at her niece, who had a very tender heart despite the tragedy of losing her father.

"I do, too," she answered.

"Is Sparkle going to show up at the party?" Barrett asked.

"I think we're going to have to see about that next week," Faith answered her son. "He's been acting a little down the past few days."

Celeste frowned at her sister. "What's wrong with him?" she asked, alarmed.

"Oh, I'm sure it's nothing," she answered. "He's just off his feed a bit. I ended up bringing him up here to his stall at the main barn to see if being back with the horses for a day or two would cheer him up."

Sparkle had a particularly soft spot for Mistletoe, an old mare who used to be Uncle Claude's. "I'm sure that's it," Celeste said.

"Maybe he just misses *you*, CeCe," Hope suggested. "You haven't been down to see him in a while."

Celeste rolled her eyes. "Right. I'm sure he's pining away."

It was true that she and Sparkle were old friends. The reindeer was warm and affectionate, far more than most of their small herd.

"You ought to go down to the barn to say hello while you're here," Faith suggested.

"Can I go meet Sparkle?" Olivia asked, her eyes huge as she followed the conversation. "I would *love* to."

She *had* told the girl she would take her to meet the inspiration for the books she loved so much. "He enjoys company. I'm sure he would love to meet you."

"Can we go now?" the girl pressed.

She looked at the table laden with delicious dishes she had done nothing to help prepare. Yes, she could claim a good excuse—being busy directing the show and all—but Uncle Claude and Aunt Mary had always been clear. If you didn't help cook a meal, you were obligated to help clean it up.

"I need to help clear these dishes first," she said.

"Oh, don't worry about this," Faith said.

"Right. We can take care of things," Hope insisted.

"Yes, dear," Aunt Mary added. "We've got this completely covered. It won't take a moment to clean this up.

Meantime, why don't you take our guests down to the barn to meet Sparkle?"

Who were these women and what had they done with her family members? She frowned, fighting the urge to roll her eyes at all of them for their transparent attempts to push her together with Flynn. For heaven's sake, what did they think would possibly happen between the two of them with his daughter along?

"I don't know," Flynn said, checking his watch. "It's getting late."

"It's not even eight o'clock yet!" Olivia protested. "Since I don't have to get up for school, I haven't been going to bed until nine thirty."

"I suppose that's true."

"So we can go?"

He hesitated, then shrugged. "If Celeste doesn't mind taking us. But we can't stay long. She's already had a long day."

"Oh, yay!" Olivia jumped up instantly from the table and headed for her coat.

"Does anyone else want to go down to the barn with us?" Celeste asked.

She didn't miss the way Barrett practically jumped out of his chair with eagerness but subsided again with a dejected look when his mother shook her head firmly.

Oh, she hoped Flynn hadn't noticed her crazy, delusional, interfering sisters.

He rose. "We'll probably need to head out after we stop at the barn. It's late and I have to get this young lady home to bed, whatever she says."

"Understandable," Aunt Mary said with a warm, affectionate smile for both of them.

With a sweet, surprising charm, he leaned in and

kissed her aunt's plump cheek. "Thank you for the delicious meal. We both truly enjoyed it."

She heard a definite ring of truth to his words, even as he looked a little surprised by them. She had the feeling he hadn't expected to enjoy the meal—which again made her wonder why he had agreed to come.

"You are most welcome," Aunt Mary said. "I hope both of you will come again before you return to California. Your grandmother was a dear, dear friend, and I miss her terribly. Having you and your daughter here helps ease that ache a little."

He looked touched. "I miss her, too. I only wish I could have visited her more the past few years."

Mary patted his hand. "She told me you called her every Sunday night without fail, and sometimes during the week, too. She was very proud of that fact, especially as so many young people these days get so busy with their lives that they forget that their parents and grandparents might be a touch lonely without them."

"A phone call was nothing. I can't tell you how much I appreciate all of her friends here in Pine Gulch who helped keep her busy and involved."

Celeste liked to consider herself one of that number. Charlotte had volunteered at the library almost up to the end of her life, never letting her physical ailments or the frailties of age prevent her from smiling and trying to lift someone else.

"She was always so proud of you," Mary went on. "Especially because of what you came from."

He gave a snort at that. "What I came from? Beverly Hills? Yeah. I overcame so much in life. I don't know why nobody has come out with a made-for-television movie about my sad life."

Mary made a face. "Charlotte was proud of many things about you, but perhaps most of all that despite every advantage you had, you always stayed grounded and didn't let your head get turned by your mother's fame or fortune. Now that I've met you, I understand what she meant. You're a good boy, Flynn Delaney."

She smiled and patted his hand again. Flynn looked a bit taken aback at anyone calling him a boy, but he only had time to give Aunt Mary a bemused sort of look before Olivia cut off anything he might have said in response.

"Are you ready, Daddy? I can't wait to see Sparkle. I can't *wait*."

"Yes. I'm ready. We can grab our coats on the way out. Thank you all again."

"You're so welcome," Faith and Hope said at the same time, almost as if they had rehearsed it. Chase and Rafe both nodded in the odd way men had of speaking volumes with just a simple head movement.

"Bye, Olivia. We'll see you at the next practice," Louisa said cheerfully.

They put on their coats quickly and headed out into the December evening.

The snow had increased in intensity, still light but more steady now. The air was still, though, with no wind to hurl flakes against them.

The night seemed magical somehow, hushed and beautiful with the full moon trying to push through the cloud cover.

Celeste was fiercely aware of him as they made their way to the barn. He was so very...male, from the jut of his jaw to his wide shoulders to the large footsteps his boots made in the snow beside her much smaller ones. He made her feel small and feminine in comparison.

To her relief, she didn't have to make conversation. Olivia kept up a steady stream of conversation about the ranch. She couldn't help noticing the girl had talked more that day than she had in all their previous encounters combined. Either she was more comfortable with Celeste now, or she was beginning to return to the girl she had been before the shooting.

If she wasn't mistaken, the girl had hardly limped that afternoon or evening. That had to be a good sign, she supposed.

"Here we are," she said when they reached the barn. The smell of hay and animals and old wood greeted them, not at all unappealing in its way.

She flipped on the lights and heard Mistletoe's distinctive whinny of greeting. She took time as they passed the old horse to give Misty a few strokes and an apple she pulled from her pocket before she led them to Sparkle's stall next door.

"Olivia, this is Sparkle. Sparkle, meet my good friend Olivia."

After a moment of coyness, the reindeer headed to the railing of the stall.

"I've never seen a real reindeer before. He's small!"

"Reindeer are generally much smaller than people think they should be." She petted him, much the way she had Mistletoe. He lipped at her, trying to find a treat.

"Would you like to feed him an apple?"

"Can I?"

She glanced down at the girl and decided not to miss this opportunity. "I don't know. You'll have to use your left arm. He prefers it when people feed him from that side."

That was an out-and-out lie. Sparkle would eat with

great delight any apple that came his way, but she decided Olivia didn't need to know that.

Flynn made a low sound of amusement beside her that seemed to ripple down her spine. She barely managed to hold back her instinctive shiver as she handed the apple to Olivia.

The girl narrowed her gaze at Celeste, obviously trying to figure out if this was some kind of a trick. In the end, the appeal and novelty of feeding a reindeer outweighed her suspicions.

She took the apple with her injured left hand and, with effort, held it out to the reindeer, who nibbled it out of her hand. Olivia giggled. "Can I pet him?"

"Sure. He won't hurt you."

She rubbed his head for a moment. "What about his antlers?"

"Go ahead. Just be gentle."

She reached out and tentatively touched an antler. "It's hard and soft at the same time. Weird!"

Sparkle visited with her for a moment, and it was plain he was happy to find a new friend. Any malaise the reindeer might have been feeling was nowhere in evidence. Maybe he really *had* been pining for her, but she doubted it. Maybe, like the rest of them, he just needed a little break from the hectic pace of the holiday season.

"What's special about this particular reindeer?" Flynn asked.

She considered how to answer. "Well, he was the first reindeer Uncle Claude ever obtained, so he's been here the longest. And he's always been so much more affectionate than the others—not that they're mean or anything, just…standoffish. Not Sparkle. He's always been as friendly as can be. It rubs off on everyone."

They watched the reindeer a few moments longer. When she heard a little sound from the stall at the end of the barn, she suddenly remembered what other treasure the barn contained. Clearly, she didn't spend enough time here.

"I nearly forgot," she said. "There's something else here you might like to see."

"What?" Olivia asked eagerly. The girl loved animals; that much was obvious. Perhaps she and Flynn ought to look into getting a dog when they returned to California.

She didn't want to think about that now, not when the night seemed hushed and sweet here in the quiet barn.

"Come and see," she answered. She led the way and pulled open the stall gate. Olivia peered in a little warily but her nervousness gave way to excitement.

"Puppies! Dad, look!"

"I see them, honey."

The half dozen black-and-white pudgy things belonged to Georgie, one of the ranch border collies.

"Can I pet them?"

"Sure. I'll warn you, they're probably not super clean. You're going to want to wash your hands when you're done."

"I will. I promise."

She knelt down and was immediately bombarded with wriggling puppies.

Celeste felt her throat tighten as she watched this girl who had been through so much find simple joy in the moment. Flynn had almost lost her. It seemed a miracle that they were here in this barn on a snowy night watching her giggle as a puppy licked her hand.

"She did all right today at the rehearsal," she said in a low voice to Flynn as they watched together. "I know you were concerned about the noise and confusion, but she handled it well. Wouldn't you agree?"

They were standing close enough together that she could feel his sigh. "I suppose."

"Does that mean you'll bring her to the next rehearsal, then?"

He gave a small sound that was almost a laugh. "Anybody ever tell you that you're relentless?"

"A few times, maybe," she said ruefully. *More than a few* was closer to the truth.

Needing a little distance, she eased down onto the bench next to the stall. To her surprise, he followed and sat beside her.

"Fine," he answered. "You win. I'll bring her to the next one. That doesn't mean I have to like it."

She glanced at his daughter playing with the puppies a dozen feet away, then turned back to Flynn. "Why do you have a problem with her performing?" she asked, her voice low. "Especially when it seems to be something she enjoys?"

"I don't *want* her to enjoy it," he answered in an equally low tone. "If I had my way, I would have her stay far away from any kind of stage or screen."

She frowned at the intensity of his words. "Because of your mother or because of Elise?"

"Either. Both. Take your pick." He watched as a puppy started nibbling on Olivia's ponytail, which only made her giggle again as she tried to extricate it from the little mouth.

After a moment he spoke with fierce resolve. "I want my daughter to find happiness in life based on her own decisions and accomplishments, not because of how many pictures of her holding a latte from Starbucks showed up in the tabloids this week. There's an artificiality to that world that crumbles to nothing in a heartbeat. Take it from someone who grew up on the edge of that spotlight."

She thought of what Aunt Mary had said about his grandmother's pride in him for staying grounded. Unlike his mother or his wife, he hadn't sought that spotlight. He had gone into a career outside Hollywood and had built a successful business on his own merits. She had to admire that.

"That must have been tough for you," she said.

He shrugged. "How can I complain, really? It sounds stupid, even to me. I grew up with the sort of privileges most people only dream about. A-list celebrities hanging out in my swimming pool, a BMW in the driveway on my sixteenth birthday, vacations in Cannes and Park City and Venice."

By worldly standards, her family had been very poor. Her parents had given everything they had to helping others, to the point that she remembered a period in their lives when she and her sisters each had had only two or three outfits that they swapped back and forth.

She hadn't necessarily enjoyed moving from country to country, never feeling as if she had a stable home. In truth, she still carried lingering resentment about it, but she had always known she was deeply loved.

She had a feeling that for all his outward privilege, Flynn had missed out on that assurance, at least from his parents. She was grateful he had known the unwavering love and devotion of his grandmother.

"We don't get to choose the circumstances of our birth families, do we?" she said softly. "The only thing we have control of is the life we make for ourselves out of those circumstances."

His gaze met hers and the intensity of his expression left her suddenly breathless. Something shimmered between them, something bright and fierce. She couldn't seem to look away, and she again had the oddest feeling he wanted to kiss her.

Now? Here? With his daughter just a few feet away? She must have been imagining things. Still, the idea of him leaning forward slightly, of his mouth sliding across hers, made nerves jump in her stomach and her knees feel suddenly weak.

She felt as if she stood on the brink of something, arms stretched wide, trying to find the courage to jump into the empty space beyond.

She could lose her heart so easily to this man.

The thought whispered into her mind and she swallowed hard. With the slightest of nudges, she would leap into that empty space and doubtless crash hard back to earth.

Careful, she warned herself, and looked away from him, pretending to focus on his daughter and the cute, wriggling puppies.

After a long pause, he finally spoke. "Despite everything you and your sisters have been through, you've made a good life for yourself here in Pine Gulch."

"I'd like to think so." Okay, maybe she was a little lonely. Maybe there were nights she lay in bed and stared at the ceiling, wondering if she was destined to spend the rest of her nights alone.

"I guess you know a little about being in the spotlight now, don't you?" Flynn said.

She forced a little laugh. "Not really. My particular spotlight is more like a flashlight beam. A very tiny, focused flashlight. That's the nice thing about being only a name on a book cover."

"That will change when the Sparkle movie hits the big screen," he predicted.

Oh, she didn't want to think about that. Just the idea made her feel clammy and slightly queasy. "I hope not," she said fervently. "I like being under the radar."

He frowned. "Why agree to let someone make the movie, then? You had to know that's only going to increase your celebrity status. You won't be able to stay under the radar for long."

In her heart, she knew he was right. What had she gotten herself into?

She hadn't had a choice, she reminded herself. Not really.

"I love my family," she said. "They're everything to me."

"It only took me a few minutes at dinner tonight to figure that out. You have a great family. But what does that have to do with signing a movie deal you don't appear to want?"

For someone who loved the magic and power in words, sometimes in conversation she felt as if she never could manage to find the right ones.

"Things haven't been…easy around here the past few years, even before my brother-in-law's accident. My uncle was a wonderful man but not the best businessman around, and the ranch hasn't exactly been thriving financially."

"I'm sorry to hear that."

"The, um, increased interest in The Christmas Ranch after the first Sparkle book came out last season helped a great deal but didn't completely solve the cash flow woes." She felt her face heat a little, as it always did when she talked about the astonishing success of the book. "With the deal Hope and I will be signing for the movie rights, we can pay off the rest of the ranch's debts and push the operation firmly into the black, which will lift considerable pressure from Faith. How could I turn down something that will benefit my family so much?"

He studied her for a moment, that funny intensity in his expression again. "So it's not necessarily what you really want, but you're willing to go through with it anyway for your family."

"Something like that," she muttered.

"If having a movie made out of your book doesn't sit well with you, couldn't you have found an alternative revenue stream?"

She shrugged. "Hope and I talked at length about this. Our agent and publisher were clear. *Someone* was going to make a Sparkle movie—which, believe me, is an amazing position to find ourselves in. The terms of this particular deal were very favorable for Hope and for me, and we were both impressed by the other projects this particular production company has engineered. The moment seemed right."

"I'm *glad* they're making a Sparkle movie," Olivia said suddenly. Celeste had been so busy explaining herself, she hadn't realized the girl had left the puppies on the floor of the stall and rejoined them. "I can't wait to see it."

Flynn smiled at his daughter with that sweet tenderness that tugged at her heart. "We'll probably be back in California, and you can tell everyone else at the movie theater that you actually had the chance to meet the real Sparkle and the women who created the fictional version."

"I guess." Olivia didn't look as excited about that prospect as Celeste might have expected. In fact, she appeared downright glum.

Why? she wondered. Was the girl enjoying her time in Pine Gulch so much that she didn't like thinking about their eventual return to California?

"Maybe we could come back and see the movie here," Olivia suggested.

"Maybe."

Celeste felt a sharp little kick to her heart at the noncommittal word. They wouldn't be back. She was suddenly certain of it. After Flynn sold his grandmother's house, he would have no more ties here in Pine Gulch. She likely would never see him or his daughter again.

This was why she needed to be careful to guard her heart better. She already hurt just thinking about them leaving. How much worse would it be if she let herself take that leap and fell in love with him?

He stood up and wiped the straw from the back of Olivia's coat where she had been sitting on the floor of the stall.

"We should probably take off," he said. "You need to tell Celeste thank-you for bringing you out here to meet Sparkle and to play with the puppies."

"Do we have to go?" she complained.

"Yes. It's late and Celeste probably has to work at the library tomorrow."

She nodded and was suddenly overwhelmed by a wave of fatigue. The day had been long and exhausting, and right now she wanted nothing more than to be in her comfy clothes, cuddled up with her animals and watching something brainless on TV.

"Okay," Olivia said in a dejected voice. "Thank you

for bringing me down here to meet Sparkle and play with the puppies."

"You are very welcome," Celeste said. "Anytime you want to come back, we would love to have you. Sparkle would, too."

Olivia seemed heartened by that as she headed for the reindeer's stall one last time.

"Bye, Sparkle. Bye!"

The reindeer nodded his head two or three times as if he was bowing, which made the girl giggle.

Celeste led the way out of the barn. Another inch of snow had fallen during the short time they had been inside, and they walked in silence to where his SUV was parked in front of the house.

She wrapped her coat around her while Flynn helped his daughter into the backseat. Once she was settled, he closed the door and turned to her.

"Please tell your family thank you for inviting me to dinner. I enjoyed it very much."

"I will. Good night."

With a wave, he hopped into his SUV and backed out of the driveway.

She watched them for just a moment, snow settling on her hair and her cheeks while she tried to ignore that little ache in her heart.

She could do this. She was tougher than she sometimes gave herself credit for being. Yes, she might already care about Olivia and be right on the brink of falling hard for her father. That didn't mean she had to lean forward and leave solid ground.

She would simply have to keep herself centered, focused on her family and her friends, her work and her writing and the holidays. She would do her best to keep him at arm's length. It was the only smart choice if she wanted to emerge unscathed after this holiday season.

Soon they would be gone and her life would return to the comfortable routine she had created for herself.

As she walked into the house, she tried not to think about how unappealing she suddenly found that idea.

Chapter Nine

She didn't have a chance to test her resolve, simply because she didn't see Flynn again for longer than a moment or two over the next few days.

At the Thursday rehearsal, he merely dropped Olivia off and left after making sure to give Hope—not Celeste—a card with his cell phone number on it.

She supposed she should take that as some sort of progress. From what she gathered, he hadn't let Olivia out of his sight since the accident. She had to feel good that he felt comfortable enough with her and her family to leave the girl at The Christmas Ranch without him.

On the other hand, she had to wonder if maybe he was just trying to avoid her.

That really made no logical sense. Why would he feel any sort of need to avoid her? *He* wasn't the one who was developing feelings that could never go anywhere.

Still, she had to wonder, especially when he did the same thing Saturday morning for their final practice before the performance, just dropping Olivia off as most of the other parents had done.

She should be grateful he'd brought the girl at all, especially when he obviously wasn't thrilled about the whole thing.

It was too bad, really, because Olivia was a natural in front of an audience. She seemed far more comfortable onstage than the other children.

The performance was nothing elaborate, a rather hodgepodge collection of short Christmas skits mixed with songs and poems, but considering the few practices they'd had, the show came together marvelously.

When they finished the second run-through Saturday morning, Celeste clapped her hands.

"That was amazing!" she exclaimed. "I'm so proud of each one of you for all your hard work. You are going to make some people very, very happy next week."

Jolie Wheeler raised her hand. "Can we take the costumes home to show our moms and dads?"

None of the costumes was anything fancy, just bits and pieces she and Hope had thrown together with a little help from Faith and a few of the parents. "We need to keep them here so we can make sure everyone has all the pieces—the belts and halos and crowns—they need for the performance. When you take them off, put your costume on the hanger and everything else in the bag with your name on it in the dressing room. Remember, you will all have to be here at five thirty sharp so we can get into costume and be ready for the show. We'll have the performance first, and then you are all welcome with your families to stay for dinner with our guests, if you'd like. There should be plenty of food for everyone."

"Then can we take the costumes home?" Jolie asked.

She smiled at the adorable girl. "We need to keep them here just in case we decide to do another show at The Christmas Ranch next year."

"Rats," Jolie complained and a few others joined her in grumbling. What they wanted to do with a few hokey costumes, Celeste had no idea, but she had to smile at their disappointment.

"You'll all just have to be in the show next year so you can wear them again," she said.

Not that she intended to be part of it, even if Hope begged her. Writing the little show had taken her almost as long as a full-fledged children's book.

"Thank you all again for your hard work, and I'll see you Tuesday evening at five thirty if you need help with your hair and makeup."

The children dispersed to the boys' and girls' dressing rooms—really just separate storage spaces that had been temporarily converted for the show. She cleaned up the rehearsal space and supervised the pickup of the children.

Finally, only Louisa, Barrett, Joey and Olivia were left. They didn't seem to mind. Indeed, they had gone to the game drawer Hope kept in her office to keep the children occupied when they were hanging out at the lodge and were playing a spirited game of Go Fish with a Christmas-themed deck of cards.

Though she had a hundred things to—including finishing the paint job on the backdrop for the little stage they had rigged up—she sat down at the table near the refreshment booth where they were playing.

"You did so well today. All of you."

"Thanks," Louisa said. "It's really fun. I hope we do it again next year."

Not unless Hope found some other sucker to be in charge, she thought again.

"I've had lots of fun, too," Olivia said. "Thanks for inviting me to do it."

"You're very welcome. How are things going at your great-grandmother's house?"

As soon as she asked the question, she wished she hadn't. It sounded entirely too much as if she was snooping. She might as well have come out and asked when they were leaving.

"Good, I guess. We have two more rooms to do. My dad said we'll probably go back to California between Christmas and New Year's."

She tried to ignore the sharp pang in her chest. "I'm sure you'll be glad to be back in your own house."

"You're lucky! You can go swimming in the ocean," Louisa said.

"Sometimes. Mostly, it's too cold, except in summer."

"And you can go to Disneyland whenever you want," Joey added.

"No, I can't," she protested. "I have to go to school and stuff."

They talked more about the differences between their respective homes. Olivia was quite envious that they could ride horses and go sledding all winter long while the other children thought California was only palm trees and beaches.

While the seasonal staff of The Christmas Ranch started arriving and getting ready for the busiest day of their season, the children continued their game, and Celeste sat at the table next to them working on a drawing for a complicated part of the stage she was hoping Rafe could help her finish later that day.

Finally, about forty-five minutes after practice ended, Flynn burst through the front doors looking harried. "Sorry I'm late. I was taking a load of things to the county landfill and it took longer than I expected."

"Don't even worry about it. The kids have been enjoying themselves. Haven't you?"

"Yep," Barrett said. "'Cause I won Go Fish three times and Joey and Olivia both won once. Louisa didn't win any."

"Next time, watch out," his sister declared.

Flynn smiled at the girl, that full-fledged charming smile Celeste remembered from when he was a teenager. She had to swallow hard and force herself to look away, wondering why it suddenly felt so warm in the lodge.

"How was practice?" he asked.

"Good," she answered. "Great, actually. Everyone worked so hard."

"I can't wait for you to see the show, Dad," Olivia declared. "It's going to be *so* good. Celeste says all the ladies will cry."

He looked vaguely alarmed. "Is that right? Will I cry, too? I'd better bring a big hankie, just in case."

She giggled hard, then in the funny way kids have, she looked at Barrett and Louisa and something in their expressions made her laugh even harder, until all three were busting up. Their laughter was infectious and Celeste couldn't help smiling.

Flynn gazed at the three children, certain he was witnessing a miracle.

This was really his daughter, looking bright and animated and…happy.

This was the daughter he remembered, this girl who found humor in the silliest things, who was curious about the world around her and loved talking with people. He'd feared she was gone forever, stolen by a troubled man who had taken so much else from her.

Seeing her sitting at a table in the St. Nicholas Lodge, laughing with Celeste and her niece and nephew, he wanted to hug all three of the children. Even more, he wanted to kiss Celeste right on that delicious-looking mouth of hers that had haunted his dreams for days.

Her smiling gaze met his and a wave of tenderness washed over him. She had done this. He didn't know how. She had seen a sad, wounded girl and had worked some kind of Sparkle magic on her to coax out the sweet and loving girl Olivia used to be.

Her smile slid away and he realized he was staring. He drew in a deep breath and forced himself to look away.

His gaze landed on a piece of paper with what looked like a complicated drawing. "I didn't know you were an artist."

She looked embarrassed. "I'm *so* not an artist, Hope is. I'm just trying to work up a sketch I can show Rafe. I'm trying to figure out how to build wings on the side of the stage so the children have somewhere to wait off-stage. There's no time to sew curtains. I just need some sort of screen to hide them from view.

He studied her sketch, then took the paper from her and made a few quick changes. "That shouldn't be hard," he said. "You just have to build a frame out of two-by-fours and then use something lightweight like particle board for your screen. If it's hinged and connected there, it should be solid and also portable enough that you can store it somewhere when you're not using it."

She studied the drawing. "Wow. That's genius! You know, I think that just might work. Can you just write down what supplies you think it might need? Rafe will be back from Jackson Hole shortly, and I can put him to work on it if he has time."

He glanced at the stage, then at his daughter, still smiling as she played cards with the other two children. Though he knew he would probably regret it—and he certainly had plenty of things still to take care of at Charlotte's house—he spoke quickly before he could change his mind.

"If you've got some tools I can use and the two-by-fours, I can probably get the frame for it done in no time."

She stared at him, green eyes wide behind those sexy glasses she wore. "Seriously?"

He shrugged. "I started out in carpentry. It's kind of what I do. This shouldn't be hard at all—as long as Olivia doesn't mind hanging around a little longer."

"Yay!" Louisa exclaimed. "She can come to the house and decorate the sugar cookies we made last night with Aunt Celeste while our mom was Christmas shopping."

Olivia looked suitably intrigued. "I've never decorated sugar cookies."

"Never?" Celeste exclaimed. She looked surprised enough that Flynn felt a pinch of guilt. Apparently this was another area where he had failed his daughter.

Olivia shook her head. "Is it hard?"

"No way," Louisa answered. "It's easy and super, super fun. You can decorate the cookies any way you want. There's no right or wrong. You can use sparkly sugar or M&M's or frosting or whatever you want."

"The best part is, when you mess it up, you get to eat

your mistakes," Barrett added. "Nobody even cares. I mess up a *lot*."

Olivia snickered and Flynn had a feeling *she* would be messing up plenty, too. What was it with all these Christmas traditions that filled kids with more sugar when they least needed another reason to be excited?

He had struck out miserably when it came to Christmas traditions this year. At least they had the little Christmas tree at his grandmother's house for decoration, but that was about it.

Olivia had insisted she hoped Santa Claus wouldn't come that year, but he had disregarded her wishes and bought several things online for her. A few other presents would be waiting back in California, sort of a delayed holiday, simply because the new bike her physical therapist suggested was too big for the journey here in his SUV.

Next year would be different, he told himself. By this time next year they would be established in a routine back in California. They could hang stockings and put up a tree of their own and decorate all the sugar cookies she wanted, even if he had to order ready-made plain cookies from his favorite bakery.

The idea of returning to a routine after the stress of the past few months should have been appealing. Instead, it left him remarkably unenthused.

"May I go, Dad? I really, really, *really* want to decorate cookies."

He was torn between his desire to keep her close and his deep relief that she was so obviously enjoying the company of other children. She would enjoy the cookie decorating far more than she would enjoy sitting around and watching him work a band saw.

"Are you sure your aunt won't mind one more?" he asked Celeste.

"Are you kidding? Mary loves a crowd. The more the merrier, as far as she's concerned." She smiled a little. "And look at it this way. You'll probably come out of the whole thing with cookies to take home."

"Well, in that case, how can I say no? A guy always needs a few more cookies."

"Yay! I can go," Olivia told the other children as if they hadn't been right there to hear her father's decision.

"Put the cards away first and then get your coats on. Then you can walk up to the house."

"You're not coming?" Olivia asked.

"I'll be up later," she answered with a smile. "But first I have to finish painting some of the scenery."

The children cleaned up the cards and returned them to a little tin box, then put on their coats, hats and mittens. As soon as they were on their way, Celeste turned to him with a grateful smile. She looked so fresh and lovely that for a crazy moment, he wished they were alone in the lodge with that big crackling fire.

Instead, an older woman was setting out prepackaged snacks in what looked like a concessions area and another one was arranging things on a shelf in a gift store. Outside the windows, he could see families beginning to queue up to buy tickets.

"Is there somewhere I can get going on this? A workshop or something?"

"Oh." She looked flustered suddenly and he wondered if something in his expression revealed the fierce attraction simmering through him. "Yes. There's a building behind back where Rafe keeps his tools. That's where I've been painting the scenery, too. I'll show you."

She led the way through the lodge to a back door. They walked through the pale winter sunshine to a modern-looking barn a short distance away.

In a pasture adjacent to the barn, he saw several more reindeer as well as some draft horses.

"This is where we keep the reindeer at night during the holiday season," she explained. "There's Sparkle. Do you see him?"

As far as he could tell all the reindeer looked the same, but he would take her word for it. "Is he feeling better?"

"Much. Apparently he only wanted a few days off."

"Olivia will be happy to hear that."

"He'll need his strength. This afternoon and evening will be crazy busy."

"For the reindeer, too?" he asked, fascinated by the whole idea of an entire operation devoted only to celebrating the holidays.

"Yes. Hope will probably hook them up to the sleigh for photo ops and short rides. The draft horses, of course, will be taking people on sleigh rides around the ranch, which is a highlight of the season. You should take Olivia. She would love it. It's really fun riding through the cold, starry night all bundled up in blankets."

It did sound appealing—especially if he and Celeste were alone under those blankets…

He jerked his brain back to the business at hand. He really needed to stop this.

"We're only open a few more nights," she said. "But if you want to take her, let me know and I'll arrange it."

As much as he thought Olivia would enjoy the sleigh ride, he wasn't at all certain that spending more time at The Christmas Ranch with Celeste and her appealing family would be good for either of them.

"We'll see," he said, unwilling to commit to anything. "Shall we get to it?"

"Right. Of course."

She led him into a well-lit, modern building with stalls along one wall. The rest seemed to be taken up with storage and work space.

She led him to an open area set up with a band saw, a reciprocating saw, a router and various other power tools, as well as a stack of two-by-fours and sheets of plywood.

"You might not need to have Rafe run to the lumber yard. You might have everything here."

"Great."

She pointed to another area of the barn where other large pieces of plywood had been painted with snowflakes. "I need to finish just a few things on the scenery, so I'll be on hand if you need help with anything."

The best help she could offer would be to stay out of his way. She was entirely too tempting to his peace of mind, but he couldn't figure out a way to say that without sounding like an idiot, so he just decided to focus on the job at hand.

"Do you mind if I turn on some music?" she asked.

"That's fine," he answered. Her place, her music.

It wasn't Christmas music, he was happy to hear. Instead, she found some classic-rock station and soon The Eagles were harmonizing through the barn from a speaker system in the work area.

She returned to her side of the area and started opening paint cans and gathering brushes, humming along to the music. Though he knew he needed to get started, he couldn't seem to look away.

He liked watching her. She seemed to throw herself into everything she did, whether that was directing a ragtag group of children in a Christmas show, telling stories to a bunch of energetic school kids or writing a charming story about a brave reindeer.

He was fascinated with everything about her.

He had to get over it, he told himself sternly. He needed to help build her set, finish clearing out his grandmother's house and then go back to his normal life in California.

He turned his attention to the pile of lumber and found the boards he would need. Then he spent a moment familiarizing himself with another man's work space and the tools available to him. Rafe Santiago kept a clean, well-organized shop. He would give him that.

The moment he cut the first board, he felt more centered than he had in a long time. He was very good at building things. It gave him great satisfaction to take raw materials and turn them into something useful, whether that was a piece of furniture or a children's hospital.

For nearly an hour, they worked together in a comfortable silence broken only by the sounds of tools and the music. He made good progress by doing his best to pretend she wasn't there, that this growing attraction simmering through him would burn itself out when it no longer had the fuel of her presence to sustain it.

The barn was warmer than he would have expected, especially with the air compressor going to power the tools, and soon he was down to his T-shirt. Before she started painting, she had taken off the sweater she wore, but it wasn't until he took a break and looked up from connecting two boards that he saw the message on it: Wake up Smarter. Sleep With a Librarian.

For an instant his mind went completely blank as all the blood left his head at the image. Unfortunately, his finger twitched on the trigger of the unfamiliar nail gun, which was far more reactive than any of the guns he was used to.

He felt a sharp biting pain as the nail impaled the webbing between the forefinger and thumb of his left hand to the board. He swore and ripped out the nail, mortified at his stupidity.

It wasn't the first time he'd had an accident with a nail gun or a power tool—in his line of work, nobody made it through without nicks and bruises and a few stitches here or there, especially starting out—but it was completely embarrassing. He hadn't made that kind of rookie mistake in years. Apparently, she wasn't very good for his concentration.

"What happened?" she asked.

"Nothing. It's fine." It was, really. The nail hadn't gone through anything but skin.

"You're bleeding. Let me see."

"It's just a poke. Hazard of the job."

"I think Rafe keeps a first-aid kit somewhere in here." She started rifling through cabinets until she found one.

"I don't need anything. It's almost stopped bleeding."

It still burned like hell, but he wasn't about to tell her that.

"I'll feel better if you let me at least clean it up."

"Really, not necessary."

She ignored him and stepped closer, bringing that delicious springtime scent with her that made him think of sunlit mornings and new life.

"Hold out your hand."

Since he was pretty certain she wouldn't let up until he cooperated, he knew he had no choice but to comply. Feeling stupid, he thrust out his arm. She took his injured hand in both of hers and dabbed at it with a wipe she'd found inside the kit.

"It's not bad," she murmured. "I don't think you're going to need stitches."

He did his best to keep his gaze fiercely away from that soft T-shirt that had caused the trouble in the first place—and the curves beneath it.

The gentle touch of her fingers on his skin made him want to close his eyes and lean into her. It had been so long since he'd known that kind of aching sweetness.

She smiled a little. "Do you remember that time I fell on my bike in front of your grandmother's house?"

"Yes." His voice sounded a little ragged around the edges, but he had to hope she didn't notice.

"You were so sweet to me," she said with soft expression as she applied antiseptic cream to the tiny puncture wound. "I couldn't even manage to string two words together around you, but you just kept up a steady stream of conversation to make me feel more comfortable until my aunt Mary could come pick me up. I was so mortified, but you made it feel less horrible."

He swallowed. He'd done that? He didn't have much memory of it, only of a quiet girl with big eyes and long dark hair.

"Why would you be mortified? It was an accident."

She snorted a little. "Right. I ran into your grandmother's mailbox because I wasn't paying attention to where I was going. It was all your fault for mowing the lawn without your shirt on."

He stared down at her. "*That's* why you crashed?"

She looked up and he saw shadows of remembered embarrassment there. "In my defense, I was thirteen years old, you were a much older boy and I already had a huge crush on you. It's a wonder I could say a word."

"Is that right?" he asked softly. Her fingers felt so good on his skin, her luscious mouth was *right there* and he wanted nothing but to find a soft spot of hay somewhere for the two of them to collapse into.

"Yes," she murmured, and he saw answering awareness in her eyes. "And then you made it so much worse by being so kind, cleaning me up, calling my aunt, then fixing my bike for me. What shy, awkward bookworm alive could have resisted that, when the cutest boy she'd ever met in real life was so sweet to her?"

He didn't want to be sweet right now. At her words, hunger growled to life inside him, and he knew he would have to appease it somehow.

Just a kiss, he told himself. A simple taste and then they both could move on.

He lowered his mouth and felt her hands tremble when his lips brushed hers.

She tasted just as delicious as he would have imagined, sweet and warm and luscious, like nibbling at a perfectly ripe strawberry.

She froze for just a moment, long enough for him to wonder if he'd made a terrible error in judgment, and then her mouth softened and she kissed him back with a breathy sigh, as if she had been waiting for this since that day half a lifetime ago.

Her hands fluttered against his chest for just a moment, then wrapped around his neck, and he pulled her closer, delighting in her soft curves and the aching tenderness of the kiss.

Chapter Ten

Life could take the strangest turns sometimes.

If someone had told her a week ago that she would be standing in The Christmas Ranch barn on a Saturday afternoon kissing Flynn Delaney, she would have advised them to see somebody about their delusions.

Here they were, though, with her hands tangled in his hair and his arms wrapped around her and his mouth doing intoxicating things to her.

She wanted the moment to go on forever, this sultry, honeyed magic.

Nothing in her limited experience compared to this. She'd had a couple of boyfriends in college, nothing serious and nothing that had lasted more than a month or two—and absolutely nothing that prepared her for the sheer sensual assault of kissing Flynn.

She made a little sound in her throat and he deepened

the kiss, his tongue sliding along hers as his arms tightened around her. Sensation rippled through her, and she could only be grateful when he pushed her against the nearest cabinet, his mouth hot and demanding.

She couldn't seem to think about anything other than kissing him, touching him, finding some way to be closer to him. She wrapped her arms more tightly around his neck, wanting this moment to go on forever.

They kissed for a long time there with the scents of sawdust and hay swirling around them. Even as she lost herself in the kiss, some tiny corner of her brain was trying to catalog every emotion and sensation, storing it up so she could relive it after he was gone. The taste of him, of coffee and mint and sexy male, the silky softness of his hair, the delicious rasp of his whiskers against her skin, his big, warm hands slipping beneath the back of her T-shirt to slide against her bare skin…

"Celeste? Are you in here?"

She heard her brother-in-law's voice and felt as if he had just thrown her into the snow. Rafe and Hope must have returned earlier than they'd planned.

She froze and scrambled away from Flynn, yanking her T-shirt back down and trying frantically to catch her breath.

He was having the same trouble, she realized, as he quickly stepped behind one of the power tools to hide the evidence of his arousal.

Had *she* done that to him? She couldn't quite believe it.

"Celeste?" she heard again.

"In…" The words caught in her throat and she had to clear them away before she spoke again. "In here."

An instant later Rafe walked into the work space. He

stopped and gazed between the two of them and she saw his mouth tighten, a sudden watchful glint in his eyes.

Rafe was a tough man, extremely protective of each Nichols sister—probably because he had once saved all their lives. His sharp gaze took in the scene and she doubted he could miss her heightened color, her swollen lips, their heavy breathing.

She was sure of it when he aimed a hard, narrow-eyed look at Flynn.

She could feel herself flush more and then told herself she was being ridiculous, feeling like a teenager caught necking on the front porch by her older brother. She was a grown woman, twenty-eight years old, and she could kiss half the men in town if she wanted.

She'd just never wanted to before.

"Hope said you might need some help building a few things for the set."

"Flynn has been helping me."

"So I see," Rafe drawled.

"Thanks for letting me use your shop," Flynn said. "I tried to be careful with the tools, but your nail gun got away from me." He held up the hand she had bandaged.

"It's got a fast trigger. Sorry about that. Anything I can do to help you wrap things up so you can get out of here?"

"Another pair of hands never hurts," Flynn answered.

Celeste finally felt as if her brain cells were beginning to function again.

"I'm about done painting. I…think I'll just clean my brushes and leave you to it. I should probably head up to the house to help Aunt Mary with the cookie decorating."

She couldn't meet either of their gazes as she walked past the men, feeling like an idiot.

"Nice shirt," Rafe murmured in a low voice as she passed him.

Baffled, she glanced down and then could have died from mortification. It was the Sleep with a Librarian shirt that Hope and Faith had given her one Christmas as a joke. She never wore it, of course—it wasn't her style *at all*—but she'd thrown it on that morning under her sweater, knowing she was going to be painting the scenery later and it would be perfect for the job.

She gathered her brushes quickly and headed for the sink in the small bathroom of the barn.

While she cleaned the brushes, she glanced into the mirror and saw it was worse than she had thought. Her hair had come half out of the messy bun, her lips were definitely swollen and her cheeks were rosier than St. Nicholas's in "'Twas the Night Before Christmas."

Oh, she wanted to *die*. Rafe knew she had just been making out with Flynn, which meant he would definitely tell Hope. Her sisters would never let her hear the end of it.

That was the least of her problems, she realized.

Now that she had kissed the man and knew how amazing it was, how would she ever be able to endure not being able to do it again?

What just happened here?

Even after Celeste left to clean her brushes, Flynn could feel his heart hammering, his pulse racing.

Get a grip, he told himself. It was just a kiss. But for reasons he didn't completely understand, it somehow struck him as being so much more.

He couldn't seem to shake the feeling that something

momentous had occurred in that kiss, something terrifying and mysterious and tender.

Why had he kissed her?

The whole time they'd shared the work space, he had been telling himself all the reasons why he needed to stay away from her. At the first opportunity and excuse, he had ignored all his common sense and swooped right in.

What shy, awkward bookworm alive could have resisted that, when the cutest boy she'd ever met in real life was so sweet to her?

She'd once had a crush on him. He didn't know why that made him feel so tender toward the quiet girl she had been.

That kiss had rocked him to the core and left him feeling off balance, as if he'd just slipped on the sawdust and landed hard on his ass. For a moment, he closed his eyes, remembering those lush curves against him, her enthusiastic response, the soft, sexy little sounds she made.

"What are you doing here?" For one horrible moment he thought Rafe was calling him out for kissing Celeste, until he realized the other man was gazing down at the set piece he was building.

Focus, he told himself. Get the job done, as he'd promised.

"She wants some kind of wings on the side of the stage for the children to wait behind until it's their turn to go on," he explained. He went into detail about his plan and listened while Rafe made a few excellent suggestions to improve the design.

"This shouldn't take us long to finish up," the other man said. "In fact, I probably could handle it on my own, if you want to get out of here."

That sounded a little more strongly worded than just

a suggestion. "I'm good," he answered, a little defiantly. "I like to finish what I start."

He was aware as they went to work of her cleaning up her brushes, closing up the paint cans, putting her sweater back on to hide that unexpectedly enticing T-shirt.

He was also aware that she hadn't looked at him once since she'd jerked out of his arms when her brother-in-law had come in.

Was she regretting that they had kissed? He couldn't tell. She *should* regret it, since they both had to know it was a mistake, but somehow it still bothered him that she might.

Did he owe her some kind of apology for kissing her out of the blue like that? Something else he didn't know.

He had been faithful to his vows, as misguided as they had been, and his relationships since then had been with women who wanted the same thing he did: uncomplicated, no-strings affairs.

Celeste was very different from those women—sweet and kind and warm—which might explain why that kiss and her enthusiastic response had left him so discombobulated.

A few minutes later she finished at the sink and set the brushes to dry.

"I guess that's it," she said, still not looking at Flynn. "The brushes are all clean and ready for Hope when she has time to come down and finish. I'm just going to head up to the house to check on the cookie decorating. Thanks again for doing this, you guys."

She gave a vague, general sort of smile, then hurried out of the barn.

He and Rafe worked in silence for a few more moments, a heavy, thick tension in the air.

The other man was the first to speak.

"Do you know what happened to Celeste and her sisters when they were kids?"

Rafe's tone was casual, but the hard edge hadn't left his expression since he had walked into the work space earlier.

"In Colombia? Yeah. She told me. I can't imagine what they must have gone through."

Rafe's hard expression didn't lighten. "None of them talks about it very much. Frankly, I'm surprised she told you at all."

He didn't know why she had, but he was touched that she would confide that very significant part of her life to him.

He also didn't know why Rafe would bring it up now. It didn't seem the sort of topic to casually mention in general conversation. Something told him Rafe wasn't a man who did things without purpose.

"She was the youngest," the man went on. "Barely older than Louisa, only about twelve. Just a little kid, really."

His chest ached, trying to imagine that sweet vulnerability forced into such a traumatic situation. It was the same ache he had whenever he thought about Olivia watching her mother's murder.

"They went through hell while they were prisoners," Rafe went on. "The leader of the rebels was a psycho idiot bastard. He didn't give them enough to eat that entire month they were there, they were squished into squalid quarters, they were provided no medical care or decent protections from the elements, they underwent psychological torture. It's a wonder they made it through."

His hand tightened on the board he held, and he

wanted to swing it at something, hard. He didn't need to hear about this. It only seemed to heighten these strange, tender feelings in his chest.

"It affected all of them in various ways," Rafe went on. "But I think it was hardest on Celeste. She was so young and so very softhearted, from what Hope tells me. She's always been a dreamer, her head filled with stories and music. The conditions they were forced into must have been particularly harsh on an innocent young girl who couldn't really comprehend what was happening to her family."

The ache in his chest expanded. He hated that she had gone through it and wished, more than anything, that he could make it right for her.

"Why are you telling me this?"

Rafe gave him a steady look, as if weighing how to respond. He could see in his eyes that her brother-in-law knew exactly what they had been doing just before he walked in. Flynn fought the urge to tell the man to back off, that it was none of Rafe's damn business.

"I was there," Rafe finally said. "Did she tell you that?"

Flynn stared. "Where?"

"In Colombia. I was part of the SEAL team that rescued the Nichols family. It was my very first mission. A guy doesn't forget something like that."

Rafe was big and tough enough that somehow Flynn wasn't surprised he'd been a SEAL. He supposed the only remarkable thing about the situation was that the man seemed content now to live in a small town in Idaho, running a holiday attraction.

"So you saw their father get shot."

Rafe's jaw tightened. "Yeah. I saw it. And I saw Celeste weep and weep during the entire helicopter flight when she realized what had happened. I thought she would jump right out after her father."

Flynn swallowed at the image. After the past three months he hadn't thought he had much of his heart left to break, but he was most definitely wrong.

"I also shot two revolutionaries who were trying to keep us from leaving with them," Rafe went on. "You might, in fact, say I've had CeCe's back since she was eleven years old."

Yeah. The man definitely knew he had walked in on them kissing.

"She's very important to me," the other man said. "The whole Nichols family is mine now."

He met Flynn's gaze and held it as if he wanted to be perfectly clear. "And make no mistake. I protect what's mine."

He could choose to be offended, he supposed. He hadn't been called out for kissing a woman in…*ever*. Somehow he couldn't drum up anything but respect for Rafe. He was actually touched in an odd way, grateful that she had someone looking out for her.

"Warning duly noted." He made his own voice firm. "But anything between Celeste and me is just that. Between the two of us."

Rafe seemed to accept that. "I just don't want to see her hurt. Despite everything she's been through, CeCe somehow has still managed to retain a sweetness and a generosity you won't find in many people on this planet. If you mess with that, I won't be the only member of this family who won't be happy about it. Trust me. You do *not* want to tangle with the Nichols women."

This, more than anything else the man had said, resonated with truth. She had become a friend, someone he liked and respected. He didn't want to hurt her, either, but he couldn't see any other outcome. He had a business, a life in LA. Beyond that he wasn't in any position right now to start a new relationship with anyone, not when Olivia was still so needy.

He had made a mistake, kissing her. A mistake that couldn't happen again.

He gave the other man a steady look. "I got it. Thanks. Now can we just finish this job so I can grab my daughter and go home?"

After a moment, Rafe nodded and turned back to work, much to Flynn's relief.

The walk from the lodge to the main house helped a great deal to cool her flaming cheeks, but it didn't do much for the tumult inside her.

Oh, that kiss. How was she supposed to act around him now when she was afraid that every second she was near him she would be reliving those wild, hot moments in his arms? His hands on her skin, his mouth on hers, all those muscles pressing her against the cabinet.

She shivered in remembered reaction. How was she supposed to pretend her world just hadn't been rocked?

It had happened. She couldn't scrub those moments from her memory bank—indeed, she had a feeling they would haunt her for a long time—but surely she was mature enough to be able to interact with him in a polite, casual way. What other choice did she have?

When she reached the house, she drew in a deep breath, hoping all trace of those heated moments was gone from her features in case either of her eagle-eyed sisters was inside, then she pushed open the door.

The scents of cinnamon and pine and sugar cookies greeted her and the warmth of the house wrapped around her like one of Aunt Mary's hand-knitted scarves. As she stood in the entry, she had a sudden, familiar moment of deep gratitude for her aunt and uncle who had taken in three lost and grieving girls and given them safe shelter from the hard realities of life.

This was home. Her center.

Some of the storm inside her seemed to calm a bit. This was how she made it through, by focusing on what was important to her. Her family, her stories, the ranch. That was what mattered, not these fragile feelings growing inside her for Flynn and Olivia.

Before she could even hang up her coat, she heard the click of little paws on the floor. A moment later Linus burst into the room and greeted her merrily. She had nearly forgotten she'd brought him up to the house during the rehearsal to hang out with Mary, since Lucy had been in one of her snooty moods where she just wanted to be left alone.

"Hi, there. There's my darling boy." She scooped him up in her arms, and he licked her face and wriggled in her arms as if they had been away from each other for years instead of only a few hours.

"Have you been good?" she asked. He licked her cheek in answer, then wiggled to be let down again. She followed him and the sound of laughter to the kitchen, where she found her niece and nephews decorating cookies with Aunt Mary and Olivia.

"Look at all our cookies!" Barrett said. "The old people are going to *love* them."

He was such an adorable child, with a huge reservoir of compassion and love inside him for others.

This was a prime example—though she decided at some point she probably would have to gently inform him that the senior citizens coming to the show next week might not appreciate being called "old people."

"What a great job."

"Look at this one, Aunt CeCe. See how I made the stars sparkle with the yellow sugar things?" Joey, joined at the hip with Barrett, thrust his cookies at her.

"Fabulous."

"And look at my Christmas trees," Barrett said.

"I see. Good work, kid. And, Lou, I love how you swirled the icing on the candy canes. Very creative."

She turned to Olivia. "What about you? Have you decorated any?"

"A few." She pointed to a tray where a dozen angel cookies lay wing to wing. They all had hair of yellow frosting, just like the blonde and lovely Elise Chandler. Celeste had a feeling that wasn't a coincidence.

"I love them. They're beautiful, every one."

"Decorating cookies is *hard*," Joey declared. "You have to be careful you don't break them while you're putting on the frosting."

"But then you get to eat them when they break," Barrett pointed out.

"They've all been very good not to eat too many broken cookies," Aunt Mary said from the stove, where she was stirring something that smelled like her delicious ham-and-potato soup.

"Can you help us?" Louisa asked.

She had a million things to do before the show—not to mention a pile of unwrapped gifts in the corner of her office at home—but this suddenly seemed to take precedence over everything else.

"Of course," she answered her niece with a smile. "I can't imagine anything I would enjoy more."

Mary replaced the lid on the stockpot on the stove and turned down the burner. "Since you're here to supervise now, I think I'll go lie down and put my feet up. If you don't mind anyway. These swollen ankles are killing me today."

"Go ahead, my dear. You've done more than enough."

"I've got soup on the stove. The children had some earlier, but there's more than enough for anyone who pops in or out."

Celeste left the children busy at the table and headed over to hug her aunt before she reached in the cupboard for a bowl. "I know Hope and Rafe are back. I bumped into Rafe." She felt herself blush when she said it and hoped Aunt Mary wouldn't notice. "What about Faith? Is she around?"

"No. She ran into Idaho Falls for some last-minute *g-i-f-t-s*," Aunt Mary spelled, as if the children were tiny instead of excellent readers. Fortunately none of the children seemed to be paying attention to them.

"Poor girl," her aunt went on. "She's been too busy around the ranch to give Christmas much thought, and now here it is just a few days away."

The reminder instantly made Celeste feel small. She was fretting about a kiss while her sister had lost a husband and was raising two children by herself—albeit with plenty of help from Aunt Mary, Rafe, Hope and Celeste.

She was so grateful for her loving, supportive family—though she experienced a pang of regret for Flynn, who had no one.

She sat down at the table with her soup and listened to the children's chatter while she ate each delicious spoonful. When she finished, she set her bowl aside and turned to the serious business of cookie decorating.

"All right. Help me out, kids. What kind of cookie should I decorate first?"

"The angels are really hard," Olivia said.

Well, she'd already faced down a bunch of holiday-excited children and been kissed until she couldn't think straight. What was one more challenge today? "Bring on an angel, then."

Aunt Mary always had Christmas music playing in the house and the children seemed to enjoy singing along. Olivia didn't join them, she noticed. The girl seemed a little withdrawn, and Celeste worried maybe the day had been too much for her.

After she had decorated her third cookie, the song "Angels We Have Heard on High" came over the stereo.

"Ooh, I love this one," Louisa said. Her niece started singing along to the Glorias with a gusto that made Celeste smile.

"My mom is an angel now," Olivia said in a matter-of-fact sort of tone that made emotions clog Celeste's throat.

"I know, sweetheart," she said softly. "I'm so sorry."

"Our dad is an angel, too," Barrett informed her.

"Mom says he's probably riding the prettiest horses in heaven right now," Louisa said.

"My mom is in jail," Joey offered. That made her just as sad for him.

"Aren't you lucky to have Uncle Rafe and Aunt Hope, though?"

"Yep," he answered.

Barrett nodded. "And we still have our mom. And you have your dad," he reminded Olivia.

"Your mom *and* your dad are angels, aren't they?"

Louisa said to Celeste. "I asked my mom once why Barrett and me don't have a grandma and a grandpa, and she told me."

The pain of losing them still hurt, but more like an old ache than the constant, raw pain she remembered.

"They both died," she agreed. "It's been a long time, but I still feel them near me."

At some moments she felt them closer than others. She was quite certain she had heard her father's voice loud and clear one wintry, stormy night when she was driving home from college for the holidays. As clear as if he had been sitting beside her, she'd heard him tell her to slow down. She had complied instantly and a moment later rounded a corner to find a car had spun out from the opposite lane into hers. She was able to stop in time to keep from hitting it, but if she hadn't reduced her speed earlier, the head-on collision probably would have killed her and the other driver.

"Do you ever *see* your mom and dad angels?" Olivia asked, studying Celeste intently.

Oh, the poor, poor dear. She shook her head. "I don't see them as they were, but whenever I see the angel decorations at Christmastime, it helps me think about them and remember they're always alive in my heart."

"I really need to ask my mom something," Olivia said, her little features distressed. "Only I don't know how."

Celeste reached for the girl's hand and squeezed it. Oh, how she recalled all those unspoken words she had wanted to tell her parents, especially her father, who had died so abruptly. With her mother, she'd had a little more time, though that didn't ease the difficulty of losing her.

She chose her answer carefully, trying to find the right words of comfort.

"When you see an angel decoration you really like, perhaps you could whisper to the angel what you need to say to your mom. I believe she'll hear you," she said softly, hoping she was saying the right things to ease the girl's grief and not just offering a useless panacea.

Olivia considered that for a long moment, her brow furrowed. Finally she nodded solemnly. "That's a good idea. I think I'll do that."

She smiled and gave the girl a little hug, hoping she had averted that particular crisis. "Excellent. Now, why don't we see how many more cookies we can decorate before your father comes in?"

"Okay."

They went to work, singing along to the Christmas music for another half hour before the doorbell rang.

"I'll get it!" Joey announced eagerly. He raced for the door and a moment later returned with Flynn.

She had known it would be him at the door, but somehow she still wasn't prepared for the sheer masculine force of him. Suddenly she couldn't seem to catch her breath and felt as if the vast kitchen had shrunk to the size of one of Louisa's dollhouse rooms.

The memory of that kiss shivered between them, and she could feel heat soak her cheeks and nerves flutter in her stomach.

She shoved aside the reaction and forced a smile instead. "That was faster than I expected. Are you finished?" she asked.

He shrugged. "Your brother-in-law is a handy dude. With both of us working together, it didn't take us long."

"Wonderful. I can't tell you how much I appreciate it, especially with everything else you have going on. Thank you."

He met her gaze finally, and she thought she saw an instant of heat and hunger before he blinked it away. "You're very welcome."

His gaze took in the table scattered with frosting bowls, sugar sprinkles and candy nonpareils. "This looks fun," he said, though his tone implied exactly the opposite.

"Oh, it is, Daddy," Olivia declared. "Look at all the cookies I decorated! About a hundred angels!"

More like fifteen or sixteen, but Celeste supposed it had felt like much more than that to a seven-year-old girl.

She handed over one of the paper plates they had been using to set the decorated cookies on when they were finished. "Here, fill this with several cookies so you and your dad can take some home to enjoy."

"They're for the old people, though, aren't they?"

"I think it would be just fine for you to take five or six. We'll have plenty. Don't worry," she answered, declining again to give a lecture on politically correct terminology.

"Are you sure?"

"Yes. Go ahead. Pick some of your favorites."

Olivia pondered her options and finally selected five cookies—all blonde angels, Celeste noted—and laid them on the paper plate while Celeste found some aluminum foil to cover them.

"Here you go," she said, holding them out to Flynn.

"Thanks," he murmured and took the plate from her. Their hands brushed and she gave an involuntary shiver that she seriously hoped he hadn't noticed.

His gaze met hers for just an instant, then slid away again, but not before she saw a glittery, hungry look there that made her feel breathless all over again.

"Find your coat," he told his daughter.

"Can we stay a little bit longer?" Olivia begged. "Louisa and Barrett and Joey said they're going to have sleigh rides later. I've never been on a sleigh ride."

"We have a lot to do today, bug. We've already hung around here longer than we probably should have."

If he and his daughter had left earlier, the kiss never would have happened. Judging by the edgy tension that seethed between them now—and despite the flash of hunger she thought she had glimpsed—Celeste had a feeling that was what he would have preferred.

"Please, Daddy. I would *love* it."

As he gazed at his daughter a helpless look came into his eyes. She remembered him saying he hated refusing Olivia anything after what she had been through.

"How long do these sleigh rides take?" he asked Celeste.

"Less than an hour, probably."

"They're super fun at night," her niece suggested helpfully. "You could go home and do your work and then come back later. Then you can see all the lights and stuff. There's even caroling."

"Ooh. Caroling!" Olivia looked delighted at the idea, while her father looked vaguely horrified.

"I must agree. It is really fun," Celeste said.

He sighed. "Would that work for you, Liv? We can go home and try to finish another room at the house, and then come back later."

"Will you all be there?" she asked her new friends.

"Sure! We love to take the sleigh rides."

Olivia looked enchanted by the idea.

"Our last sleigh ride for regular visitors of The Christmas Ranch is back at the St. Nicholas Lodge about 8:00 p.m.

Why don't you meet us at the lodge a little before that, and we can take one that's not as crowded?"

"Oh, yay! I can't wait!" Olivia exclaimed. She spontaneously hugged Celeste, and she looked so adorably sweet with her eyes bright and pink frosting on her cheek that Celeste couldn't help it, she kissed the top of the girl's head.

When she lifted her head, she found Flynn gazing at her with a strange look on his features that he quickly wiped away.

"I guess we'll see you all later tonight, then," he said.

He didn't sound nearly as thrilled as his daughter about the idea.

Chapter Eleven

All afternoon Celeste did her best not to dwell on that stunning kiss.

Knowing she would see him again that evening didn't help. The whole busy December day seemed filled with sparkly anticipation, even though she tried over and over again to tell herself she was being ridiculous.

It didn't help matters that her sisters both attempted to back out of the sleigh ride and send her alone with the children. She couldn't blame them, since it had been completely her idea, but she still wanted them there. Though she knew the children would provide enough of a buffer, she didn't want to be alone with Flynn.

Finally she had threatened Hope that if she didn't go on the sleigh ride with them, Hope would have to direct the show Tuesday night by herself.

As she expected, Rafe had obviously told Hope what

he had almost walked in on earlier in the barn. Her sisters hadn't come out and said anything specific about it, but after the third or fourth speculative look from Hope—and the same from Faith—she knew the word was out in the Nichols family.

If not for her beloved niece and nephews, she sincerely would have given some thought to wishing she had been an only child.

"You owe me this after dragging me into the whole Christmas show thing," Celeste said fiercely to Hope at dinner, when her sister once more tried to wriggle out of the sleigh ride.

Hope didn't necessarily look convinced, but she obviously could see that Celeste meant what she said. "Oh, all right," she muttered. "If I'm going out in the cold that means you have to come, too, Fae."

Faith groaned. "After an afternoon of tackling the stores on the busiest shopping day of the year, I just want to put my feet up and watch something brainless on TV."

Barrett added his voice. "You *have* to come, Mom. It won't be as fun without you. You've got the *best* caroling voice."

"Yeah, and you're the only one who knows all the words," Louisa added.

Faith gave her children an exasperated look but finally capitulated. "Fine. I guess somebody has to help you all carry a tune."

After dinner they all bundled up in their warmest clothing and traipsed down to the St. Nicholas Lodge. Even Rafe came along, which she supposed she was grateful for, though he kept shooting her curious little looks all evening.

They arrived at the lodge just as Flynn and Olivia

walked in from the parking lot. Olivia wore her pink-and-purple coat with a white beanie and scarf. She looked adorable, especially when she lit up at the sight of them.

"Hi, everybody! Hi!" she said. "We're here. Dad didn't want to come, but I told him we promised, so here we are."

Celeste had to laugh at that, especially when Flynn's color rose. "It's good to see you both," she said.

It wasn't a lie. The December night suddenly seemed magical and bright, filled with stars and snow and the wonder of the season.

Olivia skipped over to her, hardly even limping in her excitement for the evening. "Guess what, Celeste?"

"What, sweetheart?"

"Today when we were cleaning we found boxes and boxes and *boxes* of yarn and scrapbook paper and craft supplies. Would you like to have them for your story times at the library? Dad said he thought you might."

"Seriously?" She stared, overwhelmed and touched that he would think of it.

"You don't have to take them," he said quickly. "I just didn't want to send everything to Goodwill if you could find a use for it."

"Are you kidding?" she exclaimed. "Absolutely! I can definitely use craft supplies. Thank you so much!"

"Good, because they're all in the back of the SUV. I took a chance that you would want them and figured if you didn't, I could drop them in the box at the thrift store in town after we were done here."

"Smart." She considered their options. "My car is still here in the parking lot from this morning. I can just pull next to you, and we can transfer them from your SUV to mine."

"Do you want to do it now or after the sleigh ride?"

"Go ahead and do it now while you're thinking about it," Hope suggested. Celeste narrowed her gaze at her sister, wondering if this was some sneaky way to get the two of them alone together, but Hope merely gave her a bland look in response.

"Sure," she said finally. "That way we won't forget later."

They walked out into the cold air, and she tried not to think about the last time they had been together—the strength of his muscles beneath her hands, the delicious taste of him, all those shivery feelings he evoked.

"I'm parked over there," he said, pointing to his vehicle.

"I parked at the back of the lot this morning to leave room for paying guests. Just give me a minute to move my car next to yours."

"I could just carry the boxes over to where you are."

"It will only take me a minute to move." She took off before he could argue further and hurried to her very cold vehicle, which had a thin layer of soft snow that needed to be brushed away before she could see out the windshield. Once that was done, she started it and drove the few rows to an open spot next to his vehicle, then popped open the hatch of her small SUV.

By the time she opened her door and walked around to the back, he was already transferring boxes and she could see at least half dozen more in the back of his vehicle.

She stared at the unexpected bounty. "This is amazing! Are you sure Olivia wouldn't like to keep some of this stuff?"

He shook his head. "She went through and picked out a few pairs of decorative scissors and some paper she really liked, but the rest of it was destined for either Goodwill or the landfill."

"Thank you. It was really kind of you to think of the library."

"Consider it a legacy from Charlotte to the library."

"I'll do that. Thank you."

He carried the last of the boxes and shoved it into her cargo area, then closed the hatch.

"There you go."

"Thanks again."

She expected him to head directly back to the lodge. Instead, he leaned against her vehicle and gave her a solemn look. The parking lot was mostly empty except for a family a few rows away loading into a minivan, probably after seeing Santa Claus inside.

"Do I owe you an apology?" he asked.

She fidgeted, shoving her mittened hands into her pockets. "An apology for what?"

He sighed. "We both know I shouldn't have kissed you, Celeste. It was a mistake. I didn't want to leave you with the...wrong impression."

Oh, this was humiliating. Was she so pathetic that he thought because she had told him she'd once had a crush on him, she now thought they were *dating* or something, because of one stupid kiss?

Okay, one *amazing*, heart-pounding, knee-tingling kiss. But that was beside the point.

"You don't owe me anything," she said.

He gazed up at the stars while the jingle of the sleigh returning to the lodge and the sound of shrieking children over on the sledding hill rang out in the distance.

"Here's the thing. Right now, my whole attention has

to be focused on helping my daughter. I'm not…looking for anything else. I can't."

She leaned against the cold vehicle next to him and tried to pretend she was sophisticated and experienced, that this sort of moment happened to her all the time—a casual conversation with a man who had kissed her deeply just a few hours ago and was now explaining why he couldn't do it again.

"It was a kiss, Flynn. I get it. I've barely given it a thought since it happened."

He wasn't stupid. She didn't doubt he could tell that was a blatant lie, but he said nothing. He simply gave her a careful look, which she returned with what she hoped was a bland one of her own.

"Good. That's good," he said. "I just wanted to clear the air between us. The last thing I want to do is hurt you or, I don't know, give you the wrong idea. You've been nothing but kind to Olivia and to me."

"Do you really think I'm so fragile that I could be hurt by a single kiss?"

The question seemed to hang between them, bald and unadorned, like a bare Christmas tree after the holidays.

He had a fierce wish that he'd never started this conversation, but the implications of that kiss had bothered him all afternoon as he'd carried box after box out of Charlotte's house.

He meant what he said. She had been very sweet to him and Olivia. His daughter was finally beginning to heal from the trauma she had endured, and he knew a big part of the progress she'd made the past week was because of all the many kindnesses Celeste and her family had shown them.

It seemed a poor repayment for him to take advantage of that because he couldn't control his base impulses around her.

He also couldn't seem to shake the guilt that had dogged him since that conversation with Rafe. The other man hadn't come out and blatantly told him to leave her alone, but Flynn hadn't missed the subtle undercurrents.

"Your brother-in-law and I had quite a talk this afternoon while we were finishing the screens for you."

"Is that right?"

Her cheeks looked pink in the moonlight, but he supposed that could have been from the cold night air.

"He's very protective of you and wanted to be clear I knew you had people watching out for you."

She made a low noise in the back of her throat. "My family sometimes drives me absolutely crazy."

Despite the awkwardness of the conversation, he had to smile. "They're wonderful, all of them. It's obvious they love you very much."

"A little too much, sometimes," she muttered. "They apparently don't think I can be trusted to take care of myself. Sometimes it really sucks to be the youngest sibling."

He couldn't imagine having any siblings. While he was lucky to have very tight friends, he knew it wasn't the same.

"I think it's nice," he answered. "Having your sisters close must have been a great comfort after you lost your parents."

Her lovely features softened in the moonlight. "It was," she murmured. "They may drive me crazy, but I would be lost without them. Don't tell them I said that, though."

He smiled a little. "I wish I had that same kind of support network for Olivia, but I'm all she has right now. I can't forget that."

"I understand. You're doing a great job with her. Don't worry. Children are resilient. She's working her way over to the other side in her own time."

His sigh puffed out condensation between them. "Thanks."

"And you can put your mind at ease," she said briskly. "You're not going to break my heart. Trust me, I don't have some crazy idea that you're going to propose to me simply because we shared one little kiss."

"It wasn't a little kiss. That's the problem," he muttered.

As soon as he said the words, he knew he shouldn't have, but it was the truth. That kiss had been earthshaking. Cataclysmic. He would venture to call it epic, which was the entire problem here. He knew he wouldn't forget those moments for a long, long time.

He wasn't sure how he expected her to respond but, as usual, she managed to surprise him. She flashed him a sideways look.

"What can I say? I'm a good kisser."

The unexpectedness of her response surprised a laugh out of him that echoed through the night. She seemed like such a sweet, quiet woman, but then she had these moments of sly humor that he couldn't seem to get enough of.

It made him wonder if she had this whole secret internal side of herself—contained and bundled away for protection—that she rarely showed the rest of the world.

She intrigued him on so many levels, probably because she was a study in contradictions. She could be tart and sweet at the same time, firm yet gentle, deeply vulnerable yet tough as nails.

Most of all, she seemed *real*. For a guy who had grown up surrounded by the artificial illusion of Hollywood, that was intensely appealing.

"It looks as if the other sleigh ride is done," she finally said. "The kids are probably anxious to get going."

"Right. Guess I'd better get my carol on."

She laughed, as he had hoped. At least the tension between them since the afternoon had been somewhat diffused.

As they walked, he was aware of a jumble of feelings in his chest. Regret, longing and a strange, aching tenderness.

For just a moment, he had a crazy wish that things could be different, that he had the right to wrap his hand around hers and walk up to the sleigh ride with her, then sit beneath a blanket cuddled up with her while they rode in a horse-drawn sleigh and enjoyed the moonlit wonder of the night together.

He could handle the regret and the longing. He was a big boy and had known plenty of disappointments in his life.

But he didn't have any idea what to do with the tenderness.

Celeste decided a sleigh ride through the mountains on a December evening was a good metaphor for being in love.

She was bumped and jostled, her face cold but the rest of her warm from the blankets. It was exhilarating and exhausting, noisy and fun and a little bit terrifying when they went along a narrow pass above the ranch that was only two feet wider on each side than the sleigh.

She'd been on the sleigh ride dozens of times before. This was the first time she'd taken one while also being in love, with these tangled, chaotic feelings growing inside her.

She was quickly reaching the point where she couldn't deny that she was falling hard for Flynn. What else could explain this jumbled, chaotic mess of emotions inside her?

"Oh. Look at all those stars," a voice breathed beside her, and she looked down to where Olivia had her face lifted to the sky.

She wasn't only falling for Flynn. This courageous, wounded girl had sneaked her way into Celeste's heart.

She would be devastated when they left.

When they'd climbed into the sleigh, Olivia had asked if she could sit beside Celeste. The two of them were sharing a warm blanket. Every once in a while the girl rested her cheek against her shoulder, and Celeste felt as if her heart would burst with tenderness.

"I never knew there were so many stars," Olivia said, her voice awestruck.

"It's magical, isn't it?" she answered. "Do you know what I find amazing? That all those stars are there every single night, wherever you are in the world. They're just hidden by all the other lights around that distract us away from them."

The whole evening truly *was* magical—the whispering jingle of the bells on the draft horses' harnesses, the creak of the old sleigh, the sweet scent of the snow-covered pines they rode through.

Except for Mary—who had stayed behind in the warm house—Celeste was surrounded by everyone she loved.

"I wish we could just go and go and never stop," Olivia said.

Unfortunately, the magic of sleigh rides never lasted forever. She had a feeling that, at least in her case, the magic of being in love wouldn't last, either. The *in love* part would, but eventually the heartache would steal away any joy.

"We'll have to stop at some point," the ever-practical Faith said. "The horses are tired. They've been working all night and are probably ready to have a rest."

"Besides that," Joey added, "what would we eat if we were stuck on a sleigh our whole lives?"

"Good point, kid," Rafe said. "We can't live on hot chocolate forever."

Olivia giggled at them and seemed to concede their point.

"I thought we were supposed to be caroling. We haven't sung *anything*," Louisa complained.

"You start us off," her mother suggested.

Celeste was aware that while both her sisters seemed to be dividing careful looks between her and Flynn, they did it at subtle moments. If she were very lucky, he wouldn't notice.

Louisa started, predictably enough, with "Jingle Bells." The children joined in with enthusiasm and soon even the adults joined them. Flynn, on the other side of Olivia, had a strong baritone. Under other circumstances, she might have been entranced by it, but Celeste's attention was fixed on his daughter as she sang.

Why hadn't she noticed during their rehearsals and the songs they had prepared that Olivia had such a stunning voice, pure and clear, like a mountain stream? It was perfectly on pitch, too, astonishing in a child.

She wasn't the only one who noticed it, she saw. Hope and Faith both seemed startled and even Rafe gave her a second look.

Flynn didn't seem to notice anything, and she thought of those stars again, vivid and bright but obscured by everything else in the way.

"What next?" Joey asked. "Can we sing the one about Jolly Old St. Nick?"

"Sure," Faith said. Of the three sisters, she had the most musical ability, so she led the children as the sleigh bells jingled through the night. With each song, Olivia's natural musical talent became increasingly apparent to everyone on the sleigh, but both she and Flynn seemed oblivious.

"What's that place with all the lights?" Olivia asked after they finished "Silent Night."

"That's the Christmas village," Barrett answered her. "It's awesome. Can we stop and walk through it?"

"You've seen it, like, a million times," his sister chided.

"Yeah, but Olivia hasn't. It's way more fun to see it with somebody else who has never been there. It's like seeing it for the first time all over again."

"You are so right, kiddo," Hope said, beaming at the boy. "Bob, do you mind dropping us off here so we can take a little detour through the village?"

"Not at all. Not at all."

The driver pulled the team to a stop, and everybody clambered out of the sleigh and headed toward the collection of eight small structures a short distance from the main lodge.

This was one of her favorite parts of the entire Christmas Ranch. With the lights strung overhead, it really did feel magical.

Each structure contained a Christmas scene peopled with animatronic figures—elves hammering toys, Mrs. Claus baking cookies, children decorating a Christmas tree, a family opening presents.

"This is quite a place," Flynn murmured beside her.

"The Christmas village is really what started the whole Christmas Ranch. You probably don't know this, but my family's name of origin was Nicholas. As in St. Nicholas."

"The big man himself."

"Right. Because of that, my aunt and uncle have always been a little crazy about Christmas. Before we came to live with them, my uncle Claude built the little chapel Nativity over there with the cow who nods his head at the baby Jesus and the two little church mice running back and forth. It became a hobby with him, and after that he came up with a new one every year."

With a pang, she dearly missed her uncle, a big, gruff man of such kindness and love. He had taught her and her sisters that the best way to heal a broken heart was to forget your troubles and go to work helping other people.

"He decided he wanted to share the village with the whole community, so he opened the ranch up for people to come and visit. The reindeer herd came after, and then he built the whole St. Nicholas Lodge for Santa Claus, and the gift shop and everything."

"This is really great. I have no idea how he did it. It's a fascinating exercise in engineering and physics."

She frowned up at the star above the chapel, just a dark outline against the mountains. "Usually the star up there lights up. I'm not sure what's wrong with it. I'll have to mention it to Rafe. He has learned the ins and outs of all the structures in the village. I don't know how everything works. I just love the magic of it."

Olivia appeared to agree. The girl seemed enthralled with the entire village, particularly the little white chapel with its Nativity scene—the calm Madonna cradling her infant son, and Joseph watching over them both with such care while a beautiful angel with sparkly white wings watched overhead.

"You guys are welcome to hang out, but we're going to head back to the house," Faith said after about fifteen minutes. "It's cold and I know my two are about ready for bed."

"We need to go, too," Hope said, pointing to a sleepy-looking Joey.

"Thank you all for taking us on one more ride," Flynn said. "I appreciate it very much. Olivia loved it."

"You're very welcome," Hope said. "It was our pleasure."

The rest of her family headed back up to the ranch house while Celeste and Flynn walked with Olivia to the lodge's parking lot.

"I'm glad you both came," Celeste said when they reached their vehicles.

"This is definitely a memory we'll have forever, isn't it, Liv?" Flynn said as he opened the backseat door for his daughter. "When we're back in California enjoying Christmas by the ocean, we'll always remember the year we went caroling through the mountains on a two-horse open sleigh."

She had to smile, even though his words seemed to cut through her like an icy wind whipping down the mountain.

"We'll see you Tuesday for the performance."

He nodded, though he didn't look thrilled.

"We'll be there. Thanks again."

She nodded and climbed into her own vehicle, trying not to notice how empty and cold it felt after the magic of being with them on the sleigh ride.

Chapter Twelve

"Are you sure we're not too early?" Flynn asked his daughter as they pulled up in front of the St. Nicholas Lodge on the night of the show. "It doesn't start for quite a while."

She huffed out her frustrated-at-Dad sigh. "I'm sure. She told me five thirty. This is when I'm supposed to be here, Celeste said, so they can help me get ready with my hair and makeup and stuff. I get to wear makeup onstage so my face isn't blurry."

Yeah, he was terrible with hair and didn't have the first idea what to do about makeup. Here was a whole new stress about having a daughter. Soon enough she was going to want to know about that stuff. Good thing he had friends in LA with wives who could help a poor single dad out in that department.

She opened the passenger door the moment he pulled

into a parking space. "Okay. Thanks, Dad. I'll see you at the show."

When he turned off the engine and opened his own door, she gave him a look of surprise. "You don't have to come in yet."

He shrugged. "I'm here. I might as well see if they need help with something—setting up chairs or whatever."

"Okay," she said, then raced for the door without waiting to see if he followed. Clearly, he was far more nervous about this whole performance thing than she was.

She had made amazing progress in a short time. In a matter of days she already seemed much more at ease with herself and the world around her than she had been when he brought her to Pine Gulch. She used her arm almost without thinking about it now, and she hardly limped anymore.

He wasn't foolish to think all the pain and grief were behind them. She would be dealing with the trauma for a long time to come, but he was beginning to hope that they had turned a corner.

Children are resilient. She's working her way over to the other side in her own time.

He gave no small amount of credit to the Nichols family, for their warmth and acceptance of her. She had made friends with the children and she also completely adored Celeste.

Would he be able to keep that forward momentum when they returned to California? He had no idea, but he would sure as hell try—even if that meant figuring out the whole hair-and-makeup thing on his own sometime down the line.

He pushed open the front doors after her and walked

into the lodge, only to discover the place had been transformed into an upscale-looking dining room.

What had been an open space was now filled with round eight-top tables wearing silky red tablecloths and evergreen and candle centerpieces. The huge Christmas tree in the corner blazed with color and light, joined by merry fires flickering in the river-rock fireplaces at both ends of the vast room. Glittery white lights stretched across the room and gleamed a welcome.

The air smelled delicious—ham and yeasty rolls and, if he wasn't mistaken, apple pie.

Like iron shavings to a magnet, his gaze instantly found Celeste. She was right in the middle of everything, directing a crew of caterers while they laid out table settings.

His stomach muscles tightened. She looked beautiful, with her hair up in a dark, elegant sweep and wearing a simple tailored white blouse and green skirt. Again, the alluring contradictions. She looked prim and sexy at the same time.

"Hi, Celeste," Olivia chirped, heading straight to her for a hug, which was readily accepted and returned.

He didn't understand the bond between the two of them, but he couldn't deny the strength of it.

"Looks as if you've been busy," he said, gesturing to the tables.

"Hope and Rafe did all this while I was working at the library today. It looks great, doesn't it?"

"Wonderful," he agreed. "I was going to see if there was anything I could do to help, but you seem to have everything under control."

"I don't know if I'd go that far," she answered with a rather frazzled-sounding laugh. "I don't know what I was thinking to agree to this. If Hope ever tries to rope me into one of her harebrained ideas again, please remind me of this moment and my solemn vow that I will never be so gullible again."

He smiled even as he was aware of a sharp ache in his chest. He wouldn't be around to remind her of anything. Some other guy would be the one to do that—a realization that he suddenly hated.

"Thanks for bringing Olivia early. She wanted her hair fixed the same as Louisa's."

"She said it was going to be a big bun on her head," Olivia said. "That's what I want."

Celeste smiled at her. "Find your costume first, and then Louisa's mom is on hair and makeup duty in the office, and she'll help you out."

"Okay," she said eagerly, then trotted away.

Without the buffer of his daughter, he suddenly couldn't escape the memory of that earthshaking kiss a few days earlier. When she smiled like that, her eyes huge behind her glasses, he wanted to reach out, tug her against him and taste her one more time.

"How are you?" she asked.

He didn't know how to answer. That strange, irresistible tenderness seemed to twist and curl through him like an unruly vine. As he had no idea what to do with it, he said the first thing he could think of in a futile effort to put distance between them.

"Good. It's been a busy few days. We've made a lot of progress with Charlotte's house. We're now down to one room and a few cupboards here and there."

She didn't answer for about three beats, and he thought he saw her hand tighten. Would she miss them when they left? Olivia, no doubt. What about him?

"That's a huge job," she finally said. "I imagine you must be relieved to be nearing the finish line."

Relieved? No. Not really. It had been a strange, disquieting experience sorting through the pieces of his grandparents' lives, all the treasures and papers and worthless junk they had left behind. It made a man wonder what would remain of his own life once he was gone. Right now he didn't feel as though he had all that much to show for his years on the planet.

"I thought it would take me until at least New Year's, but we're ahead of schedule."

"That's great," she said. Was that cheerful note in her voice genuine or forced?

"At this point, I'm thinking we'll probably take off the day after Christmas. Maybe we'll drive to San Diego for a few days before we head back up the coast to LA."

"Oh. So soon? I… That will be nice for you, to be back in the warmth and sunshine after all this snow we've had."

Logically, he knew it *should* be what he wanted, to go home and begin cobbling together the rest of their lives, but he still couldn't manage to drum up much enthusiasm for it.

"If I don't get the chance to talk to you again, I wanted to be sure to give you my thanks for all you've done to help Olivia."

Surprise flickered in those lovely eyes. "I didn't do anything," she protested.

"You know that's not true," he said. "You have been nothing but kind to her from the first moment we met you at the library that day. You gave her an unforgettable birthday celebration and have helped her feel the Christmas spirit when I would have thought that impossible this year. She's beginning to return to her old self, and I give a great deal of the credit for that to you and your family."

Her smile was soft and sweet and lit up her face like a thousand twinkly lights. He was struck again by how truly lovely she was, one of those rare women who became more beautiful the more times a man saw her.

"She's a remarkable girl, Flynn. I feel honored to have had the chance to know her. I'll miss her. I'll miss both of you."

Before he could come up with a reply to that—before he could do something stupid like tell her how very much he would miss her, too—one of the catering crew came up to her to ask a question about the dessert trays. After an awkward little pause, she excused herself to help solve the problem.

I'll miss her. I'll miss both of you.

The words seemed to echo through the vast lodge. While his daughter's life had been changed for the better because of their stay here in Pine Gulch, he wasn't sure he could say the same thing for his own.

He would miss Celeste, too. Rather desperately, he realized suddenly. As he stood in her family's holiday lodge surrounded by the trappings of the season, he realized how very much she had impacted his world, too.

"Got a minute?"

He had been so lost in thought he hadn't notice Rafe come in. Though there was still a certain wariness between the two of them, Rafe seemed to have become much more accepting of him after their time together working in the barn the other day.

He liked and respected the other man. In fact, Flynn suspected that if he and Olivia *were* to stick around Pine Gulch, he and Rafe would have become friends.

"I have more than a minute," he answered. "I'm just the chauffeur right now, apparently, delivering Olivia to get her hair fixed."

"Perfect. While you've got your chauffeur hat on, I've got about twenty older ladies in need of rides. None of them likes to drive after dark, apparently, and especially not when it's snowing. Naturally, Hope promised them all she would find a way to get them here without thinking of the impossible logistics of the thing. Chase was supposed to help me shuttle them all, but he got tied up with something at his ranch and won't be free until right before the show starts. Everybody else is busy right now with the kids, so I'm in a pinch."

He was honored to be asked, even though he wasn't part of the community. "Sure. I'm happy to help, but I don't know where anybody lives. You'll have to tell me where to go."

"I've got a list right here with addresses and names. I figure if we split it up, we'll have time to get everybody here before the show, but it's going to be tight. You sure you don't mind?"

He didn't. It felt good to be part of something, to feel as though he was giving back a little for all that had been done for him and Olivia.

"Not at all. Let's do it."

"Where's my dad?" Olivia asked. "I thought he was going to be here to watch."

She looked absolutely beautiful in the little angel costume she wore for the show—and for the special part they had just practiced at the last minute.

The costume set off her delicate features and lovely blond hair to perfection.

Celeste's gaze drifted from her to the other children in their costumes. They all looked completely adorable. Somehow, by a Christmas miracle, they were really going to pull this off.

"Do you see my dad?" Olivia asked.

She frowned and looked around the beautiful screens Rafe and Flynn had built to serve as the wings to their small stage. She saw many familiar, beloved neighbors and friends, but no sign of a certain gorgeous man.

"I can't see him, but I'm sure he'll be here."

"Who are you looking for?" Hope asked, looking up from adjusting Joey's crooked crown.

"Flynn."

"I don't think he's back yet from picking up the last group of ladies."

Celeste stared at her sister. "What ladies?"

"Oh, didn't you know? Rafe asked him to help shuttle some of the ladies who wanted to come to the dinner and show, but didn't want to be stuck driving after dark."

She gaped at her sister. "Seriously? Flynn?"

"Yeah. He's already dropped off one carload earlier, and then I think Rafe sent him out again."

She pictured him driving through the snow to pick up a bunch of older ladies he didn't even know, and her throat seemed suddenly tight and achy. What a darling he was, to step up where he was needed.

How was she supposed to be able to resist a man like that?

She was in love with him.

She drew in a shaky breath as the reality of it crashed over her as if the entire plywood set had just tumbled onto her head. It was quite possible that she had been in love with him since that summer afternoon so many years ago when he had picked her up from her bike, dried her tears and cleaned up her scratches and scrapes.

Was that the reason she had never really become serious about any of the other men she dated in college? She'd always told herself she wasn't ready, that she didn't feel comfortable with any of them, that she was too socially awkward. That all might have been true, but perhaps the underlying reason was because she had already given her heart to the larger-than-life boy he had been.

In the past few weeks she truly had come to know him as more than just a kind teenager, her secret fantasy of what a hero should be. She had come to admire so many other things about him. His strength, his goodness, the love he poured out to his daughter.

How could she *not* love such a wonderful man? She loved him and she loved Olivia, too. Her heart was going to shatter into a million tiny pieces when they left.

"What if he doesn't make it back?" Olivia fretted now. "He'll miss my big surprise."

Celeste drew in a breath and forced herself to focus on the show. There would be time for heartbreak later.

"He'll make it back. Don't worry. He wouldn't miss seeing you."

Actually, Flynn missing Olivia's big surprise might not be such a bad thing. She wasn't quite sure he would like it, but it was too late for regrets now.

Olivia still seemed edgy as the music started. Her uneven gait was more pronounced than usual as she followed the other children onstage for their opening number.

Just as the last child filed on, she saw him leading three older women: Agnes Sheffield, her sister and their friend Dolores Martinez.

She watched around the wings as he took their coats, then helped them find empty seats. Agnes touched his arm in a rather coquettish way. As he gave the octogenarian an amused smile, Celeste fell a little in love with him all over again.

Darn man. Why did he have to be so wonderful?

At last, when everyone was settled and the children were standing on the risers, Destry Bowman, one of the older girls, took the microphone.

"We welcome you all to the first ever holiday extravaganza at The Christmas Ranch. Consider this our Christmas gift to each of you."

The children immediately launched into the show, which was mostly a collection of familiar songs with a few vignette skits performed by the older children. After only a few moments, she could tell it was going to be considered an unqualified success.

She saw people laughing in all the right parts, catching their breath in expectation, even growing teary eyed at times, just as she'd predicted to the children. Most of all, she hoped they had a little taste of the joy and magic of the season, which seemed so much more real when experienced through the eyes of a child.

This was different from writing a book. Here she could see the immediate impact of what she had created and helped produce.

Seeing that reaction in real time made her rethink her objections to the upcoming Sparkle movie. Maybe it wouldn't be such a bad thing. The story was about finding the joy and wonder of Christmas through helping others, as Uncle Claude and Aunt Mary had taught them. If Sparkle could help spread that message, she didn't see how she could stand in the way.

Finally, it was time for the last number, which they had changed slightly at the last minute.

"Are you ready, sweetheart?" she whispered to Olivia.

The girl nodded, the tinsel halo of her angel costume waving eagerly.

As all the children were onstage, she stepped out to the audience so she could watch. From this vantage point, she had a clear view of Flynn. His brow furrowed in confusion at first to see Olivia at the microphone, then when the piano player gave her a note for pitch and she started singing the first verse to "Silent Night" by herself a cappella, his features went tight and cold.

Her voice was pure and beautiful, as it had been the other night while they were caroling, and she sang the familiar song with clarity and sweetness. She saw a few people whispering and pointing and thought she saw Agnes Sheffield mouth the words *Elise Chandler* to Dolores.

When Olivia finished, the piano started and all the children sang the second verse with her, then Destry Bowman signaled the audience to join in on the third.

What they might have lacked in musical training or even natural ability, the children made up for in enthusiasm and bright smiles.

Beside her, Hope sniffled. "They're wonderful, CeCe. The whole show is so good."

She smiled, even though emotions clogged her own throat.

They finished to thunderous applause, which thrilled the children. She saw delight on each face, especially the proud parents.

A moment later, Hope took the stage to wrap up

things. “Let’s give these amazing kids another round of applause,” she said.

The audience readily complied, which made the children beam even more. The show had been a smashing success—which probably meant Hope would want to make it a tradition.

“I have to give props to one more person,” she went on. To Celeste’s shock, Hope looked straight at her. “My amazing sister, Celeste. Once again, she has taken one of my harebrained ideas and turned it into a beautiful reality. Celeste.”

Her sister held out her hand for her to come onstage. She had never wanted to do some serious hair pulling more than she did at right that moment.

She thought about being obstinate and remaining right where she was, but that would only be even *more* awkward. With no choice in the matter, she walked onstage to combined applause from the performers and the audience.

Face blazing, she hurried back down the stairs and off stage as quickly as possible, in time to hear Hope’s last words to the audience.

“Now, Jenna McRaven and her crew have come up with an amazing meal for you all, so sit back and enjoy. Parents, your kids are going to change out of their costumes and they’ll be right out to join you for dinner. As a special treat for you, the wonderful Natalie Dalton and Lucy Boyer are going to entertain you during dinner with a duet for piano and violin.”

The two cousins by marriage came out and started the low-key dinner music Hope had arranged while the caterers began serving the meal.

“You all did wonderfully,” Celeste told the cast when they gathered offstage. “Thank you so much for your hard work. I'm so proud of you! Now hurry and change then come out and find your family so you can enjoy all this yummy food."

With much laughing and talking, the children rushed to the two dressing rooms they had set aside. She was picking up someone's discarded shepherd's crook when her sister Faith came around the screen.

"Great work, CeCe. It was truly wonderful." She gave one of her rare smiles, and in that moment, all the frenetic work seemed worth it.

"I'm glad it's over. Next year it's your turn."

"Great idea." Hope joined them and turned a speculative look in Faith's direction.

"Ha. That will be the day," Faith said. "Unlike Celeste, I know how to say no to you. I've been doing it longer."

Celeste laughed and hugged her sisters, loving them both dearly, then she hurried back into the hallway to help return costumes to hangers and hurry the children along.

Just before she reached the dressing room, Flynn caught up with her, his face tight with an emotion she couldn't quite identify.

Still caught up in the exhilaration of a job well done, she impulsively hugged him. "Oh, Flynn. Wasn't Olivia wonderful? She didn't have an ounce of stage fright. She's amazing."

He didn't hug her back and it took a moment for her to realize that emotion on his face wasn't enthusiasm. He was furious.

"Why didn't you tell me she was going to sing a solo?"

She didn't know how to answer. The truth was, she *had* worried about his reaction but had ignored the little niggling unease. For his own reasons, Flynn objected to his daughter performing at all, let alone by herself.

But the girl's voice was so lovely, Celeste had wanted her to share it.

Her heart sank, and she realized she had no good defense. "I should have told you," she admitted. "It was a last-minute thing. After we went caroling and I heard what a lovely voice she had, I decided to change the program slightly. I didn't have a lot of time to fill you in on the details since we decided to make the change just tonight, but I should have tried harder."

"You couldn't leave well enough alone. I told you I didn't want her doing the show in the first place, but my feelings didn't seem to matter. You pushed and pushed until I agreed, and then you threw her onto center stage, even though I made my feelings on it clear."

"She loved it!" she protested. "She wasn't nervous at all. A week ago, she was freaking out in a restaurant over a bin of dropped dishes, and today she was standing in front of a hundred people singing her heart out without flinching. I think that's amazing progress!"

"Her progress or lack of progress is none of your business. You understand? She's my daughter. I get to make those choices for her, not some small-town librarian who barely knows either of us."

She inhaled sharply as his words sliced and gouged at her like carving knives.

Her face suddenly felt numb, as frozen as her brain. That was all she was to him. A small-town librarian who didn't even know him or his daughter. It was as if all the closeness they had shared these past few days, the tender moments, didn't matter.

As if her *love* didn't matter.

She drew in another breath. She would get through

this. She had endured much worse in her life than a little heartbreak.

Okay, right now it didn't exactly seem *little*. Still, she would survive.

"Of course," she said stiffly. "I'm sorry. I should have talked to you first. Believe it or not, I had her best interests at heart. Not only do I think she has an amazing voice, but I wanted her to know that even though something terrible has happened to her, her life doesn't have to stop. She doesn't have to cower in a room somewhere, afraid to live, to take any chances. I wanted to show her that she can still use her gift to bring light and music to the world. To bring joy to other people."

The moment she said the words, realization pounded over her like an avalanche rushing down the mountain.

This was what the Sparkle books did for people. It was what *she* did for people. All this time she had felt so uncomfortable with her unexpected success, afraid to relish it, unable to shake the feeling that she didn't deserve it.

She had a gift for storytelling. Her mother and father had nurtured that gift her entire life, but especially when their family had been held captive in Colombia.

Tell us a story, CeCe, her father would say in that endlessly calm voice that seemed to hold back all the chaos. He would start her off and the two of them would spin a new tale of triumph and hope to distract the others from their hunger and fear. She told stories about dragons, about a brave little mouse, about a girl and a boy on an adventure in the mountains.

Tears welled up as she remembered how proud and delighted her parents had been with each story. Maybe that was another reason she'd struggled to accept her Sparkle success, because they weren't here to relish it with her.

Yes, it would have been wonderful. She would have loved to see in the pride in their eyes, but in the end, it didn't matter. Not really. Her sisters were here. They were infinitely thrilled for her, and that was enough.

More important, *she* was here. She had a gift and it was long past time she embraced it instead of feeling embarrassed and unworthy anytime someone stopped her to tell her how much her words meant to them.

"Excuse me," she mumbled to him, needing to get away. Just as she turned to escape, her niece, Louisa, came out of the dressing room holding a book.

"Aunt CeCe, do you know where Olivia went? We were talking about *The Best Christmas Pageant Ever.* She'd never read it, and I told her I got an extra copy at school and she could have it. I want to make sure I don't forget to give it to her."

She turned away from Flynn, hoping none of the glittery tears she could feel threatening showed in her eyes.

"She's probably in the dressing room."

"I don't think so. I just came from there and I didn't see her."

"Are you looking for Olivia?" Barrett asked, joining them from the boy's dressing room. "She left."

She frowned at her nephew even as she felt Flynn tense beside her. "Left? What do you mean, she left?"

He shrugged. "She said she wanted to go see something. I saw her go out the back door. I thought it was kind of weird because she didn't even have a coat on, just her angel costume."

Celeste stared down at the boy, her heart suddenly racing with alarm. The angel costume was thin and not at all suitable for the wintry conditions in the Idaho mountains. Even a few minutes of weather exposure could be dangerous.

"How long ago was this?" Flynn demanded.

"I don't know. Right after we were done singing. Maybe ten minutes."

"She can't have gone far," Celeste said.

"You don't know that," Flynn bit out.

He was right. Even in ten minutes, the girl *might* have wandered into the forest of pine and fir around the ranch and become lost, or she could have fallen in the creek or wandered into the road. In that white costume, she would blend with the snow, and vehicles likely wouldn't be able to see her until it was too late.

Her leg still wasn't completely stable. She could have slipped somewhere and be lying in the snow, cold and hurt and scared…

Icy fingers of fear clutched at her, wrapping around her heart, her lungs, her brain.

"We can't panic," she said, more to herself than to him. "I'll look through the lodge to find her first, and then I'll get Rafe and everyone out there searching the entire ranch. We'll find her, Flynn. I promise."

Chapter Thirteen

He heard her words as if from a long distance away, as if she were trying to catch his attention with a whisper across a crowded room.

This couldn't be real. Any moment Olivia would come around the corner wearing that big smile he was beginning to see more frequently. He held his breath, but she didn't magically appear simply because he wished it.

Cold fear settled in his gut, achingly familiar. He couldn't lose her. Not after working so hard to get her back these past few months.

"We'll find her, Flynn," Celeste said again, the panic in her voice a clear match to his own emotions.

She cared about his daughter, and he had been so very mean to her about it. He knew he had hurt her. He had seen a little light blink out in her eyes at his cruel words.

Her progress or lack of progress is none of your busi-

ness. She's my daughter. I get to make those choices for her, not some small-town librarian who barely knows either of us.

He would have given anything at that moment to take them back.

He didn't even know why he had gotten so upset seeing Olivia up onstage—probably because he still wanted to do anything he could to protect her, to keep her close and the rest of the world away.

He didn't want her to become like her mother or his, obsessed with recognition and adulation. At the same time, he had been so very proud of her courage for standing in front of strangers and singing her little heart out.

None of that mattered right now. She was missing and he had to find her.

He hurried to find his coat, aware of a bustle of activity behind him as Rafe jumped up, followed by Hope and Faith.

The instant support comforted him like a tiny flickering candle glowing against the dark night in a window somewhere. Yeah, they might be temporary visitors in Pine Gulch, but he and Olivia had become part of a community, like it or not.

Celeste's brother-in-law stopped for an instant to rest a hand on Flynn's shoulder on his way to grabbing his own coat off the rack. "Don't worry, man. We'll find her. She'll be okay."

He wanted desperately to believe Rafe.

He couldn't lose her again.

They would find her.

A frantic five-minute search of the lodge revealed no sign of one little girl. She wasn't in any of the bathrooms, the kitchen area, the closed gift shop or sitting beside any of the senior citizens as they enjoyed their meal, oblivious to the drama playing out nearby.

Rafe texted Celeste that he had searched through the barn with no sign of her. Faith and Hope had gone up to the house to see if they could find her there. Rafe told her he wanted to take a look around the reindeer enclosure for a little blond angel next and then head for some of the other outbuildings scattered about the ranch.

As soon as she read the word *angel*, something seemed to click in her brain. Angel. She suddenly remembered Olivia's fascination the other night with the angel above the little chapel in the Christmas village.

Excitement bubbled through her, and she suddenly knew with unshakable certainty that was where she would find the girl.

She grabbed her coat off the rack—not for her, but for Olivia when she found her—and raced outside without bothering to take time throwing it on.

Though Hope and Rafe had elected to close the rest of the ranch activities early that night—the sleigh rides, the sledding hill, the reindeer photography opportunities—because all hands were needed for the dinner and show, they had chosen to keep on the lights at the Christmas village for anyone who might want to stop and walk through it.

She nodded to a few families she knew who were enjoying the village, the children wide-eyed with excitement, but didn't take time to talk. She would have to explain away her rudeness to them later, but right now her priority was finding Olivia.

When she reached the chapel, she nearly collapsed with relief. A little angel in a white robe and silver tinsel halo stood in front of it, hands clasped together as she gazed up at the Madonna, the baby and especially the angel presiding over the scene.

Before she greeted the girl, Celeste took a precious twenty seconds to send a group text to Flynn, her sisters and Rafe to call off the search, explaining briefly that she had found Olivia safe and sound at the Christmas village.

With that done, she stepped forward just in time to hear what the girl was saying.

"Please tell my mom I don't want to be sad or scared all the time anymore. Do you think that's okay? I don't want her to think I don't love her or miss her. I do. I really do. I just want to be happy again. I think my daddy needs me to be."

Oh, Celeste so remembered being in that place after her parents had died—feeling so guilty when she found things to smile about again, wondering if it was some sort of betrayal to enjoy things like birthday cakes and trick-or-treating and the smell of fresh-cut Christmas trees.

She swallowed down her emotions and stepped forward to wrap her coat around Olivia. As she did, she noticed something that made her break out in goose bumps.

"If it means anything," she murmured, "I think your mom heard you."

The girl looked up. Surprise flickered in her eyes at seeing Celeste, but she gave her a tremulous smile and took the hand Celeste held out. "Why do you think so?"

"Look at the star."

Sure enough, the star above the chapel that had been out the other night flickered a few times and then stayed on.

Celeste knew the real explanation probably had to do with old wiring or a loose bulb being jostled in and out of the socket by the wind. Or maybe it was a tiny miracle, a sort of tender mercy for a grieving child who needed comfort in that moment.

"It *is* working," Olivia breathed. "Do you think my mom turned it on?"

"Maybe."

The star's light reflected on her features. "Do you… do you think she'll be mad at me for being happy it's Christmas?"

"Oh, honey, no." Heedless of the snow, Celeste knelt beside the girl so she could embrace her. "Christmas is all about finding the joy. It's about helping others and being kind to those in need and holding on to the people we love, like your dad. I heard what you said to the angel, and you're right. It hurts his heart to see you sad. Dads like to fix things—especially *your* dad—and he doesn't know how to fix this."

"When I cry, he sometimes looks as if he wants to cry, too," she said.

Celeste screwed her eyes shut, her heart aching with love for both of them. She didn't know the right words to say. They were all a jumble inside her, and she couldn't seem to sort through to find the right combination.

When she looked up, the peaceful scene in the little church seemed to calm her and she hugged the girl close to her. "It's natural to miss your mom and to wish she was still with you. But she wouldn't want you to give up things like sleigh rides and Christmas carols and playing with your friends. If that angel could talk, I think that's exactly what she would tell you your mom wanted you to hear."

Olivia seemed to absorb that. After a moment she exhaled heavily as if she had just set down a huge load and could finally breathe freely. She turned to Celeste, still kneeling beside her, and threw her arms around her neck.

That ache in her chest tightened as she returned the embrace, wondering if this would be her last one from this courageous girl she had come to love as much as she loved her father.

"Thanks for letting me be in the show," Olivia said. "It made me really happy. That's why I wanted to come out here, to see if the angel could ask my mom if it was okay with her."

Celeste hadn't known Elise Chandler, but from what little she did know, she had a feeling the woman would love knowing her daughter enjoyed entertaining people.

"I'm glad you had fun," she answered. "Really glad. But you scared everybody by coming out here without telling anyone. In fact, we should probably find your dad, just to make absolutely sure he got the message that you're safe."

"I'm here."

At the deep voice from behind them, she turned around and found Flynn watching them with an intense, unreadable look in his eyes.

Her heartbeat kicked up a notch. How much had he heard? And why was he looking at her like that?

Olivia extricated herself from Celeste, who rose as the girl ran to her father.

Flynn scooped her into his arms and held her tight, his features raw with relief.

"I'm sorry I didn't tell you where I was, Daddy."

"You know that's the rule, kiddo. Next time, you need to make sure you tell me where you're going so I know where to find you."

"I will," she promised.

As he set her back to the ground, her halo slipped a little and he fixed it for her before adjusting Celeste's baggy coat around the girl's shoulders. "I've been worried about you, Livie."

He didn't mean just the past fifteen minutes of not knowing where she was, Celeste realized. He was talking about all the fear and uncertainty of the past three months.

Her love for him seemed to beam in her chest brighter than a hundred stars. How was she going to get through all the days and months and years ahead of her without him?

"I don't want to be sad anymore," Olivia said. "I still might be sometimes, but Celeste said the angel would tell me Mom wouldn't want me to be sad *all* the time."

His gaze met hers and she suddenly couldn't catch her breath at the intense, glittering expression there. "Celeste and the angel are both very wise," he answered. He hugged her again. "You'll always miss your mom. That's normal when you lose someone you love. But it doesn't mean you can't still find things that make you happy."

"Like singing. I love to sing."

He nodded, even though he did it with a pained look. "Like singing, if that's what you enjoy."

The two of them were a unit, and she didn't really have a place in it.

She thought of his words to her. *She's my daughter. I get to make those choices for her, not some small-town librarian who barely knows either of us.*

They stung all over again, but he was right. For a brief time she had been part of their lives, but the time had come to say goodbye.

"Since you're safe and sound now, I really should go,"

she said with bright, completely fake cheer. "Why don't you hurry back to the lodge and change out of your angel costume, then you can grab some dinner?"

"I *am* hungry," Olivia said.

She smiled at the girl, though it took all her concentration not to burst into tears. A vast, hollow ache seemed to have opened up inside her.

"I'm sure Jenna McRaven can find both of you a plate. It all looked delicious."

"Good idea."

"I'll see you both later, then," she answered.

Even though they would be heading in the same direction, she didn't think she could walk sedately beside him and make polite conversation when this ache threatened to knock her to her knees.

Without waiting for them, she hurried back toward the lodge. As she reached it, the lights gleamed through the December night. Through the windows, she saw the dinner still in full swing. Suddenly, she couldn't face all that laughter and happiness and holiday spirit.

She figured she had done her part for the people of Pine Gulch. Let her sisters handle the rest. She needed to go home, change into her most comfortable pajamas, open a pint of Ben & Jerry's and try to figure out how she could possibly face a bleak, endless future that didn't contain a certain darling girl and her wonderful father.

By another Christmas miracle, she somehow managed to hold herself together while she hurried through the cold night to her SUV, started the engine and drove back to the foreman's cottage.

The moment she walked into the warmth of her house, the tears she had been shoving back burst through like a dam break and she rushed into her bedroom, sank onto her bed and indulged herself longer than she should have in a good bout of weeping.

She was vaguely aware that Linus and Lucy had followed her inside and were watching her with concern and curiosity, but even that didn't ease the pain.

While some part of her wanted to wish Flynn had never returned to Pine Gulch so that she might have avoided this raw despair, she couldn't be so very selfish. Olivia had begun her journey toward healing here. She had made great progress in a very short amount of time and had begun regaining all she had lost in an act of senseless violence.

If the price of her healing was Celeste's own heartache, she would willingly pay it, even though it hurt more than she could ever have imagined.

After several long moments, her sobs subsided and she grew aware that Lucy was rubbing against her arm in concern while Linus whined from the floor in sympathy. She picked up both animals and held them close, deeply grateful for these two little creatures who gave her unconditional love.

"I'm okay," she told them. "Just feeling sorry for myself right now."

Linus wriggled up to lick at her salty tears, and she managed a watery smile at him. "Thanks, bud, but I think a tissue would be a better choice."

She set the animals back down while she reached for the box on the table beside her bed.

She would get through this, she thought as she wiped away her tears. The pain would be intense for a while, she didn't doubt, but once Flynn and his daughter returned to California and she didn't have to see either of them all the time, she would figure out a way to go forward without them.

She would focus instead on the many things she had to look forward to—Christmas, the new book release, the movie production, a trip to New York with Hope to meet with their publisher at some point in the spring.

With a deep breath, she forced herself to stop. Life was as beautiful as a silky, fresh, sweet-smelling rose, even when that beauty was sometimes complicated by a few thorns.

She rose and headed to the bathroom, where she scrubbed her face in cold water before changing into her most comfortable sweats and fuzzy socks.

The mantra of her parents seemed to echo in her head, almost as if they were both talking to her like the angels Olivia had imagined. If they were here, they would have told her the only way to survive heartache and pain this intense was to throw herself into doing something nice for someone else.

With that in mind, she decided to tackle one more item on her holiday to-do list—wrapping the final gifts she planned to give her family members. It was a distraction anyway, and one she badly needed. She grabbed the gifts from her office and carried them to the living room, then hunted up the paper, tape and scissors. With everything gathered in one place, she turned on the gas fireplace and the television set and plopped onto the floor.

Lucy instantly nabbed a red bow from the bag and started batting it around the floor while Linus cuddled next to her. She had just started to wrap the first present when the little dog's head lifted just seconds before the doorbell rang.

It was probably one of her sisters checking on her after

her abrupt exit from the dinner. She started to tell them to come in, then remembered she had locked the door behind her out of habit she developed while away at school.

"Coming," she called. "Just a moment."

She unlocked the door, swung it open and then stared in shock at the man standing on the porch. Instantly, she wanted to shove the door shut again—and not only because she must look horrible in her loose, baggy sweats, with her hair a frizzy mess and her makeup sluiced away by the tears and the subsequent cold water bath.

"Flynn! What are you doing here?"

He frowned, concern on his gorgeous features. "You didn't stick around the lodge for dinner. I tried to find you to give your coat back but you had disappeared."

"Oh. Thanks."

She took the wool coat from him, then lowered her head, hoping he couldn't see her red nose, which probably wasn't nearly as cute as Rudolph's.

Though she didn't invite him in, he walked into the living room anyway and closed the door behind him to keep out the icy air. She should have told him not to bother, since he wouldn't be staying, but she couldn't find the words.

"Are you feeling okay?" he asked.

Sure. If a woman who was trying to function with a broken heart could possibly qualify as *okay.* She shrugged, still not meeting his gaze. "It's been a crazy-busy few days. I needed a little time to myself to get ready for Christmas. I've still got presents to wrap and all."

She gestured vaguely toward the coffee table and the wrapping paper and ribbon.

He was silent for a moment and then, to her horror,

she felt his hand tilt her chin up so she had no choice but to look at him.

"Have you been crying?" he asked softly.

This had to be the single most embarrassing moment of her life—worse, even, than crashing her bicycle in front of his grandmother's house simply because she had been love struck and he hadn't been wearing a shirt.

"I was, um, watching a bit of a Hallmark movie a little earlier and, okay, I might have cried a little."

It wasn't a very good lie and he didn't look at all convinced.

"Are you sure that's all?" he asked, searching her expression with an intensity she didn't quite understand.

She swallowed. "I'm a sucker for happy endings. What can I say?"

He dropped his hand. "I hope that's the reason. I hope it's not because you were upset at me for acting like an ass earlier."

She tucked a strand of hair behind her ear. "You didn't at all. You were worried for your daughter. I understand. I was frantic, too."

"Before that," he murmured. "When we were talking about Olivia's solo in the show. I was cruel to you, and I'm so, so sorry."

She didn't know how to respond to that, not when he was gazing at her with that odd, intense look on his features again.

"You were a concerned father with your daughter's best interests at heart," she finally said. "And you didn't say anything that isn't true. I *am* a small-town librarian, and I'm very happy in that role. More important, I don't have the right to make decisions for Olivia without asking you. I should have told you about her solo. I'm sorry I didn't."

He made a dismissive gesture. "That doesn't matter. While she was missing, I prayed that if we found her, I would drive her myself to acting lessons, singing lessons, tap-dancing lessons. Whatever she wants. As long as she's finding joy in the world again and I can help her stay centered, I don't care what she wants to do. She's not my mother or Elise. She's a smart, courageous girl, and I know she can handle whatever comes her way. These past few months proved that."

In that moment she knew Olivia would be fine. Her father would make sure of it. It was a great comfort amid the pain of trying to figure out how to go on without them.

"I realized something else while we were looking for Olivia," Flynn said. He stepped a little closer.

"What's that?" she whispered, feeling breathless and shaky suddenly. Why was he looking at her like that, with that fierce light in his eyes and that soft, tender smile?

Her heart began to pound, especially when he didn't answer for a long moment, just continued to gaze at her. Finally, he took one more step and reached for her hand.

"Only that I just happen to be in love with a certain small-town librarian who is the most caring, wonderful woman I've ever met."

Nerves danced through her at the words, spiraling in circles like a gleeful child on a summer afternoon.

"I… You're what?"

His hand was warm on hers, his fingers strong and firm and wonderful. "I've never said that to anyone else and meant it. Truly meant it."

She took a shaky breath while those nerves cartwheeled in every direction. "I… Exactly how many other small-town librarians have you known?"

He smiled a little when she deliberately focused on the most unimportant part of what he had said. "Only you. Oh, and old Miss Ludwig, who had the job here in Pine Gulch before you. I think my grandmother took me into the library a few times when I was a kid, and I *definitely* never said anything like that to her. She scared me a little, if you want the truth."

"She scared me, too," she said. *You scare me more,* she wanted to say.

He leaned down close enough that only a few inches separated them. "You know what I meant," he murmured, almost against her mouth. "I've never told a woman I loved her before. Not when the words resounded like this in my heart."

"Oh, Flynn." She gave him a tremulous smile, humbled and awed and deeply in love with him.

He was close enough that she only had to step on tiptoes a little to press her mouth to his, pouring all the emotion etched on her own heart into the kiss.

He froze for just a moment and then he made a low, infinitely sexy sound in his throat and kissed her back with heat and hunger and tenderness, wrapping his arms tightly around her as if he couldn't bear to let her go.

A long while later he lifted his head, his breathing as ragged as hers and his eyes dazed. She was deliriously, wondrously happy. Her despair of a short time earlier seemed like a distant, long-ago memory that had happened to someone else.

"Does that kiss mean what I hope?" he murmured.

She could feel heat soak her cheeks and all the words seemed to tangle in her throat. She felt suddenly shy, awkward, but as soon as she felt the urge to retreat into herself where she was safe, she pushed it back down.

For once, she had to be brave, to take chances and seize the moment instead of standing by as a passive observer, content to read books about other people experiencing the sort of life she wanted.

"It means I love you," she answered. "I love you so very much, Flynn. And Olivia, too. I lied when I told you I was crying over a television show. I was crying because I knew the two of you would be leaving soon, and I…I didn't think my heart could bear it."

"I don't want to go anywhere," he said. "Pine Gulch has been wonderful for Olivia *and* for me. She might have been physically wounded, but I realized while I was here that some part of me has been emotionally damaged for much longer. This place has begun to heal both of us."

He kissed her again with an aching tenderness that made her want to cry all over again, this time because of the joy bubbling through her that seemed too big to stay contained.

She didn't know what the future held for them. He had a company in California, a life, a home. Perhaps he could commute from Pine Gulch to Southern California, or maybe he might want to take Rafe's advice and open a branch of his construction company here.

None of that mattered now, not when his arms and his kiss seemed to fill all the empty corners of her heart.

A long time later, he lifted his head with reluctance in his eyes. "I should probably go find Olivia. I left her with Hope and Rafe at the lodge. I'm sure she's having a great time with the other kids, but I hate to let her out of my sight for long."

"I don't blame you," she assured him.

He stepped away, though he didn't seem to want to release her hands. "I doubt Rafe was buying the excuse when I told him that I needed to return your coat. Something tells me he knows the signs of a man in love."

She could feel her face heat again. What would her family say about this? She didn't really need to ask. They already seemed to adore Olivia, and once they saw how happy she was with Flynn, they would come to love him too.

"Do you want to come with me to pick her up?" he asked.

She wanted to go wherever he asked, but right now she still probably looked a mess. "Yes, if you can give me ten minutes to change."

"You look fine to me," he assured her. "Beautiful, actually."

When he looked at her like that, she felt beautiful, for the first time in her life.

"But if you *have* to change—and if I had a vote—I'm particularly fond of a particular T-shirt you own."

"I'll see what I can do," she answered with a laugh. She kissed him again while the Christmas lights from her little tree gleamed and the wind whispered against the window and joy swirled around them like snowflakes.

Epilogue

"Are you ready for this?"

Celeste took her gaze from the snowflakes outside to glance across the width of the SUV to her husband.

"No," she admitted. "I doubt I will *ever* be ready."

Flynn lifted one hand from the steering wheel to grab hers, offering instant comfort, his calm blowing away the chaotic thoughts fluttering through her like that swirl of snow.

"*I'm* ready," Olivia piped up from the backseat. "I can't *wait*."

"You? You're excited?" Flynn glanced briefly in the rearview mirror at his daughter. "You hide it so very well."

Olivia didn't bother to pay any attention to his desert-dry tone. "This is the coolest thing that's ever happened in my whole life," she said.

Since Olivia wasn't yet a decade old, her pool of experiences was a little shallow, but Flynn and Celeste both declined to point that out.

The girl was practically bouncing in the backseat, the energy vibrating off her in waves. Celeste had to smile. She adored Olivia for the lovely young lady she was growing into.

The trauma of her mother's tragic death had inevitably left scars that would always be part of her, but they had faded over the past two years. Olivia was a kind, funny, creative girl with a huge heart.

She had opened that big heart to welcome Celeste into their little family when she and Flynn married eighteen months earlier, and Celeste had loved every single moment of being her stepmother.

Now Olivia breathed out a happy sigh. "I think I'm more excited about the Pine Gulch premiere of *Sparkle and the Magic Snowball* than the real one in Hollywood tomorrow."

"Really?" Celeste said in surprise. "I thought you'd be thrilled about the whole thing."

Olivia loved everything to do with the film industry, much to Flynn's dismay. Celeste supposed it was in her blood, given her mother's and her grandmother's legacies. Someday those Hollywood lights would probably draw her there, too—something Flynn was doing his best to accept.

"It will be fun to miss school and fly out and stay at our old house. I mean, a movie premiere in Hollywood with celebrities will be glamorous and all. Who *wouldn't* be excited about that?"

In the transitory glow from the streetlights, her features looked pensive. "But I guess I'm more excited about this one because this is our home now," she said after a moment. "This is where our family is and all our friends. Everyone in Pine Gulch is just as excited about the new Sparkle movie as I am, and I can't wait to share it with them."

Oh. What a dear she was. If the girl hadn't been safely buckled in the backseat, Celeste would have hugged her. It warmed her more than her favorite wool coat that her stepdaughter felt so at home in Pine Gulch and that she wanted all her friends and neighbors to have the chance to enjoy the moment, too.

"Good point," Flynn said, smiling warmly at his daughter. "The whole town has been part of the story from the beginning. It's only right that they be the first to see the movie."

"Yep. That's the way I feel," Olivia said.

Her father gave Celeste a sidelong glance before addressing Olivia again. "Good thing your stepmother is so fierce and fought all the way up to the head of the studio to make sure it happened this way. What else could they do but agree? They're all shaking in their boots around her. She can be pretty scary, you know."

Olivia giggled and Celeste gave them both a mock glare, though she knew exactly what he was doing. Her wonderful husband was trying to calm her down the best way he knew how, by teasing away her nerves.

She *had* fought for a few things when it came to her beloved Sparkle character, but wanted to think she had been easygoing. That was what the studio executives had told her anyway. She considered herself extremely fortunate that her vision for the characters and the story matched the studio's almost exactly.

A moment later, Flynn pulled up to the St. Nicholas

Lodge, which had been transformed for the night into a theater.

Somebody—Rafe, maybe—had rented a couple of huge searchlights, and they beamed like beacons through the snowy night. The parking lot was completely full and she recognized many familiar vehicles. Unfortunately, they couldn't fit everyone in town into the lodge so the event had become invitation only very quickly. For weeks, that invitation had become the most sought-after ticket in town.

Though the official premiere the next night in California would be much more of a full-fledged industry event, a red carpet had been stretched out the door of the lodge, extending down the snowy walkway to the edge of the parking lot.

Had that been Faith's doing? Probably. Where on earth had she managed to find a length of red carpet in eastern Idaho? Their older sister was proud of and excited for both Celeste and Hope.

The past two years since they'd signed the contract licensing the Sparkle stories to the animation studio they had chosen to work with seemed surreal. Besides two more bestsellers, they now had a *second* Sparkle animated movie in the works.

Now that she was here, about to walk into the makeshift theater to see people enjoying *her* story come to life on the screen—and it would be enjoyable, she knew, given what she had seen so far of the production—Celeste felt humbled and touched. It didn't seem real that life and fate, her own hard work and her sister's beautiful artwork had thrust her into this position.

"A red carpet," Olivia squealed as she finally noticed—and caught sight of the people lined up in the cold on either side of it, as if this was the real premiere filled with celebrities to gawk over. "How cool is that? That looks like my friend Louise from school. Oh, there's Jose. And Mrs. Jacobs. My whole class is here!"

"I guess you can't escape Hollywood, even here in Pine Gulch," Celeste said quietly to Flynn as he parked in the VIP slot designated for them. "I'm sorry."

He made a rueful face, but she knew him well enough after these deliriously happy months together to know he didn't really mind. He had been her biggest supporter and her second most enthusiastic fan—after Olivia, of course.

"For you, darling, it's worth it," he replied. He tugged her across the seat and pulled her into his arms for a quick kiss. "I'm so proud of you. I hope you know that. I can't wait for the whole world to discover how amazing you are."

Her heart softened, as it always did when he said such tender things to her.

Two years ago, she'd had a pretty good life here in Pine Gulch—writing her stories, working at the library in a job she loved, spending time with her sisters and her niece and nephew and Aunt Mary.

But some small part of her had still been that little girl who had lost both of her parents and was too afraid to truly embrace life and everything it had to offer.

Flynn and Olivia had changed her. At last, she fully understood the meaning of joy. Sparkle might have his magic snowball that could save Christmas, but the true magic—the only one that really mattered—was love.

These past two years had been a glorious adventure—and in seven months, give or take a few weeks, they would all be in for a new turn in their shared journey.

She pressed a hand to her stomach, to the new life

growing there. Flynn caught the gesture and grinned—a secret smile between the two of them. He pressed a hand there as well, then reached for his car door.

"Let's go meet your adoring public," he told her.

She didn't need an adoring public. She had everything she needed, right here, in the family they had created together.

* * * * *

FALLING FOR MR DECEMBER

KATE HARDY

To Fi, my best friend, with much love.

CHAPTER ONE

SAMMY LAUGHED AS the penny finally dropped. 'So you want me to photograph naked men for you?'

Ayesha, who chaired the Friends of the London Victoria Hospital, squirmed and stared into her latte. 'Put like that, it sounds terrible!'

'I know what you meant. Do it *artistically*,' Sammy said, still smiling. 'A calendar of hot men to raise funds for the cancer ward. It's a great idea. So do you have a bunch of sexy doctors lined up to pose for me?'

'A couple,' Mari, the vice-chair, said. 'But we were thinking maybe we can include other people who've been involved with the ward.'

'Cured patients, so you can say that this is what a cancer survivor looks like? That could work well.' And, for a cause like that, Sammy would seriously think about going public and baring her own leg, if they couldn't get enough models.

'We were thinking relatives of patients,' Ayesha said. 'Ones with high profiles locally. We've got an actor, a musician, a chef, a gardener…'

'So I could maybe shoot them in their own locations, doing their job. That'd work really well,' Sammy said.

'And they're all happy about posing naked—provided I preserve their modesty?'

'Ye—es,' Ayesha said.

The hesitation told her everything. 'You didn't actually tell them it meant posing naked, did you?' Sammy asked.

'We're going to,' Mari said. 'We can talk them into it.'

'As I'll need signed model release forms before I can let you use the photographs, I'm afraid you'll have to do that.' Sammy looked at her diary. 'If you're using the hospital as a location, I could shoot the whole lot in a day, but if I need to go to different places then I'll have to work out a schedule based on the locations and the availability of the models.' She scribbled some notes down on a pad. 'These are the best times for me to do it, but I can also work round a couple of other things if you need me to. Talk to your models and let me know where and when you want me to do the shoots.'

'Sammy, you're a star. Thank you so much,' Ayesha said.

Sammy shrugged off the praise. 'It's the least I can do. If it wasn't for the treatment I had here when I was a teen—' and again two years ago '—then I wouldn't be here. And this means I can give something back.' She smiled. 'This is going to be fun. And we're going to raise a ton of money for the ward.'

Nick folded his arms and looked at his sister. 'All right, Mandy. Out with it.'

'Out with what?' she deadpanned.

'Amanda Kennedy, I've known you for thirty-five years.'

'At least one year of which you wouldn't remember, because you were a baby at the time,' she retorted.

'Agreed,' he said, 'but I can always read your expression. So don't ever take up playing poker, will you?'

She sighed. 'I guess.'

Nick had known that tonight wasn't just about his sister giving him an update on his nephew's cancer treatment. Despite going through a messy divorce, Mandy still believed in love and happy endings. And all too often she tried to fix him up with someone she thought would be his perfect date. Nick had stopped believing in love years ago, and he'd learned the hard way that you couldn't be successful both in love and in your career. So after the break-up of his marriage he'd gone for the safe option and concentrated on his career.

No doubt this was another of Mandy's friends who really needed a plus-one for a dinner party and he'd fit the bill perfectly. OK. He'd help out, but he'd make it clear that he wasn't looking for a relationship. Nowadays he didn't do anything deeper than casual dating.

Then his sister said something he really hadn't expected. 'The Friends of the Hospital are doing a calendar to raise funds for the ward.'

He didn't need to ask which ward. The cancer ward. The one that had treated his nephew Xander for osteosarcoma. Well, he could do something to help there, too. 'If they're looking for a sponsor to cover production costs, count me in.'

Mandy reached across the table and squeezed his hand. 'Aww, Nick. I knew you'd offer to help before I could ask you. But they already have a sponsor for printing costs.'

'OK. What else do they need to cover? Distribution? Warehouse? Paying the photographer?'

'Um—not that, either. The photographer's doing it for nothing.'

'Then what?'

She took a deep breath. 'They want you to be one of the models.'

'Me?' He looked at her, totally shocked. He knew his sister had been under a lot of stress recently, but had she gone temporarily insane? 'Why?'

Mandy raised her eyebrows. 'Need I remind you that you actually got approached by a model agency when you were seventeen?'

'And I didn't take up their offer.' He might have considered it, to fund his way through university; but a couple of weeks later their parents had split up and life had disintegrated into chaos. Nick had forgotten all about the modelling offer and retreated into his studies. Concentrating on his books was what had got him through all the upheaval of his parents' divorce. Just as concentrating on his job had got him through the misery of his own divorce.

'Seriously, Nick—will you do it? They're looking for people who are connected with the ward.'

As Xander's uncle, he definitely had that connection.

'And they want people with interesting jobs.'

'A barrister isn't that exciting,' he said.

'Yes, it is. You look like a film star in your wig and gown.'

He rolled his eyes. 'Mandy, I'm just an ordinary guy.'

'Like hell you are. Apart from the fact that you're my little brother, which would make you special in any case, can I remind you that you're one of the youngest ever barristers appointed to being a QC?'

He grimaced. 'Why would anyone be interested in that?' About the only people who would even know what a QC was were people who had needed to brief one. Or maybe fans of certain types of TV crime drama.

'And you'd be helping raise money for the ward. Money they really need for new equipment.'

That was an unbeatable argument, and they both knew it. How could he possibly say no? This was to help other kids who were in Xander's position. And a little voice in his head added selfishly that maybe if he did it, then that would persuade Fate to give Xander a break and keep him in remission. And for that Nick would do almost anything.

'Will you do it?' she asked.

He closed his eyes briefly. 'All right.'

She smiled. 'Good. Thank you. I'll give your phone number and email to them, then—I'll do that now, if you don't mind, because they're waiting on my answer.'

'OK.' But Mandy was still hiding something, he was sure. 'And the rest of it?' he asked.

She blinked. 'What do you mean?'

'You're holding something back.'

She shrugged and tapped a message into her phone.

'Just save us both the time and tell me the rest of it, Mandy,' he said, leaning back and eyeing her over his glass of water.

'OK.' She sat back in her own chair and looked at him straight. 'Since you ask, you're going to be naked.'

'What?' He'd just taken a sip of water and he nearly choked on it. Naked? He must've misheard. No way would his sister have done this to him.

'You won't be *showing* anything,' she said.

'Define naked,' he said grimly.

'In court. Wearing your wig and robe.'

He shook his head. 'I'm afraid I can't do that, Mandy. The Head of Chambers would never agree to it.'

'Um, he already has.'

He blinked hard. Was he hearing things? Leo had already said yes? But—how? 'You what?'

'I talked to your clerk this morning,' she said. 'And he thinks it's a great idea.'

Now Nick was beginning to understand all the knowing smiles that had greeted him all afternoon. The news must've gone round chambers in ten seconds flat—gossip that juicy would never be ignored. And they'd all known that he didn't have a clue what was going on, making it even more fun for them.

'So what exactly did Gary say?' he asked, keeping his voice low and even and meanwhile planning how he was going to make his clerk grovel hugely in the morning.

'He put me through to your Head of Chambers. Then I told Leo all about it and he said he thought it was really a good idea, too. And he's getting clearance for us so you can do the shoot in the local court. He says he'll cover any photographic permission costs at the court himself.'

'Oh, good God.' With his boss on side, there was no way Nick could get out of it. He covered his face with his hands. 'Please tell me this is some weird, surreal dream. Please tell me it's a nightmare and I'm going to wake up. Preferably right now.'

'Nick, I've already told them you said yes,' Mandy said plaintively.

'That was before I knew I was going to be naked. This is a seriously bad idea, Mandy,' he said softly. 'I'm a senior barrister. I have to respect the dignity of the court. Which doesn't mean posing naked—or near-naked—for a calendar shoot, no matter how noble the cause is.'

'But Leo said it would be OK. And… Nick, we need you,' Mandy pleaded. 'And it's not as if you're the only one with a responsible job. One of the surgeons at the hospital is doing it.'

'Which is publicity for his own place of work.'

'And I think there's an actor and a musician on their list. And a chef.'

'All of whom would get a career boost from the publicity,' he pointed out.

'Please, Nick. For me. And for Xander.'

'It doesn't look as if I've got much choice,' he said grimly. 'But promise me you'll never, ever pitch a stunt like this again.'

'I promise. I'm sorry, Nick.' She bit her lip. 'But the ward needs the money.'

Lack of money meant lack of equipment. Which in turn meant that some kids wouldn't get the treatment they so badly needed. And that meant that those kids might even die.

Which was Nick's worst nightmare regarding his nephew.

And he was in a position to change that. To give more kids a chance of life—the same amazing chance that Xander had been given. All he had to do was pose for one little picture that would help to publicise the cause and encourage people to donate.

One little *naked* picture.

It really went against the grain. But far worse was

the thought of his nephew dying and the way it would shatter all their lives and devastate his elder sister.

'All right,' he said, blowing out a breath. 'But I need to double-check this with Leo myself, first, and make sure that he's absolutely clear on all the details. And if he changes his mind and says that I can't do it, then I'll sell calendars by hand for you—and I'm very persuasive, so I'll sell tons of them to everyone in the whole of Inner Temple and Middle Temple. Plus I'll also give a personal donation to match those sales. Double.' Time *and* money. They'd be a good alternative to posing naked for a calendar, wouldn't they?

And hopefully he'd be able to persuade his Head of Chambers that having one of his barristers naked and in the focus of the press might not be such a good idea…

CHAPTER TWO

AND OF COURSE Leo still said yes. Even when Nick pointed out exactly what was involved.

So, two weeks later, Nick found himself heading to the local Crown court. Leo had arranged for Court Number Two to be used outside the normal court working hours, though there was still a chance that Nick might bump into someone he knew who'd want to know what he was doing hanging round the court building when he wasn't in a trial—especially when he looked as scruffy as he did right now.

S. J. Thompson, the photographer, had sent him a couple of very business-like texts to arrange the photo shoot and explain that Nick needed to dress casually and remove anything that might cause a mark on his skin—socks, collars, waistbands and the like—at least two hours before the shoot.

For putting him through something as embarrassing as this—not to mention the teasing he knew he'd get from his colleagues when the calendar actually came out—Fate had *better* keep Xander safe, Nick thought grimly.

When he got to the court, carrying his court attire in its usual boxes, there was nobody waiting outside. The only person he could see in the lobby was a woman who looked to be in her late twenties or so, wearing black trousers, a black silky short-sleeved top and black shoes. Her blonde hair was cropped so short as to be almost a military cut. She didn't look remotely like the man Nick was here to meet.

She looked up from her book, then closed it, stood up and walked towards him. 'Nick Kennedy, I presume?'

He blinked. Was she the photographer's assistant or something? 'Yes.'

'Thank you for being on time. I'm S. J. Thompson—though you can call me Sammy, if you like.' She held out her hand for him to shake.

'*You're* S. J. Thompson?' Even as the words came out, he realised how dim they sounded. And how stupid of him to assume that the use of initials meant that the photographer was male.

She gave him a slight smile. 'I'm afraid so.'

Clearly he wasn't the first to have made that mistake. 'I—er—nice to meet you,' he said, feeling totally wrong-footed.

And, when he shook her hand, awareness zinged through every pore. Sammy Thompson was the most striking woman he'd met in a long time. And that severe haircut only served to highlight how pretty and feminine her face was. There was nothing masculine at all about her. Her mouth was a perfect rosebud, and he found himself wanting to trace her lower lip with his fingertip. Worse still, he could picture himself doing that before leaning in and kissing her. Lightly at first, a touch as light as a butterfly's wing, and then deepening the kiss as she responded…

He shook himself mentally. Oh, for pity's sake.

This was *business*. OK, maybe not the normal kind of business he'd conduct here in the court, but it was still business. And he wasn't exactly known for having ridiculous flights of fancy.

But he did feel uncomfortable right now.

It was nothing to do with sexism—as far as he was concerned, it was how you did your job that mattered, not what your gender or your sexual orientation or your religion was—but Sammy's gender made this situation a little more difficult. Because it meant that now he was going to be stripping off in front of a woman he'd never met before.

Either his doubts showed on his face or she was used to this reaction from the people she photographed, because she said softly, 'It's not going to be as bad as you think. And, if it helps, remember that I'll be seeing you simply as a life model rather than as an actual person. I don't tend to hit on my models.'

'I—yes. Of course. Sorry.' How long had it been since he'd felt in a whirl, like this? He was never this pathetic and woolly. And he really hoped he didn't look as if he was staring at her. He forced himself to look away. 'I believe we have Court Number Two booked.'

'My equipment's already in there, though I haven't set it up fully yet,' she said. 'Once we've decided precisely where you're going to stand, it won't take me long. Oh, and we really ought to cover the legal details now.'

Legal details? That got his attention.

'Firstly, I have public liability insurance, which covers any damage to person or property while we're in the location—not that there will be any—and secondly I'll need you to sign a model release form,' she said.

'It's pretty standard wording, but I'd still prefer you to read it thoroughly before you sign it.' There was just the slightest twinkle in her sea-green eyes as she added, 'Though I guess in your case I don't really need to tell you to ask me to explain any legal wording you don't understand.'

'Quite,' he agreed, trying to sound cool and professional. Even though Sammy Thompson was making him feel decidedly hot under the collar. What was it about her that made him feel like this?

'Shall we?' She gestured for them both to go in to the court room, and put a note on the door saying *Filming in progress: do not enter.*

'I take it you've worked in here before, or at least somewhere like this?' she asked.

'Yes.'

'Good. Then you'll be comfortable with the setting,' she said approvingly.

True, but he really wasn't comfortable with what he was about to do. 'Usually I'm fully dressed when I'm in this room,' he said.

She indicated his cases and suit carrier. 'This lot contains what you wear in court, I assume?'

He nodded. 'I brought all of it because I wasn't sure what you'd need.' Though he knew it would be a lot less than he would prefer.

'OK. Talk me through it,' she invited.

He took his work clothing out of the cases he'd brought with him, piece by piece, and laid each one in turn on the judge's bench. 'Tunic shirt, waistcoat, pinstripe trousers and frock coat.'

'You don't wear a normal business suit under your lawyer's gown?' she asked, sounding surprised.

'I did before I took silk,' he said. 'That is, before I became a QC—a Queen's Counsel.'

'Which is a senior barrister, right?'

'Yes. So that's why I wear the frock coat.' He took out the gown. 'And this.'

'And that gown's silk, I assume?' she asked.

'Yes.'

'May I touch it?'

He frowned. 'Why?'

'So I can move it about and see how the light affects it,' she said. 'Obviously I'll be careful with it. One of my best friends is a wedding dress designer, and I've taken most of the shots for her portfolio and website, so I understand how to handle material without marking it.'

'Ah. Of course.'

His fingers brushed against hers as she took the gown from him, and it felt as if pure electricity were running through his veins. What on earth was the matter with him? He never reacted like this. Especially to a complete stranger.

Maybe he was overreacting because he hadn't dated in a while, and his body's natural urges were making themselves felt because Sammy was really attractive. Well, tough. This was business and he really didn't have time for this. Behave, he told his libido mentally. You know relationships are a disaster zone.

She peered at the material carefully from several angles, then nodded in seeming satisfaction. 'OK. Do you wear lace at your collar, or am I thinking of something else?'

'That'd be ceremonial legal dress,' he said. 'Normally in Crown court a male barrister wears a wing collar that attaches to the shirt, and court bands.' He took them out of their cases for her.

'So the bands are the things that hang down like a two-pronged white tie?'

Despite himself, he smiled. 'Yes. Actually, they're symbolic. The Lord Chief Justice said back in the sixteenth century that they were two tongues. One for the rich, for a fee, to reward our long studies; and one without reward to defend the poor and oppressed.'

'I like that,' she said. 'So you defend the poor and oppressed?'

'I'm usually a prosecutor,' he said, 'but English barristers can defend as well as prosecute. I guess in either case I'd be defending my client's interests, and it's not for me to call them poor or oppressed.'

Sammy liked that little bit of humility. Given that Nicholas Kennedy QC was a top barrister, she'd half expected him to be a bit on the arrogant side, but she instinctively liked the man she'd just met. He had kind eyes, a deep rich brown. And, even though he clearly wasn't very comfortable with the idea of being part of a shoot for the charity calendar—especially now he knew the photographer was female—he'd obviously made a promise to someone and had the integrity to keep that promise.

She could see exactly why the committee had asked him to pose for their calendar. Talk about photogenic. His bone structure was gorgeous. He could've been a model for a top perfume house, advertising aftershave. It was rare to have that kind of beauty teamed with an equally spectacular intellect. And it made him almost totally irresistible.

But she was going to have to resist the pull of attraction. She was here to work, not to drool over the eye candy. Right now she was supposed to be putting the man at his ease. And hadn't she just told him that she never hit on her models?

Well, this wasn't going to be a first for her.

Be professional, she reminded herself. She wasn't going to let herself remember the little shiver of desire that had rippled down her spine when he'd shaken her hand. Or wonder how that beautiful mouth would feel against her skin. She was going to focus on her job.

Besides, he was probably committed elsewhere. He wasn't wearing a wedding ring, but that didn't prove anything. A man that beautiful would've been snapped up years ago.

'Your hair's very short,' she commented. 'Do you have a military background, or is the haircut necessary because you have to wear a wig in court?'

'It makes the wig a little more comfortable, yes,' he said. 'Speaking of which…' He took out the wig next.

There were short, neat rows of curls all the way round the pale grey wig, and two tiny tails hanging down at the back with neat curls at the ends.

'The wig is what everyone associates with lawyers in court,' she said. 'You'll definitely be wearing that, and probably the gown—though I might do some shots without the gown as well.'

'What else do I get to wear?' he asked hopefully.

'Not the trousers, the coat or the shirt, I'm afraid. Even though they're nicely cut and made from good material.'

He flinched.

'You can wear the collar and tie thingies.'

She could see in his expression that he was dying to correct her terminology—but he didn't. Clearly he was resisting the temptation to be nit-picky and was trying to be co-operative. Teasing probably wasn't the kindest or most appropriate thing she could do right now.

'Thank you. I think,' he said.

She smiled. 'As I said, to me you'll be simply a life model.'

But she needed him to relax so the strain wouldn't show on his face when she photographed him. Given what he did for a living—and that he'd agreed to wear some of his court dress for the shoot—she guessed he'd be more comfortable talking about his work. 'Talk me through the court layout, so I can decide where to put you.' Even though she knew perfectly well where she was going to ask him to stand. She'd done her research properly, the way she always did before she took a portrait.

'Right in front of us is the judge's bench.'

'Where he bangs his gavel, right?'

He laughed. 'I think you've been watching too many TV dramas. English judges don't use gavels.'

She knew that, but he didn't need to know that she knew. It looked as if her plan to make him more comfortable was working. Except, when he laughed like that, it made him look sexy as hell—and that made it much more difficult for her to keep her part of the bargain, to be detached and think of him as a life model.

Not that Sammy was looking for a relationship right now. She was too busy with her job, and she was fed up to the back teeth with dating Mr Wrong—men who ran for the hills in panic, the second they learned about her past, or who saw themselves as her knight in shining armour and wrapped her so tightly in cotton wool that she couldn't breathe. None of them had seen her as a woman.

Then again, she wasn't really a whole woman any more, was she? So she couldn't put the blame completely on them.

And after Bryn had finally been the one to break her heart, Sammy had decided that it would be much easier to focus on her family, her friends and her job and forget completely about romance.

Though the wedding she'd photographed a couple of months ago had made her feel wistful; now both her best friends were loved-up and settled. And although she was really happy for both of them, it had left her feeling just the tiniest bit lonely. And the tiniest bit sorry for herself. Even if she ever did manage to meet her Mr Right, there was no guarantee of a happy ending. Not if he wanted children of his own, without any kind of complications. She couldn't offer that.

She pushed the thought away. Enough of the pity party. She had a great life. A family who loved her—even if they were a tad on the overprotective side—friends who'd celebrate the good times with her and be there for her in the bad times, and a job that really fulfilled her. Asking for more was just greedy.

'No gavel, then. So what else am I looking at?'

'OK. In front of the judge you have the clerk of the court, the usher, and the person who makes the sound recording of the trial or a stenographer who types it up as the trial goes along. They face the same way as the judge.' He walked over to the benches facing the judge's bench. 'This is where the barristers sit, though we stand when we're addressing the court. The defence barrister is nearest to the jury—' he indicated the seats at the side of the room '—and the prosecution barrister is nearest to the witness box. The solicitors sit behind the barristers, and at the back is the dock where the defendant sits. Over there behind the witness box you have the public gallery and the press bench.'

'So it'd make the most sense to photograph you where you'd normally stand in court,' she said. Exactly where she'd always planned for him to pose—and where her equipment just so happened to be waiting. 'OK. Can you stand there for me?'

'Dressed like this?' he asked.

She smiled. 'For the moment, yes—though if you wouldn't mind putting on your gown, that'd help with the light meter readings.'

He shrugged on his gown and went to stand at the barristers' bench. She noticed that he was looking nervous again.

'You're really not going to end up on the front page of the newspapers with headlines screaming about "top barrister flashes his bits",' she reassured him. 'The point of the calendar is to sell gorgeous men posed artistically.' And Nick definitely fitted the bill on both counts. 'If the bench doesn't cover your modesty, so to speak, then you can hold a bunch of papers in a strategic place. Don't you normally have a bunch of papers with you in court, tied with a pink ribbon?'

'A brief,' he said. 'It's the instructions from my client. The defence has a pink silk ribbon and the prosecution uses white.'

Though he still didn't look convinced about the shoot.

She sighed. 'Look, just stand there for a second.'

As he did so, she took her camera body out of its carrying case, fitted a lens so she could take a quick photograph, then came over to show him the digital picture on the screen. 'This obviously isn't a proper composition—for the real one I'll be quite a bit more nit-picky about the lighting and the lens—but it should be enough to prove to you that your dignity will remain intact. OK now?'

'Sorry.' He blew out a breath. 'I know I'm being ridiculous about this. I guess this just isn't the normal sort of thing I'd do in a day's work.'

'That's pretty much what everyone's said so far.' She grinned. 'Well, except for the actor. He didn't mind stripping off, but I guess he'd done it a few times before. All in the name of art, of course.'

'Of course,' Nick echoed, still looking uncomfortable.

'And what you do in court—you have a persona, and that's a bit like acting, isn't it?'

'A bit, I suppose,' Nick said. 'But, as I said, at work I'm normally wearing quite formal dress—not standing in the middle of the room, almost naked.'

'For what it's worth,' Sammy said, 'I think what you're doing is really special. It takes guts—everyone's happy enough to put their hand in their pocket and donate money to a good cause, but you're doing something out of the ordinary. Something that's going to make a lot more of a difference. And I bet whoever you're doing this for is hugely proud of you.'

'My sister,' he said, 'and my nephew.'

'The ward treated your nephew?' she asked softly.

He nodded. 'Xander's in remission at the moment.'

She guessed the bargain he'd made in his head: if he

did this to help raise money, then Fate might smile on his nephew and keep him in remission. She knew her own sister had made the same bargain, and it was why Jenny had her hair cropped at the same time as Sammy did, every two years.

She wondered briefly why Xander's father hadn't offered to do the calendar shoot. Or maybe it was just that Nick had a more photogenic job. It was none of her business, anyway. She was just here to do the shoot.

'OK. I'm happy with that position. Now, there aren't any windows in here; plus we've got a notice on the door, so nobody's going to walk in on us. It's quite safe. So, while I'm setting up properly here, do you want to lose the clothes?'

No, Nick didn't want to lose the clothes. At all.

But he'd promised he'd do it, and he wasn't going to break his word. 'What do you want me to wear out of the court dress?' he asked, drawing on his usual court demeanour and trying to sound as if he was completely unflustered.

'Wig, collar and bands, and we'll try some shots with the gown and some without,' she said. 'I take it you followed my instructions to avoid marks on your skin?'

'Yes.'

'Good. Let's do this.'

Nick felt incredibly self-conscious stripping off. Putting on the collar and bands without his tunic shirt felt *weird.* Though the silk gown was soft against his skin, and he gathered it in front of him to cover himself and went to stand by the bench.

'We'll do some shots sitting down, first,' Sammy

said. 'I guess you need some papers spread out on the bench in front of you.'

Luckily he'd thought to bring a brief with him. He fetched it and sat down.

'Do you wear glasses?' she asked.

'No.'

'Pity. I should've thought to bring some frames with me.'

He frowned. 'Why do you want me to wear glasses?'

'To make you look clever.'

He wasn't sure if she was teasing him or not. Then he looked her straight in the eye and saw the mischievous twinkle. 'Very funny.'

'Yes, m'lud—or should I say Your Honour?'

He rolled his eyes. 'That's what I'd say to the judge. You'd refer to me as My Learned Friend.'

Her mouth quirked, and heat flooded his body. That impish smile transformed Sammy Thompson to a pure beauty.

And this was totally inappropriate.

He damped his feelings down. For all he knew, she was married or involved with someone. OK, so she wasn't wearing a ring, but that didn't mean anything. And he wasn't looking for a relationship anyway; the disintegration of his marriage to Naomi three years ago had put him off the idea of opening his life to someone else ever again. The one woman he'd thought was different. The one he'd thought had supported his ambitions and understood him. Yet it had all been a sham. That wasn't a mistake he intended to repeat. Even if he did find Sammy Thompson attractive, he wasn't going to act on that attraction. Dating seriously wasn't something he did any more.

He focused on posing for Sammy and following her instructions. He stood up, changing position when she told him to.

'OK. Now you can lose the gown for the next set of shots.'

'Are you quite sure about this?' he asked, wishing he were a hundred miles away.

'Tell you what, shy boy,' she drawled. 'Do the rest of the shoot for me without making any more fuss, and I'll buy you dinner.'

He blinked. Was she asking him out? 'Dinner? Why?'

'Because I've already shot two other models for the calendar today and I didn't have time for lunch, which means that right now I'm starving—I'll apologise now in case my stomach starts rumbling during the shoot. So I think we should have dinner while we look through the shots and you tell me which ones you approve to put forward to the Friends of the Hospital,' she said. 'Unless you have a girlfriend or a wife who'd have a problem with that, in which case please call her now and ask her to join us, because I really don't want to have to wait for too long before dinner.'

He shrugged slightly. 'No wife. No girlfriend.' And this was feeling more and more like agreeing to a date. Something that pushed him even further outside his comfort zone. He paused. 'Would it be a problem for your partner if you ate with me?'

'Not if I had one, because this is my job.'

So she was single. Available…

He squashed those thoughts. No, no and no. He didn't date any more. Not seriously.

'The quicker we get this done, the quicker I get food,' she continued, 'and the less likely it is that I'll get grumpy with you. You need to focus, m'learned friend. Lose the gown. And think yourself lucky.'

'Lucky?' He very nearly had to shake his head to clear it. Was she talking about *him* getting lucky?

'You're Mr December. I could've made you wear a Santa hat. Or pose holding a bunch of mistletoe. Or—' She flapped a dismissive hand. 'Insert a cheesy Christmassy pose of choice.'

Ah. *That* kind of lucky. Nothing to do with sex, then.

And would his head please, please start playing by the rules and stop thinking about lust and other inappropriate things? Because right now he was naked, and it would be impossible to hide his physical reaction to her.

'Noted,' he said dryly. He took off his gown, folded it neatly, and set it on the bench where it would be out of sight of her camera.

Wearing just his barrister's wig, collar and bands, Nick Kennedy was spectacular, Sammy thought. Broad shoulders, beautiful biceps, enough hair on his chest to be sexy without him looking like a total gorilla, and a definite six pack.

Mr December was going to be the best page on the calendar. He could probably sell the calendar all by himself.

But now he'd said there was no wife or girlfriend, she couldn't help wondering: how come a gorgeous man with a good brain and kind eyes was single? Was it because he was a workaholic and his girlfriends tended to get fed up waiting for him to notice them? Or had she missed some major personality flaw?

'What?' he asked, clearly noting that she was staring at him.

'Nothing,' she said, embarrassed to discover that her voice was slightly croaky. She really had to get a grip. The last thing she needed was for her skittish model to work out that she was attracted to him. And Nicholas Kennedy was bright. He couldn't be more than five or six years older than Sammy's own thirty years, and he was at the top of his profession. Scratch bright: that kind of background meant he had to be super-bright. So he'd be able to work it out quickly.

She got him to do a few more poses. To her relief, he'd relaxed enough with her by now to trust her, even when she moved round and took some shots from the side and some others from the back. And, oh, his back was beautiful. She'd love to do some proper nude studies of him. In a wood, looking for all the world like a statue of a Greek god.

Not that he'd agree to it. Not in a million years.

But a girl could dream…

'OK. That's a wrap. You can get dressed now,' she said, 'and by the time I've loaded everything on to my laptop we'll be ready to go to dinner.'

'The stuff I was wearing is hardly dressy enough for going out,' he said.

She laughed. 'As I wasn't planning to take you to the Dorchester or Claridge's, I think you'll be just fine.'

She put the memory card in the slot on her laptop and downloaded the photographs while she packed away the rest of her equipment. Once she'd finished downloading the pictures, she saved the files. 'Is it OK for me to turn round now?' she asked with her back still towards Nick.

'Sure.'

Rather than putting on the ratty T-shirt and tracksuit

bottoms again, he was wearing the white tunic shirt—without the collar—the waistcoat and his court trousers.

Sammy's heart skipped a beat. Right now, with his formal dress very slightly dishevelled, he looked as sexy as hell. She could imagine him with the shirt undone, especially as she'd actually seen his bare chest. If his hair was ever so slightly longer and someone had ruffled her hand through it to suggest that he'd just been thoroughly kissed, he'd look spectacular. In fact he'd go straight to number one in the Sexiest Man in the World list. She itched to get her camera out again. And this time she'd make him pose very differently.

'OK?' he asked.

No. Not OK at all. She was all quivery and girly, and that really wasn't good.

So she'd have to fall back on acerbic humour to hide how she really felt. 'Sure. Lucky, lucky me—I get to have dinner with a half-dressed man.' Her mouth quirked. 'Are you really so vain that you couldn't go out to eat in an old tracksuit and T-shirt?'

'I'm not vain,' he protested. 'I just feel a little more comfortable in this than I do in the scruffy stuff.'

'It'd serve you right if I took you to a fast-food burger restaurant now—and then you'd really look out of place,' she teased.

'I'll bluff it. There's nothing wrong with burgers.'

Did he really expect her to believe that? She'd just bet he was the kind of guy who went for fine wines and Michelin-starred dining. 'When was the last time you went to a fast-food place?' she challenged.

'Last weekend, with my nephews,' was the prompt reply. 'Next question?'

Ouch. She'd forgotten about his nephews. If they

were teens, like her own nephews, then she knew he'd be very familiar with fast-food places. She screwed up her face. 'OK, now it's my turn to apologise. Blame my rudeness on low blood sugar. Because I am a grumpy, starving photographer right now.'

He smiled, and she wished she'd kept her mouth shut. Stuffy and uncomfortable, she could deal with, but relaxed and sexy was another kettle of fish entirely.

Right now, Nick Kennedy could be very dangerous to her peace of mind.

'Let's go and eat,' Nick said, 'and you can show me how much of an idiot I've made of myself.'

He hadn't made an idiot of himself at all. He was utterly gorgeous and he'd be the star of the calendar—even more so than the actor and the musician who'd posed for her earlier in the week, because they were aware of how pretty they were and Nick wasn't. But Sammy knew she needed to keep her libido under control. She'd learned her lesson well, after Bryn.

No.

More.

Relationships.

Make that underlined and with three exclamation marks. And covered in acid yellow highlighter to make sure she didn't forget it.

'My car's outside,' she said.

'So is mine.'

She took a coin from her purse. 'Let's toss for it. The winner gets to drive. Heads or tails?'

'Heads.'

It was heads.

'My car, then,' he said.

'Do you mind if I bring my equipment with me?' she

asked. 'I'd prefer not to leave it unattended, even if it's locked out of sight in my car.'

'It would make more sense,' Nick said, 'if we got a takeaway and ate it at my place. Then neither of us would have to worry about leaving expensive work equipment unattended in the car.'

'Why your place and not mine?'

He coughed. 'Because I just won the coin toss.' He paused. 'You can ring my sister and ask her to vouch for me, if you're worried about going to a stranger's flat.'

'A stranger who's willing to put himself out of his comfort zone to help raise money for an oncology ward, and whose day job means he skewers the baddies in court and gets them sentenced for their crimes? I think I'll be safe enough with you,' Sammy said. Plus all her instincts were telling her that Nick was one of the good guys, and her instincts—except when it came to dating—were pretty good. 'But I'll follow you in my car. That makes more sense than getting the Tube back here afterwards.'

'You won't have to get the Tube back here. I'll give you a lift.'

'So you're going to drive home, then back here, then home again? That doesn't make sense either.' She took her phone out of her bag. 'Give me your address, just in case I get stuck in traffic and can't follow you over a junction or something, and end up having to use my satnav.' She tapped in the details as he dictated them. 'Great. Let's go.'

'Can I carry anything for you?' he asked.

She indicated his armful of boxes and carriers. 'I think you've got enough of your own, and anyway I'm used to lugging this lot about.'

'Fair enough.'

She took the notice off the court door, told the security team that it was fine to lock up, and packed all her equipment into her car. And all the time she was berating herself mentally. She must be crazy. Why hadn't she just done what she'd agreed with her other models and emailed him a choice of half a dozen photographs that she could go on to present to the calendar committee? Why was she letting him review the whole shoot with her?

The truth was because she wanted to spend more time with him. Because she was attracted to him.

But she also knew that her relationships were a disaster area. She had a three-date rule, because agreeing to more than that risked her having to tell the truth about her past—and in her experience men reacted badly to the information. Besides, she was pretty sure that Nick Kennedy was a total workaholic who wouldn't have time for a girlfriend—that was still the only reason she could think of why someone as gorgeous and good-hearted as him would be single—so it was better not to start anything. So she'd be sensible and professional when they looked at the photographs. They'd grab some food; and then she'd say a polite goodbye and never see him again.

Pity.

But, since Bryn, Sammy had learned to be sensible. It was the safest way.

And she was never getting her heart broken again.

CHAPTER THREE

AS HE DROVE back to his flat, Nick wondered if he'd just gone completely crazy. Why on earth had he invited Sammy Thompson back to his flat?

Then again, she'd had a fair point about not leaving expensive equipment unattended in a car. Horsehair wigs and silk barrister gowns weren't exactly cheap, either, and he wouldn't want to leave them in his car—just as she clearly hadn't wanted to leave her camera equipment in hers.

Out of the few dates he'd been on since the end of his marriage, he hadn't invited a single one of his girlfriends back to his flat. And he was far too sensible to invite a complete stranger back to his flat.

Yet that was exactly what he'd just done. Today was the first time he'd met Sammy. He knew practically nothing about her, other than that she was a photographer and she'd been commissioned to shoot the calendar by the Friends of the London Victoria.

Then again, he had good instincts—except perhaps where his ex-wife was concerned, he admitted wryly—and he'd liked Sammy immediately. She was business-like and capable, and she had a sense of humour that appealed to him.

And he was going to have to ignore the fact that she was utterly gorgeous. Slender yet with curves in all the right places, maybe six inches shorter than his own six foot one, and she was strong enough to carry heavy boxes of photographic equipment around without it seeming to bother her. Her bright blonde hair—which he was pretty sure was natural rather than dyed—was cut in a short pixie crop that framed her heart-shaped face, and her sea-green eyes were serious when she was working and teasing when something amused her.

Then there was her mouth. A perfect cupid's bow. A mouth that he'd wanted to trace with the tip of his finger before exploring it with his own mouth…

This was bad. He hadn't waxed poetic over anyone like this for years—maybe not since he was a teenager. So he'd better get it into his head that Sammy Thompson was simply the photographer who was working on the charity calendar, and he'd probably never see her again after today. Except maybe if the ward held some kind of launch event when the calendar went on sale and they both happened to attend it, and then they could just be polite to each other.

Be professional, he told himself. Treat her as if she's a client, or a colleague. Keep it business-like, choose the photographs, and then you can just let her walk out of your life and go back to what you normally do. Work, being there for Mandy and the boys, and more work. A perfectly balanced life.

Sammy was glad that she'd taken Nick's address and put the postcode into her satellite navigation system before they left the court's car park, because as she'd half expected she ended up losing him at a junction.

Following the satnav's directions, she ended up driving through one of the prettiest tree-lined streets in Bloomsbury, where the five-storey town houses all had wrought iron railings, tall white-framed sash windows that would let huge amounts of light flood into the rooms, and window boxes full of bright, well-manicured geraniums. She could see Nick's car towards the end of the street, and thankfully there was a parking space on the road behind it. Nick himself was waiting for her by his car.

When she climbed out of her car, Nick handed her a parking permit to place inside her windscreen. 'I'm sorry I lost you at that junction,' he said. 'I did slow down, but I couldn't see you behind me.'

'No worries,' Sammy said with a smile. 'That's precisely why I took your address.'

'Come in,' he said.

'And you don't mind if I bring all my stuff in?'

'That's fine.' He was still laden with his own cases, but even so he picked up the heaviest of her boxes and took it to the door of the Georgian house on the corner.

It was exactly the kind of building that made Sammy itch to get her camera out. The front door was painted black, with white columns and narrow bands of stucco either side to turn the entrance from a rectangle to a perfect square. Above the entrance was a filigree fanlight, the pattern within the arched window reminding her of a spider's web. The door knocker, handle and letterbox were all shiny brass, the front doorstep was scrubbed clean, and on either side of the step there was a bay tree in a black wooden planter, its stem perfectly straight and its leaves clipped into a neat ball.

Everything was discreet, tidy—and clearly wealthy

without being ostentatious about it. It was a house that had been looked after properly.

Clearly her interest showed on her face, because Nick smiled. 'You like the architecture?'

'It's gorgeous,' she said. 'I have to admit, architectural detail is one of my biggest weaknesses. Especially windows like that one.' She indicated the fanlight above the front door.

'Come on up and I'll give you the guided tour.' And then he looked slightly shocked, as if he hadn't meant to say that.

Tough. He'd said it now, and Sammy wasn't going to pass up the chance to look round such a gorgeous building.

'My flat's the ground floor and first storey,' he said.

'Not the whole house?'

He smiled. 'I live on my own, so I don't really need a whole town house. The flat gives me enough room for work, guests and entertaining.'

Though even a flat in a building like this—and in an area like this—would cost an eye-watering amount, Sammy thought. Especially a duplex flat. It would be way out of her own price range.

'Let's base ourselves in the kitchen,' Nick said. 'We can order some food, and then I'll show you round.'

'Sounds good to me.'

Nick's kitchen was small, but perfectly equipped. It had clearly been fitted out by a designer and it was the kind of shabby chic that didn't come cheap, with distressed cream-painted doors and drawer fronts, light wood worktops and pale terracotta splash-backs and floor tiles. There was a terracotta pot of herbs on one of the windowsills, and an expensive Italian coffee-maker and matching kettle, both in cream enamel; apart from that, everything was tucked neatly away.

Either Nicholas Kennedy was a total neat freak, or he didn't actually use this room much himself, she thought.

She set her boxes on the floor next to the light wood table at one end of the kitchen and put her laptop on the table itself. 'Is it OK to leave these here?'

'Sure.' Nick opened a drawer and brought out a file. Sammy had to bite her lip to stop herself grinning when she realised that his takeaway menus were all filed neatly in punched plastic pockets. She'd bet they were in alphabetical order, too.

Clearly he didn't have a clutter drawer with menus and all sorts of bits and pieces stuffed into it, unlike everyone else she knew. He was a neat freak, then. But that didn't mean he was totally buttoned-up. After all, he'd agreed to do a naked photo shoot. Someone totally stuffy would've refused to do that.

'Would you prefer Indian, Chinese, or Thai?' he asked.

'I eat practically anything,' Sammy said, 'except prawns. Fish, yes; crustaceans, no. Other than that, anything you like, as long as it's here as soon as possible.'

'Because you're starving. Noted.' He gave her a slight smile. 'How about a mix of Chinese dishes to share, then? And I promise, no prawns.'

'That'd be lovely.'

'Crispy duck?'

'Love it. Thank you.'

She set up her laptop while he was ordering their meal.

'They'll be here in forty minutes,' he said. 'OK. I promised you a guided tour.'

Sammy didn't quite dare ask if she could bring her camera. 'Lay on, Macduff,' she said with a smile.

'Living room,' he said, showing her through the first door.

Like the hallway, it had a stripped pale wooden floor. There were two huge sash windows dressed with floor-length dark green curtains; the walls were painted dark red and there was an antique-looking glass chandelier hanging from the high ceiling. It looked more like the effort of a designer than personal choice, Sammy thought.

The sofas were all low, upholstered in dark green leather and looked comfortable, and there was a light-coloured wooden coffee table in the middle of the room, set on a green silk patterned rug. There was a black marble fireplace with a huge mirror above it, reflecting the chandelier and the state-of-the-art television and audio-visual centre. Between the two sash windows, there was an enormous clock with a white face and dark roman numerals. There were plenty of silver-framed photographs on the mantelpiece, which she assumed were of his family.

But what really grabbed her attention was the painting on the wall. It wasn't exactly out of place, but she would've expected the designer to choose a couple of period portraits or maybe some kind of still life, to go with the rest of the decor. This painting was a modern landscape of a bay at dusk where the sea, cliffs and sky blurred together in the mist. It was all tones of blue and grey and silver—really striking. 'That's beautiful,' she said.

'Yes. I liked it the moment I set eyes on it,' he said.

So this was his taste rather than his designer's? She liked it. A lot.

Just as she had a rather nasty feeling that she could like Nick Kennedy rather a lot, if she got the chance. He was more than easy on the eye, and she liked what she'd learned about him in the short time she'd known him.

He ushered her in to the next room. 'My office.'

It was another room with dark red walls and stripped wood floors, but this time the curtains framing the two huge sash windows were cream voile and the patterned silk rug in the centre was dark red. The chandelier was wrought iron, and one wall was completely filled with books, most of which she guessed would be legal tomes. There was a desk against the opposite wall, teamed with what she recognised as a very expensive office chair—the kind she'd dreamed about owning but couldn't justify the price tag—and a state-of-the-art computer sat on his desk.

She could imagine him working here, with a bunch of papers spread out on the desk, his elbow resting on the table and his hand thrust through his hair while he made notes with a fountain pen. Because Nicholas Kennedy was definitely the kind of man who would use a posh pen rather than a disposable ballpoint.

'Dining room,' Nick said, showing her the next room.

Like the other rooms, the dining room had stripped floors; but it was much lighter because the walls were painted cream rather than dark red. There was a huge mirror above the white marble fireplace, reflecting the light from the sash windows and the antique glass chandelier. A light-coloured wooden table that seated eight sat in the centre of the room, teamed with matching chairs upholstered in cream-and-beige striped silk, which in turn matched the floor-length curtains. The silk rug here was in tones of cream and beige. She loved the room; she could just imagine sitting on the window-seat with a book, sunning herself while she read.

And there was another striking piece of art on the wall—a close-up of a peacock with its tail spread, and it looked as if it was painted in acrylics. 'The colours are glorious,' she said softly, enjoying the splash of orange among the turquoise, blues and greens. And it was so very different from the other picture; clearly Nick's taste was diverse.

But the artwork that really made her gasp was in his bedroom. The room was large, but for a change not painted dark red; it had blue and cream Regency striped wallpaper, floor-length navy curtains, stripped floors and a dark blue silk patterned rug to reflect the curtains.

She couldn't take her eyes off the black and white photograph that had been sliced vertically into three and framed in narrow black wood: a shot of the steel and glass roof of the Great Court at the British Museum. 'That's one of my favourite places in London.' And she had quite a few shots of that roof in her own collection. 'I adore that roof.'

'Me, too,' he said. 'It's the pattern and the light.'

'Did you know that no two panes of glass in the roof are the same?' she asked.

'No, but now you've said it, I'm going to have to look.'

'There are more than three thousand of them,' she pointed out. 'And the differences are tiny. It's only because of the undulations.' But the sudden light in his eyes now they were talking about art made her wonder. 'Did you ever think about being an artist or an architect rather than a barrister?'

He smiled. 'Absolutely not. I can barely draw a straight line with a pencil.' And then he changed the subject, making her wonder even more. 'Given that I already know you're starving, can I make you a coffee and offer you some chocolate biscuits to tide you over until the takeaway arrives?'

'That would be lovely. Thank you,' she said. 'Your flat's beautiful. Though I wouldn't have put you down as someone who'd choose dark red walls.'

'An interior designer organised most of the place for me just before I moved in,' he admitted. 'Maybe my living room and office are a little dark.'

Just a tad, but she wasn't going to be rude about it. '"Strikingly masculine" is probably the official phrase,' she said with a smile.

He ushered her back to the kitchen. She sat at the table and opened the file of photographs on her laptop while he made the coffee; and then he brought over two mugs of coffee and a plate of really good chocolate biscuits.

'Help yourself,' he said. 'And don't be polite. You said you'd missed lunch.'

'Thank you,' she said gratefully, and devoured two. 'These are scrumptious.'

'They're my sister's favourites,' he said. 'I keep a stock in for her.'

Nick was the kind of man who paid attention to details and quietly acted on them, she thought. She'd just bet he had a stock of his nephews' favourite treats, too. And the coffee was better than that served in most upmarket cafés; though, given that posh coffee machine sitting on his kitchen worktop, it wasn't so surprising. If you had an expensive machine, it stood to reason that you'd use good coffee in it. 'Would you like to see the photographs now?' she asked.

'Sure.' He viewed them in silence, then nodded with what she was pretty sure was relief. 'You were very discreet. Thank you.'

'The point is to raise money, not to embarrass people,' she said softly. 'And it's meant to be fun, so I think we should discount this one, this one and this one—' she pointed to them on the screen '—as you look very slightly uptight in them.'

'Agreed,' he said. 'I have to admit, picking out your own photographs is a bit…' He grimaced.

'It makes everyone squirm. It's much, much easier to look at someone else's photographs and choose the best ones in a set than it is to choose your own,' she said.

'Which ones would you choose?' he asked.

'Honestly? This, this and this.' She pointed them out. 'Mainly because of the expression on your face. You look more relaxed here.' And really, really sexy, which was the whole point of the calendar. Selling pictures of hot men to make money for the ward. Not that she was going to say it; she knew it would make him uncomfortable.

'OK. I'm happy with those ones,' he said.

'Great.' She took the model release form from her bag. 'So we'll put the shot numbers in here.' She wrote them down. 'Would you like to check that you agree with the numbers before you sign?'

He smiled. 'You sound like a lawyer.'

'I sound like a professional photographer who likes to get things right,' she corrected.

He checked the numbers on the form against the numbers on her laptop, then signed the form. 'I'm impressed with what you did. Can I see any of the other calendar shots?'

Sammy shook her head. 'Sorry. Only the Chair of the Friends and the committee members she chooses to work with her on the project can see them until the proofs are printed,' she said.

'Fair enough. I was just curious.'

'About the other models?' she asked.

'About your work,' he said, 'given the way you reacted to that picture of the British Museum's roof.'

'Ah. If you want to see my portfolio, that's a different matter entirely.' She pulled up a different file for him. 'Knock yourself out.'

He looked through them. 'You've got a real mixture here—lots of people and a few landscapes.'

'They tend to go with profiles of people in magazines and Sunday supplements,' she said. 'That's my bread-and-butter work. So if the profile is of someone who's set up an English vineyard, I'd take a portrait of that person and then whatever else is needed to illustrate the interview or article. Say, the vineyard itself, or a close-up of a bunch of grapes, or the area where the wine's produced or bottled.'

'What about the photographs you take for you?'

'What makes you think I don't take these ones for me?' she parried.

'Apart from the fact that you admitted that they were work, it was the look on your face when you saw the house—as if you were dying to grab your camera and focus in on little details. Particularly the fanlight window.'

'Busted,' she said with a rueful smile. 'Architecture's my big love—I never wanted to be an architect and create the buildings myself, but what I like is to make people focus in on a feature and see the building in a different light instead of just taking it for granted or ignoring it entirely.' And, although she'd never normally show her private shots to someone she barely knew, something about the way Nick looked at her made her want to open up. She went into another file. 'Like these ones.'

'They're stunning,' Nick said as he scrolled through them. 'And I mean it—I'm not just being polite. I'd be more than happy to have any of these blown up, framed and hung on my walls.'

She could see in his face that he meant it. And it made her feel warm inside. Some of her exes had scoffed at her private photography, calling her nerdy and not understanding at all what she loved about the architecture. And others had wanted her to give it all up so they could look after her—because a cancer survivor shouldn't be pushing herself to take photographs from difficult positions. Hanging off a balcony to get a better angle for her shot really wasn't the sort of thing a delicate little flower should do.

She'd wanted a relationship, not a straightjacket. And being protected in such a smothering way had made her feel stifled and miserable, even more than when the men she'd dated had backed off at the very first mention of the word 'cancer'.

'So when do you take this kind of shot?' Nick asked.

'When I get a day off, I walk round London and find interesting things. And sometimes I go to the coast—I love seascapes. Especially if a lighthouse or a pier's involved.'

'And you put your pictures on the internet?'

'I have a blog for my favourite shots,' she admitted.

'So did you always know you wanted to be a photographer?' he asked.

'Like most kids, I didn't have a clue what I wanted to do when I grew up,' Sammy said. 'Then, one summer, my uncle—who was a press photographer before he retired—taught me how to use a proper SLR camera.' Nick didn't need to know that it was because she'd been cooped up in one place, the summer when she'd had treatment for osteosarcoma; she'd been bored and miserable, unable to go out with her friends because she had been forced to wait for the surgical wounds to heal and to do her physiotherapy. Uncle Julian had shown her how she could get a different perspective on her surroundings and encouraged her to experiment with shots from her chair. 'I loved every second of it. And I ended up doing my degree in photography and following in his footsteps.'

'A press photographer? So you started out working for a magazine?'

'For the first couple of years after I graduated, I did; and then the publication I worked for was restructured and quite a few of the staff were made redundant, including me. That's when I decided to take the leap and go freelance,' she explained. 'Though that also means I don't tend to turn work down. You never know when you're going to have a dry spell, and I like to have at least three months' money sitting in the bank so I can always pay my rent.'

'And you do weddings as well?' He pointed to one of the other photographs.

'Only for people close to me. That one's Ashleigh, one of my best friends, on Capri last year.'

'It's a beautiful setting.'

'Really romantic,' she agreed. 'The bridesmaid is my other best friend, Claire. She and I went to the Blue Grotto, the next day. It was for a commission, I admit, but I would've gone anyway because the place is so gorgeous. You had to lie down in the boat to get through the entrance, but it was worth the effort. The light was really something else.' She flicked into another file and showed him some of the photographs. 'Look.'

'I like that—it's another of the sort of scenes I'd like to have on my wall,' he said.

She nodded. 'Like that misty seascape in your living room. That's the kind of thing I like to shoot at dawn or dusk. If you do it with a long exposure, the waves swirl about and look like mist.'

'That's clever,' he said.

She smiled. 'No. That's technique. Anyone can do it when they know how.'

When their food arrived, Sammy put her laptop away while Nick brought out plates and cutlery.

'Would you like a glass of wine?' he asked.

She shook her head. 'Thanks for the offer, but I'm driving so I'd rather not. A glass of water's fine, thanks.'

He poured them both a glass of water from a jug in the fridge—filtered water, she thought. Nick Kennedy clearly dotted all his I's and crossed every T.

'Help yourself,' he said, gesturing to the various dishes in the centre of the table.

'Thank you.' She noticed that he eyed her plate when she'd finished heaping it. 'What?'

'It's refreshing, eating with someone who actually enjoys food.'

'That sounds as if you've been eating dinner with the wrong kind of person,' she said dryly. 'Most people I know enjoy food.'

'Hmm.'

She finished stuffing one of the pancakes with shredded duck and cucumber, added some hoi sin sauce and took a taste. 'And this is seriously good. I haven't had crispy duck this excellent before. Nice choice, Mr Kennedy.' She paused. 'As we're going halves on this, how much do I owe you?'

'My house, my hospitality, my bill,' he said. 'No arguments.'

'Thank you.' Though there was more than one way to win an argument. Maybe she could print one of her seascapes for him, the one he'd really liked, to say thank you for the meal. 'So you like modern art rather than, say, reproductions?' she asked.

'Some. I'm not so keen on abstract art, which probably makes me a bit of a philistine,' he admitted.

'No, you like what you like, and that doesn't make you a philistine—it makes you honest,' she said. 'And your taste is quite diverse. I'm assuming they're original artworks, given that one of them is acrylics?'

He nodded. 'I like to support local artists where I can. There's a gallery not far from my chambers. The gallery owner gives me a call if something comes in that she thinks I'll like.'

'That's fabulous. It means both the artist and the art-lover win. Well, obviously, and the gallery owner, because she gets her commission.'

'Something like that.' He paused. 'Can I ask you something personal?'

Her heart skipped a beat. From his body language

and the way he'd relaxed with her, she had a feeling that the attraction was mutual. Was he going to ask her out?

And, if he did, would she have the courage to act on that attraction and say yes?

'Sure,' she said, affecting coolness.

'Your hair,' he said. 'What you said about me being in the military—is that why your hair's so short, too? You spent time in the Forces?'

The question was so unexpected that she answered it honestly before she realised what she was saying. 'No. I have a crop like this every two years.'

He blinked. 'Why two years?'

She could try and flannel him and say that it was a fashion statement, but he was observant. She was pretty sure he would've picked up the cues. 'Because it takes that long for my hair to grow twelve inches.'

He looked puzzled. 'Why do you need to grow your hair twelve inches?'

'Because seven to twelve inches is what they need for wigs,' she said softly.

The penny dropped immediately. 'You donate your hair?'

She nodded. 'There's a charity that makes wigs for kids who've lost their hair after chemotherapy. My sister Jenny and I have our hair cut together every two years. We normally get people to sponsor us as well, and the money goes to the ward so they can buy things for the kids. You know, things to keep them occupied and cheer them up, because being stuck in hospital isn't much fun—especially when you're a kid.' The hair cut before last had been on the actual day of Sammy's test results. She and Jenny had celebrated the news with a hair cut and a bottle of champagne.

'That's a really nice thing to do. I take it your sister's your connection to the ward?'

'Uh-huh,' Sammy said. It wasn't a total fib. Her sister was one of the connections. Just Sammy herself happened to be the main one. Not that Nick needed to know that.

'So that's why you're taking the photographs.'

She nodded. 'I take photographs for the ward every Christmas—so the families do at least get to have some Christmas pics together with their children, and with Santa for the younger ones. That's why Ayesha knew I was up to the job and would waive my fee, because I always do where the ward's concerned.'

'I assumed you were a photographic student who wanted to do it for his portfolio, and you'd been interviewed with half a dozen others.'

'No,' she said. 'Though you have a point about the portfolio. Maybe I should've given someone else the chance to work with me.'

'But then your styles would've been different,' he said.

'I guess. But I ought to think about that in future.'

When they'd finished their meal, Sammy refused the offer of more coffee. 'I'd better let you get on.'

Which Nick guessed was a polite way of saying that she needed to get on. And now, he thought, this was where she left and they'd say a polite goodbye, and they'd never see each other again.

Except his head and his mouth were clearly working to different scripts, because he found himself asking, 'When's your next day off?'

'I'm actually on holiday at the moment,' she said.

'I'm doing the last four shoots for the calendar tomorrow and the day after, but other than that my time's my own.'

'You're using your holiday to shoot the calendar?' And yet she'd said she was a freelance who never turned work down. Her time off must be precious.

She shrugged. 'It's not a big deal.'

But she wouldn't meet his eye. And she'd said that her sister was her connection to the ward. So maybe she'd made the same kind of silent bargain with Fate that he had, Nick thought—do the job and it'd keep her loved one safely in remission.

'So, thanks for dinner. And for being patient at the shoot,' she said. 'I know it can be a bit wearing, being told exactly how to stand and moving your head or your shoulders just a fraction.'

'You were very professional and made it easy,' he said, meaning it.

This was his cue to say goodbye. But his mouth had gone into reckless mode. 'Would you spend the day with me on Sunday?' he asked. 'Maybe we could have lunch, and you could show me some of the places you really like in London.'

'Urban hiking, one of my American friends calls it.' She smiled. 'I'd like that. OK. But there's a string attached.'

He frowned. 'What?'

'You bought dinner tonight, so I'm buying lunch on Sunday. No arguments.'

He wasn't surprised; Sammy had already struck him as someone who was seriously independent. He wasn't going to argue for now, but he'd find a way to get round her reservations on Sunday. 'OK. What time?'

'Half past nine?' she suggested.

'OK. It's a date.'

Even though he'd promised himself he wouldn't date again. Because Sammy Thompson intrigued him. And he wasn't quite ready to say goodbye to her yet.

CHAPTER FOUR

'SO HOW WAS the photo shoot?' Mandy asked.

She sounded ever so slightly guilty, Nick thought. 'It was fine,' he reassured his sister. 'The photographer was nice. She put me at my ease, and she let me choose the shots to give to the committee.'

'*She?* But I thought…' Her voice trailed off.

'So did I,' Nick said wryly.

'Oh, no. It must have been so embarrassing, taking all your clothes off in front of a woman you'd never met before.'

Nick laughed. 'She was at pains to tell me before the shoot that she saw me only as a life model, not as a person.'

'Right.' Mandy sounded intrigued. 'So was she young? Old?'

'It's immaterial, Mandy. Don't even think about trying to match-make.' And no way was he admitting to his elder sister that he was seeing the photographer for lunch on Sunday. It probably wouldn't come to anything, anyway. By then his common sense would be back in place. He and Sammy would have a nice walk through the city together, talk about art and architecture, have lunch, and then not see each other again.

Except Nick discovered the next morning that his common sense was very far from being back in place. When he walked into the narrow lanes off Fleet Street to his chambers, he found himself looking at the buildings with a photographer's eye.

Sammy would love this area, he thought.

And she'd really love the hidden gem in the middle.

He couldn't resist texting her.

I have a bright idea for Sunday.

Details? she texted back.

Just bring your camera. Which Tube line are you on?

There was a short pause before she replied: Northern.

Meet you at Embankment Tube station at 9.30? he suggested.

Her reply was a smiley face and a slightly sassy note.

Hope good coffee is involved.

He grinned and typed back: It will be.

On Sunday, Sammy felt ridiculously nervous. This was her first date in months—and it was with someone whose working life and whole lifestyle were so very different from her own.

She'd liked Nick Kennedy instinctively. She was attracted to him. And it was definitely mutual.

But how would he react if she told him she'd had osteosarcoma as a teen?

She didn't think he'd be one of the men who ran

for the hills—his nephew had the same condition, so he'd understand instead of panicking at the c-word. But would he be overprotective, the way her family was, making a big deal out of every twinge she felt and worrying that it might be the first sign of something more sinister?

And, if he was close to his nephews, did that mean he liked kids? That maybe he'd want some of his own, some day? That could be a problem, because—thanks to the demands of her treatment—she might not be able to have kids in the future. There were possibilities, but no actual definites, because she'd had to have her eggs frozen before her first chemotherapy—and IVF didn't come with a cast-iron guarantee that it would work.

Part of her wanted to make up an excuse and call the whole thing off. Not because she was a coward, but because over the years her boyfriends' reactions to the complications had worn her down. It had left her feeling less of a woman and more of a freak.

Though part of her was intrigued by Nick. He was a man with a buttoned-down, highly respectable job, and yet he'd actually posed naked for a charity calendar. That took guts; and it also hinted at an unconventional streak.

So maybe this could even be the start of something good. She'd have to take that leap of faith and try to trust that it wouldn't go the same way as her last few relationships had.

Maybe Nick Kennedy was different.

But, until she knew him a little better and could work out what his reaction would be, she'd keep quiet about the fact that she'd had bone cancer and was in remission.

* * *

Nick's heart skipped a beat as he saw Sammy at the Tube station. Again, she was dressed completely in black, though this time her T-shirt was more of a vest top, in a nod to the warm September weather, and she wore a silver necklace decorated with deep green beads that matched the studs in her ears.

And she looked stunning.

Not that she seemed to realise she was turning heads. That was something else he liked about Sammy Thompson. She was just herself, comfortable in her own skin. And that in itself made her easy to be with.

He greeted her with a kiss to her cheek. 'So you're being the Mysterious Woman in Black again?' he teased.

She smiled at him. 'I never thought about it before but, yes, I probably do wear too much black. Sorry. I guess it's a hangover from art college.'

'Don't apologise. Actually, it suits you,' he said. 'And I like your jewellery.'

'The green stuff? It's malachite,' she said. 'One of my art school friends became a jeweller when she graduated. I love Amy's work—all the strong lines and the colours. She uses very different semi-precious stones, too.'

'My sister likes that kind of thing, and she's got a birthday coming up. Perhaps you can give me your friend's details and maybe she can design something for me,' he said.

'Sure I can. Remind me when we stop for coffee—and I haven't forgotten that you promised me good coffee.'

'I did indeed.' He smiled at her. 'Shall we?'

Together they walked out of the Tube station, then headed down the Embankment with the Thames on their right.

'So where are we going?' she asked as he turned left and took her into a maze of narrow passageways.

'This is Inner Temple—one of the Inns of Court,' he explained.

'Where you work?'

He was pleased that she'd realised that. 'Yes. We're not going to my actual office, but I thought you'd like to see some of the area around it.' He led her into a courtyard. All the way round, there were dark brick buildings with tall sash windows and stone doorways. At each end of the courtyard was a white stone arched entranceway, and in the middle were trees, slatted benches and stone troughs containing bright pink geraniums.

'This is absolutely gorgeous,' she said. 'Is it OK to take photographs here, or do I have to ask permission from someone?'

'It's fine as long as they're not for commercial use—then you'd need to talk to the media relations team first,' he said.

'Do you mind…?'

'Be my guest,' he said with a smile. He watched her as she looked around the courtyard and bent down to take various shots, moving position to change the angle of whatever had caught her eye. It had never occurred to him to do that; whenever he'd taken a photograph, he'd just framed a snap in the viewfinder.

Which was probably why his photographs were snaps and hers were a true art form.

'This was a really good choice, Nick,' she said. 'I like this place. A lot.'

And he thought that she might like what he was about to show her even more. 'Come this way,' he said, and led her through the archway. In the next courtyard was a church built of honey-coloured stone; part of it was completely round, with a smaller round tower perched on top.

'This is the original Crusader church in London—one of the four remaining round churches in England,' he said softly. 'And the reason I brought you here now is so you can explore it as much as you like before the Sunday service starts.'

'I had no idea this was even here,' she said, looking entranced. 'So we can actually go inside?'

He nodded. 'And it's got the Templar effigy tombs. I think you'll like them.'

She did. Not just the round church itself, but also the way the blues, purples and reds from the sunlight coming through the stained glass windows shone onto the dark marble pillars surrounding the Templar effigy tombs. This was her idea of the perfect day—and it had come from a very unexpected source.

'That's William Marshal. He served under four English kings, and was the regent for Henry III,' Nick explained as they stood in front of the tombs. 'Next to him is his son William.'

Stone effigies that were nearly a thousand years old, darkened by age, portraying knights wearing their mail armour, holding a shield and sword, with dogs at their feet. Sammy was entranced by them, particularly the little dogs, and took plenty of detail shots.

'I love this church. It's so peaceful,' she whispered. 'Though inside it doesn't look as old as it actually is.'

'It was badly damaged in the second world war during the Blitz,' Nick whispered back, 'so it had to be restored. But I can show you something really, really old.'

It turned out to be a Norman doorway with a rounded decorated arch, with beautiful geometric ironwork spreading across the wood. Again, Sammy took plenty of photographs, focusing on the details that caught her eye.

'Come with me,' Nick said, and took her into the gardens.

There was a long, tree-lined avenue that Sammy found irresistible, and she made him pose in the centre of it.

'This is the Broadwalk,' he said. 'The London plane trees were planted here in Victorian times.'

And in the Peony Garden there was an ancient wall and an iron railing with wisteria tumbling down it. 'It's amazing that these gardens are smack in the middle of the city and only a few steps away from the Thames,' Sammy said. 'They're stunning. I thought I knew London pretty well, but I had absolutely no idea they were here.'

'Most people don't—though the gardens are open to the public,' Nick said, 'and it's the perfect place to chill out on a summer lunchtime. If I'm not in court, I'll sometimes eat a sandwich out here. It's a good place to think, too, when you're stuck on some knotty legal problem.'

Sammy found the brass sundial in the centre of one of the gardens equally fascinating. 'Why is there a Pegasus in the middle of the sundial?' she asked.

'It's the symbol of Inner Temple. It's said that it was chosen for Robert Dudley.'

'The guy Elizabeth the First was in love with?'

'At the time, he was her Master of the Horse,' Nick said. 'He took part in the Christmas revels here in the middle of the sixteenth century, and his followers all wore the symbol of Pegasus. It's thought to come from there.'

'It's a beautiful piece of brasswork,' she said. 'Though I still think Dudley was a bit of a baddie. It was a little bit too convenient how his wife fell down the stairs and broke her neck. So did Amy Robsart trip or was she pushed?'

'We'll never know the truth,' Nick said.

She paused. 'Would you have defended Robert Dudley in a court of law if he'd been up on a charge of murdering his wife?'

He didn't hesitate. 'If I was asked to, yes.'

She looked at him. 'Would you defend someone you absolutely knew was a criminal?' Because that was something she really couldn't get her head round. 'How could you defend someone you knew was guilty?'

Nick smiled. 'That's the first question everyone asks a barrister. First of all, in law, everyone is presumed innocent unless proven guilty. Secondly, everyone has a right to representation and we're not allowed to refuse to represent someone just because we don't like them, or because we don't believe in their case,' he explained. 'Barristers work under strict rules of ethics, and we're subject to the law. So if my client's guilty, I can't say in court that he's innocent, and I can't call anyone to give false evidence on his behalf, because that's perjury—I'd be struck off.'

'So would he get away with it?'

'It's the prosecution's job to prove the case to a jury

so they're absolutely sure that the person in the dock committed the crime. The jury has to hear from both sides for the justice system to work properly,' Nick said. 'So as a barrister I care about my client having the same human rights and entitlements as anyone else.'

OK, so Nick was professional. But what about the ethics he'd spoken of earlier? What about doing the right thing? 'But if they'd admitted to you that they'd done whatever they'd been accused of?'

'Then I would advise them to plead guilty to the charge, because the truth would come out in court,' he said simply.

'And if they said they were still going to plead not guilty?'

'Then I could walk away, because my first duty is to the court. And I could also refuse to take the case if I was going to be a witness in the case, because there would be a conflict of interests.' He shrugged. 'Though sometimes innocent people appear guilty, and sometimes guilty people appear innocent, so it's really important that both sides are heard properly and all the evidence is put to the jury so they can reach a verdict.'

'So you wouldn't try to get your client off if they were guilty?' That made her feel better about the situation.

'Guilt isn't actually that black and white,' he said.

She frowned. 'How do you mean?'

'OK. Supposing I have a client—let's call him Tom—who's been accused of taking an expensive pen from a shop.'

'That's theft,' Sammy said promptly.

'Only if he intended to deprive the shop-owner of the pen permanently and dishonestly. Supposing he'd taken it accidentally and was on his way to give it back? Or maybe someone had threatened him—if he didn't take the pen, then that person would hurt someone he loved, which means he took it under duress. Or maybe,' Nick continued, 'Tom's only nine years old—which means he's under the age of criminal responsibility. Or he has dementia, to the point where he's not responsible for his actions and didn't realise he'd taken the pen.'

Sammy looked thoughtfully at him. 'So if Tom did take the pen, in those cases he wouldn't actually be guilty of theft.'

'Exactly. Guilt's a really tricky question,' Nick said. 'As I said, it's important that all the facts are known so the jury reaches the right verdict. Both sides have to be heard for the system to work properly.'

'You really love your job, don't you?' she asked. She could see his passion for it in his expression and hear it in the way he talked about it.

'Guilty as charged,' he said with a smile. 'Though not everyone gets that.'

If you had workaholic tendencies, it could play havoc with your relationships if your partner didn't understand how important your job was to you. Sammy knew that from experience. Was that why Nick was single? Because his girlfriends got fed up with coming second to his job all the time? Not that it was any of her business. She wasn't going to be pushy and ask. 'I really love my job, too,' she said, smiling back. 'There's nothing wrong with that.'

'I'm glad you get it,' he said softly. 'And there's something else I wanted to show you.' He took her back through to the maze of buildings.

'Old-fashioned street lamps,' she said with delight

when they came to a stop in front of one. 'They're gorgeous. I love that shape—like the lanterns you see on Christmas cards. I can imagine people bustling past wearing top hats and capes and crinoline dresses.'

'Absolutely right, because this is the Victorian bit. These are working gas lamps,' he said. 'It's really atmospheric at night—like being back in Dickens' time. In fact, there are several bits of Middle Temple that he described in his books.'

With the stucco-fronted buildings and the narrow passageways, she could imagine it. 'This is amazing. You work in such a beautiful area, Nick.'

'I'm very privileged,' he said. 'And I promised you good coffee. Do you think it's too early for brunch?'

Sammy glanced at her watch. 'Whoops. Sorry. I had no idea I'd spent so much time photographing things. I'm afraid I can get a bit carried away. I…' She blew out a breath. 'Sorry.'

'Hey, no need to apologise. It was my idea to bring you here, and I'm really glad you liked it as much as I hoped you would,' he said, his eyes crinkling at the corners.

'Coffee and brunch,' she said, 'is a great idea. And, remember, we had a deal. It's my bill. No arguments.'

He looked as if he wanted to protest but, to her relief, he nodded. 'OK. Let's go this way.'

Nick had had a feeling that Sammy was going to be stubborn about paying her share. So had her ex been the controlling type who never listened to her? He couldn't think of any reason why someone as vibrant and gorgeous as Sammy Thompson would still be single, other than that someone had let her down. Badly.

His own track record wasn't great. And he didn't believe in love. So it wasn't fair of him to let this continue, see where things took them—because the chances were that she'd end up hurt. They'd have lunch and then he'd find a nice way of saying goodbye. Because, after all, it wasn't her fault; *he* was the problem.

He walked alongside her, half lost in thought. His hand brushed against hers once, twice, making his skin tingle. The third time, he ended up catching her fingers loosely between his. She didn't pull away, but she didn't look at him or make a comment, either.

Shy?

Weirdly, he felt the same. Like a teenager holding hands with his girl for the first time. And it was a very, very long time since anyone had made him feel like that. Enough to make him rethink his earlier decision. Would it be so bad, seeing where things went? Would it necessarily mean that one or both of them would get hurt? Could he take the risk?

Eventually they reached the café he'd had in mind. 'Is this OK with you?' he asked.

She looked at the menu in the glass case by the door. 'Very OK, thank you. Though it's going to be quite hard to choose, because I like absolutely everything on the menu.'

Again, he found her attitude to food so refreshing; his last couple of dates had been with women who were so focused on watching what they ate that they forgot to enjoy it. Meaning that he hadn't enjoyed his food, either. And he'd made polite excuses not to see them again.

The waitress greeted them as they walked through the door, showed them to a quiet table for two, and took their order for coffee while she gave them time to browse through the menu.

In the end, Sammy sat back in her chair and sighed. 'I just can't decide between the hazelnut waffles with berries and Greek yoghurt, or the eggs Florentine—or the scrambled eggs with smoked salmon and sourdough bread,' she finished, looking rueful. 'And I don't quite have room for all of them.'

'There are two ways of sorting that out,' he said.

'Which are?'

'Either we come here for brunch again and the next time we choose whatever we don't have today,' he said. 'Or we order two different dishes and share them.'

Or, better still, do both. Because, the more he got to know Sammy, the more he liked her and the more he discovered that he wanted to spend time with her. Even though this wasn't the way he normally did things.

'If we share,' she said, 'what do you suggest?'

'The smoked salmon and the waffles.'

'Done,' she said. 'And freshly squeezed blood orange juice as well as the coffee.'

'Sounds perfect,' he said.

When the waitress came back, Sammy ordered for them. Nick wasn't quite used to that, but he rather liked her independent streak.

She sighed happily once she'd taken a sip of her juice. 'This is almost as good as Venice.'

'Venice?'

'When we had breakfast on the Grand Canal,' she said. 'It was amazing. We sat there watching the gondoliers at the stand next to us. One of them noticed and actually serenaded us—we loved it.'

'Who's "we"?' he asked.

'Me, Claire and Ashleigh. Claire and Ash knew each other from school, and I met Claire at art school—she was studying textiles and I was studying photography. We were the Terrible Trio.'

'Were?' he prompted.

'They're the ones in the wedding pictures I showed you. The bride and the bridesmaid in Capri—that was Ash getting married last year, and Claire got married in the spring this year.' She shrugged, and gave him a super-bright smile. 'Obviously I still get to spend time with them when I'm in London. But we won't be going on holiday together any more, just the three of us.'

Something she'd clearly miss. Meaning that Sammy was feeling just a little bit lonely right now? he wondered. He felt lonely, sometimes. When he woke at three in the morning, the bed feeling way too wide and nobody to cuddle up to. And then his father's words from all those years ago would echo in his head. *Love's not reliable, the way work is. Give your job your heart and you'll get to the top. Give love your heart and it'll just cheat on you and break you.*

With age and maturity, Nick had come to realise that his father had been speaking from hurt and anger at the disintegration of his marriage. And Edward Kennedy had never recovered from the divorce—he'd buried himself in work, and moved to Brussels to take his career ambitions further when Nick was halfway through his degree. Edward had done well for himself and reached the top of his particular tree, but Nick often thought his father was lonely and there was a gap in his life.

It wasn't the kind of life Nick wanted for himself—all work and no love. He'd wanted to have both. He'd met Naomi and she'd seemed to understand his drive to be the best at what he did. She'd encouraged him. He'd thought he had it all.

But then he'd come home early and found out that his marriage wasn't what he thought it was. His father's words had turned out to be all too true: because she'd cheated on him and broken his heart. Just like the way his mother had done to his father. Or maybe some of that had been his own fault, for paying too much attention to his work and not enough to his wife—even though at the time he'd thought she was OK with the hours he worked.

He pushed the thought away. Not here. Not now.

When their food arrived, Nick noticed that Sammy went straight for the waffles.

'Aren't you supposed to eat the savoury stuff first and then the sweet?' he asked.

She shook her head. 'Haven't you heard? Life's short, so eat dessert first. It's a good philosophy.'

He thought of Xander and guessed that she was thinking of her sister. Wanting to push away the sadness, he said, 'Can I be nosey and look at the photographs you took earlier?'

'Sure.' She took her camera out of her bag and handed it to him. Again, their fingers touched and adrenalin rippled through him. From the brief widening of her eyes, Nick thought it might just be the same for her, too. Instant attraction. Something he had a feeling neither of them really had time for. And yet something about Sammy made him want to explore this thing between them further. Even though he didn't do love any more. Or maybe it would be different with Sammy, because she loved her job as much as he loved his. And she was direct. He didn't think she'd say one thing and mean another, the way Naomi had.

'These photographs are amazing,' he said. 'I'd never really noticed the kind of details you picked out. The stonework, the windows, the ironwork. You've made me see my workplace in a completely different way.'

'It's what I do,' she said simply. 'The same as you made me think a bit differently this morning, when we talked about people being innocent or guilty.'

'It's what I do,' he said. 'Sammy, are you busy this afternoon?'

'I've got nothing planned. Why?'

He decided to take the risk. 'Because I've really enjoyed spending time with you and I'm not really ready for that to end just yet.'

'Oh.' There was the faintest slash of red in her cheeks. 'Me, too,' she said, her voice ever so slightly croaky.

'Given that we're just round the corner from Trafalgar Square, I'm tempted to suggest going to the art gallery,' he said. 'But it kind of feels wrong to take a photographer to an art gallery.'

She laughed. 'Don't worry about that. I never need an excuse to go to the National Portrait Gallery. That's not work. It's pure pleasure.'

'And you love your job anyway,' he finished.

'Like you. And I'm guessing you get nagged by your family as much as I do about overdoing things,' she said.

'My sister's favourite words are, "You work too hard."' He rolled his eyes. 'But how else are you really going to be good at your job and get to the top of your profession unless you put the hours in?'

'Absolutely. I guess in some areas you could get to

the top by nepotism, but it wouldn't mean that you were any good at your job,' she mused. 'And I want to be the best photographer I can be.'

Her views were so like his own. Nick had a feeling that he'd just met the one woman who might actually understand him. Then again, he'd made that mistake before. He'd thought that Naomi had encouraged his ambitions—to the point where he'd considered easing back on his hours to spend more time with her and start a family. And yet he'd ended up making the same error as his dad and his sister. He'd put his trust in someone who seemed to see things his way on the surface, but had a hidden agenda. Someone weak, who'd lied to get her own way.

'Nick?'

'Sorry. Wool-gathering.' He forced himself to smile. 'Let's go to the gallery.'

When she excused herself to go to the toilet, he asked the waitress for the bill. Except he discovered that Sammy had beaten him to it and already paid it on her way to the ladies'.

'Thank you for brunch,' he said when she came back to their table.

'Pleasure. But it was my turn anyway,' she said, 'because you bought the takeaway, the other night.'

He couldn't argue with that. But it was refreshing to be with someone who believed in fair shares instead of expecting to be treated all the time.

On the way to the National Portrait Gallery, they ended up holding hands again. This time, Sammy slanted Nick a sideways glance, at exactly the same time that he looked at her.

She burst out laughing. 'Is it just me, or do you feel seventeen again?'

'Something like that,' he said, and tightened his fingers round hers. 'I feel as if I should have greasy hair that's badly cut, acne, and be quoting terrible poetry at you.'

She laughed. 'I bet you were a beautiful teen.' And then she blushed. 'Um, that's with my photographer's head on.'

'I'll accept the compliment very happily,' he said. 'For the record, I bet you were a beautiful teen, too.'

'Nah. I was very ordinary,' Sammy told him with a grin.

He didn't believe that at all.

They spent the afternoon wandering round the gallery, and Sammy taught him how to read a portrait. 'The whole point of a portrait is to tell you about the subject. With the older paintings, the background's important and you need to look at what the person chooses to be painted with. In modern photographic portraits, you try to stop the background noise coming through and concentrate on your subject.'

There was a mischievous glint in his eye. 'I love it when you talk technical.'

She grimaced. 'Sorry. I can be very boring on my pet subject.'

'I'm not bored in the slightest. This is totally new stuff to me.' He smiled at her. 'Besides, I rambled on enough about law earlier.'

When she'd said how she loved her job, too. She'd understood something about him that Naomi never had. And it was crazy that it made him feel so warm inside.

'Do you have any portraits on display here?' he asked.

She laughed. 'Sadly, I'm not *quite* in the same league as David Bailey or Lord Lichfield. Maybe one day.'

'What's your favourite portrait you've taken?' he asked.

She looked thoughtful. 'I can probably name you half a dozen. But my absolute favourite is probably Freddy, the free runner.'

'You mean, one of those people who run around London and jump off rooftops?' he asked.

'According to Freddy, it's all about expressing yourself without limiting your movement—but yes, that's what it looks like. To get the interview and the portrait, the journalist and I went with him on a free run. He said you know who you are when you know how your body moves and what you're capable of doing. That if you learn to overcome obstacles in your environment you'll also learn how to overcome obstacles and stress in your daily life—and that fascinated me.'

'So you actually did the jumping off roofs bit with him?' Now that he hadn't expected.

'Not with my camera, no—the insurance would never have covered that kind of risk.' She smiled. 'But I did have a go when the journo looked after my camera.'

He raised an eyebrow. 'So are you brave, or are you a thrill seeker?'

'Neither,' she said. 'Life's short, so it's always worth taking the chance to experience something new, even if it seems a bit scary at first. Because that way you push yourself beyond your boundaries and you live life to the full—you don't get left with a pile of regrets at the end.'

'That's a good philosophy,' he said. 'So what's on your bucket list?'

For a moment he thought he saw her flinch. But it must've been his imagination. Or maybe it was a phrase that made her think about her sister. 'Sorry. That could've been phrased better.'

'Things I really want to do before I die.' She pursed her lips. 'Top of my list would be the chance to go to the edge of the earth's atmosphere—the bit where you see the blue curved line of space and all the blackness above. I'd love the chance to see that for myself and photograph it.' She looked straight at him. 'How about you? What's on your list?'

'Most of the places I want to see are in the middle of political turmoil right now,' he said, 'so it's not sensible to travel there. But on the doable list, I'd love to see the whales and polar bears in Canada. And see the Northern Lights.'

'Book the trip,' she said immediately.

Yeah. Except he wanted to share it with someone. 'When work isn't quite so busy,' he said, knowing that it was a feeble excuse.

'Being busy at work is fine,' she said softly. 'But it's important to remember to take time to play as well. To give yourself a chance to refill the well.'

Clearly his expression said that he thought that was totally flaky, because she grinned. 'I just believe in living life to the full. Work hard and play hard.'

He persuaded her to let him buy her coffee and cake in the gallery's café. When they'd finished, he said, 'May I see you home?'

'Thank you, Nick, but I'm an adult. I'm perfectly capable of getting myself home.'

There was a slight edge to her voice that surprised him. He'd thought they'd had a good time together. Clearly it was time to back off. 'Sorry. I was brought up to be a bit old-fashioned.'

'Courtesy—yes, I can understand that. Sorry for biting your head off.' She took a deep breath. 'Let's just say in the past my family's tried to wrap me up in cotton wool, and that drives me crazy.' There was a flash of panic in her eyes, gone so fast that Nick thought he might've imagined it. And then Sammy added, 'I guess it comes from being the baby of the family.'

Nick was the baby of the family, and nobody had wrapped him in cotton wool. When his mother's affair had come to light, his sister Mandy had been away at university and Nick had been left alone with his father—who'd been too hurt and angry to put a filter over his words. Edward Kennedy had said an awful lot of bitter, unhappy things that the teenaged Nick could've done without hearing.

He shook himself. Now wasn't the time to dwell on that. 'A photographer who's actually tried free running and dreams of going to the edge of space is the last person who'd want to be wrapped in cotton wool,' he said.

She looked relieved that he actually understood her. And then she looked him in the eye. 'We could always go for the compromise.'

'What's that?'

'Walk me to the Tube station?' she suggested.

'Works for me,' he said.

And he was pleased that this time she was the one to tangle her fingers with his as they walked.

At the entrance to the Tube station, he turned to her.

'I've had a really nice day. Thank you.' He bent his head, intending to kiss her politely on the cheek—but somehow his lips ended up brushing against hers. Once, twice. Clinging. Exploring the softness of her mouth, the sweetness.

And it made him feel as if an electric shock had run through him.

When he pulled back, he could see the shock and surprise in her own eyes, so clearly it had affected her in the same way.

'Nick. I…' The words dried up and she shook her head helplessly.

'Yeah. Me, too,' he said softly. And, because he could see just the faintest bit of panic on her face, he backed off. 'See you later.' Even though he had the strongest feeling that he might not. And he didn't look back once as he headed on the half-hour walk back to his flat.

Sammy really hadn't expected that kiss. She didn't think Nick had intended to kiss her like that, either. He'd probably been aiming for her cheek—just as she'd been doing. Except then they'd both turned the wrong way and their mouths had accidentally collided.

She brooded about it all the way home.

Part of her didn't want to risk another relationship where she'd get let down.

And yet she'd told him her view on life. *It's always worth taking the chance to experience something new, even if it seems a bit scary at first. Because that way you push yourself beyond your boundaries and you live life to the full—you don't get left with a pile of regrets at the end.*

Dating Nick Kennedy was a scary prospect. One she wasn't sure she was brave enough to handle. What if he was disgusted by her scars and it made him back away? He wouldn't be the first. And, even if he wasn't repulsed by her leg, would she be enough of a woman for him? It was a bone-deep fear that she hadn't even discussed with her sister and her best friends. She knew they'd tell her she was being ridiculous and they were probably right, but that didn't shift the fear. The fact that she'd have difficulty conceiving—that if she met someone who wanted to have a family with her, they'd have to go through IVF using her frozen eggs, and there was no guarantee it would work—made her feel less of a woman. In her head, she knew it was stupid, but in her heart she couldn't help worrying about it.

But, if she walked away from Nick, would she end up with a pile of regrets?

Was this sudden burst of loneliness just a reaction to the fact that Claire and Ashleigh had both got married and she was the only one of the Terrible Trio who was single now? Or was it something more?

There was only one way to find out.

She texted him.

Very carefully.

Thank you. I had a really good time today.

He took his time in replying.

Me, too.

Was he being polite? Or was he being wary, given that she'd bitten his head off so unfairly?

Bravery time again. And this would be their second official date, so it was safely within her three-dates-and-end-it rule. She could do this. Keep it casual. Unthreatening. She tapped into her phone.

Maybe we could do something next week, if you're free.

That was the crunch suggestion. If he made an excuse and backed off, so would she. If he didn't…then maybe they could have some fun together.

He took even longer replying, this time. And she only realised how tense she was when her phone beeped and she saw his message.

Day or evening?

Either. I'm still on holiday next week. Nothing planned.

His reply was swift.

Am in court for at least three days but can do evenings.

Good. How are you with heights?

Instead of texting her, this time he called her. 'What do you have in mind? Is this something to do with free running?'

'No. Just heights. Something off my bucket list that I hope you'll enjoy.'

'The top of the Shard?' he suggested. 'Sure. Heights aren't a problem.'

'Not the Shard. Something else,' she said. 'Dress casually. I'll text you with the times and directions when I've booked it. *Ciao.*'

And then she hung up before she made a fool of herself.

CHAPTER FIVE

ONCE SAMMY HAD booked tickets for the outing she'd planned, she sent Nick a cheeky text.

M'learned friend, do you possess such a thing as a pair of jeans?

Clearly he was in court, because he didn't reply until lunchtime. And then he called her rather than texted her. 'Of course I own a pair of jeans, Sammy. Why?'

'Because I need you to wear them when you meet me on Thursday night. Trainers would be good, too, but they're not essential.'

'Jeans and trainers? Why? What are we doing?'

'Something fun,' she said. 'Because as I told you before, I believe in working hard, but I also believe in playing just as hard.'

'Fair enough. Are you at least going to tell me the location, or am I supposed to be developing my mind-reading abilities?'

She laughed. 'North Greenwich Tube station. And that's all you need to know for now. I'll text you the time.'

'Hmm,' Nick said, but she could hear the smile in his voice.

* * *

When Nick met Sammy on Thursday evening, she did a pirouette in front of him. 'I hope you notice that I'm not wearing black today,' she said.

She was wearing faded jeans, which clung to her like a second skin, a hot pink T-shirt, and canvas shoes that matched her T-shirt. And Nick was slightly shocked to realise how much he wanted to carry her off to his flat and peel her clothes off her. Very, very slowly.

'You look very nice,' he said, hoping that his thoughts weren't showing on his face and that she hadn't developed mind-reading skills. 'So where are we going?'

'The O2 Arena. We're booked in for the sunset climb,' she told him. 'I've already bought the tickets and this is my idea, so don't even *think* about offending me by offering to pay. Got it?'

'Yes, ma'am,' he said, saluting and clicking his heels together.

'Good. I'm glad you know your place, m'learned friend.'

And he loved the teasing glint in her eyes. With Sammy, he was starting to rediscover his sense of fun—something he'd lost after the break-up of his marriage, except for the time he spent with his nephews. 'So we're actually walking over the top of the Dome?'

'Yep. You were the one talking about bucket lists. This happens to be on mine. One of my best friends is totally scared of heights, but you said you were OK with them, so I thought I'd dragoon you into doing it with me.' She paused and frowned. 'Oh, wait. You haven't done this already, have you?'

'No.' Though this was definitely something that his nephews would love to do, he thought. Maybe it was something he'd suggest doing with them. Maybe he'd ask Sammy to join them—though he didn't know whether she actually liked children. Plus it was way too soon to suggest meeting his family. This was, what, their second date? Yeah. Way too soon. They needed time to get to know each other, first.

Live for the moment, he reminded himself. 'I'm looking forward to this.'

'Me, too.' She looked gleeful. 'This is going to be huge fun.'

He agreed. Particularly because he was going to be sharing the experience with her.

After a safety briefing with the guides, they joined the rest of their group in putting on their climb suits and boots. Next they put on a harness with a latch that they'd been told to clip to the walkway; and finally they climbed the stairs up to the suspended walkway.

The person at the front of the line stumbled partway up the steep incline, and the walkway rippled with the impact. The person in front of Sammy stopped dead, clearly worried, and Sammy had to stop short.

Nick almost collided with her and rested his hands on her shoulders to steady them both. 'OK?' he asked Sammy.

'I'm fine,' she said. 'Apparently this happens a bit, especially on the way down. I'm sure we'll both be fine.'

The gradient levelled out, and finally they found themselves in the viewing platform on the centre above the Dome. Sammy took her mobile phone out of her pocket and took snaps of the panoramic view. Nick recognised the cable car, Canary Wharf, the Shard and the Gherkin, along with Royal Greenwich and the sculpture at the Olympic Park.

But best of all was the sunset, just to the side of the buildings of Canary Wharf. He could see exactly why this had been on her bucket list. It was a photographer's dream view.

'This is an amazing view,' he said.

She beamed. 'I hoped it would be like this—and I love the way all the skyscrapers are lit up, too, now it's dusk. Hey, can I take a selfie with you?'

He laughed. 'That sounds *really* weird coming from a professional photographer.'

'Don't knock it. A good selfie can still be a good shot. If you hold your arm out far enough and zoom in, then you're not going to end up with a bulbous nose or big ears.'

'Bulbous nose?'

She laughed. 'Like that shot where the monkey stole that camera from the photographer and managed to take a selfie. I've seen a few of those in my time.' She took a few snaps of them together on the edge of the walkway, with the iconic masts from the Dome sticking out on either side of them. And Nick enjoyed the fact that he got to put his arm round her, even if they were both in climb suits and he wasn't actually touching her skin.

'So now we're up here,' Sammy said to their guide, 'do we get to do the James Bond bit now, minus the bullets?'

'Sliding down the side of the Dome, you mean?' He laughed. 'I'm afraid that would be a no.'

'Pity,' she said, and clipped her harness back on the walkway to start the descent.

At the bottom, once they'd changed out of their climb suits and boots and walked away from the area, Nick teased, 'What with your yen for outer space, the free running stuff and now this, I think you were totally bluffing about bravery and you're really a thrill seeker at heart.'

'No. The free running stuff was work, anyway, and I haven't actually done it since. I just think it's a good idea to get out of your comfort zone every so often, because life is short and you need to appreciate every second of it,' she said. 'In fact, I have a very good idea right now…' She stood on tiptoe, cupped his face with her hands, and pressed her mouth to his.

Her lips were warm and soft and she tasted of strawberries. And Nick couldn't help responding, wrapping his arms tightly round her and nibbling at her lower lip to persuade her to deepen the kiss.

Sammy Thompson made his head spin.

And he couldn't remember the last time he'd reacted so strongly to someone. He'd always thought of himself as careful—that he'd get to know someone over a few months before going to bed with them. But Sammy made him want to take all his brakes off and he wanted to make love with her right now. He wasn't sure if that was more exhilarating or frightening.

'Great idea,' he said when she finally broke the kiss. 'Apart from the fact that my head's totally scrambled now, thanks to you.'

'So you're outside your comfort zone?' she asked.

'Yes and no.' He stole another kiss. 'I think I could get to like this very much indeed. You?'

She fanned herself. 'I don't normally do this sort of thing with complete strangers.'

'We're not complete strangers now. Plus you've seen me naked,' he pointed out, 'which puts you at rather an unfair advantage.'

To his amusement, her face went bright scarlet, clashing with her T-shirt. 'Nothing untoward was on show when you modelled for me,' she reminded him.

'I was naked, so it still counts. And I think this means I need to get to see you naked, to even things up.'

Her eyes were sparkling. 'Oh, do you now?'

He pulled her closer and nibbled her ear. 'That was the best idea I've had all day.' She was still deliciously pink. And he noticed that she wasn't making excuses and backing away. Anticipation skittered through him. Were they both about to break their own rules and fast-track to the next stage?

'I think we should feature you on the front cover of the calendar,' she said thoughtfully. 'Because, with your bare chest and your abs, we'll sell tons of copies for the ward.'

Which answered his question. This was teasing banter, not a statement of intent. Best to keep it playful, then. He groaned theatrically. 'OK. Shutting up now. Do you have to rush off, or shall we have dinner?'

'Dinner would be good,' she said. 'Shall we go to one of the restaurants here?'

'Here's fine. And dinner's on me, seeing as it was my idea and you bought the tickets to the climb.'

'Thank you,' she said with a smile.

They went to one of the bars inside the Dome, and looked through the menu.

'You're going to choose dessert first, aren't you?' he asked.

She wrinkled her nose. 'Yes, but it looks as if most of the puddings on the menu are chocolate.'

'Problem?' he asked.

She nodded. 'I hate chocolate puddings.'

'You don't like chocolate?' He was surprised. Every female he knew loved chocolate.

'No, I love chocolate,' she said, 'but I don't like chocolate puddings or chocolate ice cream. And I already know that makes me weird. I've been told that often enough.'

He grinned. 'Someone rather wise once told me that you like what you like and it doesn't mean you're a philistine—or, in this case, weird.'

She laughed back, clearly recognising that he was throwing her words back at her. 'I guess.'

She chose the salted caramel cheesecake—the only non-chocolate pudding on the menu—and they ordered a mix of sharing plates between them: ginger and lemon chicken, pulled pork, sweet potato fries, quinoa salad and stuffed peppers.

'What do you want to drink?' he asked.

'They can apparently mix a cocktail to suit you,' she said. 'And I'm really torn between a glass of Prosecco and a cocktail.'

'You could always have a cocktail based on Prosecco, and that way you get the best of both worlds,' he pointed out. 'Why not ask the barman? And I'll join you.'

Once they'd told the bartender what they'd chosen to eat, and Sammy explained that she wasn't much of a spirits drinker, he made them a cocktail of Prosecco mixed with ginger liqueur and limoncello.

'Excellent choice, m'learned friend,' she said to Nick with a grin after the first sip. 'I like this.'

'Me, too,' he agreed.

The food was just as good but the company was even better. Nick found himself relaxing with Sammy, laughing and talking about a complete mixture of subjects. Every so often, his fingers brushed against hers as they chose something else from their sharing platter, and adrenalin fizzed through his veins.

Plus there were those kisses. He couldn't get them out of his head. Her mouth was beautiful, her lips soft and warm, and he wanted to kiss Sammy again. Explore her. Find out where she liked being touched, where she liked being kissed. What made her curl her toes with pleasure.

There was definitely something special about Sammy Thompson. But would she be prepared to take a chance on him? Nick still hadn't worked out why she was single. She was bright, she was charming, and she made him see the world in a slightly different way. Someone, he guessed, must have hurt her and made her wary of relationships.

But maybe she could learn to trust him.

And maybe he could learn to trust her.

Because she wasn't like Naomi. Sammy struck him as very straightforward and honest. She wasn't the sort to spin a web of lies and turn someone into the bad guy when he hadn't actually done anything wrong.

After their meal, they walked hand in hand back to the Tube station. 'Sammy, I know you're old enough and tough enough to look after yourself, but this time will you please let me see you home to your front door?' he asked. At her raised eyebrows, he gave her a rueful smile. 'OK, I admit—it's because I've enjoyed tonight and I want to spend a few more minutes with you, and seeing you home feels like a good excuse.'

'And once you see me to my front door, then I'm supposed to invite you in for coffee?' she asked.

'It's not essential,' he said, 'though it would be nice.' He paused. 'And, if you offered, I'd accept.'

'Even though the coffee's not going to be made with a posh Italian coffee machine like yours?' she tested.

He laughed. 'You could give me a chipped mug of decaf instant coffee made with long-life milk that was almost out of date and that would be absolutely fine.'

She laughed back. 'No way—with a coffee machine like yours, you're used to the best and you might even verge on being a coffee snob. And none of my mugs are chipped, thank you very much.'

But she agreed to let him walk her back to her front door. It turned out that she lived in a small flat in Camden, among a row of terraced houses painted ice cream colours. Cute—and the area suited her, he thought. Vibrant, with something interesting round every corner.

'I'll give you the guided tour of the flat,' she said. 'It's going to take us all of two minutes—and that's provided I talk a lot while I show you round.'

He smiled. 'Sounds good to me.'

She hadn't been exaggerating that much; her flat was compact and much, much smaller than his. All the floors were stripped and varnished wood, but that was the only thing their flats had in common. Her walls were all painted cream and the windows had neutral-coloured roman blinds rather than floor length curtains. Though he guessed that made it easier to focus on the artwork; there were framed photographs grouped together on the walls that seemed to have either a similar theme or a similar colour.

'Are these all your own pictures?' he asked.

She nodded. 'I change them round every so often.

But it's nice to use the shots rather than just leave them languishing out of sight on my hard drive.'

Her kitchen was open plan. 'I guess it's fairly self-explanatory—I use the dining table as a desk as well as to eat,' she said.

'It's a nice room,' he said. 'Comfortable.' The other half of the room was the living room and contained a sofa, a stereo system, a bookcase, a cupboard where he guessed she kept most of her photographic equipment, and a small television.

Her bathroom was only just big enough to contain a bath with a shower over it, the toilet and a sink; there wasn't a window, but the room was small enough for the overhead light to keep things bright. Her bedroom was equally bijou, with just enough room for a double bed with an iron frame, a small pine bedside cabinet, and a matching chest of drawers and wardrobe.

And he suddenly had the clearest picture of being in that double bed with her, curled up together and talking after they'd made love. Her face would be flushed with passion and her eyes sparkling. And he couldn't resist spinning her into his arms and kissing her until he felt dizzy.

'Well, now,' she said when he broke the kiss, sounding flustered.

'Sorry.'

She lifted an eyebrow. 'Are you?'

'For kissing you, no,' he admitted. 'For being pushy, yes.'

She smiled and stroked his face. 'I don't think either of us knows how to handle this. I don't usually invite men home after a second date. But here you are.'

'I don't usually invite complete strangers home, either,' he said. 'But I invited you back to my place after the shoot.'

She laughed. 'You don't strip off in front of strangers, either. But you did for me.'

It would be oh, so easy to pick her up and carry her to her bed. Suggest that he stripped for her again. Better still, suggest that she undressed him. Very slowly. With a lot of kissing in between.

But rushing things would just make life way too complicated.

He needed to cool things down. As in right now, before he did something reckless and they both got burned. 'Talk to me,' he said. 'Tell me about your job. Does it mean a lot of travelling?'

'I go wherever the photograph needs to be taken,' she said, ushering him back to her living room and then switching on the kettle to make coffee. 'Sometimes it's in London, but often it's further afield.' She lifted a shoulder. 'I've done some work in LA, some in New York, and some on various film locations. The best bit is when I get a chance to explore while I'm away and take some shots for myself, too.'

'Like your architectural stuff?'

She nodded. 'And seascapes.'

'So do you have a dark room and an office somewhere?' he asked.

She shook her head. 'Most of my work is digital, so I don't really need a dark room. But occasionally I borrow my uncle's, if I've been experimenting with arty shots and want to do it the old-fashioned way. There's something special about watching the shot develop on the paper.'

'And is it like they show you in the movies, with trays of liquids and a red light?'

'It's called a safe light, and it can be brown or red,' she said. 'Basically, ordinary light will ruin any unexposed film or photographic paper, whereas safe light means that you can see what you're doing but it won't wreck your work.'

'Sounds like a sensible solution,' he said.

'Though you don't have to have a special room to be a dark room,' she said. 'My bathroom doesn't have an outside window, so in theory it wouldn't take much to turn it into a dark room, provided I block out all the light round the door. And I could use my bath as a bench for the chemicals.'

He looked at her, surprised. 'But wouldn't they ruin your bath?'

'No, because you wash the chemicals away too quickly for them to do any damage—besides, the bath is the same kind of plastic as the trays.'

'So how does it work?'

'Basically you have four trays set up,' she explained. 'You expose the photographic negative onto the paper—the length of time you expose it controls what you see on the final image—and then you put the paper into developer trays so you can actually see the image. Once it looks exactly how you want it, you move the paper from the developer tray to the stop bath, so the picture doesn't develop any more. From there you move the paper to the fixer so you can look at the image in normal light later without it being ruined; and finally you rinse the paper in water to get rid of the last bits of chemicals.'

'And then you peg it up on a line to dry?' he asked.

'Just like in the movies. Yup.' She smiled. 'Actually, I love making black and white prints. I could take you to Uncle Julian's and show you how it's done sometime, if you like. It's magical when you see the image emerging, like a ghost at first and then getting stronger. And it's fun playing about with different contrasts, and different sorts of paper.'

'No. You have a passion for your job,' he said softly, 'and it shows.'

And he really wanted to see that passion in her eyes again.

Except he wanted to be the one to put it there. Like he had when he'd kissed her a few minutes ago.

When she finished making coffee, she came to join him on the sofa and set her mug on the floor. And that was the perfect cue for him to slide his arm round her shoulders. From there it was easy to twist round to face her, and to brush his lips against hers. Her mouth was soft and sweet and giving, and she slid her hands round his neck to draw him closer.

The next thing he knew, he was lying full length on her sofa, she was lying on top of him, and his hands were splayed against her back, underneath her T-shirt.

Her skin was so soft, so warm. Touching wasn't enough. He wanted to see, too.

Which was crazy. He never behaved like this, so out of control. He didn't do love. And he didn't want to hurt Sammy. He should back off. Now.

Except he couldn't.

He blew out a breath. 'Sorry. I'm taking this a bit too fast again.'

Her face was flushed and her eyes were sparkling. 'You and me both.'

'I'm sorry. I don't normally behave like this,' he said.

'Neither do I.' Her face was rueful. 'I might say outrageous things, but I don't tend to walk the talk,' she admitted.

'There's just something about you that makes me want more than I should ask for,' he said softly, holding her closer because he wasn't quite ready yet to relinquish the feel of her skin against his fingertips.

'Me, too. But, Nick, this probably isn't a good idea. Our lifestyles are too different.'

'Actually, they're probably too similar,' he corrected. 'We're both workaholics.'

'I guess so.'

He stole a kiss. 'So maybe it could work between us. But I agree. We need to cool this very slightly. Much as I'd really like to scoop you up and take you to your bed right this very minute—and believe me I've wanted to do that all evening—I can't do that, because I don't actually carry condoms around with me.'

'I don't have any either.'

His heart skipped a beat. Was she saying that, if she'd had condoms, she would've been fine with him taking her to her bed? For a second, he couldn't breathe.

'Rain check,' she whispered, and climbed off him.

The sensible thing, Nick thought, would be for them to sit at opposite ends of her sofa. Except her sofa was so compact that even when they tried it in tacit agreement, they were still close enough to touch.

Take it down a notch, he told himself, and took her hand instead.

'I'm trying to take it slower,' he said by way of explanation.

She smiled. 'OK. Let's pick a safe subject. We did something on my bucket list this evening. What's on yours, apart from polar bears, whale-watching, the

Northern Lights and some places that are too dangerous for tourists?'

Making love with you.

Not that he was going to say that out loud.

And he was still a bit stunned that she'd actually remembered what he'd told her.

He thought about it for a while. 'A proper afternoon tea in a very posh hotel,' he said. 'With a cake stand and a silver teapot and someone playing the piano in the lobby.'

'Oh, come off it,' she scoffed. 'You're a barrister and you work in the middle of London. You must've done that before.'

'Actually, no. My clients don't generally tend to take me to tea at a posh hotel,' he said mildly, 'and in the afternoons if I'm not in court then I'm in my chambers, up to my eyes in paperwork. If I'm *very* lucky I might be able to sweet-talk my clerk Gary into making me a mug of tea—but usually we take turns, so whoever puts the kettle on in the kitchen usually checks to see who else wants a cuppa.'

'Seriously? You don't have a secretary?'

'Barristers have clerks,' he said. 'The clerks are responsible for the admin and business activities of the chambers. So Gary would do some secretarial things, like arranging meetings, invoicing solicitors for fees and planning case timetables in detail, but he also looks after three more barristers as well as me. He doesn't have time to wait on my every whim—and he wouldn't do that anyway,' he admitted with a grin. 'If I asked him to go and put the kettle on, he'd tell me I was old enough and ugly enough to make my own cuppa, he was already busy making phone calls on my behalf, and his is white with three sugars while I'm at it, thank you very much.'

'Right.' She smiled as if she was imagining the scene, then looked at him. 'I can't believe you've never had a proper posh afternoon tea.'

'I take it you have, then?' he asked.

'Oh, yes.' Her eyes lit up. 'Birthdays, red letter days, and any other time I can find an excuse to do it.'

'Seriously?'

'Provided the cake isn't chocolate. Then I have to talk people into swapping with me. But posh tea, dainty finger sandwiches, scones with jam and clotted cream, yummy little savouries… Yeah, I love all that. It's so decadent and such a treat. Like going out for breakfast. I think I'd rather do that than go out for dinner, even. It feels more special.'

He'd enjoyed sharing brunch with her. And he had a feeling that this particular item on his bucket list would be even more enjoyable if he shared it with her, especially as she sounded so enthusiastic about it. 'Right then, Ms Thompson, would you like to come to afternoon tea with me?'

'Thank you, m'learned friend, I would,' she said.

'Good. When?' He took his phone out of his pocket and checked his diary. 'This weekend?'

Sammy grabbed her phone to check her diary, too. 'Sorry, I can't. I'm in Somerset doing a shoot with an organic cider producer.'

'OK.' He checked the next week. 'How's Wednesday afternoon looking for you?'

Sammy nodded. 'I've got a planning meeting at one of the magazines in London that morning, so Wednesday afternoon is pretty much perfect for me.'

'Great. I'll book something tomorrow and let you know where and what time,' he said. 'Call me if there's a problem and we'll reschedule if we need to.'

'OK. That sounds good.'

'And I'd better let you get on.' He stood up, and she saw him to the door.

He kissed her goodbye, being careful to keep his libido in check. 'See you on Wednesday,' he said.

And he could hardly wait.

CHAPTER SIX

WEDNESDAY.

A seriously posh hotel.

For afternoon tea.

Panic flooded through Sammy the more she thought about it. Given that kind of venue, she could hardly turn up in her usual black trousers. But a business suit with opaque tights wouldn't be appropriate, either; they were having an Indian summer, even though it was late September. Wearing a floaty cotton dress meant having bare legs or wearing the sheerest tights; and either of those options would mean that the scar on her left leg would be clearly visible.

Even though Nick would probably be too nice to ask her what had caused the scar, she'd know that he was wondering about it. Or maybe he'd recognise it as something that he'd seen before, on his nephew's leg. And in the end she'd cave in and tell him that she'd had a strange bony lump on her shin as a teen, and when it had been investigated the doctors had told her that she had osteosarcoma.

Bone cancer.

Chemotherapy had shrunk the tumour before the operation, and the surgeon had been able to take out the tumour from the bone and put in a metal prosthesis. Sammy knew she'd been one of the lucky ones, able to have bone-sparing surgery rather than an amputation. She'd done every single breathing exercise and every single physiotherapy exercise to the letter after the operation. She'd been through more chemotherapy to mop up any last bad cells after the operation and she'd attended every single one of her regular check-ups. And she was hugely grateful that she'd come through it.

She was strong. She had the full support of her family.

And when she'd met Bryn, she'd thought she'd finally found someone different.

But instead he'd gone on to break her heart. He'd asked her to marry him just before she'd had her scare, two years before. And then he'd ended it the day she'd got the results. He'd admitted that he couldn't cope with the prospect of her having cancer again, but he hadn't wanted to be the bad guy who'd dumped the cancer patient. Instead, he'd waited until they knew she was clear—and then he'd dumped her.

Just as well they hadn't actually chosen the engagement ring.

Sammy had walked away with her head held high and her heart feeling as if it had been ground into sand. And she'd promised herself she'd never make the mistake of getting that close to anyone again. Yet, right now, she was taking a huge risk. This would be her third date with Nick—and she didn't have an exit strategy in place.

She dragged in a breath. Nick's nephew had been diagnosed with osteosarcoma, so maybe Nick would understand more than the average person.

But what if he didn't?

What if it made him back away? What if she repulsed him?

Even Bryn—who'd been engaged to her—hadn't coped with her scars. Not really. They'd always made love with the lights off, and he'd been careful never to look at her leg or touch it. She'd pretended that it didn't matter…but it had.

And it mattered now.

She really wasn't ready to tell Nick about her past yet.

She didn't want to call off their date, either; given that she'd already told him how much she liked going out for afternoon tea, she knew he wouldn't believe a feeble excuse. And, being a lawyer, of course he'd ask questions.

Probing ones.

Ones where even a silent reaction would help him to see the truth.

Sammy still hadn't worked out how to deal with the situation by the time she met up with her best friends for a long-planned evening with pizza at her flat.

Except Ashleigh and Claire had known her for long enough to guess that something was wrong.

'Spit it out,' Claire said.

'What?' Sammy asked, feigning innocence.

'You're very quiet. Which isn't you, unless you're concentrating on a shoot. So talk to us,' Ashleigh said. 'That's what best friends are for. To listen, to tell you when you're being an idiot, and to give you a hug when you need one.'

Sammy actually felt tears pricking her eyes at

Ashleigh's words, and was cross with herself for it. For pity's sake. She wasn't one of those people who bawled their eyes out at the drop of a hat.

'Did you find another lump?' Claire asked softly.

'No. Why does everyone *always* assume it's the cancer come back, if something's bothering me?' Sammy asked, losing her cool.

Ashleigh and Claire immediately put down their cutlery, stood up and enveloped her in a hug.

'We're not assuming anything,' Ashleigh said, stroking her hair. 'But we've known you for years, we can see you're upset, and we want to be here for you.'

'It's just something stupid.' Sammy swallowed hard to keep the tears back. She wasn't weak. She was independent and strong. She could do this.

'Then it's something we can help you with—and make you laugh about,' Claire pointed out. 'Don't push us away. There's a fine line between being independent and being too stubborn, you know.'

She and Ashleigh returned to their chairs, but each of them kept hold of one of Sammy's hands.

'I don't know what to wear on a date,' Sammy muttered.

'OK,' Ashleigh said carefully. 'Where are you going, and is it a first date?'

'Afternoon tea at a posh hotel.' Sammy knew this was something she should have told them about before. Because they were her best friends and they had her best interests at heart. They wouldn't judge her. They never had. 'Third date.'

Claire and Ashleigh exchanged a glance. 'Is there going to be a fourth?' Claire asked.

Was she going to break her three-date rule for Nick?

'I don't know.' She wanted to. And she didn't. All at the same time. 'It's driving me crazy,' she admitted.

'Tell us about him,' Ashleigh said.

So Sammy found herself spilling the beans. How she'd taken Nick's photograph for the charity calendar, then ended up having dinner with him—which didn't count as a date, because then that would mean that afternoon tea was the scary fourth—and they'd seen each other a couple of times since.

'Does he know about your leg?' Claire asked.

Sammy shook her head. 'It hasn't been the right time to talk about it, yet.'

'If he's involved with the calendar, he must have a connection to the ward,' Ashleigh suggested.

'Yes. His nephew had osteosarcoma,' Sammy said.

'So he'll understand,' Ashleigh reassured her. 'If you're even thinking about a fourth date with him, Sammy, it's serious. So you're going to have to tell him.'

'And you have to do it before you end up naked with him and he sees the scar,' Claire added.

Ice slid down Sammy's spine. 'Because you think he'll reject me when he sees it?' That had happened before. A mistake she'd made three times until she'd learned to keep it to herself. Until Bryn, who'd made her trust him...and then let her down even more than the run-for-the-hills boyfriends.

'No, of course not. I mean because when you have sex with him for the first time you want to enjoy it, not worry about having to explain your medical history to him beforehand,' Claire said, rolling her eyes.

'And if you think he's not going to see you for who you are, then you shouldn't be thinking about having sex with him anyway—because in that case he's not good enough for you,' Ashleigh added firmly.

'I know.' Sammy rubbed a hand over her short crop. But even if her hair had been at its longest, she wouldn't have been able to hide behind it because her best friends knew her so well. 'He's a good man—he's ethical and honest.'

'Unlike a certain person I'd like to stake out in a field of fire ants while he was covered in honey,' Claire said darkly. Sammy knew she was referring to Bryn.

'Why can't you wear your usual black trousers, maybe with a top that's a bit more dressy than usual?' Ashleigh asked.

'Because it's the kind of place where I need to wear a dress.'

'Where are you going?' Claire asked.

When Sammy told them the name of the hotel, they both whistled.

'The afternoon tea there is meant to be amazing,' Ashleigh said. 'You have to go and tell us so we can live vicariously through you. Don't chicken out.'

The problem was, Sammy wanted to chicken out. This was the third date. Crunch time. And she knew she was making a fuss about what to wear so she could avoid facing the real reason why she didn't want to go—that she was afraid it would all go wrong and she'd end up hurt again.

'Actually, you can wear a dress, Cinderella. Because your fairy godmother just happened to get some new material delivered last week that would be perfect for you,' Claire said. 'It's purple and I think it's got your name written all over it.'

Her best friend was going to make her a dress, especially for her date? 'Claire-bear, I can't ask you to—' Sammy began.

'You're not asking, I'm offering,' Claire cut in. 'In fact, I'm telling you.'

'If you make me a dress,' Sammy said, 'I'm paying for it, and I don't mean mates' rates.'

'What, like you let me pay you for my wedding photographs and all the shots you took for my website—*not*?' Claire scoffed. 'No. I'm doing it because I want to make you a dress. Just occasionally, Sammy, it's nice to be able to do something as a treat for one of my best friends, OK? So shut up and say yes instead of being over-independent.'

'OK. And sorry. And I really, really appreciate you,' Sammy said.

Claire cuffed her arm playfully. 'So you should, Sammikins. I was thinking an empire line maxi dress, with a V-neck, in two layers—plain underneath and chiffon on top.'

It always amazed Sammy how Claire could see the perfect dress for someone whenever she looked at them. And Claire's creations were stunning. Ashleigh's wedding dress had been amazing.

'You've got heels to go with it?' Claire asked.

'Just because I tend to live in trousers, it doesn't mean I don't own any pretty shoes,' Sammy said.

'Good. Bring them tomorrow night for your fitting so I can make sure the hem's right,' Claire said.

'And what about jewellery?' Ashleigh asked. 'Because Mum had a string of black pearls that'd look fabulous with what Claire's just described. I'll bring them with me tomorrow.'

Sammy had to swallow the lump in her throat.

Ashleigh's parents had been killed in a car accident eight years ago, so for Ashleigh to offer to lend her friend something so very precious… 'Thanks.'

'Hey.' Ashleigh hugged her. 'You're worth it.'

'You do know that when you two start having babies, I'll take portraits of the babies every single month for you. As a best friend gift,' Sammy said. The same way she'd done their wedding photographs and had refused to take any payment for even the photographic paper.

'Godmother gift, not just best friend,' Claire corrected. 'And I'm really glad you brought the subject up, because…' She paused for dramatic effect. 'Well, there's something I need to ask you both. Sean agrees with me. Will you both be godmothers?'

Sammy's jaw dropped. 'Oh, my God. You're actually having a baby?'

'In six months' time,' Claire confirmed.

'Oh, that's fantastic.' Sammy hugged her. 'I'm so pleased for you and Sean.'

Ashleigh coughed. 'Seeing as we're doing news, I guess I have a little announcement, too.'

'What?' Sammy stared at her in amazement. 'You and Luke, too?'

'In six months' time, too.' Ashleigh nodded. 'And I'll be looking for you both to be godmothers as well.'

'I'm the only one of us who can drink alcohol now, or I'd rush out and buy a bottle of champagne,' Sammy said. 'Both of you, expecting at the same time. That's *amazing*. Such brilliant news.'

'So, if this thing works out with your barrister, you're absolutely not allowed to get married to him until after we've had the babies,' Claire said, 'because I'm not planning to walk down the aisle behind you in a maternity matron of honour dress.'

'Seconded,' Ashleigh said. 'And we are so drinking champagne at your wedding. Which we can't do when we're pregnant.'

'Two babies,' Sammy said, beaming at both of them. 'That is, I'm assuming neither of you are having twins?'

'Not me,' Claire said.

'Just one baby here, too. But we're waiting until the baby's born to find out if we're having a girl or a boy. Luke and I agreed we wouldn't ask,' Ashleigh said.

'That's fabulous. Really fabulous.' Sammy was thrilled for her friends, she really was.

But at the same time there was a tiny chunk of ice in the middle of her heart.

One of the downsides of having chemotherapy at sixteen was that she'd had to have some eggs frozen in case she wanted to have children when she was older. But there were no guarantees that IVF would work—and she knew that could be a deal-breaker for any potential partner.

Including Nick. She thought about Nick. She had no idea whether he wanted children or not, and she couldn't think of an easy way to ask him. In any case, it was way too early to ask him right now. They'd only been out together twice. So she'd have to add it to the list of difficult conversations they'd need to have if things worked out between them. Cancer, fertility…no wonder her exes had panicked and run. And she was pretty sure that Nick had some issues, too. No way could someone with such a good heart and a keen intellect—perfect partner material—be single at his age without some emotional baggage.

Or maybe she was over-thinking it and she should just treat this whole thing as a chance to have some fun.

Whatever, she knew that she had to tell him the truth about herself.

But not just yet…

The following evening, Sammy met her best friends at Claire's shop for the dress fitting. She put on the high heels she planned to wear with the dress, and Claire adjusted the hem.

'You look a million dollars,' Ashleigh said, and looped the black pearls round Sammy's neck.

'Totally stunning,' Claire agreed. 'Your barrister isn't going to know what hit him.'

And there wasn't a single inch of leg displayed above Sammy's ankle. The dress was floaty, feminine and gorgeous, and Sammy didn't quite recognise herself in the mirror.

'Thank you. Both of you.' The lump in her throat made her voice all croaky.

'Hey. We want to see you as happy as we are,' Ashleigh said softly. 'Which doesn't mean we're trying to marry you off—you don't have to be married to be happy. But I know you've been lonely since Bryn.'

'Hey. I have a brilliant family and the best friends I could ask for,' Sammy said. 'Asking for more is greedy.'

'No, it's not,' Claire said. 'You deserve it. Enjoy your date.'

So what would his mysterious Woman in Black be wearing today? Nick wondered. Something dressy, given their surroundings. But he was pretty sure it would be black.

As he became aware of someone entering the room, he looked up from checking the emails on his phone and did a double take.

Not black, then.

And very, *very* dressy.

He'd never have believed that Sammy scrubbed up so well. She took his breath away. She was wearing only the lightest make-up, but that dress…

He stood up when she walked over to their table. 'You look amazing,' he said.

She blushed. 'Thank you.'

'Really amazing,' he said, sitting down again after the waiter had seated her.

'And note that I'm not wearing black,' she said with a self-deprecating smile.

He smiled. 'I'd guessed that you'd wear a little black dress. I'm glad I was wrong.'

'I did tell you that my best friend's a dress designer. And she's amazingly talented.'

'I'll second that,' he said.

The waiter ran through the list of teas. 'I'd recommend one of the black or green teas with the sandwiches and savouries,' he said, 'and then a fruit infusion with the sweet selection.'

'That sounds perfect,' Sammy said. 'Could I have Earl Grey, please?'

'And for me, too,' Nick said.

'I've never been here,' she said when the waiter had gone. 'Claire and Ash—my best friends—would love this. It's like a proper Regency drawing room. And there's even a pianist.'

Nick raised an eyebrow. 'He could be playing this one especially for you right now.'

'Debussy's "Girl with the Flaxen Hair".' She smiled back. 'Maybe.'

'Not a fan of Debussy?' he asked.

'Beethoven all the way for me,' Sammy said.

Romantic. Why didn't that surprise him?

The waiter brought over their tea in a silver pot, and a sage-and-cream striped porcelain tray to match their cups, saucers and tea plates, filled with a selection of sandwiches and savouries.

'I'm really glad I skipped lunch,' Sammy said. 'I don't know where to start. The sandwiches—smoked salmon, roast beef, ham, or cucumber and cream cheese?'

'I'd say the Welsh rarebit first, as it's hot,' Nick suggested. 'Then maybe we should start at one end of the tray of sandwiches and work our way through.'

'Great idea. This is such a treat. Thank you so much for inviting me.'

'I can't think of anyone I'd rather share this with,' Nick said. And he realised how true it was. He enjoyed Sammy's company hugely. Strange that this was only their third official date. It felt as if he'd known her for years and years. He was comfortable with her, felt that he could be himself—and that was such a rare feeling. Something that made him want to take things a lot further between them. Because maybe Sammy was the one he could learn to trust. The one who'd help to mend his heart again.

Once they'd finished the savoury platter, he excused himself and had a quiet word with the pianist.

When the waiter brought the fruit teas—lemon verbena for him and strawberry and rhubarb for Sammy—

with the three-tiered cake stand containing the sweet selection, Sammy looked at Nick with slightly narrowed eyes. 'Did you just say something to the pianist?'

'I might've done,' he said, lifting one shoulder in a shrug.

'The Moonlight Sonata is my favourite piece of music in the world,' she said softly. 'And it's perfect right now. Perfect music, perfect food—and perfect company.'

His thoughts entirely. He gave her a tiny bow. 'Why, thank you, ma'am.'

They made short work of the scones with clotted cream and jam, the lavender shortbread and the tiny rich selection of pastries.

'Oh, yes—a verrine,' Sammy said, looking at the shot glass filled with panna cotta. 'I love it when I get a commission in Paris. It means I get the chance to go to a certain patisserie and have one of their deconstructed desserts.'

'Want to swap mine for your super-chocolatey brownie?' he asked.

She blinked. 'You remembered that I don't like chocolate cake?'

'Of course.' Why was she so surprised? Or maybe she'd just dated the wrong kind of man in the past. Someone who was selfish and never put her first. That would explain why she was single: dating someone selfish would definitely put you off relationships. Naomi had put him off relationships just as badly.

'I've really enjoyed this,' she said when they'd finished. 'Though I don't think I'm going to eat again for a week!'

'Agreed. Though could I tempt you to a glass of wine back at my place?' he asked.

She smiled. 'I'd like that.'

He ordered a taxi to take them back to his flat.

Nick already had half a dozen bottles of his favourite white wines chilling in his wine cooler; he swiftly opened one and poured them both a glass.

'This is lovely,' Sammy said when she'd taken a sip. 'What is it?'

'Montrachet,' he explained. 'It's one of the grand cru chardonnays.'

'It's gorgeous. Really smooth.'

He hooked up his phone to his stereo system, and set some Beethoven piano music playing. And when Sammy put her wine glass on the low coffee table, she ended up curled against him on the sofa, with her head resting on his shoulder.

They didn't even have to talk; and it felt so good, just being together. She felt more relaxed with Nick than she ever had with anyone else—even in the early days with Bryn, before he'd killed her love stone dead and broken her heart.

She knew she ought to tell Nick about her past and explain about her leg; but she just couldn't find the right words, and she didn't want to spoil what had been such a perfect afternoon.

She reached up to trace the curve of his mouth with a forefinger. 'I really enjoyed today.'

'Me, too,' he said.

Even though she knew it was being greedy, wanting something she couldn't have, she couldn't resist stealing a kiss. He responded instantly, wrapping his arms tightly round her and kissing her back.

Everything about this man felt right.

But the fear was still there. Would she repulse him? When push came to shove, would he too think she wasn't enough of a woman for him?

'Nick, I really have to go,' she said softly. 'I've got a train to Edinburgh at the crack of dawn tomorrow, and it's a four-and-a-half-hour journey.'

'Can I drive you home? I've only had one glass of wine, so I'm below the limit for driving. And yes, I know you're perfectly capable of taking the Tube,' he added swiftly, 'but you're wearing high heels and that gorgeous dress and it won't be much fun keeping the hem out of the way on the escalators.'

True. And she liked the way he was thinking of her. 'Thank you. That would be nice,' she said. Plus it meant she got to spend just a little bit more time with him.

'So what are you doing in Edinburgh?' he asked as he drove her home.

'I'm taking a portrait of a sculptor for one of the Sunday magazines. Actually, it's someone whose work I've admired for a while, so I'm really looking forward to meeting him,' she said. 'What about you?'

'Preparing for a trial which starts next week and might go on for a fortnight or so. How long are you away for?'

'Three days,' she said. 'Shall I call you when I get back?' And maybe on that long train journey she'd find the right words to tell him about her leg. And, if they managed to negotiate that and come out the other side in one piece, maybe they could do Date Four. Take another step towards a real relationship.

'I'd like that,' he said. He parked outside her flat.

'And I'm guessing you have to pack, check over your equipment and charge up various batteries.'

'Something like that,' she said.

'Then I won't ask to come in for coffee.' He cupped her face in his hand and kissed her goodnight so sweetly that she felt the tears prick her eyelids. 'Sleep well,' he said softly.

'You too,' she said, and stole a last kiss before climbing out of his car.

There was a message on her phone when she got up the next morning. Short, sweet and to the point: Safe journey.

Have a good day in chambers, she typed back.

She could really get used to dating Nick Kennedy.

But before she got too comfortable she really had to tell him the truth about herself…

CHAPTER SEVEN

WHILE SAMMY WAS in Edinburgh, she had a chance to explore some of the shoreline of the Firth of Forth; the sculptor whose photograph she was taking was inspired by it, and took her and Ben, the journalist, for a short drive from the city down to Yellowcraigs. They headed off the beaten track, down through a pretty village to the parking area, and then walked out to the beach.

The long, sweeping cove was beautiful. 'I love this sky. I could take your picture here,' Sammy suggested.

'Or on Fidra.' Jimmy McBain pointed to the island. 'I thought we could get a boat over there this morning.'

'Sounds good to me.' Sammy smiled at the journalist. 'OK with you, Ben?'

'I'm not the world's best sailor,' the journalist admitted, 'but I'll give it a go.'

'Just as well I told you to bring your walking boots in a plastic bag,' Jimmy said with a grin. 'And we'll cheer you up when we get back with a wee dram.'

Sammy took a few shots of Jimmy on the beach while he chatted to them about the area.

'So why is the name Fidra familiar?' Ben asked.

Sammy knew the answer to that one. 'Robert Louis Stevenson spent his holidays there as a boy.' When Ben still looked puzzled, she said, 'Pieces of eight? Long John Silver?'

'Oh—*Treasure Island*.'

'That's the one,' Jimmy said, looking pleased. Sammy took a few more shots of the cove while Jimmy was talking to the skipper of a boat, and she thought of Nick and his misty shoreline painting. He'd love it here, she was sure. On impulse, she took a snap of the island on her phone and sent it to him.

Guess where I am?

Clearly he was in chambers rather than in court, because he answered straight away.

I thought you said you were going to Edinburgh?

I did. We're half an hour or so's drive away. This is the island of Fidra.

Fidra?

She smiled.

Tsk. You must've read Treasure Island when you were a kid?

That's Treasure Island?

Jimmy the Sculptor says that's what inspired Robert Louis Stevenson. I think you'd like it here. Ice creams, cafes, miles of sand, and apparently just down the road is biggest colony of puffins on the east coast.

Sounds great, was the response.

Had they been dating long enough to think about going away together? She typed, Wish you were here, then stopped herself. She did wish that she were sharing this with Nick, but was telling him a step too far? She went to delete the message but accidentally pressed the wrong button and sent it instead.

Oh, no.

This time, there was no reply.

Well, it served her right for being way too forward. Of course it was too soon to think about going away together. How ridiculous of her to think otherwise.

Thankfully right then they had to get on the boat, and after that her time was caught up taking photographs, so it stopped her brooding about the situation.

Then her phone beeped on their way back to the city.

Sorry about earlier. I was called back to court so my phone was off. Wish I was there, too.

It made Sammy feel all warm inside.

And it clearly showed on her face, because Jimmy patted her arm. 'Message from your man, was it?'

'Yes.'

'He's a lucky lad. You'd have plenty of admirers up here, even though your haircut's…well.' He rolled his eyes. 'You'd be a bonnier lass if you'd let it grow.'

She smiled back. 'It's short right now because I donate my hair to make wigs for children who've had cancer.'

Jimmy whistled. 'So you've a good heart, too. That's rare. Bonny, and with a good heart.'

'And it'd make a great story,' Ben said, looking interested.

'Agreed. I can get you some people to interview, if you like,' Sammy said. 'Especially as I happened to shoot a calendar which is going to raise money for the cancer ward. You could maybe do an article on that. Hot men stripping off to raise money.'

'It'd be a good human interest story.' Ben held her gaze. 'And I can start by interviewing you.'

She shook her head. 'I'd rather stay behind the lens.'

He could see that she meant it and he left it there rather than nagging, but Sammy found herself thinking about it on the way back to London, the next morning. Maybe if she went public about her experience, it would help someone else to get through their own situation. And talking to Ben about it might be a good test run, something that would give her the courage to talk to Nick.

'Ben—did you mean it about that interview?' she asked.

'Which one?' He groaned. 'Sorry. My brain is totally scrambled. Never let me agree to drink with a Scots guy again.'

'Or a cider producer in Somerset—I'm sure you had a hangover after that interview, too,' she said with a grin. 'I mean the article about the charity calendar and why I donate my hair.'

'Yes, I meant it. Though give me a while for my brain to unscramble so I can work up some decent questions.'

'Sure. I'll get you a cup of tea and a bacon sandwich from the buffet.' And she'd better hope that her courage didn't fail her in the time between now and when her colleague had recovered from his hangover.

It didn't. And Ben was incredibly kind with his questions.

'I had no idea that you'd been through all that,' he said when he'd finished the interview.

'I don't talk about it because I don't want cancer to define me,' she said simply.

He nodded. 'I admired you before, because you're always so professional and you deliver every single time. But knowing you had to cope with all that as well—you're really amazing, Sammy.'

'That isn't why I told you. It's not about my ego. I want to give other people some hope so they know you really can come out the other side of the experience and it'll be OK,' she said. 'Though is there any way you can do the piece without actually revealing who I am?'

He raised an eyebrow. 'You think people might not want to hire you because you're a cancer survivor?'

'Some people don't react so well,' she said. Personally as well as professionally. Not that she wanted to explain that.

Ben gave her a pithy response about precisely what that kind of people could do.

'I still have to earn my living,' she said.

'I'll talk to my editor and see if we can find a way round it,' he said. 'But thank you. Now I know your story—well, I'm really proud to call myself your colleague.'

'And friend,' she said. 'Now shut up before I start being wet.'

He grinned. 'That's the last word I'd ever use to describe you.'

Talking to Ben had been so easy.

But was that simply because he was a journalist, used to asking questions and teasing the real story out of reluctant interviewees? Would it be as easy, talking to Nick?

Ben was her colleague. Her friend. She'd known him for years. There was no way that her past could change their relationship.

Whereas Nick was…

Help.

Not her lover. Not yet. Though she wanted him to be. 'Boyfriend' sounded twee. Partner? They hadn't been together that long. But she really felt she'd clicked with him. While she'd been away in Edinburgh, she'd really missed him, and it had shocked her how much she'd wanted to share all her new experiences with him. Had he missed her? Or had he been so busy that he'd barely registered her absence?

She was probably over-thinking things again.

Why couldn't she be like she was in every other area of her life? Why couldn't she just step up and do it? Tell him?

'You are such a coward, Samantha Jane Thompson,' she told herself grimly.

Back at her flat, she found a rectangular parcel waiting for her. It had fitted perfectly through her letterbox, and she recognised the box as one from a very exclusive chocolatier.

There was a note with it in bold script that was clearly from a fountain pen:

Welcome home. Missed you.

So he *had* missed her as much as she'd missed him. And what a welcome home. She hardly knew where to start when she opened the box; they were glorious, and each one was a treat. Best of all was the dark chocolate violet crème.

She glanced at her watch. It was a Saturday, but Nick had said that he was preparing for a trial. He was probably knee-deep in paperwork. Better not to disturb him, then. She texted him instead of calling.

Thank you so much for the chocolates. They're sublime. Might not be any left by the time I see you! *insert guilty smiley*

When he didn't reply, she knew that her guess about him being really busy was right. But, to her surprise, he called her at half past five.

'Hey. So did you find any treasure on your island?'

'I took some good shots, if that counts.' She laughed. 'And thank you for the chocolates. They're amazing. Though, um, there aren't many left to share with you.'

'My pleasure. Besides, they're meant for you, not for sharing.' His voice was full of warmth. 'I just wanted to welcome you back.'

And how. Which gave her the courage to suggest Date Four. Something she hadn't done in a long, long time. 'Are you busy tonight, or do you want to do something?'

'Aren't you tired after that long train journey?' he asked.

'A bit,' she admitted, 'but if you're not busy maybe we could have a quick drink or something.'

'I really missed you,' he said softly. 'How about we compromise and I'll come over to you with a takeaway?'

She'd been away for three days so she hadn't had a chance to restock her fridge, apart from the carton of milk she'd grabbed at the train station. She padded over to it and glanced inside. 'It seems I have a bottle of Prosecco in the fridge,' she said. She opened the freezer door. 'And some posh ice cream.'

'Perfect. I'll order something to be delivered to yours and be with you at seven.'

'Sounds good to me.'

At precisely seven, her doorbell rang. She opened the door and greeted Nick with a hug. 'Hey.' Then she stepped back and took in his appearance; he was wearing an expensively cut wool suit, a handmade white shirt and an understated silk tie.

'I feel very scruffy compared with you,' she said. 'I wish now I'd changed.'

'Instead of working?' He smiled. 'You had a long journey and it was sensible to dress for comfort.'

'I can change now.'

'Too late. Dinner's just arrived,' he said, indicating the white van emblazoned with the name of a Thai restaurant that had pulled up outside her flat. 'Perfect timing, too.'

Over dinner, she showed him some of the shots of Fidra.

'That beach looks amazing,' he said.

'It's gorgeous. That sweeping cove…'

'Maybe,' he said, 'we could go there together sometime.'

Maybe. If he still wanted to know her, once she'd told him about her past.

But for a workaholic like Nick to suggest taking some time away… 'I'd like that,' she said.

They ended up stretched out on her sofa, all warm and smoochy. Sammy's legs were entangled with his,

his hands were flat against her back underneath her T-shirt—and how good his skin felt against hers—and her arms were wrapped round his neck.

It would be oh, so easy to suggest that they moved from her sofa to her bed, where they could shut the world away. Where they could take the time to explore each other, discover where each other liked being touched and kissed.

Except…she still hadn't told him.

And letting him find out by seeing her scar—or, worse, touching it by accident—would be totally wrong.

'Sammy? Is everything OK?'

Clearly he'd picked up on her tension.

'Just tired,' she fibbed. 'It's been a long few days with a lot of travelling.'

Nick kissed her gently. 'I'd better go and let you get some sleep.'

Now. Tell him now. Don't be such a coward. He's not going to run for the hills. He's not going to react the way Bryn and the others did.

'Sorry,' she said, chickening out.

'It's fine. I'll call you tomorrow.' He gave her a last lingering kiss. 'I'll see myself out. Sweet dreams.'

And, even though she was tired, she couldn't sleep. She lay there in the dark, regretting her cowardice. Why was it so hard to tell him the truth?

Over the next couple of weeks, Sammy and Nick spent as much time together as they could. The more she got to know him, the more she liked him, and she hoped it might be the same for him. They had similar tastes in music; they both liked complicated whodunnit dramas—though he always made some comment about the legal bits being wrong—and they both liked outrageous stand-up comedy and long walks on the beach and browsing through little art galleries.

This could be perfect. With Nick, she felt as if she really fitted.

All she had to do was tell him.

The truth, the whole truth and nothing but the truth.

How hard could it be?

She even practised it in front of the mirror. *Nick, there's something I need to tell you. I'll understand if you want to call the whole thing off, but fourteen years ago I had...*

Six letters.

Two syllables.

A word that could explode someone's whole world and leave nothing but rubble.

Three dates on the trot, she tried to tell him—and failed.

Then he said to her, 'On Saturday, Mandy's going on a spa day with a couple of her friends—it's a birthday present from them. I promised her I'd look after the boys for her.' He paused. 'I was wondering, would you like to spend the day with us?'

He wanted her to meet his family?

This was serious.

And this was his nephew who'd had osteosarcoma.

Oh, help. She really, really needed to tell him about her past, but she still hadn't found the right time or the right words to tell him.

There was a wary look in his eyes; clearly he was half expecting her to refuse. It would probably be sensible to refuse, yet at the same time she didn't want to hurt him. How could she throw the offer back in his face? She had a feeling this wasn't the kind of thing he suggested very often.

'Actually,' she said, 'I like kids very much. I have two nieces and two nephews myself, and my family's really close. How old are the boys?'

'Xander's twelve and Ned's eight.'

'Good ages,' she said. Stupid. Any age was a good age. 'My nephews are very slightly older.' And now she was babbling. Focus, Sammy, she told herself. 'Maybe we could go to the park if it's a nice day, or somewhere like the Natural History Museum if it's wet.'

'That's a great idea,' he said. 'I'll pick you up.'

Tell him. Tell him now.

'Nick…'

'Yes?'

For a split second, she glimpsed vulnerability in his face.

No, she couldn't tell him right now.

'What?' he asked.

She thought on her feet. 'Please don't think I'm being nosey here, but I just need to know if there are any topics of conversation I ought to steer clear of on Saturday?'

He nodded. 'Xander's a bit sensitive about his leg. And we don't talk about their father.'

She winced inwardly. 'I take it from that, he let them down?'

'Big time,' he said, his face tightening. 'Mandy doesn't want anyone to badmouth him in front of the boys, in case he ever decides to come back into their lives, but…' He looked grim. 'I can't ever see that happening. Warren the Weasel walked out on them the day they got Xander's diagnosis, eighteen months ago, and they haven't seen him since.'

Sammy sucked in a breath, shocked beyond measure. She could just about get her head round the reasons why someone might not be able to cope with their partner's diagnosis and walk away, but to do something like that to their child… 'That's pretty rough on your sister and the boys.'

'Yeah.' His lip curled. 'Warren's the most selfish man I've ever met. He hasn't even sent the boys a birthday or Christmas card since he left. Mandy's been trying to keep the lines of communication open and she takes them to see his parents. Warren's mother always makes excuses for him, saying he's "sensitive"—' Nick made exaggerated quote marks with his fingers as he said the words '—but he's certainly not sensitive to his sons' feelings. Or to his ex-wife's. The only people he cares about are me, myself and I.' He blew out a breath. 'Thankfully Mandy had the sense to divorce him for unreasonable behaviour, and he had the sense not to dispute it.'

With a hotshot barrister as an ex-brother-in-law, Warren would have been very stupid indeed to try to contest a divorce petition, Sammy thought. And it sounded as if Nick seriously disliked the man.

'I'm sorry,' she said.

Nick shrugged. 'It's not your fault.'

'I know, but still a horrible situation for you all to deal with.' She took a deep breath. 'And that's empathy speaking, not pity.' She'd had enough pity after her diagnosis to last a lifetime; no way would she ever give pity to someone else.

He drew her into his arms and held her close. 'Thank you. It's appreciated.' He sighed and brushed his mouth against her hair. 'We're not very good at marriage in my family.'

So was this the reason why he was single? Because he'd been so badly bitten that he didn't want to risk falling in love again? Not sure what to say, she stroked his face.

'Sorry. I shouldn't burden you with my woes,' he said, looking guilty.

'No, that's fine. And it's not going any further than me.'

He kissed her lightly. 'I know. And thanks. Again.' He grimaced. 'I guess you ought to know what you're getting yourself into. My parents split up when I was seventeen. My sister—well, I've told you about the weasel she married. And I'm divorced as well. So we're not a good bet, the Kennedys.'

'Or maybe you haven't met the right person for you yet.' She worked it out. He would've been in the middle of his exams when his parents split up. A really vulnerable, impressionable time.

'Maybe,' he said. 'Dad kind of buried himself in work after my mother left.'

Not 'Mum', she noticed. It sounded as if he wasn't close to his mother. Did he blame her for the divorce? But asking felt too much like prying.

'Do you see much of your parents?' she asked carefully.

'Dad lives in Brussels, so we don't see him that often.' He gave her a rueful smile. 'He specialises in European law. I guess he hoped I'd follow in his footsteps, but I like London too much.'

'What about your mother?'

He shrugged. 'She's even further away, in Cornwall.'

She frowned. 'How can Cornwall be further away from London than Brussels?'

'It's quicker to get the Eurostar to Brussels than to drive to the far depths of Cornwall,' he said.

She had a feeling that there was a bit more to it than that, but pushing would be unfair. 'So they don't get to see much of their grandchildren, then?'

'No. Which is a shame, because Mandy could've done with their support after Warren left. Dad's very busy in Brussels, and our mother has her B&B to think about. But Mandy knows she can always rely on me, even though I'm the baby of the family.' He smiled. 'And it's not a burden—not at all. Xander and Ned are nice kids. Plus it means I have a cast-iron excuse to see all the superhero films at the cinema, because I can take them.'

'Sounds good. I do something similar with my nephews and nieces,' she said lightly.

Guilt seeped through her. Nick had been open with her. She really ought to tell him what he was getting into, too. The spectre of cancer, fertility issues, the fact she wasn't really a whole woman…the Sammy Thompson he'd met was a fake.

But the words dried up in her throat when she tried to utter them.

She'd tell him.

Soon.

And was it so wrong to want to feel like a normal person without complications for just that little bit longer, instead of turning into Sammy-the-cancer-survivor?

CHAPTER EIGHT

SATURDAY DAWNED BRIGHT and sunny. Although it was the beginning of October it was still really warm.

Nick called Sammy's landline. 'We're outside in the car,' he said.

'Great. I'm coming out to join you,' she told him.

To her secret amusement, although he was wearing jeans he was also wearing another of those white hand-made shirts; she guessed he was always going to have that touch of formality.

The boys were both sitting in the back of the car. Sammy could see the family resemblance to Nick in their dark hair and dark eyes. She was curious as to how he was going to introduce her to them: as his friend or as his girlfriend?

'Boys, this is my friend Sammy,' he said. 'Sammy, these are my nephews, Xander and Ned.'

Friend, then—which was sensible. Especially given the situation with their father; Nick obviously wouldn't want to introduce the boys to a string of 'aunties', feeling that they'd had enough change in their life already. She could understand that.

The boys chorused hello, both looking slightly shy.

Sammy smiled at them. 'It's very nice to meet you

both. Nick says we're going to the park—is that OK with you?'

Ned looked thrilled. 'They have a really cool zip-wire at the park.'

'That sounds like fun,' she said. 'Are adults allowed on it?'

'You like zip-wires?' Ned asked, his eyes round with surprise.

'I love them,' she said. 'Race you?'

'You're on,' Ned said with a grin.

Nick drove them to a park that the boys clearly knew well. There was a play area with a massive slide wide enough to take four people at a time and a low zip-wire, and the boys spent most of their time there. Sammy raced Nick down the slide and joined the boys on the zip-wire.

Then she noticed a stall selling water pistols and nudged Nick. 'My brothers, sister and I loved that sort of thing when I was a kid. I bet the boys will, too.'

He raised his eyebrows. 'You're challenging us to a water fight?'

'Ah, no. I was thinking me and the boys versus you.'

'Three against one? That's totally unfair.' But he was laughing, so she was pretty sure he was up for it. 'Where are we going to get water from?' he asked.

She gestured to the kiosk at the other side of the playing field. 'I'm pretty sure they'll sell bottled water. That'll do the job.'

'Hmm.'

'Ned, Xander—team huddle,' she said, beckoning the boys over.

'Team huddle?' they asked, mystified, but went with her.

'Water fight. Us versus Uncle Nick,' she explained economically. 'What do you think?'

'Yeah,' they chorused, each pumping a fist into the air.

She bought four water pistols and two large bottles of still water, and she enjoyed charging round with the boys and doing her best to soak Nick with water. Though she noticed that Xander was looking tired at almost the same time as Nick clearly did, because Nick stopped dead and said, 'Right, time for a truce.'

'Not a chance,' she said.

He came over to her and lowered his voice. 'They've been running around like mad and Xander's in danger of overdoing it. He needs to rest.'

She murmured back, 'I know. Trust me.' Then she turned to Xander. 'I've been thinking—with three of us, we're getting in each other's way. I reckon we need a master strategist to direct us, and I think out of the three of us you'd be the best one to do that.'

The boy looked slightly suspicious. 'Master strategist? Really?'

'Really,' she confirmed. 'Come and sit down here by this tree so you've got the best view of the field. Now, imagine you're the shepherd, Ned and I are the sheepdogs, and Uncle Nick's the big fat sheep who's about to get a bath.'

'And?'

'So you need to direct us,' she said. 'And if you do it right, then we win and your Uncle Nick gets totally soaked.'

Xander stopped looking suspicious and grinned. 'Let's do it.'

She and Ned followed Xander's shouted directions, and finally managed to soak Nick from head to foot.

'OK, I surrender,' Nick said, laughing.

And, with that white shirt and his jeans plastered to his skin so the outline of his pectorals and gluteus maximus were perfectly defined, he looked utterly gorgeous. Sammy had already noticed how many female heads he was turning during the water fight, and several more seemed to be showing interest in a hot, wet man.

'We won, Sammy!' Ned crowed. He rushed over to her and hugged her.

'That's because we had a great strategy director,' she said, and high-fived Xander and then Ned, who both beamed at her.

'Not that brilliant,' Nick said calmly. Before Sammy realised what he was planning to do, he'd picked up all four water pistols and soaked her. 'Revenge,' he said with a grin, 'is sweet.'

'Oh, you monster—you'd already surrendered so that's totally cheating,' she said, laughing. 'For that you can buy me an ice cream, and I'm going to sit down here and get Xander to protect me.' She took one of the water pistols from Nick, refilled it, and handed it to Xander. 'You're my bodyguard.'

'Cool,' Xander said.

'Can we have ice creams, too? A whippy one with a chocolate flake?' Ned asked hopefully, adding belatedly, 'Please?'

'Whippy ice cream with a chocolate flake—is there any other kind?' Sammy teased.

'Hint taken.' Nick rolled his eyes. 'Come on, Ned. Let's go and queue up.'

Xander had gone quiet, she noticed. 'Are you OK?' she asked softly when Nick and Ned had left.

The boy sighed. 'I just wish… I hate my stupid leg. I know you're just being nice about letting me rest.'

'Hey. We needed you as our strategy director,' she said. 'And now to protect me against sneaky water attacks from Nick.'

'I'm twelve, not a baby like Ned—I knew what you were doing. But my leg had started hurting a bit so I went along with it.' Then he glanced at her. 'Sorry, Uncle Nick and Mum would be mad at me for being rude to you.'

'You're not being rude, just honest—and if your leg starts aching of course it's going to make you feel fed up and grumpy.'

'It aches nearly all the time,' Xander said with a sigh. 'They had to take part of my bone away, so there's a metal thing in my leg they have to expand when the rest of my bones grow.'

'Meaning you don't have to have lots of operations, just the one? That's really good,' she said.

He blinked at her. 'Uncle Nick says you know someone who had what I did. That's why you photographed him and everyone else for the calendar.'

'I do.' She paused. This was a huge risk—but it might help the boy to feel a bit happier. 'Want to know a secret?'

'What sort of secret?'

'A really, really big secret. But you have to promise not to tell anyone,' she warned.

'Cross my heart and hope to die,' he said, making the sign of a cross over his heart with his fingertip.

Sammy glanced over towards Nick. He and Ned

were in the queue at the ice cream van so they probably couldn't see, but even so she shifted so she could hide her legs from Nick's view in case he turned round, and pushed up the left leg of her jeans to her knee.

Xander's eyes went wide. 'You've got a scar in the same place as me.'

'Yes, and for exactly the same reason,' she said softly. 'But I was a little bit older than you—I was sixteen when I had my op.'

'Did it hurt?'

'My leg?' At his nod, she said softly, 'After the op, yes.'

'Does it hurt now?'

'No.'

'And you had to have more than one op?'

'Luckily not, because I'd pretty much stopped growing at sixteen—but some of my friends did.' She swallowed hard. 'This is your and my secret, Xander, OK?'

'OK,' Xander said.

'Good. And it's important to do your exercises, even when they're boring and even when they hurt a little bit.'

'Why?' he asked.

'Because it means you get strong,' she said. 'And, next time you think you can't do something and your leg's holding you back, remember that I go all over the world in my job. It doesn't hold me back.'

'Have you been to Australia?' he challenged.

'And America, and Japan.' She paused. 'And I climbed Mount Kilimanjaro three years ago.'

His eyes went wide. 'Really? You climbed a mountain? Even after...you know?'

'Yup. I can show you the photographs. I went as the

team photographer, but obviously I had to go where they went, so that meant climbing with them.'

He looked impressed. 'That's *so* cool.'

'I know. Though I guess I should admit that it isn't the climb that's the hard thing—it's not like rock-climbing where you see people sticking an axe into the cliff or what have you and hauling themselves up. It's the altitude that makes it difficult. The air's really thin, so you have to walk incredibly slowly or you can't breathe and get dizzy. And sleeping on the hard ground for five or six nights really makes you ache all over. But it was worth it. The views were amazing.' She high-fived him. 'And if I can do anything I like after having osteosarcoma, then so can you. Never, ever let your cancer define you. Because you're more than that.'

For a second, his eyes glistened with tears, but he blinked them away. 'Thanks, Sammy.' His voice was a little hoarse.

'Any time,' she said. 'And any time you want to talk to me, you can—I'll keep whatever you tell me confidential. Uncle Nick's got my phone and email.'

'Thanks—it's really nice having someone who understands.'

Sammy had the strongest feeling that he wanted to tell her something. So she waited, knowing from experience as a photographer that people always filled a silence if you gave them the time.

And he did.

'Uncle Nick always makes me stop and rest before I'm really ready.'

'It's because he loves you,' she said gently, 'and he worries about you, and he's scared you'll overdo it and give yourself a setback.' Just what her family had said to her, when she'd finally lost her temper with everyone and yelled about how being wrapped in cotton wool drove her crazy.

'But I won't overdo it—I'm *twelve*, not stupid.'

'He knows that,' she said, 'but sometimes when you love someone and you're scared for them, that kind of stops you thinking straight.'

'So what do I do?'

'Tell him,' she said simply, knowing that she was the biggest hypocrite in the world—because she hadn't told Nick what he really ought to know, had she? 'Sit down with him and tell him what you told me. Tell him you're doing all your exercises and you want to get strong, so you're not going to overdo it because you know that'll mean you have to wait even longer before you're fully recovered. Promise him you'll always say when you're tired or you've had enough, and then he'll relax a bit.'

'Is that what you did?'

'Eventually. After a big fight.' And even now she knew she sometimes overdid the independence bit, but she couldn't help it.

Xander nodded. 'I love Uncle Nick. He's a better dad to me than…' He dragged in a breath. 'I'm not supposed to talk about that, either.'

'That your dad left?'

He nodded. 'I hate him. He left us when Mum really needed him. She still cries when she doesn't think I can hear her. I used to think it was my fault for getting sick, but Uncle Nick said it wasn't that at all. I once heard him call my dad a—well, he's right, but Mum would kill me if I used that word.'

Sammy's heart bled for him. She still couldn't get

her head round how anyone could be so selfish as to put themselves before their child, especially when their child really needed them. She gave him a hug. 'Xander, if I had a magic wand, I'd fix this—but people are complicated. Maybe your dad was just really scared.'

'Uncle Nick's scared. Mum's scared. Ned's scared. But they didn't leave.' He lifted his head. 'Did your dad leave you when you got cancer?'

'Nope. But some of my boyfriends did.'

'Because they were scared?'

'Something like that.'

'Then they were weasels and you deserve better,' Xander said. 'That's what Uncle Nick says about Dad to Mum.'

'When he thinks you can't hear?'

The boy nodded. 'And because she'd yell at him for using the other word.'

She ruffled his hair. 'I take it they don't know you have ears like a bat, then.'

Xander smiled. 'No. I sometimes think I'd like to be Batman, though.'

'You and me both. Though I'd rather be the Black Widow.'

'In the Avengers? Yeah. She's awesome.'

They were still laughing when Nick and Ned came back with the ice creams.

'What's so funny?' Nick asked.

'We're talking about superhero movies,' Sammy said.

'Sammy wants to be the Black Widow,' Xander informed him.

Nick stood so that the boys couldn't see him and mouthed, 'That works for me—she's hot.'

Sammy had a hard time keeping a straight face and dealing with the rush of heat that went through her.

'I want to be Spiderman,' Ned said.

'And I'm Batman,' Xander said. 'Who would you be, Uncle Nick?'

He sighed. 'You've already bagsied both my favourites.'

'You can be Robin,' Xander said kindly.

Nick shook his head. 'No. I think I'll be Iron Man.'

Sammy shifted so that only Nick could see her face, caught his eye, and mouthed, 'Works for me—*he's* hot.' She had the satisfaction of seeing colour slash across Nick's cheeks. Yeah. Two could play at that game.

And she pushed away the fact that she still hadn't told him the truth.

They went to a fried chicken place for lunch on the way home. Nick turned to Sammy when the boys were out of earshot. 'Thank you—you found a nice way to make Xander rest and not feel that he was missing out. And I apologise. I thought at first you were pushing him too hard.'

She nodded grimly. 'A word to the wise—don't wrap him in cotton wool, because he'll resent it later. You need to find a way of keeping him right in the middle of things and yet resting at the same time.'

'That sounds like experience talking.'

'Uh-huh.' She certainly couldn't tell him what Xander had confided in her, as she'd promised to keep it to herself.

'Would this be your sister who was wrapped in cotton wool?' Nick asked softly.

No, it had been her, for the first week. But, after that huge fight, Sammy's family had learned to support her instead of smothering her. Most of the time. She knew they still panicked, which was why she didn't always tell them if she felt any kind of twinge in her leg. 'I'd rather not talk about it,' she said.

'Your sister's not…?' He stopped and winced. 'I'm sorry. I didn't mean to rip the top off your scars.'

'My sister's fine. Now let's change the subject. I'm sorry for soaking you.'

'I got my own back.'

'Yeah, and your car's a bit soggy.'

'It'll dry,' he said. 'Thank you. You're good with the boys.'

'I'm an aunt of four,' she reminded him, 'so I jolly well ought to be good with kids by now.' She pushed back the surge of longing. She had to be realistic and recognise that she might have to content herself with being an aunt or a godmother. But she'd deal with it when she had to.

'My ex wasn't good with kids,' he said. 'She never really enjoyed spending time with the boys.'

Because she wanted kids of her own and his attention had been focused on them? Sammy wondered. 'That's a shame,' she said.

He gave her a thin smile. 'Yeah. There wasn't a maternal bone in Naomi's body.'

Ah. So she'd got it wrong and Nick's ex hadn't wanted kids. And it sounded as if it had been an issue between them. Maybe one of the issues that had led to their divorce.

Did Nick want children? Sammy wasn't brave enough to ask—because she knew this might be the deal-breaker for their relationship. If he wanted kids and she couldn't give them to him, what then?

Sammy was still damp by the time they got back to his sister's house.

'I can't make you sit around in wet clothes,' Nick said. 'Look, you're about the same size as Mandy. I can go and get something for you to change into. She won't mind.'

Sammy went cold—supposing he brought down a skirt? Something that would show him her scar? That wasn't the way she wanted to tell him. And she wished she'd been brave enough to tell him before. 'No, it's fine,' she said with a smile. 'I'll soon dry out in the back garden.' She indicated the patio table and chairs. 'Do you have a pack of cards?'

'We do,' Xander said, and went to fetch them while Nick organised drinks.

Sammy shuffled the cards. 'This was my favourite card game when I was your age. It's called Cheat—you go round in turn and put down the next named card. So if I start with an ace, Xander would put down a two, Nick would put down a three, and Ned would put down a four.'

Ned frowned. 'But that doesn't sound like fun.'

'Oh, yes, it is,' she said. 'Because you put the cards face down on the table, and nobody knows if I've put down say four aces, or four completely different cards.'

'So if you put down three fives and I don't have any sixes, I put down a card and pretend it's a six?' Xander asked.

'Exactly. And if I've got four sixes, I know you haven't put down a six, so I'd say Cheat and you'd have to pick up all the cards on the table. But if I've got three sixes and someone else has got one six, we won't know if you're cheating or not…unless you giggle and give yourself away.' She smiled. 'Uncle Nick should be good at this. He'll be able to see if people aren't telling the truth.'

He did. And Sammy let him win the first round.

And then she played the way she had with her family, half a lifetime ago. As a total card sharp. With a grin, she put down her last cards, saying, 'Three fours.'

Nick frowned. 'Hang on, you laid down three fours last time it was fours—and there aren't seven fours in a pack of cards.' He pointed a finger at her. 'Cheat!'

She turned over the last three cards, one by one. The four of diamonds, the four of clubs and the four of hearts.

'But—how?' Nick asked plaintively.

She laughed. 'Because I cheated massively last time and you didn't spot it.'

'You're really good at this,' Xander said admiringly.

She winked at him. 'My dad taught me how to play when I was Ned's age—and I have two big brothers and a big sister, so I had to learn to be really good at this or they'd sit on me.'

'Really sit on you?' Ned's eyes went wide.

She laughed. 'No, not *really*, but when you're the littlest it's hard to come last all the time, and I always knew if they were being kind and let me win.'

'I don't like it when Xander lets me win,' Ned confided in a whisper.

She ruffled his hair. 'Then, young Spiderman, let me give you some tips…'

Mandy came back just before tea time.

'Thank you so much,' she said to Sammy, shaking her hand. 'I feel so guilty about dumping my parental responsibilities on Nick and on you, especially as I hadn't even met you!'

'Not at all,' Sammy said firmly. 'Apart from the fact that it's your birthday weekend, I had a really good afternoon and your boys are lovely. And it's tough being a single mum. Having a break means you're refreshed and can enjoy the kids more.'

Mandy blinked. 'Wow, that's... I'm not used to people being that understanding.'

Sammy smiled. 'Remember, I'm a photographer. I've met an awful lot of people and heard an awful lot of life stories over the years.' She blew on her nails and polished them against her T-shirt. 'Very wise that makes me, young Padawan.'

Mandy laughed. 'If you're Yoda, then how old does that make me?'

Sammy laughed back. 'About the same age as my oldest brother, I'd guess. Which is—ooh—*ancient*.'

Mandy grinned. 'I like you. Would you stay and have dinner with us?' She wrinkled her nose. 'Though I guess you'd want to spend some time alone with Nick.'

'If you're offering me just about anything followed by birthday cake that isn't chocolate,' Sammy said, 'I'm all yours. *And* I'll do the washing up.'

'Deal, even though I'd always pick chocolate cake first,' Mandy said with another grin. 'I take back what I said. I *really* like you.'

Sammy smiled. 'If you're like your brother and your sons, then I like you, too.'

'I like your hair—it's a pretty radical cut, but you've got the bone structure to get away with it.'

'Thank you,' Sammy said, 'but I don't have it cut this short for fashion.'

'What, then?'

'Didn't Nick tell you? I grow my hair and donate it every two years, when it's long enough to make a child's wig,' Sammy explained.

'A kid who's had chemo?' Mandy swallowed hard. 'Xander lost his hair when he had chemo.'

'That's the downside of chemo—but he's doing just fine,' Sammy said softly. 'Thanks to you, he's really well adjusted.'

'I hope so.'

Sammy saw the sheen of tears in Mandy's eyes and hugged her. 'Sorry, I didn't mean to make you cry.'

'It's not you—it just catches me unawares sometimes. I never met anyone who donated hair before. Maybe that's something I can do in the future,' Mandy said thoughtfully.

'My sister's a teacher. She makes everyone in the staff room sponsor her before we have our hair cut,' Sammy said.

Mandy nodded. 'I could do that, too.'

'And if you don't want to do it on your own, join us—except it's going to be another two years before our hair's long enough to do it again.'

'I'll do it next week,' Mandy said. 'And then I'll join you in two years.'

'It's a deal,' Sammy said.

She enjoyed sharing pizza, garlic bread and birthday cake with Nick's family. Later that evening, Nick took her home. 'Thank you,' he said as they sat in the car outside her flat. 'You've been brilliant.'

'I had a great day,' she said. 'I loved the zip-wire. And the water fight.'

His eyes went hot. 'Yeah. Me, too.'

She kissed him. 'You have no idea how many of the mums were ogling you.'

'You have no idea how many of the dads were ogling *you*,' he countered. 'You're a natural with kids.' He paused. 'I probably shouldn't ask you this, but would you think about having your own, some day?'

'Maybe,' she said carefully. And this really was the crunch question, as far as she was concerned. Now he'd brought it up, she'd have to be brave and ask him. 'What about you?'

'Some day.' He looked sad. 'I wanted them about five years ago, but my ex wasn't keen.'

'Is that why you broke up with her?' She realised how bad that sounded and clapped her hand to her mouth. 'Sorry. I was being intrusive. You don't have to answer that.'

'No, that's fine. And no, it isn't why we broke up. You could say that my job got in the way.'

From the look on his face, Sammy was pretty sure there was more to it than that, but now wasn't the time to pry. 'I'm sorry,' she said again.

'It wasn't your fault, so there's no need to apologise.' He leaned forward and stole a kiss. 'But every cloud has a silver lining. It means that you and I got to meet.'

'There is that to it.' But he definitely wanted kids, and she might not be able to do that. She needed time to think. Time to work out how to tell him the truth about herself. She kissed him lingeringly. 'I would invite you in, but—'

'—you've got an early start tomorrow?' he guessed. 'Even on a Sunday?'

'That's the thing about being a freelance—you never

really know what hours you're going to work from week to week,' she said lightly.

'Yeah. Call me later,' he said softly, 'and maybe we can do something when we're both free.'

'Great idea.' She stroked his face. 'Thank you for letting me share today with you.'

'My pleasure.'

Mandy called Nick later that evening. 'I really like her, and so do the boys. They haven't stopped talking about her since she left.'

'Uh-huh,' Nick said, knowing that there was going to be more.

'She's a million miles away from Naomi—that one would never have had a water fight with the boys.'

No. Naomi had never really taken to them. 'Or ganged up on me so blatantly,' he said. 'You know the three of them soaked me in the park?'

'Suck it up and deal with it, you big baby,' Mandy said, laughing. 'But, seriously, Nick, Xander thinks she's amazing. She had a chat with him in the park—he wouldn't tell me what she said, but his attitude's changed. He said he wasn't going to let cancer define him.'

'Sammy's sister had cancer,' he said.

'The one who donates her hair for wigs, too?'

'Yes,' he said.

'And I bet Sammy was there for her every step of the way.' She paused. 'Nick, I know how you feel about relationships, but I'm telling you now that Sammy's different. She's a keeper.'

Yeah, he knew.

But sometimes he thought he could see something in

Sammy's eyes—something she was holding back. He really wasn't sure if she felt the same way about him that he was starting to feel about her.

Did he have the spirit to risk his heart again?

And, knowing that relationships weren't his strong point, was it fair to her?

CHAPTER NINE

LATER IN THE WEEK, Sammy had a girly pizza night with Claire, Ashleigh and her sister Jenny. She ended up telling them about the interview she'd given Ben. And admitting that she'd met Nick's family.

'Have you told Nick about your leg, yet?' Claire asked.

'I've tried telling him a few times,' Sammy said miserably. 'But I keep chickening out at the last minute. And what if he reacts badly when he realises I've kept it from him all this time—especially as I've had loads of chances to tell him the truth?'

'He might be a bit upset at first that you kept it from him,' Jenny said, 'but then he'll think about it and realise that it's a hell of a thing to tell someone. And then it will be fine.'

'Hmm.' Sammy wasn't so sure.

'Give him a chance, Sammy,' Ashleigh urged. 'Tell him.'

'I'll do it when I get back from New York next week, I promise,' Sammy said.

And she really meant to do it.

Except, when she got back to the airport, Nick was waiting for her right by the arrivals gate. Seeing him so unexpectedly totally threw her.

He took her suitcase and the heaviest of her photographic boxes from her. 'How was your flight?'

'Fine.' She frowned. 'Hang on, what are you doing here?'

'The trial finished at lunchtime and I had some time to kill. I thought you might like a lift home.'

She knew part of that was a fib—following one trial, Nick would be in the middle of doing prep work for the next one, so he'd clearly taken time off just to meet her here—but it was so good to see him.

'Did you eat on the plane?' he asked.

'I had a sandwich, so I'm fine.'

He gave her a sidelong look. 'I've never seen you in a business suit before.'

'I'm not always a complete scruff,' she said. And she was very glad that she was wearing thick opaque tights, to hide her scars and avoid any awkward questions.

'No, I didn't mean that,' he said. 'I'm just used to you wearing black trousers. Smart ones.' He stopped and kissed her. 'You look fabulous. And I've missed you.'

'I've missed you, too,' she admitted, kissing him back.

He loaded her luggage into his car and drove her back to her flat.

'Do you want to come in for a coffee?' she asked.

'I'd love to.'

Her heart hammered. She was going to tell him now. Give him the choice to walk away, the way Bryn and the others had, or to accept her for who she was.

She slid her jacket off and hung it over the back of a chair, switched the kettle on and practised the words in her head. *There's something I need to tell you. Nothing to worry about. Just so you know, nearly half a lifetime ago I had osteosarcoma, but I'm absolutely fine now.*

But when Nick had put the visitor parking permit inside his windscreen, he walked back into her kitchen and kissed her stupid, and all the words flew out of her head.

She kissed him back, loving the way his mouth teased hers, warm and coaxing and sexy as hell.

'You make me feel light-headed,' she whispered.

'That's how you make me feel, too.' He drew her closer. 'Sammy. I know this is soon, I know it's crazy, but I've never felt a connection like this before. Not even with…' He shook his head, clearly not wanting to talk about his ex. 'This is ridiculous. In court, I'm articulate and I'm never stuck for what to say. Right here, right now, I'm making a total mess of this.' He brushed his mouth over hers. 'What I'm trying to say is, I want you. I really, *really* want you. And right now there's nothing more I'd like than to carry you to your bed.'

The smouldering heat in his eyes knocked every bit of common sense out of her brain. She'd never been looked at with such desire before. The feeling was heady, and she gave in to her body's urging. How could she possibly resist? She couldn't think about anything else other than what he'd just said and how much she wanted that to happen, too. 'Then what are you waiting for?' she asked, sounding a little hoarse.

He gave her the most sensual smile she'd ever seen, scooped her up and carried her to her bedroom.

When he set Sammy down on her feet next to the bed, her heart felt as if it were hammering so hard against her ribs that the whole world could hear it.

'Curtains,' she whispered. She switched on her bedside lamp, closed the curtains and walked back to him.

'I'm all yours,' he said softly. 'Do what you will with me.'

Need throbbed through her. She'd never wanted anyone so badly in her entire life. With shaking hands, she removed his tie, then slowly unbuttoned his collar. And then she dealt with each button on his shirt in turn.

He really was beautiful. And she couldn't resist skimming her fingertips over his pectorals and down to his abs.

'When I was photographing you for the calendar,' she said, 'I really wanted to photograph you for myself.'

'Oh?' He looked interested.

'In a green glade somewhere,' she continued.

'Wearing what?' he asked.

She grinned. 'The same as any other Greek statue.'

He raised an eyebrow. 'Just a fig leaf?'

She laughed. 'No fig leaf. You have beautiful musculature.'

He frowned. 'Are you telling me you're seeing me as a life model?'

'Right now, no.' Her voice went husky. 'I'm seeing you as my lover.'

'Good.' He stole a kiss. 'I'm looking forward to learning what you like. What makes you smile. What makes you see stars.'

'I like the sound of that,' she said.

He kissed her, then undid her own white shirt, exploring and touching and teasing as he uncovered her skin. He traced the lacy edge of her bra. 'I like this,' he whispered.

'Good.' She unbuckled his belt, her hands shaking as she undid the button of his trousers; she slid the zip down and helped him ease his trousers off.

He kicked off his shoes and got rid of his socks, then kissed her again. 'I think we're a little mismatched here, Ms Thompson.'

Sammy spread her hands in invitation. 'All yours.' She smiled. 'What's the phrase you used? "Do what you will with me."'

The heat in his eyes took her breath away.

He unzipped her lined skirt and let it fall to the floor next to his trousers.

And then, as he started to roll the waistband of her tights downwards, her common sense came back.

It felt as if someone had tipped a whole bucket of ice-cold water over her.

She couldn't do this.

Not now.

Maybe not ever.

Memories echoed in her head. The disgust in her last boyfriend's eyes when he'd seen her leg. The way Bryn had always insisted on having the light off, as if he couldn't bear to see her skin. He'd said it was because he hadn't been able to bear to think about her being in pain, but she'd known the truth. Her scar had repulsed him.

She knew Nick wasn't Bryn. In her head, she knew he was a good man. That he'd understand.

But the fear was too strong. She really, really couldn't do this.

'Sammy?' Nick stopped, clearly seeing that she was upset.

She shook her head. 'I can't do this. I'm sorry. I thought I could. But I can't.'

'What's wrong?' He curled his fingers round hers. 'Tell me.'

That was the point. She couldn't. Every single time she tried, her throat felt as if it had filled with sand. And she sure as hell wasn't going to show him. Apart from being unfair to him—it would come as a total shock—she couldn't bear to see the disgust or the pity in his face when he saw her leg.

Right now, she felt totally inadequate. She'd so wanted to do this. She'd so wanted to be *normal* and to make love with the most gorgeous man she'd ever met. But she wasn't normal, she never would be, and she knew she could never have the uncomplicated relationship she'd longed for.

And the panic flooding through her was far, far stronger than the voice of reason.

'I can't do this, Nick.' Her breath hitched. 'You have to go.'

He shook his head, his dark eyes filled with concern. 'Sammy, I can't just leave you on your own when you're upset.'

'Please, Nick. Just go.' She dropped her gaze. 'It's not you. Nothing you've done. It's me.' She was too scared to face the fear, too pathetic and weak and snivelling. She pulled her hand away from his and crossed her arms over her breasts.

'Sammy?'

'Please, just go,' she repeated.

She couldn't look at him. But she could hear the puzzlement in his voice, the concern. 'Sammy, you're clearly upset and I'm really not happy about leaving you on your own like this when something's obviously badly wrong. Can I ring someone for you? Your sister? Your friend who made you the dress?'

Why did he have to be so nice about it? Why couldn't

he just lose his temper and storm out? Why couldn't he be one of those horrible men she'd dated before?

Holding the tears back took so much effort. 'I can't do this, Nick. I just can't. I can't be with you.' She'd been stupid and selfish to think that this would work. 'This thing between us isn't going to work. It's not you, it's me.'

'But why?'

'It just *is*. I'm sorry. I really wish it could be different.' That at least was true. 'But we can't be together any more. It's over.'

'But—I thought we were getting closer.' His voice was full of hurt. 'You met my family. We...' He stopped.

Yeah. They had been getting closer. She really liked his family. And they'd just been about to make love.

But this wasn't fair of her. Even if he could cope with her being a cancer survivor, there were the complications. The fertility issues. She knew he wanted kids of his own, and she might not be able to offer him that. She'd been unfair and selfish to let things go this far. She should've stuck to her rules and ended it at the third date. Before either of them got hurt.

'I'm sorry,' she said. 'Please go, Nick.'

Nick dragged his clothes on in silence, too stunned to say any more.

Sammy had ended their relationship.

Just when he thought they were moving closer to the next stage. To making more of a commitment to each other.

They'd almost made love, for pity's sake.

There was clearly something very badly wrong,

something that had upset her, but she obviously didn't trust him enough to tell him what it was. Which made him feel like something that had just crawled out from under a stone.

Pain lanced through him. It looked as if he'd made the same mistake all over again. He was pretty sure that, unlike Naomi, Sammy wasn't having an affair and using his workaholic tendencies as an excuse to make him the one at fault for the break-up. But, just as he had last time, he'd invested more of himself in the relationship than his partner had. Sammy had made it clear that she didn't feel the same way about him that he felt about her.

Right now she couldn't even bear to look at him.

Feeling horrible, he left in silence and drove back to his flat. It was an effort to concentrate, and a couple of taxis beeped their horns at him for not driving on the second that the traffic lights had turned green. And he was none the wiser by the time he got home. Why something that had felt so special had just dissolved into nothingness. But he'd just have to suck it up and deal with it. He'd done it before and survived.

He tried calling her the next day. If nothing else, just to be sure that she was OK—because he was pretty sure that he'd seen fear in her face. Something was wrong, he was sure.

But she didn't answer her phone or return his messages.

Just silence.

And he wasn't pathetic enough to keep trying to talk to her when his attentions weren't welcome.

Over the next week and a half, Nick buried himself in work—that, at least, would never let him down. And he stonewalled any questions until people finally stopped asking him if everything was OK.

It wasn't OK.

But it would be.

Eventually.

Sammy's eyes felt three times the size of normal—she'd cried for so long. But she knew from experience that the best way to deal with heartache was to concentrate on her work and not leave even the tiniest moment free for the pain to make itself felt.

Though she had to tell a white lie at her photo shoot, the morning after she'd broken up with Nick. 'I've got conjunctivitis,' she said, 'so I need to wear dark glasses.'

Her eyes were sore and puffy, all right. But from crying, not from an eye infection.

It felt as if she'd made the biggest mistake of her life.

But she knew she'd done the right thing in the long run.

She just hoped it would stop hurting soon.

'I know something's wrong,' Mandy said. 'I'm your big sister. You can't fob me off with any more excuses. And Danica next door is babysitting the boys, so I can stay here until you finally tell me what's wrong.'

Nick sighed. 'OK. Sammy and I have split up.'

'What? But why did you dump her? Sammy was lovely,' Mandy said.

'I didn't dump her. She dumped me.' Nick shrugged.

'No *way*,' Mandy said, sounding shocked. 'The way she was with you—I could see how much she thought of you. You must've got it wrong.'

'She said it wasn't working for her. And you can't

force someone to feel something they don't.' He looked away. 'At least I didn't make a total fool out of myself and tell her how I felt about her before she dumped me.'

'Oh, Nick.' Mandy hugged him. 'Are you sure you're not just being a typical bloke and totally misreading things?'

'Pretty sure,' he said dryly. He wasn't going to tell his sister the circumstances. Some things weren't for sharing. 'She was quite clear about it.'

'I'm sorry. I really hoped…'

'Yeah, I know.' So had he. 'Plenty more fish in the sea.'

'Except you're not going to even put out a single line, let alone a net.'

'Hey. I have a great family, a job I love, and friends. I don't need anything more,' Nick said lightly.

And if he told himself that enough times, he'd believe it.

'What do you mean, you've split up? You're telling us he turned out to be another Bryn?' Ashleigh said.

Sammy looked away.

'You *did* tell him about your leg?' Claire asked.

'No.'

'So you dumped him without even talking about it?' Ashleigh asked, her voice filled with disbelief. 'Sammy, are you nuts? You broke your three-dates rule for him. Which means he was special.'

'He is.' Sammy bit her lip. 'It was the right thing to do. Now he's got the chance to find someone without any complications.'

'You mean, you were too much of a coward to give it a chance to work,' Claire said. When Sammy flinched, she continued, 'And yes, Ash and I can tell it to you this straight, because we're your best friends and we love you, and you've just done the most stupid thing *ever*.'

'Talk to him,' Ashleigh urged. 'Tell him you made a mistake. Tell him everything.'

Sammy shook her head. 'It's a bit late for that now.'

'It's never too late,' Claire said. 'Look, you've got the calendar launch next week. He's one of the models, so he's bound to be there. Talk to him then.'

Except Nick wasn't at the launch.

Xander, Ned and Mandy were there, but Mandy gave her a cool look and steered the boys away before they could talk to her.

And Sammy felt like the nastiest woman in the world.

She felt even worse when her phone pinged with a text from Xander.

You're not the Black Widow. You're one of the weasels.

He was absolutely right.

She went home on her own.

And then she cried herself to sleep all over again.

CHAPTER TEN

'TEA?' GARY SMILED broadly at Nick and placed the mug on his desk. 'Oh, and you might like to see this.' He handed over a press cutting. 'It's about your calendar. Which is selling like hot cakes from the clerks' room, I might add. We're getting people from every set of chambers around here coming in to buy them.'

Nick rolled his eyes. 'The next person to ask me if I'll strip off in the middle of their court case is going to get pushed into the nearest puddle.'

'Hey.' Gary punched his arm awkwardly. 'They're only teasing. What you did is pretty awesome. I'm not sure I'd have the guts to do it. Is your nephew doing OK?'

'Yeah, he is. Thanks for asking.'

'Are *you* OK?'

Nick gave his clerk a pointed look. 'I will be, if people will let me get on with my job.'

'Got it, boss.' Gary sketched a wry salute and left Nick's office.

Nick ignored the article for a while. But curiosity eventually won, and he picked it up to look at it.

It was pretty standard stuff: how a group of people connected with the oncology ward had stripped off for a charity calendar to raise money for new equipment and treatment. And it came with a montage of photographs from the calendar—including his own page. Mr December.

He was about to drop the cutting in the bin when something in the last paragraph caught his eye.

About the woman who'd photographed the calendar.

Who was a cancer survivor.

What the hell…?

He sat up, slapped the cutting back on his desk and read it more closely.

When he'd finished, he just stared at the page, stunned. He'd had absolutely no idea that Sammy had had osteosarcoma as a teen.

Why hadn't she told him? Especially when she knew that his nephew had the same condition? Did she really think it made any difference to the way he'd treat her?

The article implied that not everyone in Sammy's past had reacted well to her medical condition. OK, some people were ignorant. But, for pity's sake, she *knew* him. Surely she'd known that he wouldn't react badly? That he would never have pushed her away or made her feel ugly or anything less than beautiful? That for him, beauty was skin deep and that it was who you were rather than what you looked like that mattered?

Nick thought about it.

And then he thought some more.

He remembered that day in the park. He'd asked Sammy afterwards if she wanted children; and he'd told her that he wanted kids of his own.

According to the article, she'd had chemotherapy before and after the surgery. He didn't know that much about the side-effects of cancer treatment on women—

thankfully none of the women in his life had been affected by it—but he was pretty sure that it could make having children difficult. A quick bit of research on the internet told him that, yes, fertility could be a problem, depending on whether or not she'd had some eggs frozen before the treatment.

It's not you, it's me.

Her words took on a slightly different meaning now. Maybe she'd ended things between them not because she wasn't interested, but because she thought that having a family would be too complicated, she knew he wanted children, and she didn't want to stand in the way of his dreams. She'd pushed him away, but maybe she'd broken up with him as the ultimate in self-sacrifice rather than actually rejecting him.

She hadn't given him the chance to discuss it with her. But maybe, if she'd been hurt badly before, she found it difficult to trust. As difficult as he did.

Even though part of him was hurt and angry that she hadn't trusted him, a deeper part of him understood why. Maybe he should cut her some slack. Give her a chance to tell him herself.

When his session in court had ended, in the middle of the afternoon, Nick called her. The line went straight through to voicemail: meaning that she was busy, or she was avoiding him. He wasn't sure which. Either way, he'd leave a very clear message, so she'd be left in no doubt. 'Sammy, it's Nick. I saw the article your friend wrote about the calendar. About you. If you don't call me back, I'll come and sit outside your flat until you get home, and I don't care if I have to sit there for a whole month before you turn up. Because we really, really need to talk.'

* * *

'Answer it, you chicken,' Sammy told herself when she saw Nick's name on the screen of her mobile phone.

But she didn't quite have the nerve.

She listened to the voicemail he left her, though.

It seemed that Nick wanted to talk to her. And he wasn't planning to take no for an answer.

She dragged in a breath. He'd read the article, so he knew the truth about her now. She had absolutely no idea what was going through his head. But she knew that she owed him an explanation at the very least.

Time to be brave.

She picked up her phone and called him. 'It's Sammy, returning your call,' she said, careful to keep her voice neutral.

'We need to talk, and I'd rather not do this on the phone. Can we meet this evening?' he asked.

Sammy noticed that her hand was actually shaking. 'I—um…'

'A neutral place,' he said softly. 'Remember that place where we had brunch, just off Fleet Street?'

'Yes. I remember.'

'Shall we meet there?'

'OK. What time?'

'Any time after six is good for me.'

'Six, then,' she said. Better to get it over with as soon as possible than to wait and worry herself stupid about it.

'I'll see you there at six.'

The phone went dead. Either he was busy, or he was seriously fed up with her. Or maybe both.

Sammy just about managed to focus on her work for the next couple of hours, and then she headed for the café where they'd met before. Nick was already there—and her heart skipped a beat when he met her gaze.

Seeing him again made her realise just how much she'd missed him.

But she'd messed this up big time.

This was going to be closure, and nothing more, she reminded herself. Don't think that this is fixable. Because it's not. Your role today is to apologise for not telling him, explain, and then walk away. Don't sit there vainly wishing and hoping for things you can't have.

'Thank you for coming,' he said when she reached his table. 'What would you like to drink? Wine? Coffee?'

'Mint tea, please,' she said.

He ordered her a mint tea and himself a coffee.

Something about his message had really bugged her. 'Would you really have sat outside my flat for a whole month?'

'I would've camped on your doorstep,' he said. 'I might not have been very fragrant if you'd kept me waiting for a whole month—but yes, I would've waited.'

For the first time since he'd called her, hope flickered in her heart. So was he saying they still had a chance?

The waiter brought their drinks over before she could ask. And then it wasn't appropriate to say anything. This was a discussion they needed to have in semi-private.

'Why didn't you tell me?' he asked gently when the waiter had gone to look after another table of customers.

'And you've seen the article?' It was a rhetorical question. She already knew he had. But she couldn't think of what to say, and it was the only thing that came into her head.

'I've read it,' he confirmed. And she could hear the hurt in his voice. 'Why didn't you tell me?'

'I was going to.'

'We almost made love, Sammy,' he said softly, 'and you didn't tell me—but now I know why you never wear a short skirt unless you're also wearing thick opaque tights. Why you asked me to leave, instead of doing what we both really wanted to do.'

'Yes.' And now she felt miserable and stupid. Why hadn't she been brave enough to tell him? They'd both missed out on something that could've been amazing. All because she'd been too scared.

'You told me that your sister was your connection to the ward—that she was the one with cancer.'

She shook her head. 'No. I told you that my sister donated her hair, the same as I do. You just assumed that she was the connection to the ward, not me.'

'You obviously realised that, but you still didn't correct me.'

'And a lie of omission is just as bad as a full-on lie, I guess.' She sighed.

'Why didn't you tell me? That's what I don't understand.'

She shrugged slightly. 'Because I've found that people treat me differently when they know.'

'Xander has the same condition. Did you see me treating him any differently from the way I treat Ned?'

'No. Well, you're a bit more protective with him.'

'Which is only natural.' He glanced at her. 'Did Xander say that to you?'

'I'd rather not answer that.'

Then another thought occurred to him. His sister had said that Xander's attitude to cancer had changed since he'd talked to Sammy. 'Does Xander know about you?'

She nodded. 'I asked him not to tell anyone.'

He frowned. 'I don't get it. Why did you tell him and not me?'

'Because I wanted him to see that there was hope on the other side of the op, and having osteosarcoma didn't mean that he'd end up never being able to do anything again. I wanted him to see that not being able to play football with his mates is just temporary, and having to rest would give him a chance to find other things he likes doing just as much.'

'Mandy says he sees things differently, so obviously we have you to thank for that. I think you're right—he did need to hear something like that from someone who'd been through it,' Nick said, 'but I still don't get why you think *I'd* treat you differently.'

'I know you're not like my exes. Some of them walked away because even the word "cancer" brought them out into a cold sweat.' She paused for a moment. This wasn't something she found easy to talk about, but she knew she owed Nick the full truth now. 'Except Bryn. He was the one I thought was different,' she said softly. 'He was the one who asked me to marry him.'

Nick waited. Clearly he knew that trick too, she thought wryly.

'Two years ago, I had a scare. I found a lump in my breast. Most people my age would've just assumed that it was probably a cyst and not worried themselves stupid from the time they discovered the lump until the time they got the results back, but once you've had osteosarcoma you have a different perspective,' she said.

'Even though I had chemo before and after the surgery, it doesn't mean that they managed to zap every single bad cell. So there's always a chance that the cancer will come back somewhere else in my body. You need to understand that.'

'But you have regular check-ups, yes?'

She nodded. 'They're annual, now. I have my check-up in the morning; then, in the afternoon—if I'm clear—my sister Jenny and I go out for champagne to celebrate. Every other year, we have an appointment afterwards at a salon so we can donate our hair.'

Then he asked the crunch question, his voice so gentle that it made her want to cry. 'And was the lump cancer?'

'No. It was a cyst. I had a scan and the doctor took some fluid out of it, so they could tell me straight away it was benign. Obviously they tested the cells to make absolutely sure. But it went away by itself.'

'That's good—right?' he asked.

She swallowed hard. 'That's when Bryn broke our engagement—as soon as he knew I was OK. He didn't want to be the bad guy who dumped the woman who had cancer.'

Nick raised his eyebrows. 'But it was fine to dump you when he was sure the cancer hadn't come back?'

She nodded. 'He said he couldn't cope with the fear that it would come back in the future.'

Nick said something very pithy, and she flinched.

'It's true,' he said, 'and he wasn't good enough for you. He was one of the weasels and you had a lucky escape.'

'Xander said I was a weasel,' she said miserably.

Nick frowned. 'When?'

'At the calendar launch. And he's right. I hurt you, and I'm sorry.'

'You're not a weasel,' he said. 'And Xander—'

'—was covering your back,' she said. 'Because he loves you and he knew I'd split up with you.'

'I guess.' His frown deepened. 'I'm still trying to get my head round the fact that you think I'd be as weak and selfish as your ex. You know how I feel about Mandy's ex walking out on them when Xander was diagnosed. I'd never, ever do that to anyone I loved.'

'I know—and I panicked. I'm sorry,' she said again. 'I know you're not like them. But I… I tend to push people away when I get scared. My family and my best friends yell at me all the time for being too independent. Claire—the one who made me the dress—says there's a fine line between being independent and being too stubborn.'

'She has a point,' he said.

She bit her lip. 'I know. I guess…' She sighed. 'The men in my life either run for the hills or they wrap me in cotton wool, and that just makes me more stubborn and more independent. I'm sorry.'

'You're not the only one to blame. I should've pushed you harder and not taken your silence for an answer. I let you walk out of my life because I thought I'd made the same mistake all over again, too,' he said. 'That I felt more for you than you felt for me.'

She frowned. 'But I broke my three-date rule for you. Doesn't that tell you something?'

'What three-date rule?' he asked, looking surprised.

'I never date anyone more than three times. Then I don't have to tell them about my past. I can pretend I'm normal. That I'm a real woman.'

He stared at her as if she'd just grown another head. 'How do you work out that you're not a real woman? Because you look perfectly real to me.'

'That's not what I mean,' she said miserably. 'It's complicated.'

'I'm used to complicated situations in court,' he said softly. 'Try me.'

'Do you have any idea how hard this is to talk about?'

'Having not been through cancer myself, no. But I guess it's as hard as I find talking about my marriage. And I told you about that.'

'That she broke up with you because you're a workaholic.'

He grimaced. 'I guess that's the anodyne version.'

She frowned. 'What's the real version?'

'If I tell you,' he said, 'then you come clean with me. All of it.'

She took a deep breath. 'All of it. OK.' She bit her lip. 'I know I'm being a coward and putting it off, but… you, first?'

He reached over and squeezed her hand. 'You've been through the kind of hell most people can't cope with—and you still smile your way through life, living it to the full. You're no coward, Sammy. But, OK, me first. I thought Naomi liked our lifestyle—I worked hard, so did she, and we had a nice flat and good holidays and a decent standard of living. I knew my dad had made that mistake with my mother, focusing on his job and leaving her to be practically a single parent as well as having her own career, and I'd got to the stage where I'd started wanting a family of my own. So I came home early one night. I intended to take her out somewhere to spoil her, tell her that I was going to cut back a bit on my hours and put her first, and suggest that maybe we could start trying for a baby.'

Everything Sammy wanted.

And something she might not be able to have.

She pushed the thought away and listened to him.

'I heard voices when I got home. I thought maybe Naomi was home early and listening to the radio, or watching something on the TV.' He looked away. 'And then I walked into the bedroom. She wasn't alone.'

His ex had been having an affair?

It must have cut him to the quick.

Especially as he'd said that his mother had had an affair and his parents had split up during his late teens. It must have brought all that misery back, too.

'Her lover did the decent thing and left us to talk. And Naomi told me she'd started seeing him because she was lonely, fed up with waiting for me to come home late from the office, and our marriage was over.' He blew out a breath. 'And yet she'd always encouraged me to work late, to go for every case that would move my career forward. It was only later that I worked out she'd done that to cover her tracks and make it easier for her to see the other guy. But my job was the perfect excuse for me to be the one at fault.'

'That's...' This time Sammy was the one to make a pithy comment.

'Yeah.' He looked away. 'She lied to me.'

She reached across the table to squeeze his hand. 'And I lied to you, too. By omission, but it was still a lie. And I pushed you away without giving you a chance—just like she did.'

He said nothing, clearly not trusting himself to speak.

'I'm sorry I hurt you,' she said. 'It's not that I don't trust you. I know you're a good man, Nick. You're honourable and decent. All I can say in my defence is that I was scared.'

'We've both made bad choices in the past. That doesn't mean we'll make a bad choice this time,' Nick said.

'OK. Let me ask you straight. Can you cope with the fact that I'm in remission, but one day the cancer might come back?'

'Yes.'

'How?' she asked, wanting to believe him but not quite able to.

'Because one day you might be knocked over by a bus, or have a piano dropped on your head, or be struck by lightning,' he said. 'You can't live the rest of your life worrying about something that might not happen. Yes, there's a chance it might come back. But there's also a chance that it might not.'

'You need to be realistic about this,' Sammy said. 'Because there's more of a chance of me getting cancer again than there is of me having a piano dropped on my head. Quite a big chance.'

'It doesn't make any difference to me,' he said. 'In English law, there's the eggshell skull rule. You take your victim as you find them.' He flapped a dismissive hand. 'Well, not that you're my victim, but you get what I mean.'

'Yes.' She smiled.

'And, for the record, I'm not going to wrap you in cotton wool. I remember you telling me not to do that to Xander, and I thought you were speaking about the way people treated your sister.'

'It was the way people treated me,' she said. 'And it drives me nuts.'

'No wrapping in cotton wool, either. So that's the first elephant down,' he said. 'Want to tackle the second? Because I have a feeling that this one's the really big one. The mammoth, you might say.'

'Second?'

'This thing about not being a real woman. I'm hazarding a guess here, but I read up on the side-effects of chemotherapy.'

So he knew?

'You once asked me if I wanted children,' he said, 'and I told you that I did. But when I asked you, you fudged the issue. Is that because you don't want children, or because you don't think you'll be able to have them?'

'I do want children. I had some of my eggs frozen before the first chemo.' She dragged in a breath. 'But there's no guarantee that IVF will work. So I might not be able to have children.'

'There are other ways,' he pointed out. 'If we want children and IVF doesn't work, then we can foster or we can adopt. Or we can just enjoy being an aunt and uncle. I have two and you have four, right? I reckon that makes a five-a-side football team with one in reserve.'

Her eyes filled with tears. 'Would that be enough for you? Being an uncle and maybe a godfather?'

'If I have you in my life, yes.' His dark eyes held hers, and she knew that he meant it. Truly.

A tear spilled over her lashes and he brushed it away. 'Don't cry. I never want to hurt you, Sammy. And, believe me, as far as I'm concerned you're all woman. I don't get how you can think otherwise. Unless your ex said that—and you already know that the man's worthless and his views aren't worth listening to, yes?'

'I guess.' The wobble in her voice was obvious to her own ears. It was something she found it so hard to get her head around. 'I can't make any promises that this is going to work,' she said, 'but maybe we can start again and see how it goes?'

'Learn to trust. Together. That works for me,' he said.

She took a deep breath. 'OK. Then I think the first thing is…well, not something I want to do in the middle of this café.' A hurdle she should've tried to overcome long, long before. And one that would have to be cleared right now before they could move forward. 'Your place or mine?'

'Mine's nearer,' he said.

'Your place, then. Which Tube station?'

'The Tube changes from here are a bit messy. Actually, it's just as quick to walk—unless you want to get a taxi?' he suggested.

She shook her head. 'Walking's fine.'

He paid the bill, and they walked back to his flat hand in hand. They didn't say much on the way. Sammy grew more and more nervous, the nearer they got to his flat, but she knew she had to do this.

'What would you like to drink?' he asked when he closed his front door behind him.

'I don't want a drink.' She shook her head. 'We need to go to your bedroom.'

He sucked in a breath. 'Sammy?'

'With the curtains closed and the overhead light on full. In fact, every single light in that room on full,' she said. She remembered where his room was; she took his hand and led him there.

He guessed what she was going to do. 'Sammy, you don't have to do this.'

'Oh, but I do,' she said. 'This is the third elephant. The last one. And it's bigger than a mammoth. Getting on for Amphicoelias size, I'd say.'

'Amphicoelias?' He looked mystified.

'You don't know the name of the biggest sauropod ever? And you an uncle of two boys. Tsk. You need to bone up on your dinosaurs.' Her tone was light, but her hands were shaking as she undid the button of her jeans.

'Sammy.' Gently, he put his hands over hers. 'Do you trust me to do this?'

The lump in her throat was so huge that she couldn't speak, just nodded.

Slowly, he undid the zip, drew the denim down over her hips, then knelt down and drew the material down her thighs to her knees.

She flinched.

He leaned back and looked up at her. 'Do you want me to stop?'

She shook her head. 'No.'

'No?' His voice was so gentle. But there was no pity in his eyes. Just empathy. He understood, and he'd let her take this at her pace.

'And yes,' she admitted. This terrified her. The moment when things between them would change. When he'd start to pity her and want to protect her. When he'd see for himself that she wasn't a real woman.

As if he could read her mind, he said, 'It's really not going to make a difference between us. But you're right—I do need to see this for myself. And then I need to prove to you that it won't change a thing.'

She closed her eyes. 'Then do it.'

Gently, he pulled the jeans down to her ankles and helped her step out of each leg.

She still had her eyes closed.

Then she felt him kiss her shin. Her left shin. The scar. All the way from the bottom to the top, his mouth soft yet very sure.

A tear leaked out and slid down her face; she couldn't stop it.

'Sammy,' he said, his voice husky. 'You're so brave and so incredible and so amazing. And this is just one little part of you. The part that makes me proud, because you've been through so much and you haven't let it hold you back.' He pressed another kiss to her scar, then got to his feet; she felt him cup her face with his hands.

'Open your eyes,' he said softly. 'Open your eyes and look into mine.'

It was one of the hardest things she'd ever done. If she looked into his eyes now and saw the slightest jot of pity, then she'd walk away. She'd have regrets, but she'd still walk away, because this was a deal-breaker.

'Do it,' he said.

She held her breath and opened her eyes.

But there was no pity in his gaze, just understanding. And something else she didn't quite dare name, but she really hoped she wasn't wrong about it.

'You're brave and you're beautiful, and I love you,' he said. 'Yes, we'll have a few bumps in the road ahead of us—everyone does—but we'll face them and we'll deal with them as and when we have to. Together.'

'You love me?' she whispered.

'I love you,' he confirmed. 'I think I fell for you the day I met you. The day you bossed me around and made me strip in front of you—and then you made me talk to you until I was comfortable about what I was doing. And you had dinner with me without being fussy about what you ate. And I knew you were straightforward and honest.'

'But I lied to you,' she said.

'No, you just didn't correct me when I made a wrong assumption,' he said, 'and you didn't tell me about the thing that really scared you. And although I admit I was hurt when I found out, I understand now why you kept it from me—and it's not a problem for me any more.'

'Thank you.'

He kissed her lightly. 'We've got a chance, Sammy. Let's take it.'

She stroked his face. 'For me, it was when you let Ned soak you in the water fight. You didn't care about your dignity. You just wanted the boys to have fun.'

He coughed. 'Is that a roundabout way of saying…?'

She blinked. 'I didn't say it already?'

He looked pained. *'Sammy.'*

She smiled. 'I love you, too. Though I'm still scared it's all going to go wrong.'

'We've both been here before and it's gone wrong,' he said, 'but it doesn't mean that it'll be like that this time. Let's give it a go—see if we can help each other learn to trust again.'

'I'd like that.'

'Starting now,' he said.

'With me half-naked and you fully dressed?' she protested.

'I think we've been here before. Or something like that. Except this time I hope you're not going to ask me to leave.'

'We're in your flat. I can hardly ask you to leave.'

'Then tell me you're not going to walk away,' he said. 'Because right now I need to be close to you. I want to make love with you. And I want to prove to you that you're all woman. You're all the woman I'll ever want or need.'

She didn't need a second prompt. She leaned forward, kissed him, and began to undo his shirt.

CHAPTER ELEVEN

Two months later

NICK SET A mug of tea down on the bedside cabinet next to Sammy and placed the Sunday newspapers on the bed next to her.

'Are you quite sure you have to work today?' she asked, patting the pillow next to her invitingly. 'I was thinking we could have a lazy morning in bed, then go and look at the Christmas lights this afternoon. Hot chocolate, mulled wine, Christmas gingerbread, that sort of thing…'

'I definitely have to work, so we need to take a rain check.' He leaned over and kissed her. 'But I'll text you when I'm nearly done and you can come and meet me. We'll eat out tonight—my treat,' he said.

She smiled at him and kissed him back. 'That sounds lovely, but will you be able to get a table anywhere? Most places will be booked up for office Christmas parties.'

He grinned. 'I'm sure I can find something.'

'Trust you, you're Mr December?' she teased.

'Something like that.' His eyes crinkled at the corners. 'I love you.'

'I love you, too. See you later.'

Sammy spent the morning in bed reading the newspaper, had a light lunch and pottered round her flat in the afternoon.

Her phone pinged at three with a message.

Meet me at Temple Church and bring your camera.

Odd, she thought, or maybe Nick had found out that there was some kind of exhibition or a carol concert on today and wanted to make up for the fact that they hadn't been able to do anything Christmassy today. She locked the front door behind her, caught the Tube to Embankment, then headed for Inner Temple on foot.

As the sun set by four o'clock in December, it was starting to get dark by the time she got to the complex of buildings around the church. She couldn't resist pausing by the gas lamps and taking a few shots; she remembered Nick saying that it was like being back in Dickens' time with the streets lit by gaslight, and he was absolutely right. The light was different—much softer. All they needed was a sprinkle of snow and a few actors from a period drama walking around in crinolines or top hats and tailcoats, and the Inns of Court would look just like an old-fashioned Christmas card.

She headed to the church. It looked beautiful, with a Christmas tree scenting the air and the organ playing 'Silent Night'. But if there was a carol concert on today, it couldn't be for a while yet; the place was virtually empty, apart from a couple of stray tourists.

As she walked in, the music changed. Was the organist playing Moonlight Sonata or was she imagining it? Were they even allowed to play secular music on a church organ? she wondered.

And there definitely weren't any signs up about a carol concert today. Sammy looked around the church for Nick, but she couldn't see him. Maybe he'd been caught up with a phone call or something. Well, at least this was a nice place to wait for him. And with beautiful music playing, because it was definitely Beethoven.

When she went to take another look at the Crusader tomb effigies, a church official came over to her.

'Ms Thompson?'

'Yes.' She looked at him in surprise. How had he known her name?

'I believe there's a message for you,' he said.

From Nick? she wondered. But why hadn't Nick just called her mobile phone?

The church official gestured to the effigies and Sammy realised that propped against the little stone dog that had captured her imagination last time was a cream vellum envelope—and her name was written on it in bold black ink. She recognised the handwriting as Nick's.

Why would he leave her a note here? And why next to the little stone dog?

'Thank you,' she said, and opened the envelope. It contained a cream vellum card. On the front, there was a brief message.

Life's short—eat dessert first.

Something she'd said often enough to him. Hmm. So were they meeting somewhere for dessert rather than a full meal? Well, that was fine by her.

She opened the card, and inside there were directions to go to the café where they'd had brunch. The place where they'd talked over all the misunderstandings and agreed to start again.

Maybe he was going to meet her there, then. But it was strange that he'd asked her to come here to the church first.

'Thank you,' she said to the church official.

She also stopped by the organist, because she was starting to suspect something. 'Thank you,' she said quietly. 'The Moonlight Sonata is my favourite piece of music, and I have a feeling that you might have been asked to play it especially for me.'

The organist smiled. 'I was, my dear. And it was my pleasure. I love Beethoven, too.'

Her favourite piece of music, the Crusader tombs and the café where they'd had brunch. What was the connection? Or was Nick doing some kind of treasure trail?

She dropped some money into the church donation box on her way out, and headed to the café, intrigued. What was Nick up to?

Icicle lights were hanging everywhere on shop fronts along the Strand, and she knew that if she peeped in at Somerset House there would be skaters in the ice rink in front of a massive Christmas tree. As she passed the entrance, she could hear 'All I Want For Christmas Is You' belting out, and she could smell hot chocolate.

This was definitely something she needed to take Nick to in the future, she thought. Somewhere they could both play hard, after a day's work.

'Good evening, Ms Thompson,' the waiter said when she walked in to the café.

She wasn't even going to ask how the waiter knew her name. Nick had clearly given directions of some sort. 'Good evening,' she replied.

'Come this way,' the waiter said, and seated her at a small table with a candle in the centre, next to a sparkly reindeer with a red ribbon round its neck, and a miniature Christmas tree decorated with red and gold baubles. Though only one place was set, and there was no sign of Nick.

'Mr Kennedy says to have dessert on him,' the waiter told her.

'Dessert?' So was this going to be a mince pie, or Christmas pudding with brandy sauce? she wondered.

'He was very specific,' the waiter said. And Sammy couldn't help smiling when he brought out a tiny hazelnut waffle, finished with berries and cream, together with a small coffee. Not Christmassy, but just what they'd enjoyed on their first visit here.

'Thank you,' she said, and texted Nick.

The waffle's a very nice touch—but what are you up to?

Wait and see, he replied.

So you *are* up to something…

This time, he didn't reply. OK. If he wanted to be mysterious, she'd let him have his fun. Because this was turning out to be just as fun for her, too—trying to guess what his next move was.

She enjoyed both the waffle and the coffee. When she'd finished, the waiter handed her another cream vellum envelope. This time, she was directed to the National Portrait Gallery, to one of the portraits that Nick had really liked when they'd visited together.

She loved walking through Trafalgar Square; the massive Christmas tree next to the fountain was lit with vertical strands of white lights, and the fountain itself was lit up, the jets spraying higher than usual. The trees in Trafalgar Square and St Paul's Cathedral were two of her favourites in London, and she had plenty of shots of both in her portfolio—even so, she couldn't resist taking just a couple more.

Almost as soon as she walked into the art gallery and found the painting Nick had specified, one of the curators came over to her. 'Ms Thompson?' he asked.

'Yes.' She smiled, now absolutely sure that Nick had planned some sort of treasure trail for her. Something based on their dates, unless she was missing something.

'I have a note for you,' the curator said.

It was another vellum envelope, although this time the message was written on the back of a postcard of the portrait she'd been directed to rather than on plain cream card. The directions were to the gallery's café, and the message read:

I'm not going to make you climb over the Dome tonight as the sun's already set—but I thought you might like these.

So this trail of his was definitely based on their first few dates, she thought with a smile. Her table in the café was specially reserved for her, set with a single red rose in an exquisite crystal bud vase. After the waiter had seated her at the table, he brought over a glass of champagne and two tiny squares of toast with Welsh rarebit. Just like the afternoon tea they'd had together at the posh hotel.

'Enjoy, ma'am,' he said with a small bow.

'Thank you,' she said, and ate the Welsh rarebit before it went cold, then called Nick.

His phone went straight through to voicemail.

She sighed and left a message. 'Nick, thank you. It's very nice having a backwards dinner, complete with champagne, but it would be even nicer if I got to share it with you. Where are you?'

A few seconds later, her phone beeped with a reply.

Patience...

So he *was* there. Just not answering her. 'Arrgh,' she said, rolling her eyes, and sipped her champagne.

When she'd finished, a man wearing livery and a peaked cap came over to her. 'Ms Thompson? Please come with me.'

The next stage of Nick's trail, she thought. So wherever she was going next was clearly by car, because this man was definitely dressed as a chauffeur.

Not just a car, she discovered: a limo. Very shiny, very black, and very swish. Which, she supposed, went perfectly with a chauffeur.

There was another envelope in the car.

I do hope you meant it when you said you're not scared of heights.

Hmm. Nick had already said they weren't going to walk over the Dome tonight, so what did he have in mind?

She had no clue as the car drove along the Victoria Embankment; they were driving in the opposite direction to the London Eye, so he couldn't have meant that. But then the driver turned along London Bridge, and she could see the lights from the bridge, the riverfront buildings and the fairy lights on the trees all reflected in the dark water of the Thames. London by night was beautiful—but she'd always thought that London by night at Christmas was even more magical.

And finally the driver pulled up outside the tallest building in London—the Shard, its very top storeys lit up with the nightly-changing Christmas light show.

Now she understood what he meant about heights.

Hopefully this meant that Nick would be at the top, waiting for her.

The driver opened the door for her and ushered her inside.

She was met at the doorway by someone that she assumed was part of the attraction's PR team. 'Ms Thompson?' the man asked.

'Yes,' she said, wondering quite what was coming next.

To her surprise, he handed her a filled water pistol, together with another of the vellum envelopes. The note said:

Choose your target carefully.

She remembered the day they spent in the park with Nick's nephews and smiled. Was he planning to have another water fight with her?

'This way, please, Ms Thompson.' The man took her to a corridor. Set in the middle was a table, with three photographs set on a small ledge. As a nod to Christmas, all the photographs were decked with a sprig of holly, making her smile. The first photograph was of Nick wearing his full barrister garb; the second was Nick wearing a suit, and the last one was Nick in jeans.

Which one was she supposed to shoot?

This was a tough decision. The barrister garb was linked to the very first day she'd met him, albeit he hadn't worn much of it; the suit was what he wore whenever she met him from work; and he'd worn jeans to the park when she and the boys had ganged up on him and soaked him.

She tried to second-guess him. A barrister would be super-protective—so Nick, knowing how much over-protectiveness drove her crazy, would want her to take that target down...right?

She aimed the water pistol at the photo of Nick in his barrister dress and knocked it over.

There was another small vellum envelope underneath the photograph. She read the message:

Good choice. Now go to the lift.

So she had got it right. That was a relief.

'Um—could you direct me to the lift, please?' she asked.

'Of course, Ms Thompson,' the PR man said.

As soon as the lift doors opened, Sammy saw tasteful Christmas decorations—swathes of beautiful greenery. But there was also a handmade sign bearing a photograph of a pile of fluffy cotton wool balls, with a red X scrawled through it in pen, and she burst out laughing before grabbing her phone and calling Nick.

This time, he actually answered his phone.

'So are you telling me this is a cotton-wool-free zone?' she asked.

He laughed. 'Got it in one.'

'Where are you?'

'Not far now,' he said. 'Pay attention.'

'Yes, m'learned friend.'

He laughed again and hung up.

She wasn't quite sure what he had in mind but she was enjoying this. He'd clearly spent time setting this up and she loved how very personal it was.

The lift stopped halfway up the tower, and the PR man said, 'You need to get out at this floor.'

Nick wasn't at the top?

'OK,' she said.

But just outside the lift was another table. This one had three cards on it.

The first was a gorgeous shot of lightning—one she would've loved to have in her own portfolio. Inside, he'd written:

Chance of being struck by lightning—roughly one in a million.

To her amusement, he'd listed the source so she could look it up and prove it to herself.

The second was a picture of a piano. Inside, he'd written:

Chance of a piano falling on your head—apparently this is an old movie trope and there aren't any actual recorded cases of a piano being dropped onto someone's head.

Trust him to investigate it thoroughly and debunk the myth. She couldn't help smiling.

The third was a picture of a bumpy, lumpy road leading to the brow of a hill. Inside, he'd written:

Chance of having rough times ahead—one hundred per cent, but I'll be there to hold your hand through whatever comes. Without cotton wool. Just as I know you'll be there for me.

There was a huge lump in her throat.

He really meant this.

They'd be there for each other, no matter what lay ahead.

'Ms Thompson?' the PR man said. 'We need to go up.'

'Yes.' She smiled at him, swallowed hard and put the cards in her bag.

Another corridor stop: and this one also had cards on the table. A picture of the edge of space.

I can't promise you this right now, but once it's commercially available...

She smiled. She'd so hold him to that one.

A picture of the Northern Lights and polar bears.

Alternative suggestion to the edge of space, from my bucket list.

And finally a picture of a lighthouse.

You said you liked these. You, me, a bottle of champagne and a spa bath on New Year's Eve. How about it?

Sammy grinned. She was totally fine with that. She scooped up the cards and put them in her bag, too.

'Ms Thompson,' the PR man said, gesturing back to the lift.

This time, the lift went straight to the top—and when the doors opened Nick was right there, waiting for her.

'You,' she said, 'are amazing, Mr December.' She walked over to him, wrapped her arms round him and kissed him.

'You're pretty amazing yourself,' he said.

'I can't believe you did all that for me. And what if I'd picked the wrong target with the water pistol?' she asked.

'I had a contingency plan,' he said.

'Which was?'

'I put exactly the same message under all three,' he confessed with a grin.

She laughed. 'Nick, that's cheating.'

'Cheating?' He coughed. 'And who is the queen of a certain card game?'

'Got it.' She smiled at him. 'That treasure trail you made is like everything we've shared together, squished into a single afternoon.'

'And you liked it?'

'I *loved* it,' she said. 'I really appreciate the time and effort you put in to this.'

'Good,' he said, 'because there's something I need to say.'

She went very still. After all this, surely he hadn't changed his mind? He wasn't going to walk away from her, like Bryn had? 'What?'

'Look down from the viewing platform.' He indicated the edge.

She took his hand and walked over to the area he'd indicated. When she looked down, she saw five words spelled out in fairy lights on the roof of one of the nearby buildings.

Sammy, will you marry me?

'Nick, I...' She could barely get the words out.

He dropped to one knee beside her and took a box from his pocket containing the most beautiful, simple, solitaire diamond. 'I talked to your friend Amy about the kind of design you'd like, so I really hope you like this.'

And now she definitely couldn't speak. The ring was perfect.

'I love you, Sammy Thompson,' he said. 'I want to grow old with you, if we're lucky enough. I want to live with you and make love with you and laugh with you. Life's not always going to be full of sunshine, but I reckon we can weather the storms together. Will you please do me the honour of being my wife?'

Realistic, practical and totally honest. She knew he'd be there for her—just as she'd be there for him. And she too wanted to grow old with him, live with him and make love with him and laugh with him. 'Yes,' she said simply.

He kissed the back of her ring finger, then slid the diamond onto it. 'I'm very glad you said yes.'

'You really thought I might say no?'

'It was a risk,' he said.

'Someone wise told me the risk was one in a million for a lightning strike. Impossibly tiny for a piano falling on your head. And a hundred per cent for life not always going your way in the future—but we have each other,' she said softly.

'We have each other,' he said.

He gestured upwards, and she realised that they were standing right underneath a ball of mistletoe. 'Well, now. A Christmas proposal deserves a proper Christmas kiss, I think,' she said and kissed him lingeringly.

'And now…I promised you dinner.'

He'd said that he'd be able to find them a table, even though most places would be fully booked with Christmas parties. And she couldn't wait to see what he'd arranged. She smiled. 'You've organised dinner up here?'

'Sort of,' he said. 'Come this way, Mrs Kennedy-to-be.'

They went down one floor in the lift, and he led them into a dark room.

'She said yes,' he said into the darkness.

And then the lights came on, what seemed like a thousand party poppers went off along with much shrieking and cheering, and she realised that all their family and friends were there, ready to celebrate their engagement. Nick had clearly set this up and sworn everyone to secrecy, because she hadn't had a clue.

And smack in the middle of a table—right next to a Christmas tree covered in icicle lights and gauzy ribbon and silver baubles—was a really huge, really swish engagement cake.

'Cake first,' Nick said.

He didn't need to say the rest of it. They both already knew.

She smiled at him. 'Always.'

* * * * *

A HUSBAND FOR THE HOLIDAYS

AMI WEAVER

To the baristas at my local Biggby,
who keep me supplied with gallons of iced tea
and a place where I can write without feeling I have
to clean my house. You guys are awesome!

Chapter One

"She's back."

The grim tone of his brother's voice told Mack Lawless all he needed to know, and his heart gave an unwelcome thump. Still, since he hadn't heard from the *she* in question in almost a decade, he deliberately uncoiled more of the pine garland he was hanging on the front of his veterinary practice and kept his voice level. "Who's back?"

Chase moved so he was at the periphery of Mack's vision. Even out of the corner of his eye, Mack could see the tight set of his brother's mouth. Damn. He willed his hands not to shake. He refused to let on that the mention of *her*—even indirectly—could still affect him. He came down the ladder, leaving the boughs hanging and ignoring the sting of the snow that pelted his face. "Chase?"

Chase met his gaze. "Darcy."

Darcy. Her name was a hard punch to his gut. Still. After seven freaking years. He'd gotten over her, and yet…

And yet hearing her name tore the lid off the memories he'd worked so hard to bury.

He forced himself to hold Chase's gaze and not show anything but indifference. "Are you sure?"

Chase nodded. "Saw her at the gas station a bit ago. Thought I'd—thought I should be the one to tell you."

The wind kicked up and the tail of the abandoned garland lashed Mack in the face. He winced, caught it and turned back to the ladder. Mack and Chase were planning to buy her family's tree farm after Christmas. He hadn't thought it would matter to Darcy. She hadn't been back since their divorce, even to visit her aunt and uncle.

His brother angled so the wind was at his back. "You okay, man?"

Irritation flared, but Mack tamped it down. Chase meant well. They all would mean well. As if he was still the heartbroken mess Darcy'd left in her dust all those years ago. "Yeah. It was a long time ago." He fitted the garland over the next hook and pretended the acid in his stomach was because he'd had a burrito for lunch and not because the only woman he'd ever really loved had returned to Holden's Crossing. The woman who'd broken him into shards when she left.

But his damn heart had never fully let her go.

"All right, then. Let me know if you need anything."

In spite of the tension coiling through him, Mack laughed. "Like what?"

Chase shrugged. "Whatever you need. We can talk to her…"

"Oh, no. No talking." He could just imagine how that particular conversation would go. He could almost pity Darcy. *Almost.* "Leave her alone, Chase. I'll deal with her when I have to."

"If you say so." Chase jingled his keys, then walked away. Mack heard his brother's truck start up and forced himself to focus on his task. Now he felt exposed. Anyone who'd seen Darcy, anyone who knew the story—or thought they did—could be driving by right now, staring at him, whispering.

He hated the whispers.

He looped the last of the decoration over the final hook and secured it so the winter winds wouldn't rip it free. Since the weather was steadily getting worse, he opted to leave the Christmas lights for another day. He hoped the wind wouldn't rip them down—the way Darcy had ripped his heart.

He closed the ladder and tried damn hard to ignore the mental picture of his ex-wife, with her long coppery locks and golden brown eyes. Damn it. Now he'd have Darcy on the brain after he'd been so successful at getting her out of it. He forced himself to turn away and haul the ladder back inside, banging it hard on the door. He swallowed a curse as pain radiated up his arm.

"All done?" Sherry's voice was cheery and he relaxed for a moment. His office manager didn't know anything too personal about him, thank God. At least not yet.

"Weather's getting worse," he said as he lugged the ladder down to the hall closet. "Wind is picking up, so I'll finish tomorrow."

She gave a quick nod. "You've had a bunch of calls in the past half hour," she said. "Your family, mostly."

She held the messages out, her attention back on the computer screen.

"Ah. Thanks." He took them and beat it back to his office. He skimmed through them quickly, then dumped them in the trash. Mom. Chase. His sister, Katie. How sad was it to be a thirty-two-year-old man and have your entire family band together over an ex-wife? Had the whole thing really been that bad?

He closed his eyes, then opened them.

Well, yeah, actually it had. Worse, probably.

He stared out his office window at the snow, which had changed from pellets to flakes. The radio station playing in the waiting area announced, between Christmas tunes, that three to six inches of the white stuff was expected by morning. It'd be a white Thanksgiving. Not uncommon in northern Michigan.

Darcy's uncle would be thrilled. And so should Mack.

Mack rubbed his hand over his face. Had Joe and Marla told their niece how he'd been helping out at the farm? Would she have come back if she'd known? He liked them. He enjoyed the labor of trimming the trees, mowing, whatever Joe needed done on the farm. They'd become friends, even with their shared history, but it was funny how the older man hadn't mentioned Darcy's imminent return. Mack was supposed to go out there tonight and help with some of the prep for the tree farm's official opening the day after Thanksgiving. He wanted to make sure this last year went off flawlessly.

Canceling wasn't an option. He knew Joe needed the extra hands more than ever.

Would Joe inform Darcy of the evening's plans?

A small part of him acknowledged the appeal of

showing up and seeing her shocked reaction. Letting her see he was fine and completely over her. He'd moved on with his life. Seven years was a long time and he wasn't that man anymore.

Maybe she isn't that woman anymore, either.

It didn't matter. He didn't want to go there. He'd managed to compartmentalize his relationship with Darcy's uncle away from what he'd had with her. That part of his life was over. At least until now, when it looked as though the past had come back to haunt him.

Sherry appeared in his door. "Jim Miller and Kiko are here. Jennifer's not back from lunch yet," she said, then really looked at him and frowned. "You okay, Mack? You look as if you've seen a ghost."

She wasn't too far off the mark. In a way, he had.

"I'm fine," he assured her. "I'll be with them in a few minutes."

As she exited his office, he sighed and pulled up Kiko's chart on the computer. Kiko was one of many pets he'd see today. Jim and his wife were getting a divorce, and the older man had gotten Kiko, a Siamese cat, as company. Some marriages weren't meant to be, no matter how promising they started out.

Like his and Darcy's.

He filed the unhelpful thoughts away and went to get his patient, whom he could hear yowling from the waiting room. Still, in the back of his head, all he could think was *She's back*.

His ex-wife was back.

Darcy Kramer drove through downtown Holden's Crossing, her hometown until she'd fled after the bust-up of her marriage at the young age of twenty-three.

She'd always loved the town at Christmas. The cheery decorations, the snow, the old-fashioned charm of the buildings added up to magic for a young girl. Somehow there was comfort in knowing it hadn't really changed.

Had it really been almost eight years since she was here? She truly hadn't intended to stay away so long. Shame tugged at her conscience. She knew Mack's older brother, Chase, had seen her back at the gas station. The look he'd given her was far colder than the wind that whipped outside. Had he gone straight to Mack? Probably.

Pain bloomed in her chest. The Lawless family pulled together tight when one of their own was hurt. Except, apparently, those related only by marriage. Those weeks after the accident and the loss of their baby, as her marriage crumbled under the weight of shared grief and her guilt, they'd set themselves firmly in Mack's camp. And he'd turned to them for comfort, rather than her.

She inhaled deeply and forced the memories down. To get through these next two weeks, she had to keep Mack out of her mind as much as possible. Her focus was helping her aunt and uncle, who'd raised her after she lost her parents, with their last Christmas season with the farm.

She gripped the wheel a little tighter. One last Christmas before the tree farm went up for sale. Before he'd died, her father had asked his brother to include Darcy in the final season if they ever sold the farm. So she'd agreed to take two weeks' vacation from her PR job in Chicago and come home.

Home.

Even though she hadn't been here in many years, it was still her childhood home, entwined in her heart and her memories, both the good and not so good. She'd missed being here. But coming back—and possibly facing Mack—hadn't been an option. Until now.

She accelerated as she exited the town limits. The steadily falling snow wasn't yet sticking to the roads, though it was starting to coat the grass. Figured, she'd get up here just in time for the first real snow of the season. Good timing, really. The snow added to the festive holiday atmosphere Kramer Tree Farm prided itself on.

She flexed her fingers on the steering wheel. Two weeks. She could do it. Then she could go back to Chicago and her carefully ordered life. She'd worked so hard for some measure of peace.

She turned on the road leading to the farm. Right away she saw the fences lining the property by the road were faded, even broken in some places. She pulled over in one such spot and got out, zipping the down vest she wore over a fleece jacket to her chin as she walked over to examine the broken board.

The chill that ran through her had nothing to do with the cold. The farm's financial situation must be much worse than her aunt and uncle had let on. Why hadn't he or Marla said anything to her? She'd offered help over the years as her career took off, but they'd always turned her down. She touched the jagged end of the wood, and tears stung her eyes. Her uncle and father had always been so adamant about the appearance of the farm. She swallowed hard as she looked out over the field beyond, with its neat rows of trees. Those, at least, looked well cared for. The wind bit through her fleece jacket and she folded her arms tight over her chest as she walked back to the car.

The farm entrance came into sight up the road and

she turned into the drive with a sense of trepidation. She drove past the low-slung barn that housed handmade wreaths and other decorations, relieved to note at least here the fencing here was in good shape and the area was trimmed festively. There were a half dozen cars parked in the lot and she knew inside the barn would be four or five people making wreaths, grave blankets and other decorations. No doubt her uncle was out in one of the fields somewhere, when he should be taking it easy. The road forked just past the barn, and since her aunt had requested she come to the house first, she continued up the driveway..

The house, a white-painted bungalow with green shutters, already sported lights and garlands and little wreaths hung from wide red ribbons in every window. Smoke curled from the chimney and a sense of relief, of rightness settled in Darcy's bones. When she pictured home, this was exactly how she thought of it. She grabbed her purse and reached for the door handle.

But she couldn't open the door. She'd been gone for so long, for reasons that seemed to pale in light of the farm's plight. Even though she knew she'd done the right thing for both her and Mack, she couldn't stop the wave of guilt that washed over her.

Marshaling her courage, she got out of the car, pulled her bags out of the trunk and trudged across the drive, the snow falling on her face and stinging her cheeks. The weight of her luggage was nothing compared to the weight of the baggage she carried within her. She knocked on the back door and waited. She could see the lights in the kitchen through the curtains, see the shadow of someone hurrying toward the door. Her aunt, of course.

Her breath caught as Marla opened the door, a smile wreathing her ageless face. "Darcy Jane! So nice to see you, honey."

Darcy stepped through the door into her aunt's embrace, letting her bags slide down to the floor. "Hi, Aunt Marla," she said, breathing in her aunt's familiar scent of Jean Nate. She squeezed her eyes shut against tears. Thank God some things didn't change.

Her aunt gave her a squeeze and stepped back. "Let me look at you. My goodness, you don't look any older! You've got your mama's good genes. Come on in, let me shut the door."

Darcy stepped all the way into the kitchen and rejoiced in the smell of pot roast. She never cooked like that for herself. "Mmm. Smells wonderful in here."

Marla opened the oven and took a peek. "I try to have a hot meal for us after these long, cold days of getting ready for the opening. This roast is a bit of a splurge, since you're here. Normally, we don't eat red meat anymore. Trying to keep Joe on a better diet to help his heart."

Darcy toed off her boots. "How is Uncle Joe?"

"He's doing good. He needs to take it easy, which is very hard for him this time of year, but he restricts his working hours and we've got some wonderful employees who pick up any slack. Selling is going to be hard, but it's the right thing to do. It's time."

Darcy hesitated. "I see it needs a little work," she said softly.

Marla nodded. "We've focused on the trees, not that fence out by the road. We couldn't do it all, although—" She stopped, and Darcy could have sworn guilt crossed her aunt's face.

"Although what?"

Her aunt gave her head a quick shake. "Nothing. We've done what we can. Now it's time to turn it over to someone else." She nodded at Darcy's bags. "Why not take those up to your room, honey? It's all fresh for you. We'll eat shortly. I hope you're hungry."

Her stomach chose that moment to unleash a rolling growl. Her aunt cocked an eyebrow. Darcy gave a little laugh. "Guess that's your answer." She'd been too much of a wreck about coming back to Holden's Crossing to do much more than nibble on a protein bar in the car.

"Good thing, too. We've got a lot of food and I don't want your uncle to eat it all. Here, let me help you." Marla picked up one of her bags and Darcy grabbed the last two.

As she followed her aunt to the stairs, she noted the decor hadn't changed much, either. Clean, same plaid couch from when she'd left, same curtains. A large blue spruce stood in front of the big window, lit with hundreds of lights and covered in ornaments. A fire crackled on the hearth, which made the whole place seem homey and cozy.

Sadness gave a little twist under her heart. She'd miss this house when they sold it.

Marla set the small duffel on the bed. "I know it was hard for you to come. I just want you to know how much we appreciate it. And I wish—I wish you hadn't thought you couldn't come home."

Caught, Darcy sank down on the bed. "You know why I couldn't."

Marla held her gaze and Darcy saw understanding and compassion there. "I know why you thought you couldn't. There's a difference."

Darcy dropped her gaze to the quilt and ran her hand over it, the slightly puckered fabric cool under her hand. Leaving gave both of them a chance to start over after the divorce. "Not to me."

"I know that, too. Your dad would be proud of you for coming back. So." She headed for the door. "Come down when you're done. Dinner'll be ready soon. Then we've got work to do."

Darcy stayed on the bed, hearing the stairs creak as her aunt went downstairs. She took a deep, shaky breath.

The memories weren't going to go away. In fact, being here pretty much ensured she'd be assaulted by them at every turn. So she'd deal.

Determined, she stood up and unzipped the nearest bag. She wasn't that naive young woman anymore. She'd been to hell and back. She'd lost her baby and her marriage. There was nothing the Lawless family could dish out she couldn't take.

But she did need to make things right. So she'd apologize to Mack, make him see her intention had never been to cause him any more pain. Maybe then she could forgive herself.

Maybe.

Two hours later, at the kitchen table, her stomach full of Marla's excellent roast, she smiled at her aunt and uncle. "Thank you. That was the best meal I've had in a long time." And tomorrow was Thanksgiving. Two excellent home-cooked meals in a row. Amazing.

They exchanged glances, and then her uncle spoke, his face serious. "Darcy, there's something we need to tell you."

Worry rose so fast she thought she'd choke. "Are you okay, Uncle Joe?"

He patted her arm. "Yes. Oh, yes, Darce, it's not me. It's—well, it's just that Mack has been working here."

That couldn't be right. She clearly had her ex on the brain, because she thought she'd heard her uncle say he was working here. At the farm. Which wasn't possible. Why would Mack be out here? He was a vet. "I'm sorry. What was that?"

He met her gaze. "Mack's been helping me."

The air whooshed out of her lungs. She hadn't misheard. *No. Way.* "*My* Mack?" She winced at her mistake. He hadn't been hers for seven years. "Why?"

Marla laid her hand on Darcy's arm. "He's young and strong. He's been out here for years helping. I know this must be upsetting for you."

She looked away, betrayal humming in her veins. *Upsetting* put it mildly. But they were all adults. What right did she have to expect her family, who lived in this community, to not interact with the Lawless family? "Ah. Well, that's nice of him. I know his vet practice must keep him very busy." She gave a little shrug, trying for casual and fairly sure she'd failed. "Why would it be upsetting? It's been a long time."

Her aunt made a distressed little noise. "Oh, Darcy."

Joe cleared his throat. "One more thing. He's on his way here."

Her gaze snapped to his, panic coiling in her belly. "What?"

Marla looked at her with concern. "He's been out here every night for the past couple of weeks. I know this is a shock—"

"You couldn't have given me a little more warning?" Oh dear, was that a squeak of hysteria in her voice?

"We didn't want to upset you," Marla said simply. "We thought it would be best not to tell you. We talked about it at length, trying to decide how to handle it. Things were so hard for you after the divorce."

She shut her eyes and inhaled deeply, trying to calm her quickly frazzling nerves. Or course they meant well; she didn't doubt that. They were only trying to protect her. Mack, at least, wouldn't be blindsided. Chase would have taken care of that before Darcy got back in her car at the gas station.

"When will he be here?" Amazing, her voice sounded almost calm. Thank God.

Joe glanced at the wall clock. "He's usually here by six thirty. Please understand, Darcy. I know we should have said something before now, but…" He trailed off and looked helplessly at his wife.

She jumped in seamlessly. "But we weren't sure how you'd react. It was hard enough for you to come back as it is. I'm sorry."

Darcy managed a laugh. "I've been over Mack Lawless for years now. If he helps you out, that's great. I've got no problem with it at all."

That wasn't entirely true. But she chose to believe it was because they hadn't told her.

It had nothing to do with maybe not being over him.

Chapter Two

"Well," Marla said as she stood up and began to stack dishes. "I'm going to take care of these and then I'll join you in the barn. Darcy, if you'd rather not go out there tonight, we'd understand."

"No. I'll be fine." She hoped like crazy it was true. She couldn't let her aunt and uncle know how rattled she was.

Marla wouldn't hear of Darcy helping her clean up, which was probably a good thing, as her hands hadn't stopped shaking since they'd told her about Mack, so she got into her down jacket and boots and followed her uncle down the snowy path to the barn. Any other time, she would have found the quiet and the falling snow peaceful. Right now, she found herself too keyed up to enjoy it.

"Finances are a little tight around here, as I'm sure you noticed when you drove up," her uncle said finally.

"Mack offered to help out. He won't accept any pay. Likes the work, he says."

Her heart tugged. That sounded like the Mack she'd known and loved.

"It's okay, Uncle Joe."

He took her hand for the rest of the brief walk and she was grateful for the simple touch. In the workshop, he introduced her to his employees, then said, "We'll be in and out. You remember how to make a wreath?"

In spite of her nerves, she smiled. "I can do it in my sleep, Uncle Joe."

He gave her a quick hug. "Stay strong, honey." He headed outside with his crew and left her alone.

She took a moment to inhale the sharp scent of pine. Some things never changed, and this room was one of them, thankfully. Long scarred tables, open shelves with wire, twine, cutters, pinecones and different colors and styles of ribbon along with boxes of assorted decorations. She admired a finished wreath. It was beautiful—spruce and juniper, with berries, pinecones and a big gold ribbon.

Forcing herself not to watch the clock and failing—just how much longer till six thirty anyway?—she kept busy by gathering supplies for and starting a wreath. Her aunt walked in five minutes before Mack was due to arrive.

"I thought maybe it'd be best if I were here," she said, and Darcy gave her a tremulous smile. "I see you haven't lost your bow-tying skills."

Her aunt kept up a steady chatter, not seeming to expect Darcy to reply, which was good because she had one ear tuned for an approaching engine. When she finally heard it, she took a deep breath.

Marla gave her a sympathetic look. "Relax, honey. It'll be okay."

But Darcy barely heard her as the barn door rolled open and Mack's familiar, long-legged form stepped through. Her breath caught.

He hadn't changed. If anything, he'd gotten even better looking, even in old jeans, boots and a down vest, with a Michigan State ball cap. His brown hair was a little longer, curling slightly at the nape of his neck. He'd always hated the curl, worn it short. Somehow the new style was a sign of how much she'd missed.

His gaze landed on her and he gave her a cool nod. "Darcy. Nice to see you."

It'd been seven years since she heard her name on his lips in that delicious deep voice of his. Longer still since he'd said it with affection, love or passion. Pain and regret hit her like a tidal wave. She'd botched things so badly. She swallowed hard. "Mack." Her voice wasn't much more than a whisper.

Before she could say more he shifted his attention to her aunt. What they talked about, Darcy couldn't say. She turned back to the table to busy herself by tying bows. Her hands shook so hard she kept fumbling the ribbon.

Watching Mack now—because her gaze kept pinging over there on its own—it was clear to her that he wasn't having the same issues she was. He'd gotten over her.

That was good, right? That was why she'd left. Mission accomplished.

Too bad she didn't feel accomplished. She felt torn up inside. Raw.

She started to reach for the scissors when her neck tingled. When she looked up, her gaze locked on Mack's.

Even across the barn and over her aunt's head, she felt the heat of it to her toes.

Oh, no.

She looked down at the bow she'd botched and untied it with trembling fingers. Oh, this was bad.

True, in the years since the divorce she'd barely dated. The few times she'd gone out? Her friends had talked her into it and there'd never been a second date.

She'd never reacted to anyone the way she did to Mack.

"We need to talk."

Darcy jumped at the sound of his voice right behind her. She turned and looked up at him, at the hard set of his jaw, the iciness of his blue eyes. Oh, how she'd hurt this man she'd loved with all her heart. If only she could go back and undo the past.

But she couldn't.

"About what?" Panic fluttered in her throat. He couldn't want to get into their failed marriage already, could he?

"Why we're here."

Darcy put down the scissors she could barely hold anyway and crossed her arms over her chest, needing the barrier it signaled to both of them. "I know why I'm here. My aunt and uncle asked me to be."

His eyes flashed. "You could have come home at any time."

She inhaled sharply. "No. I couldn't. You of all people know why."

"I don't even know why you left in the first place." The words were simple but stark and sliced through her as cleanly as a sharp blade.

She lifted her chin, fought the threat of tears back.

"Of course you do. But it doesn't matter now. I'm going to help my aunt and uncle out, then I'll be out of your life."

He looked at her, his intense blue gaze unreadable. "You'll never be out of my life," he said, his voice low.

Darcy stared after him as he strode out of the barn, his words vibrating in her soul.

Marla hurried over to her. "You okay, dear?"

Darcy forced her lips into what she hoped passed for a smile. "Of course." At her aunt's skeptical look she added, "A little shaken, but I'll be fine, Aunt Marla. It's been a while."

The phone rang and her aunt glared at it, then went to answer, clearly reluctant to leave Darcy alone.

She picked her scissors back up and decided right then not to show how much the encounter had affected her. As she started a new bow, determination set in. It might be too much to hope she could get Mack to understand now what he'd been unable to back then. But she absolutely had to try so she could finally move on.

Wasn't Christmas a season for miracles?

She'd need one.

Mack strode out into the cold, thoughts whirling. He thought he'd been prepared for the shock, but he'd been wrong. Way wrong. Seeing her wasn't easier after all these years.

Especially when she looked so damn appealing.

But it'd been the look in her big brown eyes that killed him—wary, hopeful, sad all mixed together. Regretful.

Regrets. He had a few of those himself.

The still falling snow swirled around him as he approached Joe, who was readying to bale and load cut trees into a truck for delivery at a local store. Joe looked distinctly guilty as he approached.

"You saw Darcy?"

Mack gave a curt nod. "Yeah."

Joe's look was assessing and it made Mack uncomfortable. He didn't want the older man to see how rattled he was. "I'm sorry we didn't talk to you about Darcy. We were afraid you'd quit or that she wouldn't come. We didn't want either to happen."

Mack shook his head. He wouldn't have quit. And he wouldn't have discussed Darcy with her uncle anyway—it would be disloyal and he'd never ask Joe to do that. "It's all right. So where are these going?" He pulled a fresh-cut spruce off the trailer.

"Tom's. Said delivery would be first thing tomorrow." With that, Joe turned the equipment on.

It suited him.

It didn't take nearly long enough to load the truck with the trees and wreaths the grocery store owner had ordered. By the time he'd completed several other tasks and he ducked back into the barn, he didn't see Darcy.

The stab he felt wasn't disappointment. It couldn't be. He'd been there, done that.

He wasn't able to fool himself.

With a sigh, he trudged toward his truck through a good four inches of snow. Joe's voice stopped him.

"Are you going to talk to Darcy?"

Mack turned around. "About what?"

"About what happened."

Anger surged through him, but he forced it down. "There's nothing left to say. It's been a long time, Joe. A long time," he repeated, even though seeing her made it all feel like yesterday. He wanted to forget, to keep it buried. She hadn't wanted them, their family. What good was it to rehash the whole thing now?

"Maybe so. But you two have unfinished business. Talk to her." When Mack opened his mouth, Joe held up a hand. "I'm not going to say any more on this. You're adults. Thanks for the help tonight. We'll be back at it after dinner tomorrow."

Mack said good-night and swiped the fluffy snow off his windshield. He stood there for a second and watched Joe walk up the lane that led to the house. With a sigh he climbed in and started the engine. As he drove back out to the road, exhaustion washed over him. No doubt there'd be no sleep for him tonight. Or he'd dream of Darcy all night. Frankly, he'd prefer no sleep.

He turned in the driveway of his little house, the one he'd bought and restored after Darcy left. He'd needed an outlet for his grief, and this house had provided it. He came in through the front door, and was greeted by enthusiastic barking. Sadie and Lilly came barreling out of the living room and threw themselves at him, barking as if they'd thought he wouldn't be back. He rubbed ears as he waded through them and headed for the kitchen.

"You guys want out?" They zipped to the door and he let them out in the snow in the fenced-in backyard. His phone rang before he even got his coat off. A glance at the caller ID had him bracing himself.

"Hi, Mom."

"Mack. How are you?" There was concern in his mother's voice.

"Fine." And because he was feeling a little contrary with how his family assumed he wasn't, he added, "Why wouldn't I be?"

His mother sighed. "I don't know. Because Darcy is home. And you help out at the tree farm. Did you see her?"

Mack shrugged out of his jacket. "I did." There wasn't anything else to say—at least not to his mom.

"How did it go?" Her voice was gentle.

"I don't know. Fine." He raked a hand though his hair, remembering Darcy's huge, stricken eyes. "Mom. What do you think I'm going to do?"

She sighed. "I don't know. I know how torn up you were when she left. How we thought we'd lose you, too. I know you're an adult, but you're still my boy. And I don't want to see you go through that again."

Mack turned as he heard a noise at the back door. The dogs were ready to come in. He opened it and they tumbled through in a flurry of wet paws and snow and cold air. "It's all in the past, Mom."

She made a little noise that could have been disbelief. "Okay, then. I won't keep you. We'll see you tomorrow."

Tomorrow. Thanksgiving. He'd spent one of those with a pregnant Darcy as his wife. Just before—well, before. It was how he divided everything. Before. And After. He shut the images down. "Sounds good."

She talked a few more minutes and Mack made all the appropriate noises before hanging up with a promise to be on time.

He tossed the phone on the counter and sank down at one of the bar stools lining it. He covered his face with his hands and braced his elbows on the counter. Darcy. All those things he'd worked so hard to avoid were staring him in the face.

He slammed his palms on the surface, and both dogs looked up from their bowls.

"Sorry, guys," he said, and they looked at him as if they saw more than he wanted them to. Wanted anyone to, for that matter.

After a shower, he lay on his bed and turned the TV on, more for distraction than anything else. He flipped through the channels until he found a hockey game he wasn't going to watch anyway.

She'd looked shocked when he said he didn't know why she'd left. How could that be? She'd never told him, she'd just said she wanted a divorce. She'd left in a hurry after that, without so much as a glance back.

He'd been looking for her ever since.

Thanksgiving passed in a blur of fantastic food and frantic preparations for the season opening of Kramer Tree Farm the next morning. Darcy knew Mack was around, but there were so many other people and so much to be done she had no time to dwell on it.

But she was always aware he was in the vicinity. Somehow she was very tuned in to him. That wasn't a good thing.

She hadn't slept so well the previous night, dreaming of Mack. Now, fired up on caffeine and nerves, she figured tonight would be a repeat of the last.

She thought of her quiet condo in Chicago, her refuge from all this emotion and pain. She missed it and the safety it offered—even if it was apparently safety from herself and her memories.

The chatter of the employees, the Christmas music, all combined to make a festive atmosphere. The fresh six inches of snow added to it. Her aunt and uncle were thrilled. She tied the last sprig of bittersweet to the wreath she'd made as Marla came over.

"Looks lovely," she said with a smile. "You haven't lost your touch."

Darcy laughed. "I think I can make these in my sleep. Everything going okay?"

"Yes, thankfully. We're pretty much set. Can I get you to take the ATV out to the warming stations and make sure they are ready to go in the morning? Hot chocolate and coffee out there, and both that and mulled cider up here."

"Sure." Darcy left the completed wreath where it was and stripped off her pitch-sticky work gloves. It only took a couple minutes to gather the supplies she needed and put them in a bag. Outside, she fired up the ATV and drove down the plowed paths to the first—and largest—warming shed. Someone had left the lights on. She parked outside and went in.

Mack turned around, surprise on his face. Darcy squeaked.

"What are you doing here?" she blurted, and realized as his expression closed up how rude she sounded. "I mean—I didn't mean—"

"I know what you meant." He nodded toward the heating unit. "Wasn't running right, so I told your uncle I'd take a look at it."

"Oh. Well. I'll be just a minute." She held up the bag as she edged inside. "I've got cocoa mix for tomorrow. Got to stock up."

She had every right to be here. She couldn't let him intimidate her, not that he was trying. She had nothing to hide or defend to this man. Their marriage was over.

So why were her hands shaking?

When she stood back up, she bumped a can of coffee, which fell off the table and crashed on the floor, leaving a fragrant trail of grounds as it rolled around. Her face burning, she practically dived for it the same moment Mack reached for it.

"I got it," she muttered, then inhaled sharply as Mack's hand closed over hers. His palm was warm, and while she knew she should yank hers back, her gaze flew to his and locked on.

He was only inches from her. His blue eyes were serious and heat sparked in them—and an answering heat spread through her. She wanted to lean forward, just a little and close the gap, see if he tasted like she remembered—

She couldn't afford to remember. She'd spent far too long trying to forget.

"Darcy." His voice was low, a little rough. She swallowed hard and pulled away, gathering the errant coffee can in her arms like a shield. His gaze was shuttered as he sat back on his heels. "Need a broom?"

She blinked at the coffee mess on the floor. "Looks like it." Hopefully, there was a backup coffee can somewhere, or else everyone would have to make do with cocoa. "There's one in the closet. I'll just clean this up and get out of your hair."

She couldn't even tell the heater wasn't working. It was awfully hot in here right now.

She suspected it had everything to do with how Mack managed to kick up her internal temperature.

"You're not in my way," he murmured and retreated to the heater when she came back with the broom. It was as if they were performing some kind of awkward dance. She managed to clean up her mess and stock up the packets with no further incidents, even though she kept sneaking looks at his broad back as he worked on the heater.

She put the broom away and turned toward the door, wanting only to escape the oppressiveness of the room.

"Okay, well, bye," she said in an overly bright tone. "Sorry for the interruption." She made a beeline for the door, unable to resist a last look at him.

He looked up and caught her. "No apologies necessary," he replied quietly.

Darcy escaped outside and took a deep lungful of the cold, crisp air in hope it'd settle the crazy butterflies in her belly.

She didn't care so much about making a mess in front of Mack—though she really hoped Aunt Marla had an extra can of coffee on hand—but her response to him scared her. She'd worked long and hard to move on past the guilt and grief, to build a new and successful life in Chicago. It'd been a long road, and hard won. But seeing Mack threatened all those carefully constructed walls. She couldn't afford that. If she hadn't promised her dad all those years ago she'd be here for this, she'd pack up and leave on Monday.

It wasn't running away when your sanity was on the line. Right?

Chapter Three

Opening day flew by in a merry haze of families and Christmas trees. Darcy was thrilled with the number of people who came out to the farm. The weather co-operated, too, with a very light snow and no wind. She worked the register, greeting old friends and new faces alike. She saw Mack often from her post, as he was helping with tree processing and loading for anyone who needed it. She actually began to suspect there were a few women who didn't need it, but took advantage of the fact they'd get his attention for a few minutes.

She wasn't sure how she felt about that.

She tried very hard not to stare at how perfectly the faded jeans he wore hugged his butt and strong thighs. She also tried to avoid eye contact with him, but it seemed they glanced off each other every time he came into her line of sight. She did note how much the people loved him. Which made sense. As a Lawless, he'd be well-known.

And sometimes she caught him looking at her. Those small moments thrilled her in a way she knew they shouldn't. There was nowhere it could go that would end well.

Only a handful of people alluded to their past and none of them made hurtful comments, even though Darcy had been braced for the worst.

So she was relaxed and happy when they closed at eight that night. Enough that when Marla invited Mack to the house for a hot supper and a drink, she smiled at him.

He accepted without even looking at Marla.

Talk at dinner was minimal, as Marla and Joe were clearly exhausted and they were all starving. But the stew was hot and good and just spooned from the slow cooker. After dinner, Darcy sent them to relax. "I'll get the dishes."

"We both will," Mack said and stood up from the table.

Marla and Joe exchanged a look and Darcy wished he hadn't said anything. Now it was clear what her aunt and uncle were thinking. She didn't want to give them the chance to do any misguided matchmaking.

"Okay," Marla relented. "Thank you."

In silence, Darcy and Mack cleared the table. She was thankful there were only a handful—Mack was doing the suck-all-the-air-out-of-the-room routine that made it hard to concentrate. And he smelled so *good*, like fresh air and snow and pine. She wanted to burrow into his plaid flannel shirt and just breathe him in.

Wait. No, she didn't. She was over him, remember?

She turned the water on and added soap while he quietly got out a clean towel. From the living room, the TV added a nice undertone and helped fill the silence, but didn't do anything to cut the tension.

"So," she said as she slid plates into the sink, "a good day, huh?"

"Very," he agreed. He took the plate from her instead of waiting for her to put it in the drainer. She pulled away quickly. She'd have to be very careful not to touch him accidentally.

"Tell me about your job," he said.

She relaxed. This was a safe topic, not likely to venture into territory she wasn't comfortable with. She filled him in on her PR career, stressing how much she enjoyed it and the city.

Or used to. No point in mentioning the dissatisfaction she'd had over the past few years.

"You love Chicago."

It wasn't a question, almost an accusation. Surprised, she forgot she wasn't going to make eye contact and looked at him. His jaw was tense.

"I do," she said because it was true. She loved the city, the pulse, the vibrancy. The quirky atmosphere.

"So you're happy." The words were quiet, but Darcy recognized them as a minefield. No answer would be the right one. She swallowed hard.

"I am, yeah." She carefully washed the last plate and handed it over, mindful of his long fingers and the memories she had of them, both tender and erotic.

"I'm glad to hear it," he said quietly, and she looked up to catch his gaze. It was sincere and regretful at once. Her heart stuttered. Maybe she could get him to see what had been in her head and heart back then. Maybe she could apologize and he'd accept it. Maybe this was the opportunity she needed to finally move on and find peace.

"Thank you," she murmured, but couldn't look away, gripping the dishcloth because she was afraid she'd reach for him. Touch his face, with the faint shadow of whiskers on his strong jaw. Bury her hands in the longer length of his hair.

Or kiss him.

With a hard swallow, she turned back to the sink. None of those were options. Not a single one. To even think so was madness of a truly bittersweet kind.

He folded the towel and she drained the sink, bumping his arm with hers as he hung it up. She gritted her teeth against the little prickle of heat the contact generated. She didn't want this, but didn't know how to make it go away.

"How about you?" The question was more of a desperate deflection. "How's the vet practice? What else are you up to these days besides helping here?"

He leaned a hip on the counter and folded his arms across his chest. "I'm good. The practice is good. I've got another vet working with me now, too. We're a good team. The practice is expanding and we need more room, so that's why your aunt and uncle are selling to us."

She blinked and went cold. "I'm sorry. What did you say?"

He looked at her strangely, then comprehension dawned. "I'm buying the tree farm, Darce. With Chase. Didn't they tell you?"

She turned to the sink and swiped at it with the cloth,

fighting the sense of betrayal that flooded her. "It must have slipped their minds," she muttered.

What else hadn't she been told? Had things been so bad when her marriage ended they'd tried to shelter her to the point of simply not telling her anything?

He swore, then rubbed a hand over his face. "I'm sorry, I thought you knew. I wouldn't have—"

"Told me. I know. No one around here seems to think I need to know anything that's going on." She sounded put out but couldn't help it. What else didn't she know?

"You've been gone a long time," he pointed out, an edge creeping into his voice.

"I know." The words were bitter on her tongue, all the more so because he was right. "What are you going to do with it?" She wasn't sure she wanted to know.

He pushed off the counter. "Chase has an ecologically sound plan for the place, Darcy. If you stop by my office I'll show you—"

"Wait." She held up a hand. *Ecologically sound* were pretty words that hid a nasty truth. "Is he turning this into a subdivision?" The thought made her sick to her stomach. All the trees leveled, the ponds filled in, the buildings that had been here forever torn down.

"Not like you're thinking, I'm sure. The barn will hold my practice. The rest will be a sub, which will have large lots. The plan is to preserve as many of the trees as possible. It'll be natural, with trails and everything."

The roaring in her ears intensified. "You're taking my childhood home and tearing it down so you can build a subdivision."

Alarm crossed Mack's face as he narrowed his eyes. "You make it sound personal."

"Isn't it?" The bitterness spewed out of her now. "I

hurt you. Badly. I took everything from you and now here's your chance to hurt me back." This farm had always been here, always been a constant in her life. Now it'd be torn down and replaced with houses and people. And no longer part of her.

"Oh, come on, Darcy. It's been seven years! And you haven't been back since to the childhood home you love so much. Your aunt and uncle are important to me. This has nothing to do with you." His voice had risen to match hers, and she glanced at the living room, worried her aunt and uncle would overhear.

She stared at him, the final realization he'd truly moved on hitting her right in the heart. "You knew. And you're still going to destroy it."

"We gave them a fair price," he said simply. "They know my plans. They know Chase's plans. No one's destroying anything. It's why they agreed to sell to us. They had opportunities to turn us down. I'd never pressure them, Darcy. Give me some credit."

The tight edge of anger in his voice forced her to bring it down a few notches. "Right. It's not about me. As long as they are okay with selling the farm to you for a subdivision, it has nothing to do with me." Were her words for Mack, or for herself?

"No, it doesn't." There was a challenge in his eyes. "Because you'll leave. You claim to love it here, but you'll leave it without a second thought. And not ever look back." He snagged his jacket off the back of a chair. "Never mind, Darcy. I've got nothing to justify to you. It doesn't involve you."

His words followed him out the door and she resisted the urge to scream and throw something after him. Tears pricked her eyes and she swallowed hard. He had a point. She'd seen firsthand how little they needed her here, how they didn't see how much she'd loved it. How she'd dreamed of being back.

Whose fault was that? Her own. She'd needed to get away from Holden's Crossing so badly she hadn't thought about what it would mean to relationships with those she'd left behind. Even being in touch long-distance hadn't been enough, though she'd tried to convince herself it was.

It hurt they'd opted not to keep her in the loop. Worse that Mack had been the one to tell her.

Aunt Marla walked in. She looked around the kitchen. "Where's Mack?"

"Gone," Darcy said shortly. Marla frowned.

"Did you two have a fight?"

In spite of herself, she laughed. "Fight? That would imply there was something to fight over. No. He just—he told me he's buying you out."

"Oh." Marla sat down at the table. "Yes. He is."

Darcy didn't have the energy to pursue it further. Plus, it didn't matter, as Mack had made clear. "That's great."

Marla covered Darcy's hand with her own. "He and Chase will treat it with respect, Darce. It's a good choice for all of us."

Darcy's breath caught. *All of us* didn't include her, of course. And now it was too late to ask for a say. Besides, what could she do? She lived in Chicago, for Pete's sake. Her life was there. She'd spent the past seven years making sure everyone knew that. How happy she was, how successful she was, how busy she was.

It had all been a sham.

"Of course it is." She pushed back from the table. "I'm wiped. I think I'll go to bed."

Marla rose and gave her a quick hug. "I'm sorry, honey. We should have told you."

"Just out of curiosity, is there anything else I need to know?"

Marla shook her head. "No. Nothing. Darcy, I'm so sorry for how this has gone."

Being angry with them wouldn't serve anyone. Besides, the one she was mad at was herself. And Mack, no matter how unfair that was. "No harm done," she murmured and hurried up the stairs to her room.

A few minutes later there was a knock on the door. Darcy opened it to find her uncle standing there. "Can I come in?" His voice was quiet.

"Of course." She stepped back. The room was small, and he sat on the bed.

"Marla told me." He took a deep breath. "I know. We should have said something. We've really—we've really dropped the ball when it comes to all this. We thought—we thought we'd kind of ease you into it. That wasn't our intention, to shut you out."

Darcy's mind was whirling. It felt that way, but there was no point in going there. She was as much, if not more, to blame, letting them think she needed to be protected from all this. "I know. I understand." She stared out the window at the light snow that fell, dancing in the reflected light of the Christmas lights on the porch. "But—how can you sell it to them, Uncle Joe?" No matter what Mack said, that he and Chase would keep it intact and not level the whole thing to build wall-to-wall cookie-cutter houses, she couldn't believe him.

Didn't believe him. "It's just—always been here." But of course she could see the proof, that it needed more than Joe and Marla could give it.

"It's been in the family for a few generations now," Joe said. "But there's no one to carry on the farm. Unless..." His voice trailed off and Darcy, hearing the speculation in his tone, pivoted to face him.

"Unless what?"

"Unless you want to run it."

Darcy laughed and slapped her hand on her chest, incredulous. "Me? I couldn't possibly."

Joe's gaze was steady and her laughter died. "Why not?"

She scrambled for an answer. "My life. My job. It's all in Chicago." It seemed obvious. Didn't it?

"Are you happy there?"

She turned back to the window. What was up with that question? Mack had asked her the same thing. "Of course." Wasn't she happy? Was it her guilt that was eating at her?

She heard the creaking of Joe's knees as he rose off the bed and came to stand beside her. When he spoke, his voice was quiet. "As a child, you loved this place. Loved it, Darcy. Followed me and your daddy all over, helping. Even after he died, and you were so young, you kept on helping. With your PR skills, you could take this place and really turn it around. We have a verbal agreement only at this point. No papers have been signed yet."

She stared at his profile, her mind whirling. She had a closet full of stilettos, for God's sake. She'd never wear them here. She was a city girl now. And—Mack was here. Could she live in the same town and still move on with her life?

Joe looked over and slid his arm around her shoulders and pulled her into a hug. She breathed deeply of his outdoorsy, piney scent and squeezed her eyes shut. "Keep it in mind before you reject it totally, Darcy."

She hugged him back. "I can't make any promises, Uncle Joe." She didn't want them to pin their hopes on her. She just didn't see how it could ever work.

She'd worked so hard to make partner, a feat that was almost in her grasp. So hard to earn the respect of her coworkers. So hard to forget what had happened here, to move past it. To come home to stay would be like throwing away the past seven years of her life. Why would she want to undo everything she'd worked so hard for?

Why would she want to face, every day, what she'd tried too hard to forget?

Damn it. It hadn't gone away.

Mack walked into his office Monday morning in a foul mood thanks to his sleepless weekend. Ever since Darcy showed up, he'd been unable to sleep for the damn dreams.

Dreams of Darcy.

They'd managed to spend all weekend together, but not really. She spoke to him when necessary but no more than that. Eye contact was minimal but searing. Sometimes he'd catch her watching him, and he couldn't read her anymore. Wasn't sure he wanted to. It was driving him slowly insane.

Now he went into his office, tossed his coat on the coatrack and dropped in his chair to rub his forehead wearily. God help him, he'd never make it to Christmas this way. She'd kill him all over again and not even know it.

Even though Sherry would fuss at him, he went ahead and started coffee. Functioning on zero sleep required constant caffeine. Delivered by IV preferably. Since that wasn't an option, he headed for the coffeemaker.

There was a rhythm to the mornings. Check everyone, feed everyone, take out those who needed it. Medicine to those who needed it. He embraced the routine today, relieved for the constancy of it. Today he had no truly ill animals, which was always nice. By the time the coffee perked, he was feeling more relaxed.

Jennifer, another vet who worked with him, came in on a flurry of snow.

"Morning," she said, then looked at him hard. "Notice I didn't say 'Good morning,' because you look like hell."

He sputtered a laugh. He could always trust she'd get to the point. "Thanks, Jenn."

"This have anything to do with the return of the ex-wife?"

He shut his eyes for a second before reaching for a food bowl. "You heard."

"Of course. Small town means everyone eventually knows everything." She held up a hand before he could say anything. "You don't have to confirm or deny. Though one look at you is plenty of confirmation for me."

He replaced the bowl and ran his hand down the back of the cat gently. She didn't purr, but neither did she swipe at him. "There's not much to say." He knew his tone was curt but she didn't flinch.

"Maybe I'm not the one you need to talk to," she said softly.

He thought of Darcy, of her laugh, of her spill of hair, of her big brown eyes and smooth skin. Of her cute little body in worn jeans and a long-sleeved T-shirt. Of how he'd thought he was over her and somehow he wasn't.

Nope, no reason to say anything.

"I'm good," he said, and she rolled her eyes at him as Sherry entered the clinic.

The morning passed quickly. He managed to keep thoughts of Darcy to a minimum. He wasn't due to help at the Kramer farm till the weekend. With any luck he'd have this under control by then.

His last patient of the day was a cantankerous old cat. The owner, Mrs. Harris, had known him his whole life, and she still spent most of her days at the bakery she'd owned for as long as Mack could remember.

"Hello, Mrs. Harris," he greeted her as he entered the exam room. "Wolfie's not eating today?"

The older lady frowned. "No. He's just not himself."

An exam of the animal didn't reveal anything untoward, so Mack suggested a change of cat food and sent them on their way with a sample bag. He stood in the reception area, making his notes in Wolfie's chart. Afterward, he ran through the closing duties with his staff and headed out to meet his brother for dinner. It wasn't lost on him how his mother and brother checked up on him regularly. Even Katie had, all the way from California.

He tried to appreciate their concerns, but it was a little stifling.

"So. How's it going with Darcy?" Chase's question was casual, but Mack heard the concern under the words.

"There's nothing to report," he said drily. "I hardly

see her, much less talk to her." All true. She was avoiding him. He knew he should be grateful.

"Mmm. So that's why you look as if you haven't slept in a week," Chase observed, tilting his beer bottle toward Mack. "You want to try again?"

Unsure actually if that question meant change his answer or give it another go with Darcy, he gave the answer that covered both. "No."

Chase raised an eyebrow but said nothing else. Mack stared at the TV, pretending *Monday Night Football* was enthralling, even though he had no idea what the score was and the teams were just a blur, since Darcy's face kept floating through his brain. He rubbed his hand over his face.

"Have you talked to her?"

"Well, yeah. I have to work with her. I'm not going to be rude," Mack said, irritated.

"That's not what I meant."

Mack laughed. "Why would I do that, Chase? It's long over. There's nothing to say."

Other than ask questions. Like, *Why did you leave? Why didn't you love me as much as I loved you? Why wasn't I enough? Why couldn't we pull through our loss?*

And she might have one for him. Like, *Why weren't you there for me when I needed you?*

He had no answer for any of them.

"Nothing to say," he repeated flatly. "Chase. Drop it."

His brother looked at him hard and Mack managed not to flinch. Chase gave a short nod. "All right."

Mack let out a silent exhale. The only way he'd get through this was if people left him alone. All the well-meaning looks and questions were driving him crazy.

He wasn't going to self-destruct just because Darcy was home. Or because she'd leave again.

Because this time she wasn't leaving him behind. He'd walk away first.

Chapter Four

Darcy walked into Java, the local coffee shop, with her laptop bag on her shoulder. Internet at the farm was slow and spotty at best. She needed to check in at work, and this was the best way to do it. She stepped up to the counter, smiled at the barista she didn't recognize and ordered a latte. Then she settled in at a table by the window and booted up her computer.

She frowned at the sheer number of emails. It'd been only a few days since she left, and there were nearly a hundred of them. Many of them from her team on the Grant project. Her phone didn't work reliably up here, either. Apparently the farm was in a technological dead zone. With a sigh, she opened the first one, called her assistant and expected to be putting out fires.

So she didn't see Mack until he was right across from her. She looked up and her heart caught. She didn't hear what her assistant said and had to ask her to repeat. She pulled her computer closer, opening a space on the other side of the table, and gave him a nod. God only knew what this would do to gossip.

When she managed to hang up, he arched an eyebrow. “Problems?”

“I’ve got it under control,” she said, and gave a sharp little laugh. “They take credit for the good stuff, but as soon as things turn into a flaming pile of poo they bail and blame me.”

“Why do you put up with it?”

The question stopped her hand in midlift of her now cool latte. Why did she? “I don’t know. It’s just the way it is.”

Mack shook his head. “Sounds as if you need a new team.”

She set her cup down. “I’ve got it under control,” she repeated. She wasn’t sure why her temper was sparking. Why he’d touched a nerve with a simple observation. “I’ve worked very hard to get where I am. I’m not going to quit.”

“No?” His voice was deadly soft. “Isn’t that what you do?”

Her gaze snapped to his, but his was carefully blank. Temper surged, and she welcomed its heat because his words left her cold. “No. I don’t. I didn’t.”

“Sure you did. You never gave us a chance, Darcy.”

Darcy’s jaw nearly hit the table. “This is not the place for this conversation.” She snapped the laptop closed, hands shaking with fury. “In fact, there’s no place for this conversation because that would imply we had something to talk about.”

“Easy,” he said softly. “We’re being watched.”

Of course they were. She bit back a sharp retort and

slid the laptop into her bag. She offered him a stiff smile. “Enjoy your coffee.”

She stood and spun around. Her bag caught on the chair and sent it toppling to the floor. Every head turned, but Mack was off his chair before she could move. He picked up the chair and slid a hand under her elbow. “I’m sorry,” he said in her ear as he guided her to the door. She just shook her head, because any words she had for him weren’t fit for anyone to overhear. Outside she yanked her arm away and walked as fast as she could in the opposite direction of where he was. Which, she realized after about twenty steam-fueled steps, was away from her car. Which sat in front of the coffee shop. Where Mack stood.

She stopped, shut her eyes, then pivoted. He had his hands in his pockets. He tipped his head toward her car.

She lifted her chin and walked back. When she got close enough to kick him—which was awfully tempting—he caught her arm. “Darcy. I’m sorry.”

She looked him in the eye and saw the remorse there. “It’s too late, Mack. Sorry isn’t enough.”

She got in her car and managed to get onto the street with tears burning in her eyes. Oh, no, sorry wasn’t enough. It’d never be enough. And she knew that from years of being sorry for how things ended with their marriage. From knowing she could never go back and fix it. Go back and handle it differently, right down to deciding to turn left instead of right.

To save the baby he’d wanted so desperately. When she hadn’t been ready to be a mother. She’d barely been ready to be a wife. But she’d gotten pregnant and he’d insisted they marry.

As always, when it came to Mack, she'd been unable to say no.

A sob escaped her and she swiped at her eyes. He had every right to be angry—but she wasn't that young woman anymore. She hadn't been since she lost their baby. She'd grown up in those awful hours after the accident that had fractured their marriage. She hadn't needed him to take care of her. She'd just needed him to be there for her. And he hadn't been able to understand the difference.

He hadn't been wrong. She *had* quit. She'd run away because it was easier than facing everyone else's pain when she could barely tolerate her own.

So no, he hadn't been wrong.

But to hear it from him tore her up inside.

Later that afternoon, Darcy had managed to put the whole thing behind her. Mostly. Now she stood behind the cash register—an old one, nothing electric about it—and smiled at the young couple paying for the tree. They were probably a little older than she and Mack had been, but her heart tugged all the same. Had she ever been that young and in love?

She watched as the husband dropped a kiss on the woman's temple. Oh, yes. She had been. But she'd been uneasy in her marriage and Mack had been so confident. This couple didn't look unbalanced like that.

"This is our first tree together," the woman said, beaming at her husband, who gave her an indulgent smile, then left to talk to Mack, who had the tree. Darcy forced her gaze to stick to the woman in front of her.

"Congratulations," she said a little too cheerfully. "How long have you been married?"

"Eight months." The woman pulled out a check and when she stooped to write it Darcy saw the rounding of her stomach. She saw herself at the same time, the same place and the world tilted. In spite of her best efforts, her gaze shot to Mack, who had his back to her. *This is how we could have been, should have been.*

"Are you all right?" The woman frowned, tore off the check and held it out. "You look awfully pale."

Darcy forced a smile back on her face as she took the piece of paper. "Headaches. They come on fast."

The other woman's face cleared. "I'm sorry. Hope you feel better. Merry Christmas!"

"Merry Christmas," Darcy echoed and watched as she walked to her husband, who slipped a protective arm around her and dropped another kiss on her head. She tilted her chin up to him, love shining on her face.

Longing and sorrow swamped her, hard and fast, and she wrapped her arms around her middle, willing it all away. She'd been so good at not feeling anything for these past few years, and now one happy couple had undone all that hard work.

"Darce." Mack's voice, laced with concern. How had he seen? Where had he come from? She looked up at him, but his face was suspiciously blurry. She blinked.

"I need some air," she said. "Can you watch the register for me?"

Then she bolted.

Mack stood there, stunned as Darcy darted across the barn and into the back. Then he went after her, calling out to another employee to take the register. To hell with this not being his place. Something in her eyes tugged at him and he knew he was helpless to resist. Plus, he owed her after earlier, in the coffee shop.

When he came in the back room, Marla looked at him, then pointed at the door. "I'll get the front."

"Thanks," he said, and went outside.

The cold air hit him with a blast, after the warmth of the back room. She stood by the tree line, her back to him. He saw the defensiveness of her posture, her arms wrapped around herself, her head down.

The fierce need to draw her in, rest his chin on her head, to just hold her, nearly overwhelmed him. He shoved his hands into his pockets instead as he came up beside her. "What's going on? Did that woman upset you?"

Had she been thinking what he had? Seeing them as a young married couple? Wondering how their marriage had disintegrated so fast?

She went even stiffer than before, if that was possible. "Mack, why are you out here?"

"I don't know." It was God's honest truth. He came around to the front of her, but she wouldn't look up. "Darcy. Did she?"

She shook her head. "Of course not. She was very nice. Excited for their first Christmas together." Her voice cracked slightly. She cleared her throat. "I've just got a headache."

A headache. Right. And he'd just grown a third arm. "Okay. Can I get you anything?" Why had he thought she'd maybe confide? That maybe they'd seen the same thing and had the same regrets? Why would she tell him?

She lifted her gaze then, and the pain in her eyes

nearly brought him to his knees. "There's nothing you can do."

If that was the truth, then what the hell? He cupped her chin in his hand, saw her eyes widen. "I saw it, too. I felt it, too. Lie to me, but not yourself." His voice was rough in his throat. "Don't think this is easy on me, Darce. It's not." Then because he couldn't not, he bent forward and planted a soft kiss on her cold lips, lingering for a heartbeat, before he pulled away. Now there was surprise in her eyes, and that was better than pain. He ran his thumb over her lower lip, then turned to go back inside.

Because if he didn't, he'd kiss her again. For real. And once they started down that path, there'd be no going back.

"You going to turn the water off, dear?" Amusement filled Marla's voice as Darcy blinked, then yanked the handle down. *Mack kissed me.* That was a shock after the little scene in the coffee shop earlier. Marla hadn't asked any questions, and that led Darcy to believe Marla thought something had happened with her and Mack.

She wouldn't be wrong, exactly.

It had been a small kiss. A peck, really. But, oh, it—and the look in his eyes—had shot straight to her heart.

She managed a smile for her aunt's sake. "Just tired."

"Mmm-hmm." Marla folded the towel precisely and put it on the counter. "Darcy. What happened today?"

Darcy shut her eyes. She didn't want to relive it. If she'd been able to control the reaction, as she had the few times she was hit with it before, none of this would have happened. Of course, Mack hadn't been within touching distance. "I had a weak moment."

Marla sat down at the table, and the squeak of a second chair being nudged out was a clear hint that she wanted Darcy to have a seat, too. So she did, reluctantly. "Honey, this has been a shock for you. I'm not sure how much you've dealt with since you've been gone." She held up a hand as Darcy opened her mouth to deny it. "Please. Listen. Okay?" Darcy clamped her mouth shut and nodded. "Okay. You left but you never dealt with the pain. You suffered two incredibly hard losses in a short time. You wouldn't talk about it when we asked you. You kept insisting you were fine. And you were so very young to boot. You've thrown yourself into your new life, but reinventing yourself isn't any good if the foundation you've based it on isn't strong."

Tears pricked Darcy's eyes, but she folded her hands tightly in front of her on the table, not wanting to give in to the weakness. Again. Marla's gnarled hand found hers, closing tight over her own. Darcy focused on her aunt's neatly trimmed nails to try to keep the tears at bay.

"Honey. You are strong. You are one of the strongest people I know, and as stubborn as your uncle. You went through hell and back and it's okay to grieve. It's not weak. It's necessary."

Darcy shut her eyes. She appreciated this, she did, but Marla didn't know the whole story. No one did.

"Talk to Mack," Marla said gently. "You don't have to reconcile, but you do have some stuff to put behind you."

Darcy managed a smile. "I appreciate your concern. It has been a shock." That was the absolute truth. Seeing Mack had sent her off-kilter in so many ways. Knowing he was buying the farm had been the least of it. "But there's not much to say, Aunt Marla. It was a long time ago. I don't see what it would change."

Marla sat back and Darcy caught the look of disappointment that passed over her face. She swallowed hard. It was so important that she keep all this locked down. She'd worked so hard to get it to that point. She wasn't sure what would happen if she let it all out now.

The next night, she went upstairs to her room, but she wasn't sleepy, despite her restless nights and busy days. She looked out the window to see the snow had stopped. The moon was shining on the snow, gilding the trees with silver. It was still fairly early, only eight thirty.

She went back downstairs and outside. She needed more shampoo, so she'd run to Jim's to grab some. It'd get her out of her head and off the farm for a little bit.

Win-win.

She drove into town and parked in the half-empty parking lot of the grocery store. Inside, she got her shampoo but stopped dead when she saw who was in line in front of her.

Mack.

Knowing she couldn't turn and slip away once he spotted her, she lifted her chin and got in line.

"Evening," he said, and offered her a smile.

Her breath caught. The laugh lines that fanned out from his eyes added character and were surprisingly sexy. "Hi," she managed to return in a normal voice. Then, because she couldn't stand there and look at him, she dropped her attention to the items he'd put on the belt, including a garish box with a toucan on it.

"Kids' cereal?" A giggle escaped her. "Still?"

He looked sheepish. "Hey. I like them."

"I know." Now her gaze caught his and the weight of a shared past blanketed them for a heartbeat. For once, it wasn't fringed with pain. She swallowed hard.

"How are you tonight?" The cashier's chirpy voice cut through the moment and Darcy looked away, heart pounding, as Mack turned to address the young woman.

She kept her gaze fixed on the colorful box of cereal. Because then she wasn't looking at how those jeans hugged his perfect rear. If she didn't look, she didn't have to acknowledge how badly she wanted to slide her hands over it.

If she didn't acknowledge it, she could pretend everything was normal. That somehow she wasn't losing her tenuous grip on normal.

Oh, who was she kidding? He turned so his profile was to her and she couldn't help looking. He had a small scar on his jaw. That was new. Her fingers itched to touch it, to feel the roughness of the slight growth on his face. He turned to look at her then, and her face turned hot.

"See you, Darcy."

She managed a smile. "Bye."

He walked away, pushing his cart with his couple of grocery bags, and she could still see the box of cereal. It was bittersweet to know some things never changed.

She paid for her own purchase and walked out.

"Darce."

She jumped at his voice. "Mack. What are you doing?"

"Sorry. Didn't mean to scare you." He nodded to the Town Line Diner across the street. "Want to grab coffee? I'd like to make up for the other day."

Oh, yes, more than anything. Which was why, when

she opened her mouth, she fully intended to say no. "Sure."

Blame it on the darn cereal. He looked so relieved, she couldn't berate herself for her weakness. "Great. Let me just put these in the truck. I'll meet you over there."

"Okay." Darcy walked to her car, the butterflies in her midsection going full flutter. What had she done? This wasn't a good idea.

It was just coffee. Maybe a chance to smooth things over.

She sat in her car and waited until he got in his truck, then followed him to the diner. This was why Uncle Joe's suggestion she buy the tree farm was ridiculous. She couldn't imagine running into Mack all over the place. She'd never be able to breathe fully here.

Coward.

Well, yes. Yes, she was. She parked next to him, grabbed her purse and took a deep breath.

She got out of the car and walked in next to him, unable to suppress the little shiver of awareness when his arm brushed hers. Even through the thickness of their coats, she swore she could feel his heat. Neither of them spoke.

Unsettled, she followed him wordlessly to a booth in the corner. She remembered coming here as a teenager with her friends. It smelled the same, of coffee and bacon and burgers. She slipped her jacket off and tried not to look at him.

Which, as it turned out, was easier said than done.

The waitress, perky and young, came over. "Hi, Dr. Lawless. What can I get you?" Darcy swore the young woman batted her eyes at him.

"Hi, Michelle. I'll just have coffee. Darce?" He shifted

his smile from the waitress to her. She resisted the urge to bat her eyes, as well.

The waitress shifted her attention to Darcy and took her in. If she hadn't been already on the edge, she'd have found it amusing to be viewed this way by a girl who couldn't be more than twenty to Mack's thirty-two. Clearly she didn't know the story of Darcy and Mack. If she did, Darcy was willing to bet she'd find her coffee in her lap. "Same. Thanks."

Michelle pocketed her pad and headed off, a definite swing to her hips. Darcy looked back at Mack, whose gaze was on her, not the girl, and raised an eyebrow. "Still charming the ladies?"

"All but one, it seems," he said, and his tone was serious.

She dropped her gaze and toyed with her silverware. He didn't waste time getting to the point. "Why do you think charming her would work?" She meant to keep her tone light and failed.

"I don't. But nothing else does." The frankness of his words caught her. She sat back and regarded him with slightly narrowed eyes.

"What do you want, Mack?" It seemed best to just ask. Maybe they could just clear the air and move on.

He met her gaze as the waitress returned with the coffeepot. Darcy said nothing as she filled both cups, then reached for two creams when she left. "Nice to know some things don't change."

She emptied both in her cup. "Like what?"

"You've always taken your coffee the same way."

The reference to the past, which lately hovered too close to the surface, brought her up short. "I've changed a lot, Mack."

"I know."

"Do you?" She sipped the hot liquid, welcomed the burn. "I've been gone a long time."

"I know that, too." Now his gaze was steady on hers. "We've got a lot to talk about."

She shook her head. "No, not really. Nothing will change what happened and how it was handled. I will say I'm sorry." Damn it, now there were tears burning in her eyes. "I'm so sorry for how it all went down. But it's not all my fault."

He leaned forward. "You left, Darce. Just left."

"No, Mack. You let me go."

Chapter Five

He stared at her. “It was what you wanted.”

No, it hadn’t been. What she’d wanted was for him to want her—to want their marriage—enough to fight for her. Make her stay. Want her for more than just her role as mother of their child.

He hadn’t. He’d just granted the divorce, no questions asked.

He’d never actually asked her why she’d left.

She pushed her cup aside. “It doesn’t matter now, does it?”

Mack examined her, this woman who’d once been his wife. He’d so wanted to do right by her, but when it had come down to it, he’d failed her. Failed their baby. It wasn’t any less bitter a revelation now than it had been then. He thought of when she’d bolted at the sight of the happy young couple. Clearly, it all mattered to her, too, even if he couldn’t get her to admit it.

"It does matter." When she stared at him he cleared his throat. "It matters to me."

He saw regret and pain in her brown eyes. She dropped her gaze. "It was what I wanted."

Even as her words pierced him, he wondered if they were true. But this wasn't the place to push it. He reached over and took her hand, feeling its coldness in his own, but it did nothing to diminish the heat he felt when he touched her. "For what it's worth, I'm sorry, too." For all of it, even the way he'd sprung his plans for the farm on her.

She looked at their linked hands, then gave a nod. "Well, then. Friends?"

He squeezed her fingers before releasing her. "Friends." He didn't think this was settled, not by a long shot. But he'd take these first steps for what they were—a start. At least she wasn't running away in tears.

"So. Tell me about your practice," she invited, and he ran with the topic change, grateful for the chance to just be with her.

Nearly an hour later, he looked at his watch. Time to go back to the clinic. "I've got to go," he said, truly regretful. "I've got a patient to check on."

She looked at her phone, and seemed surprised at the time. "Wow. I didn't realize it was this late. Okay."

They paid the bill and walked out into the cold night. A light snow had moved in and it sparkled in the parking lot lights. Not wanting the evening to end, he turned to her. "Come with me?"

She blinked up at him, snow caught on her lashes. "Excuse me?"

"Do you want to see the clinic?"

He held his breath, not wanting to admit how important this was to him, as she clearly wrestled with the question. “Okay.”

Relief flooded him, along with something else he couldn’t name. “It’s not far. Follow me.”

She got in her SUV and followed him to the clinic. He had managed to get the Christmas lights up as well as the garland, and they were lit now—on a timer to go off at eleven, along with all the other businesses along Main Street. Darcy parked across the street and stood there, looking.

He came up next to her, closer than he knew he should. “What do you see?”

She gestured at the street. “It’s so cheery. Especially in the snow. When I think of Christmas, this is the scene I picture. I’ve missed it.”

He nearly pointed out she could have come back at any time—in fact, she’d never had to leave—but he didn’t want to ruin their new truce. “It is charming.” He swept his hand out. “Shall we?”

She gave a little giggle and stepped off the curb. God, how he’d missed her laugh. There hadn’t been much laughter after they got married. Then the accident had happened only six months in.

Pushing that thought away, he unlocked the door and reset the alarm. She stepped in behind him, noting the neatness of the waiting room. A Christmas tree stood in one corner, tags hanging off it. “What’s this?”

“A wish tree. For the humane society. Things like cat litter, dog food, towels and blankets, that kind of thing. People take a tag, drop off the items and one of us runs it out there.”

Oh, yes, this was the man she’d so loved. “What a great idea.” When he went in front of her, she took a tag off the tree. "Dry cat food," it read. She slipped it in her purse.

The waiting area had a hard floor, comfy chairs, a few magazines on a table. A bulletin board held pictures of lots of animals and their owners. Another framed picture said "Get to know Dr. Lawless" and had pictures of him and his pets. "This is sweet."

He glanced up from the chart he was looking over. "Oh. Well, people like to see my pets."

"How many?" she asked as she followed him back through a door.

"Two dogs, two cats," he said. "Sometimes more if I'm fostering somebody. Minnie is in here."

She heard the muffled barking behind another door and raised an eyebrow.

"Those are the boarders, or those that are recovering from less intense surgeries. In here I keep those who need a more relaxed environment. Trauma patients or riskier surgeries."

"And who's Minnie?" She followed him into the room, where a little beagle lay on a doggie bed. She thumped her tail when they walked up.

"Minnie was hit by a car. The guy who hit her brought her in. She was— It was touch-and-go. She needs more pain meds."

Darcy stared at the liquid brown eyes, so full of pain yet joy to see them. "Oh, what a sweet girl. Who's her owner?"

"We don't know yet. No collar, no tags, no microchip." He opened the cage door and murmured in a low voice to the dog while Darcy stood back, out of the way, watching. There was a little yelp as he gave her a shot.

Then he rubbed her head as she dozed off. "Here. You can pet her while she falls asleep."

Darcy stepped forward and rubbed the dog's head. Minnie tried to give her a little lick. "Oh, you poor sweet girl. You don't know who she belongs to?"

"No." His tone was grim.

A shudder ran through Darcy. "Abandoned?"

His face was grim. "Happens more than you'd care to know. Foreclosure, need to move, can't take care of the pets. Sometimes they just leave them in the house and walk away. Sometimes they just drop them off somewhere thinking, hey, it's an animal, it can fend for itself. They can't." Anger laced his voice. "I understand not being able to feed them. But I wish—I wish people would bring them to a shelter rather than just abandon them."

She touched his wrist with her free hand, thought of the wish tree in the lobby. "That's so sad. They've got you as an advocate, though. That counts as something."

He moved up next to her, and in the dim light she saw the weight of this on him. The grimness on his face was reflected in his tone. "It's not enough. It will never be enough. However." He reached in, his arm brushing hers, his hand touching hers as he rubbed the now sleeping Minnie's head. "We do what we can."

She looked up at him as he looked back down at her. The heat from the proximity of their bodies drowned out everything else. He was so close she could lay her head on his chest. If she angled her body slightly, she could fit against him, see if it was still as perfect as it had been all those years ago. His hand slid over hers on Minnie's head, and the rough warmth of his palm sent sparks across her skin. He withdrew both their hands together, and his hot gaze dropped to her mouth.

Minnie whimpered in her sleep and Darcy stepped back, her breath shaky, as he shifted his attention to the dog. She cleared her throat. "Will she be okay?" Her words were a little breathy.

"I hope so. So far so good." She heard the roughness of his voice and closed her eyes. This attraction wasn't welcome, yet she couldn't control her reaction to him any more than she could stop breathing.

He latched the cage and made a note in the chart. She stepped a little farther back. "Do you have to come back and check on her later?"

He shook his head. "Jennifer will check on her later tonight. There's an apartment upstairs. She lives there and usually when we have a case like this takes the middle of the night shift."

"Oh. Well. That's handy," she murmured, trying to ignore the completely irrational spurt of jealousy at the casual mention of the other woman. Stupid, and totally unwarranted.

"Yeah, it works well." He tipped his head toward the door. "I've done what I need to here. You ready?"

She followed him back out, noting the quiet with which he shut the door behind him. She nodded toward the other door. "Do they need to be taken out?"

"No, that's all been taken care of for the evening," he said, and set Minnie's chart on the front desk.

"You've done well, Mack." The observation slipped out and he turned to her with surprise. "You fit here."

He moved toward her, his gaze sharp. "As would you, Darcy."

She shook her head. "No, I'm good in Chicago. I love it there."

"Do you?" He moved closer still and she edged back, but the hallway wall stopped her. "Do you really?"

He wasn't holding her in place, but Darcy couldn't seem to move. It was as if her cells had missed him so much she needed to soak up his nearness, his heat, as if he were the sun. She swallowed. "Yes," she whispered.

He moved a little closer and braced one arm on the wall, his gaze never leaving hers, the heat and want there a mirror of her own. "Darcy," he murmured, then lowered his head to settle his mouth on hers.

Her eyes drifted closed and she savored the sweetness of the kiss, which quickly turned to fire as he nipped at her lip. She opened for him and the kiss went from sweet to spicy in a heartbeat.

She slid her arms around his neck and let her fingers play in the longer hair there. He plunged his fingers in her hair and deepened the kiss even more. Fire licked through her, and brought with it the roaring desire she'd always had with Mack.

All of a sudden he wrenched back and left her, nearly panting, against the wall. "God, Darcy, I'm sorry. I didn't mean— I overstepped."

Her face burned. Sorry. Of course he was. "Are you saying we need to just forget it happened?"

He didn't seem to sense the trap. "Yeah, I think that'd be best."

He couldn't have hurt her more if he'd physically struck her. She swallowed hard and lifted her chin. "Well. Consider it forgotten." She darted around him and he let her go.

He let out a curse as the door shut behind her. He'd made a royal mess of it. Not the first time. They'd been making strides toward a fragile peace and then he went and gave in to the need to push her, to touch her, to kiss her. To get her to admit she'd made a mistake. Now she'd be back to avoiding him.

Maybe that was for the best. Maybe they couldn't manage "friends" after all. Especially with kisses like that hanging between them.

He walked back to his office and looked out the window to confirm her car was gone. He didn't want to admit he was more than disappointed she'd left. He hadn't been able to give her a reason to stay when it mattered most, so why did he think it'd be different now?

He was a fool. A fool for Darcy Kramer. It seemed he'd learned nothing over the past several years.

She'd leave—again—and that'd be the end.

This time for good.

Mack had kissed her. Really kissed her.

And she'd melted all over.

The memory of it swirled through her system, like the snowflakes that danced in her headlights. A little shiver ran through her. No one had ever kissed like Mack did, made her feel like Mack did. Not that she had much experience outside of Mack. She'd shut that part of her down.

Of course, he'd also suggested it had been a mistake. So there was that. She tried to ignore the spike of disappointment and remind herself it was for the best.

She snapped out of her reverie when she pulled into the driveway and saw an ambulance parked there. In a heartbeat the panic set in. She threw the car in Park with a gasp and ran up to the door, where she saw her uncle strapped to the gurney and her aunt's ashen face.

"Uncle Joe! Aunt Marla, what happened?" She stood

to the side so the paramedics could load her uncle in the ambulance.

"His heart." Marla turned stricken eyes on Darcy. "He's having pain, shortness of breath, all of it."

Darcy inhaled deeply and took her aunt's arm. "I'll drive you up to the hospital," she said as the nearby paramedic nodded as they climbed into the vehicle. "Let's go."

They hurried back to her still warm car and Darcy bounced down the driveway behind the ambulance. Marla sat beside her and even in the dark, Darcy could feel the tension and fear rolling off her aunt.

Hours passed, and Marla looked up at Darcy. "You'd better call Mack. Let him know."

Darcy inhaled sharply. While she knew her aunt was right, the thought made her own heart beat irregularly. She kept her voice calm. "I don't have his number. If you can put it in my phone, I'll do that now."

Marla nodded, apparently not reading anything on her face, so Darcy pulled her phone out. It was late. Would he even answer? She'd left in such a hurry.

The phone rang twice. Then Mack's voice, low and calm. "Hello?"

Darcy took a deep breath. "It's me. Darcy," she added lamely, momentarily tangled up in the propriety of how to identify herself to the man she'd been married to yet hadn't spoken to for seven years until the past week or so.

"Darcy?" The question he didn't ask was clear in his tone. "Is everything okay?"

"Um, not really. Uncle Joe's in the hospital. Aunt Marla asked me to call you and let you know." She folded her free arm across her middle and stared out at the parking lot, at the snow sifting down on the cars parked there. The coldness of the scene reflected how she felt inside.

"What happened?" He sounded much more alert now.

Darcy explained what she knew. "So it's a waiting game now. I'm with Aunt Marla and some of her friends. They're knitting."

A little chuckle came over the line. "I'm sure they are. I'll be there in fifteen."

Darcy jumped and looked up to see Marla's gaze on her. "Um. That's not necessary. It's so late—"

"See you then."

The phone went dead in her hand and she pulled it away from her ear to stare at it, frustrated. There was no reason for him to be here. They weren't married. Joe was going to be fine.

She walked back over to her aunt, who had needles flying in her hands. She looked up, but the needles never slowed. "Did you talk to him, then?"

Darcy dropped in a chair. "Yep. He said he's on his way."

"That's good." Marla didn't miss a beat. "He'll be a good source of support for you."

"I don't need him," she said, too worried and too tired to care that this conversation had to take place in front of two of Marla's best friends, who knew what had happened with her and Mack. And she almost believed what she'd said. Almost. Truth was, she'd love to lean on him. But the price was more than she could ever pay.

Marla's needles clicked. "Maybe he needs to be here. He and Joe are close."

Of course. Now Darcy just felt foolish. Mack had relationships outside of and independent of her. One of those was with her uncle.

She fidgeted in her chair. The steady click of needles should be calming, but, God, she just hated hospitals. The smell. The feeling. The urgency, the waiting, the memories of a stay here in this hospital, where she'd lost her baby and the seeds of destruction for her marriage had begun to bloom.

Now it had Uncle Joe in its grasp.

She took a deep breath, tried to calm the nerves. Marla needed her to be strong. But it all felt like yesterday.

She laid a hand on her belly lightly, knowing no life beat there. That the last time it had beat there was seven years ago. By the time she'd gotten here after the accident, it had already been too late. And it was possible she'd never get pregnant again. And while she hadn't been ready at the time to be a mother, she'd had the opportunity ripped from her forever.

Of course, being a mother implied there was a man to get her pregnant. A marriage even. Someone who loved her and stood by her.

She thought she'd had a chance at that once, but she'd been wrong, as had the timing. Now that she was older and wiser, she was ready.

But she'd lost the only man she'd ever wanted to share the dream with. Now she was here and so was he and she needed to finally put it all behind her. And forget she was in a hospital and focus on her uncle, who'd need her help more than ever, since he'd be laid up for most of the Christmas season. Which meant what? She'd have to stay? She'd worry about that later.

She was thinking positive. He'd be okay. He was too tough not to be.

But it was so hard to beat back the fear.

Chapter Six

Mack made it to the hospital in under fifteen minutes. Darcy hadn't really said how Joe was, how Marla was. Equally important, how she was. He hurried in and up to the surgical waiting room. When he entered his gaze landed right on Darcy. She sat, arms folded over her middle, her face pinched and white, and stared at the TV, which ran a twenty-four-hour cable news show. Then he looked at Marla, whose expression was knowing despite the tension on her face.

Darcy looked over and he forgot to worry about what they thought.

She'd pulled her hair up in a clip, and pieces had slipped out and fallen all around her face. Memories of the last time they'd spent time in the hospital assaulted him, as they no doubt did her, as well. His gut twisted when she turned her pale face toward him and he saw etched on her face the pain and memories. Not to mention the fear for her uncle.

He crossed the floor but stopped short of pulling her in his arms, though every cell screamed that he needed to get closer, hold her, let her break down and get it all out.

She hadn't let him comfort her when they were married. Why would now, when they were virtually strangers, be any different?

"Mack. You came." It was Marla's voice. Not the one he wanted to hear, but he turned to her and hugged her instead. Darcy wouldn't meet his eyes over Marla's head. Marla hugged him fiercely.

"She needs you," she murmured in a low tone. "She'll never admit it. Thank you for coming," she added in a louder voice.

"Of course," he said, choosing to ignore Marla's words about Darcy. "Any news?"

Marla shook her head and he saw, with a pang, that she looked every one of her years. He'd always thought she was so strong, so youthful. Tonight, fear for her husband had aged her. "Not yet. They said hours, so—" She glanced at the clock.

Darcy came over and rubbed her aunt's back. "Time goes so slow, doesn't it?" He didn't know if Marla caught the undertone of deep sorrow, but he did. He remembered all too well.

"Can you ladies use something from the cafeteria?" He could at least be useful.

One of Marla's friends perked up. "That's a great idea, Mack. Why don't you and Darcy make a run?"

Mack turned to her. She wouldn't like that suggestion, he knew. "Darcy?"

She looked like the proverbial deer caught in headlights. Before she could say anything, Marla spoke up. "He'll need the extra set of hands, dear."

Darcy inclined her head and offered a stiff smile to him. More of a baring of teeth than a real smile. "Well, then. Let's hurry."

She strode away toward the elevator, and he couldn't help watching her slender hips sway. Jeez. What kind of guy stared at a woman's rear when she was worried and scared and suffering from memories better left buried? He tried not to think of her mouth, hot and mobile under his, just a couple hours ago.

He moved after her and stepped into the elevator as she jabbed the button for the basement and therefore the cafeteria. She leaned against the wall of the car, her arms folded tightly across her chest, her stance screaming "leave me alone."

He couldn't. "Darcy." He kept his tone gentle, his stance relaxed. Her gaze shifted to his, then away. "I know what you're going through."

At that her gaze shot to his and she straightened up. "I doubt it very much, Mack."

"You're thinking about that night. It's hard to be here."

"But yet you came," she said, and there was a thread of bitterness under her words.

"Of course I did. Joe and Marla are important to me."

Now her gaze was full of pain. "That's good," she murmured.

He moved closer, trapping her in the corner. "Am I wrong?"

She shook her head. "Not as long as you're here for them only. What went wrong with us can't be fixed, Mack."

"I lied."

She drew back, whether from the words or the heat in his tone, he wasn't sure. He forged on, pinning her in the corner with his gaze, careful not to touch her. "I'm not sorry I kissed you earlier."

She blinked and the elevator door opened. He turned and walked out, sure if he didn't get away right then, he'd give in and kiss her until the pain in her eyes went away. Until the past wouldn't wedge between them anymore.

Darcy followed him into the cafeteria, a little surprised at how busy it was for midnight. But far more shocked by Mack's arrival and his words in the elevator. She'd been working darn hard on a righteous anger and he'd just popped it like a balloon.

She needed the anger to keep her distance. To keep the fear for her uncle at bay.

Right now she was too wrung out to sulk about it.

Mack handed her a tray and proceeded to pile it with crackers, cookies and some fruit. Her hands trembled, but she managed to hold the tray.

He tipped her chin up with one finger. "Hey," he said softly. She blinked back the tears the gesture threatened to break loose. She would not cry, not here, not now, not ever…

He took the tray and set it down, then pulled her in as the dam broke. She couldn't help it, she burrowed in, and he wrapped her up tight, murmuring words she couldn't quite understand, but the tone was soothing. He pressed his lips to her hair. She felt the light kisses even as she sobbed out her fear and anger and regrets into the chest of the man she'd loved more than life itself and had lost.

Finally, she wasn't sure how long it took, but her sobs subsided into hiccups and it dawned on her where she was. She didn't have the energy to break away, even though she knew she needed to. They stood like that, the steady pound of his heart calming her, his heat seeping into places she hadn't known she was cold.

"Better?" His voice was a rumble under her ear. He didn't loosen his grip, but she nodded against his chest and pulled away slightly. He loosened his grip but didn't let her go.

"Oh, no." She touched his shirt lightly. It was wet and sported mascara smears. "I made a mess. I'm sorry." She must look a fright, but she couldn't bring herself to care, even if she was covered in snot, mascara and tears.

He ran his hands up her arms and she became aware they were in a public place, and even though it was late, they had an audience. Still, she couldn't bring herself to break the contact. "I don't care, Darce. It'll wash."

She stepped back and he let her go, with what looked like regret on his face. "Thank you," she whispered, feeling too emotionally flayed to pretend any different. It was the first time she'd cried over all this in seven years. Once she'd realized he was going to just let her walk away, she'd been unable to cry. To grieve what they'd lost. She'd locked it all down.

They paid for their purchases and headed back to the elevator. There she simply stood next to him and drew from his strength. Their arms touched, and the small contact was enough.

It felt good. She'd worry about how dangerous it was another day.

* * *

Back in the waiting room, Marla looked up when they walked in. Darcy knew her aunt took in her tear-ravaged face when her gaze softened. Mack held up the bag and inclined his head toward the cardboard container of drinks Darcy held.

"Food and coffee. Both hospital-grade, but that can't be helped."

Marla managed a small smile at his joke. "Thank you, you two." She glanced at the clock. "Shouldn't be long now."

Marla's friend Carol came over, snagged two coffees and handed one to Marla. "Not too long," she agreed.

Darcy took her aunt a cookie and set it on a napkin next to her. Marla's smile was faint but real. She reached forward and pulled Darcy into a hug.

"Oh, honey. You okay?" she whispered.

Darcy nodded. She needed to address this head-on. "I just had a moment. I'm fine now. You?"

Marla sat back. "I'm hanging in there," she said with a fierce nod. "He'll be okay."

"Yes, he will," Darcy agreed. It simply couldn't go any other way.

She couldn't sit, so she walked back to the window while Aunt Marla's needles clicked away. She held her cooling coffee in both hands and stared at the parking lot. A fine layer of snow coated all the vehicles in the lot. Mack came and stood beside her. He said nothing, just leaned against the wall near her. She decided to be grateful for that. She could allow the small chink in her armor.

As long as she fixed it tomorrow.

The phone rang and the nurse manning the station

answered, speaking in low tones. When she hung up, she said, "Family of Joe Kramer?"

Marla leaped up, Carol catching her knitting as it flew from her lap. Darcy hurried to her side, her heart pounding, her palms clammy. *Please, please, please let him be okay.* She slipped her arm around her aunt's shoulders, felt her take a deep breath. "That's us," she said.

"Come with me," the nurse said. "The doctor will talk to you back here."

They followed her wordlessly back to the room she indicated, where the surgeon was already waiting. He rose to his feet and extended his hand to Marla. "Mrs. Kramer. I'm Dr. Peterson. First of all, let me assure you your husband came through surgery just fine."

Darcy's breath whooshed out at the same time Marla said, "Oh, thank God." Darcy hugged her aunt hard, relief flooding her.

They sat and the doctor went over the details. The upshot was Uncle Joe would be sidelined for the next six to eight weeks. Darcy knew it would make him crazy.

They shook hands with the doctor and went back in the waiting room.

"He's okay," Marla said to Carol, and promptly burst into tears. Her friend opened her arms and hugged her close. Mack came over and stood next to Darcy, but didn't touch her.

"Good news," he said quietly.

She nodded and gave him a wan smile. "Very. A huge relief. They said Aunt Marla can see him soon, once he's out of recovery." She glanced at the clock. "Another forty-five minutes or so, I guess. He's got a long road in front of him, but the doctor was optimistic."

This would mean Joe couldn't work at the farm. They'd need full-time help. He'd check his schedule and see if Jennifer could take over a bit of his load, which would free him up to spend more time at the farm.

Near Darcy.

He wasn't sure yet if that was a good thing or not. Right now they were on fragile ground, because she was distracted—and because the memories that bound them were centered on this hospital. The real test would be when he spent more time at the farm.

"After I see him, you can go home," Marla said. "No point in both of us being here all night."

Darcy sent Marla a worried look. "You can come, too. Lie in your own bed, even if you can't sleep."

Marla shook her head. "I need to be here, Darcy. Please. You'll need to run the farm for now. Can you do that?"

"Of course." Her response was swift and sure.

"I'll help more," Mack said, and watched shock flit over Darcy's face. "I'll work my schedule around it as much as possible. You and Joe don't have to worry about anything but getting him well."

Marla squeezed his hands. "Thank you. I knew we could count on both of you. Don't let it get in the way of your practice, though."

"I won't," he assured her. Darcy looked less than pleased. He'd talk to her later, get her to see his point. They could work around each other just fine. He knew the peace they'd forged tonight was fragile, but they'd have to find a way to make it all work. Put aside the past for the sake of the couple they both loved.

His family would be fairly certain he'd lost his mind.

After Marla's visit, and she'd reassured Darcy she

was okay now and nearly shoved her to the elevator, she and Mack rode to the first floor in silence.

He saw the worry etched on her face and the exhaustion. “Do you want me to stay?”

Her shock showed he’d overstepped. “Excuse me?”

“At their house. I can sleep on the couch. Keep you company.” Clearly, he was so tired his mouth had separated from his common sense. Still, in for a penny…

She blinked and shook her head. “No. I’m fine. I’ll be fine,” she amended, apparently seeing him forming a rebuttal. “Really.”

He bit back a sigh. He had no grounds to push, wasn’t sure he wanted to anyway. There were lines, and tonight they’d been grayed out a bit, smudged.

Darcy collapsed on her bed after a tense ride home. Mack had followed her, damn him, reminding her what a great guy he was. She didn’t want to be reminded. It was hard enough with the past hovering between them, with the memories, with their loss. All of it combined into an overwhelming emotional morass that she could not deal with tonight on top of her worry about her uncle.

Mack had turned around in the driveway. She was grateful he hadn’t tried to talk to her. “Do you want me to stay?” indeed.

Of course she didn’t. Not after he’d kissed her and later, held her while she’d cried. He’d been so sweet. Dangerous.

She peeled her clothes off and crawled under the covers, fairly sure sleep would not come for her tonight.

She woke the next morning to light streaming through the window. With a gasp she sat up and grabbed her phone. It was nearly eight. She had to get to the hospital. Aunt Marla needed to come home and sleep and Darcy wanted to know how Uncle Joe was doing. Then she had a tree farm to run. A run through the shower was a necessity and she washed up quickly, ran downstairs as her phone rang.

"Hello?"

"Darcy, it's Aunt Marla."

Dread pooled in her stomach. "Is—"

"Everything is fine, honey. Joe is tough. He's doing exactly what he should be doing for someone postsurgery."

Relief had Darcy slumping against the wall. "Okay, then. That's good."

"It is. Carol and her husband are bringing me home. Did I catch you before you left?"

"Um, yeah. I overslept—"

"No, you didn't." Marla's voice was soothing. "Go back to bed if you can. It was a rough night for both of us."

Darcy looked at the coffee can in her hand. Not likely, but there was no point in saying so. Once she was up, she was up. "I'm good. So I'll see you soon."

"Yes. We're going to grab a little bite to eat and then I'll be there."

A few more words and Darcy hung up. Thankfully, Uncle Joe was okay. Should she tell Mack?

She stuffed the phone in her pocket. No. They'd already crossed too many lines. If he wanted to know he could call her. Or better yet, call Marla.

She started the coffee and poured a bowl of cereal, pulling the books out to peruse over breakfast. She was surprised Marla hadn't strong-armed him into computer records. The records were very complete and organized, but that would have to change— She stopped the thought. It didn't matter now. She wasn't going to use a computer when she'd only be here another week.

The schedule was spelled out in detail. Today she had to oversee the cutting of a fresh load for a big box retailer a couple towns to the south. If they'd had more of that kind of order, maybe the farm would have been okay.

The slam of a car door brought her head up for a moment from the books and her cereal. Must be Aunt Marla. When no one came in and a second door slam got her attention, she stood up and walked to the window.

Aunt Marla was just now being dropped off. So who had come before her?

Her gaze landed on the truck. Oh, no. That couldn't be—could it?

Marla and Carol came in before she could go stomping out in the snow to make sure it wasn't Mack, skipping work to help out here.

Her aunt enveloped her in a hug. Her skin was gray and she looked exhausted, but the little brackets of tension were gone around her eyes. "He'll be okay," she said, and Darcy squeezed her eyes shut against the sting of tears.

"Of course he will," she agreed. Those doctors had better be right. She didn't think her aunt could take losing her husband of so many years this early.

Marla gave her a little squeeze and stepped back. "I see Mack is out there."

Darcy sighed. "There's no need. I can handle it."

Marla exchanged a look with Carol and patted her

arm. “Accept his help, honey. The farm needs it. It’s nice of him.”

Nice. Darcy nearly snorted. He wanted this place for his own purposes, to expand his vet practice. His brother was going to build houses on it.

Marla slipped off her coat. “Besides, it’s going to take some doing to convince Joe to relax and let the farm be managed by someone else. Mack will go a long way to easing his mind.”

There was nothing to say to that, so Darcy didn’t try. Instead, she pulled her aunt in for a hug. “Are you going to catch some sleep now?”

“She’s going to try,” Carol answered firmly, and shook her head when Marla opened her mouth. “The doc told you to get some sleep, Marla. Joe needs you to be strong. I promise I’ll be back for you in a few hours.”

Marla tugged at the hem of her shirt, which was wrinkled. Exhaustion was etched clearly on her face. “I’ll try.” Then she pointed at her friend. “You, too.”

“Me, too,” Carol agreed. “I’m going home now. I’ll see you this afternoon.”

She left and Darcy steered Marla toward the stairs. “Let’s get you settled in,” she said.

“Did you sleep?” Marla asked.

“I did. You will, too.”

Marla paused in the bedroom doorway. “Accept Mack’s help, okay, Darcy? I know you’d rather not be around him, but—”

“I’ll be fine,” Darcy said, and smiled at her aunt. “We’ll make it work. Now go. Sleep.”

Chapter Seven

Mack looked up from his conversation with one of the employees to see Darcy striding toward him, a frown on her face. He excused himself from the conversation, not missing the other man's interested expression. No doubt this was best done without anyone overhearing. He met her halfway.

"Why are you here?" The anger in her tone caught him off guard, as he took in her flushed face and fisted hands. She wore a green fleece and a red vest, with a red knit cap over her hair. She looked festive. And angry. And hot.

He took a second to focus on something other than the *hot* part of the equation.

"I'm here because your uncle needs help," he said carefully.

She narrowed her eyes and he resisted the urge to pull her in and kiss her. It wouldn't help things right now.

"I can handle it," she said, lifting her chin.

So she was feeling a little territorial about the farm. He got that. "I'm sure you can. But it'll be easier with more help. You've been gone a long time." She stiffened and he guessed that hadn't been the best choice of words. He caught her arm and she didn't pull away. "Darce. I don't mean that as a criticism. I mean that as a fact. You have. And you're leaving before the season is over." And once she left, the farm would be down two people.

Her shoulders slumped a bit, then she straightened back up. "You're right, of course." Her expression was a polite mask, but he caught a hint of pain in her eyes.

He hated to see all the fight go out of her, hated that he was the one who'd done the deflating. He resisted the urge to apologize—for what? For buying the place? For being available to help? "My schedule is pretty flexible. I'm happy to help you guys out. It's no trouble at all."

Her lips curved in a smile that still didn't reach her eyes. "I know my aunt and uncle appreciate it."

"If you are that unhappy about us buying it, you can always buy it yourself." The words slipped out before he could stop them.

She snapped her gaze to his, eyes wide. "No, I really can't, Mack. My life is in Chicago. I can't just—I can't just walk away and leave it behind."

He sent her a sideways look as he started back toward the barn. "Sure you can. If you want this bad enough." His point made, he walked off, leaving her fuming in his wake.

Darcy got the order filled and sent on its way. It was a good thing they had orders to fill. That people came out here to get their trees. It made her happy.

Or would have if Mack weren't about to take it all away. To be fair, yes, it was her aunt and uncle's farm. But how could Mack and his brother look at this place, look at the families, some of whom had been coming here for decades, and decide they could just build houses on it?

And how dare Mack hint that she had a choice? That she could leave her job, leave all she'd done, just walk away from it all?

So, okay, she hadn't been super happy at work lately. She was overworked and stressed, but that was normal for someone trying to make partner as she was. Right? And yes, she felt at home here, even more so than in the city she really did love, but she'd grown up here, so it made sense.

Didn't it?

Damn Mack for making her think. She just wanted to get through all this and back to Chicago. Okay, fine, they were going to tear apart her home. A home that would someday have been their son's—if their baby had lived.

Darcy stopped in her tracks at the thought. She'd never thought of it in those terms before. That the farm would have belonged to their child. That at seven, he'd be running all over, marveling at the magic of Christmas, doubly so on a farm that celebrated Christmas. Something warm hit her face and she realized she was crying. She dashed at the tears with her gloved hands, but they were already crusted with snow.

No. Why now? She'd worked so hard to keep the loss at bay, to lock the pain away. And she couldn't even rectify it—after the accident and the miscarriage, the doctors said she'd probably never have kids. Ever.

Just another reward for her selfishness, and something she'd learned after the fact. Another reason why she'd left. Mack had been so torn up over the loss, but he'd kept saying they could have more kids. Well, they couldn't.

"Darcy. Darcy?" Mack's concern cut through her fog. She tried to ignore him, but he came up behind her. "Darcy?" Now there was concern in his voice.

The snow fell around them, and not too far away, she could hear the happy calls of a family looking for the perfect tree.

"I'm sorry you're upset about the farm," he said, and sounded sincere. "It works well for all of us."

Except me.

Darcy kept the selfish thought to herself and dug though her pockets for a tissue of some kind to wipe her face. Would he think her red face was just from the cold? She could hope.

"Well," she managed in almost normal tones, "of course it does. I mean, you're right. I've been gone. I left. I made my choices."

How could one choice have so many consequences? Over so many years?

"Yes," Mack said carefully as if he sensed a trap. Smart man.

"Okay, then. I've got to—" she checked her watch as if it would give her the answers she needed "—run."

She scooted around him and sent him a wave over her shoulder as she trekked back the way she'd come, hoping he bought her line and left her alone.

Mack watched Darcy flee as if an army of rabid dogs was on her heels. Ah, well. It was better than having her fight with him.

On the other hand, when she was mad, at least she looked at him. And damn if she hadn't sounded as though she'd been crying. But since she'd been so clear on not letting him know he'd opted to honor her. Since his buying this place upset her so much.

Which he didn't want, either. But he couldn't tell her his reasoning. Owning it kept it near him. A piece of her.

Yeah, the fact Chase was going to develop it sucked a bit. But he'd be careful and tasteful. Chase's company specialized in green environmentally sound building practices. It was a big thing up here and, all told, it was much better than some other builder buying it and putting up cookie-cutter houses. Still, he knew it was cold comfort to Darcy.

That evening, he checked in on the animals, even though he didn't doubt for a minute Jennifer was doing a great job. Minnie was doing better, looking perkier and even filling out a little. He stroked her head a bit. When she was healed he'd either find her a new home or keep her himself.

Darcy had been very taken with Minnie that evening she was here. That evening he'd broken down and kissed her, which had been all kinds of stupid, but there it was. Would she like a dog? Or would that not fit in her big-city life?

The beagle licked his hand and he rubbed her ears.

"Everything look okay?"

There was only amusement in Jennifer's tone, and some surprise he'd stopped in here.

"Of course. I just— It's a habit."

"Like tucking in a child before bed, I would imagine." She pushed off the doorjamb as his gut knifed at her comparison.

I wouldn't know. The thought speared him. Jennifer didn't know he'd lost a child. "Most likely."

If she caught the odd tone in his voice, she gave no sign. "It's been as smooth as it always is, Mack."

"Are you saying you guys don't need me here?" he joked, hoping to dispel the tension in himself that had nothing to do with Jennifer and wasn't her fault.

"Of course not." She scratched behind Minnie's ears, as well. "There's always room for a token male."

Surprise huffed out in a laugh. "Damn, girl. You don't pull any punches."

"Nope. You should know that by now." She stepped away from the cage. "You going to fix things with Darcy?"

"What?" He wasn't sure what, if anything, to say.

Jennifer held up a hand. "I have eyes. I can see. The two of you have a lot of unfinished business. I hope she's smart enough to know what she's got in you."

What she had. Past tense. They were long past the point of being able to fix things. To pick up where they'd left off and move forward.

"We're very different people now," he said simply because it was the truth. "We want very different things." He shrugged.

Jennifer made a sympathetic sound in her throat. "Too bad." She turned to walk away. "I'll leave you to your tucking in, then."

"Thanks," he managed as she left. Why couldn't he be interested in *her*? She was smart, funny, cute and he enjoyed her company. She just wasn't Darcy. Not her fault.

He sighed and finished his rounds before heading

out to his house. The house he'd bought for his wife as a present, hoping to cheer her up, to give them a project to work on together.

Instead, she'd left and he'd signed the papers alone. And renovating it had been his therapy. Maybe someday he'd show her. But not tell her the whole story. It seemed cruel somehow, to tie it in with the past.

The house was a small one-story bungalow, white, with a very traditional front porch. He pulled into the drive and up to the garage—he rarely parked in there, since he had to shovel the snow somewhere and it ended up often as not in front of the garage—and got out. The motion light came on as he entered the kitchen. It took a few minutes of blessed busyness to take care of the animals' food, water and outside needs.

He had just finished when there was a knock at the front door. He could guess from all the joy coming from the dogs that it was his mom. She always had a treat for them.

He was right. She smiled at him when he answered the door and petted the dogs, giving them their treats before greeting him with a quick hug.

"Nice that I rate below the dogs," he said affectionately, and she patted his arm.

"Oh, don't be silly. But you don't slather attention on me the way they do."

"*Slather* is the key word there," he noted drily as Lilly attempted to lick his mother's hand while she walked toward the kitchen. She washed her hands and set another bag on the counter.

"So. How's Darcy?"

Mack winced at his mother's question. "Fine, as far as I can tell."

His mother made a harrumphing noise. “As far as you can tell? How can you not know?”

Floored Mack stared at his mother, whose narrowed gaze was lasered in on him. “Why would I know?”

Exasperation laced her tone. “Mack. Because you are working with her. Because you guys have a history—”

Mack held up a hand. “History or not, we’re not chatty.” He didn’t want to explain how trying to reconnect, even tenuously, kept resulting in dead ends. It bothered him. A lot. “We’re not—it’s been a long time, Mom.”

His mother opened the fridge and examined the contents as if all the answers to her confusing offspring resided inside, then turned and grabbed the bag she’d brought. “Maybe you can make it right with her.”

Mack frowned. “I thought you didn’t want her anywhere near me.”

“Why would you think that?” Seeming truly shocked, his mother set the bag back down with a thump. “You and Darcy were perfect for each other. I don’t think—” She stopped abruptly.

“Don’t think what?” he asked softly.

She pulled out the first container, paused, then turned to him. “Honestly, I don’t think she was ready to get married.”

Mack’s jaw dropped. “How can you say that? You were pushing me to do it!”

She nodded. “I was. But looking back, I see she wasn’t ready for any of it. Not like you were. She loved you—I have no doubt about that—but she wasn’t ready for the wife-and-motherhood thing.”

“She kind of didn’t have a choice,” he pointed out, even as his stomach soured. Could his mother be right?

She looked at him, her gaze serious. “That’s exactly my point, Mack. She didn’t have a choice. And before she could even adjust to any of it, she lost all of it. I wish—” She stopped and pressed her fingers to her lips. “I wish I’d seen it then. I wish we hadn’t pushed you to do right by her, when it was clearly not what she was ready for.”

Mack sat there, stunned. “She could have said no, for God’s sake. I didn’t force her to marry me.” Had he, inadvertently? He’d certainly worked to convince her. Maybe, in retrospect, that should have been his first clue.

She reached over and rubbed his arm. “She could have, you’re right. And you were a wonderful husband. If there’d been no—accident, I think you’d have worked it all out and stayed together.”

Would they have? As soon as the going got tough, she’d abandoned him emotionally, or so he’d always believed. Now it made sense, especially if his mom was right, and she hadn’t been ready.

God, he was an idiot. Worse.

“I guess we’ll never know,” he said, and heard the note of sadness in his tone. His mother did, too, if the soft look she sent him was any indication.

“Maybe you can start again,” she suggested.

“I don’t think so.” He thought of the pain in Darcy’s eyes, and the fierce longing he had to hold her. It was a bad idea. Mack shook his head and pushed back from the counter. “It was a long time ago. We aren’t the same people anymore.”

“Exactly,” she said, so soft he almost didn’t catch it. In fact, he decided to pretend he hadn’t heard her. Best that way.

Because if she was right, he had to rethink everything he thought he’d known.

Chapter Eight

Darcy ducked into the warm-up shack. Lori, the teenager working, gave her a smile. Christmas music played softly in the background and a fire crackled in the fireplace. The little building smelled of cider, coffee and hot chocolate.

"Hey, Lori. How's it going back here? You got enough cups and cocoa and coffee?"

Lori smiled. "Yep, all good. Been pretty steady back here."

"That's good." Darcy took a moment to check the supplies. "The snow brings people out."

"Yes, it does." The bell over the door jingled and a family came in. Lori greeted them with a smile, and Darcy slipped back out into the snow. It sifted lightly down, as if Mother Nature knew it was two weeks before Christmas and was giving her all to make some magic. Enough to be pretty, not enough to hinder anyone stomping around in it.

Perfect. She walked back up to the pole barn, hearing the roar of the baler, the laughter of kids, the notes of Christmas music here and there. Despite the snow, she wasn't cold. And if it weren't for the fact her uncle was in the hospital, her ex was about to buy her childhood farm—well, no, just for a heartbeat she was happy. In this moment, she was happy,

Her therapist would be so proud of her.

She skirted the busyness but noted the full parking lot as she made her way to the house. Uncle Joe was possibly to be released from the hospital today—seemed a little early to Darcy for someone who'd had heart surgery just a few days ago—but he was doing well and Marla didn't seem alarmed, so she'd go with it.

"Ready?" she asked as she came in the warm kitchen. Marla was seated at the table, tying her bootlaces.

"I am. Let's go."

They left the house and got in Darcy's car. She brushed the fluffy snow off quickly, and they were on their way. Darcy followed her aunt to the elevators and tried to breathe normally. The panic was there, pressing in her throat, but it didn't have claws today. Marla squeezed her arm. She followed her through the maze of corridors. Marla's stride was brisk and Darcy tried not to look at anything as they went. This was not the same floor she'd been on. It wasn't even the same wing.

But it was still the same building.

Marla stopped in front of room 527 and went in. "Good morning," she said, her voice quiet but cheery. Darcy followed her in, and her stomach clenched at the sight of her uncle.

He looked far more frail than he had a few days ago. His hair was mussed—he usually wore a hat from the time he got up until he went to bed—and his skin was pale. He had an IV running from one hand, and the skin around it was bruised and swollen. His eyes were tired, but he smiled at both of them.

"There's my ladies."

Marla went over and took his free hand, pressing a kiss to his forehead, and Darcy saw the look of relief that passed her uncle's face. She came up and kissed him, as well.

"Things okay at the farm?"

In spite of herself, Darcy smiled. He was all business. "Yes. We're moving along."

He quizzed her on a few things and she answered. Fortunately, correctly. She was lucky that she'd grown up on the farm and had retained most of the knowledge from way back when.

He sat back after a few minutes and sighed. Marla touched his hand. "If you overdo it before they even discharge you, they won't let you go today." Her tone was part affection, part exasperation, and he nodded.

"I know. It's just hard. To know I'm missing it."

There was more to that statement than just her uncle wanting the season to go smoothly—more than his need to oversee it. This was the last season and it had to be perfect. And he wasn't there to make sure it happened.

"Darcy and Mack know what they're doing. They've got it all under control." Marla looked at her for confirmation and she nodded.

"Absolutely." Too bad she felt anything but under control since she'd been back here and Mack had reentered her life.

* * *

Mack was already at the farm when she pulled back in. This was the second day in a row he'd been out here early. She got out of the car and slammed the door, stomping through the snow to the barn. Kelly, one of the wreath makers, looked up when she came in.

"Hey, Darce. How's Joe this morning?"

"Good. Ready to come home."

Kelly's smile was wry. "Marla will have her hands full when he does."

Darcy smiled back. "Yes. She will. Have you seen Mack?"

By now, everyone knew she and Mack had been married. While she didn't talk about it, it had made the rounds pretty quickly. But no one asked her about it, or pressed her. "Pretty sure he went to cut the trees for the delivery today."

Of course he had. "Okay. Thanks."

Kelly went back to work and Darcy went out back. She and Mack needed to have a little chat.

Sure enough, there he was, with four other guys, cutting the trees. She stood to the side for a moment, unable to take her eyes off Mack.

Dressed in old jeans and boots, with an insulated jacket and a hat, he looked right at home among the snowy trees. He didn't hear the approach of the ATV over the sharp whine of the chain saw that felled the trees as if their trunks were made of butter. She pulled her own hat down closer over her ears and came up behind him, the snow crunching under her boots as she picked her way over the drifts to where the men were working. One of the guys saw her and gave a little wave.

Mack turned. As soon as she caught his gaze, her insides heated up.

This was bad. A kiss, and now—now she was worried about being in over her head.

He strode through the snow toward her, his strides long and sure on the uneven path. "Hey," he said when he reached her. She looked up at him, his face ruddy from the cold, and wondered what would happen if she kissed him.

No. She was here to ask him a tricky question. She needed to know. But shouting over the chain saw wasn't the place for this conversation. She leaned in and he leaned down. "Why exactly are you here?" she said into his ear, trying not to breathe in his scent of spice and fresh air.

He turned his head, and his warm breath tickled her ear. She barely suppressed a shiver. "I'm getting the trees ready for the shipment."

She shook her head and he straightened up. The chain saw had quit and the first few seconds of quiet after were almost more deafening in the ringing silence. "No. Mack, you've got a vet practice to run. Really, why are you here and not there?"

His expression turned cautious. "I told you before. Because your uncle needs the help, Darce. I've got my practice under control."

She had to ask. "Are you trying to make up for what happened?"

He stared at her, then frowned. "What happened? With what?"

"You and me."

Her words hung in the crystal-cold air for a second. The sounds of the guys dragging the trees to the wagon, their laughter and voices, all of it seemed to be coming through a kind of filter. Mack's eyes widened and then he frowned.

"What do I have to make up for, Darcy?" The words were clipped and colder than the air around them. She winced when they almost physically struck her, like shards of ice. But she couldn't say anything, because she could see she'd been wrong. Very wrong. "I'm not here for you, not in the way you seem to think. I'm here to help out, because I know your uncle is out of commission and this is important to him. He and your aunt are my friends, Darcy."

"Okay," she said, and turned to go back to the ATV. She'd read something very wrong there. But he caught her arm and, off balance in the snow, she teetered a little as she tried to turn to face him. He ended up with one hand on each of her upper arms.

"What do I need to make up for?" The intensity of his voice made her breath catch.

She blinked at him, the lump in her throat making it hard to breathe. "Nothing." He didn't get it, didn't understand what she'd been through. He didn't see his part in it. She'd made a mistake bringing it up. When his eyes narrowed she pulled away and he let her go. "I'm sorry. I was wrong."

This time when she turned and walked away he let her go.

What the hell had that been all about?

All day the odd encounter with Darcy played through Mack's mind. Over and over. He'd blamed himself for a lot that had happened with them, more maybe than he should have. He'd never viewed working with her uncle as atonement. Joe had never hinted he felt that way, either, so it caught him off guard that Darcy apparently did.

And the upshot seemed to be, it wouldn't be enough to fix—it. Whatever exactly she blamed him for. Looking back, he could see any number of things. He'd failed her in almost every possible way, and no doubt there were more he didn't even know about.

So, no. He wasn't doing this for her. Or for him. He was doing it because it was the right thing, to help out a friend who needed it. It wasn't that he didn't feel the need to make things right for her, as much as he could, but this wasn't the way he'd do it.

He let himself in the house and absorbed the dogs' ardent greeting.

He took care of the drying of paws and dishing out of food, then wandered into his bedroom to take a shower before he scrounged up something to eat. The bedroom he'd have shared with Darcy, if she were still his wife.

That wasn't a line of thought he wanted to follow.

Bone tired, he showered and dressed in sweats and a long-sleeved T-shirt. He waded through the animals to get a container of frozen stew from the freezer and popped it in the microwave. There was a knock at the front door and he frowned, glancing at the time.

He walked through the living room and opened the door to see Darcy standing there, in the dark on his porch. She gave him a tremulous smile and he shoved a hand through his hair before stepping aside. "Darcy. What brings you here? Is Joe okay?"

"Fine," she assured him as she entered, her arm brushing him as she moved past him. "And I won't stay long. I just wanted to apologize."

He closed the door behind her. “For what?”

She shoved her hands into her coat pockets. Her cheeks were pink. He didn’t know if it was nerves, the cold or the fact she was too warm in her down jacket. “For my behavior earlier. I was wrong to come after you like that.”

The microwave dinged behind him, but he didn’t turn around, even when her gaze slid in that direction and back to him. “Bad time?”

“No. Just dinner. Darce. There’s no need—no need for apologies.” He wanted her to smile, to see her relax. One of the dogs came out and shoved his head against her leg. She patted him with her bare left hand and he wondered what she’d done with her rings. Did she still have them? He had his, wrapped in a plastic bag in the bottom of his underwear drawer. Classy all the way. “That’s Sadie.”

“Hi, Sadie,” she said, her gaze still on the dog, who sat down and looked up at her adoringly.

“Do you want to stay?” The words slipped out before he could stop them. And now it was too late to call them back. “I just reheated some stew, if you’re hungry. Otherwise you can just keep me company.”

She hesitated. “I’m not hungry. But I can stay a little bit.”

After he took her coat, she followed him through the house to the kitchen. He wondered what she thought of it, if he should tell her why he’d bought it. Seeing her wary expression as she seated herself at the breakfast bar, he decided not to.

She looked around and he saw the frank curiosity on her face. “This is really nice, Mack. I like it.”

The words fill him with a silly gratitude. "Thanks. I do, too. Chase and I worked on it together."

"How long have you lived here?" She nodded when he held up a bottle of wine. He opened a cupboard and took out a glass, then met her gaze and decided he couldn't do it. Couldn't tell her the whole truth.

"A while now. Long enough to be settled in, I guess." The evasive answer was kinder. If he told her, she'd do the math and realize when he'd bought the house. That might open up more guilt, and there was no point in either of them going there.

He slid the wineglass across the counter and watched as she fingered the stem. Nervous. He seated himself near her and started in on the stew.

"Do you cook?" The surprise in her voice made him laugh around a forkful.

"God, no," he said when he'd swallowed. "My mom makes extra and drops it off. She caught me buying a TV dinner once when I ran into her at the grocery store." He grinned at the memory. Her reaction hadn't been much different than if she'd caught him buying condoms. "She was horrified. And then I started getting containers."

Darcy gave a little laugh. "I bet."

He forked up another bite. "I know I'm too old for my mother to be cooking for me. But she enjoys it. I guess it benefits both of us."

"I guess so," Darcy agreed, a slightly wistful look in her eyes.

"You should come to dinner sometime," he said, and she drew back, already shaking her head.

"Oh, no. After everything..." Her voice trailed off.

"They'd love to see you." That might be a bit of a

stretch when it came to Chase, but after what his mom had said earlier, he knew she would be welcoming.

He wanted to ask her if it was true, if she'd felt rushed into their marriage, then decided now wasn't the time. Besides, Darcy had always been straightforward. They'd talked about it at length when they found out she was pregnant. She'd never expressed any reservations about any of it at all.

She smiled at him then. "Maybe. We'll see."

No, he decided, his mother had been wrong.

The next morning, Marla sat at the table with Darcy. "I need to ask you something."

"Okay," Darcy said carefully, her pulse kicking up.

"I know you only planned to stay a few days." Marla drew in a deep breath and Darcy's heart sank. She knew what was coming. "But. We could really use your help now that Joe is out of commission. Mack can't do it all, since he's got his vet practice. I know he's putting a lot of it on Jennifer, but he can't just leave it. I can't do it all with Joe, and the farm needs someone who can give it attention full-time." Her voice trailed off and Darcy saw the misery on her aunt's face and knew how hard it had been to even ask her.

"Of course I'll stay. I'll make it work," she said with far more confidence than she actually felt. They needed her here, far more than they needed her at work. What did that say about her career? "I need to call my boss and make some arrangements."

Marla grabbed her hands and squeezed tightly. There were tears in her eyes. "Thank you, Darcy. I know—I know there are parts of this that aren't easy for you."

Darcy squeezed back. "You're welcome. It'll be fine.

You don't need to worry about anything but getting Joe back on his feet." She glanced at the clock. "I'm going to give my boss a call and get this all arranged." She had several weeks of vacation. Sad to say, she almost never used any of it. She'd convinced herself she loved her job, and she was pretty sure that was true. But more than that, she didn't have anyone to share the time off with. So really, why bother?

Somehow she'd convinced herself that was okay.

She pulled on her jacket and shoes and grabbed her bag. It'd be easier to do this in the car, without anyone overhearing. She pulled out of the tree farm and drove the little way into town, where she parked in the diner parking lot—she'd noticed earlier her phone signal was strongest there—and hit Ross's number on her phone. It was six o'clock in Chicago, an hour behind, but she knew that he'd be there. Sure enough, he answered on the third ring.

"Darcy. Please tell me you are coming back early." His voice was tense.

Darcy's heart plummeted and she gripped the phone tightly. "What's going on?"

He launched into an explanation of how one of her accounts, the one she'd worked so hard to bring in to the company, was teetering on the edge of disaster. Darcy propped her arm on the steering wheel and rested her head on her hand, the urge to scream building like a head of steam. Why hadn't she been apprised of any of this? Her team was in contact with her, but hadn't said a word. She cut Ross off. "I'll call Mally and talk to her," she said with a calmness she didn't feel. Ross could be an excellent boss, but if he sensed weakness, you'd be out on your tail before you could blink. She'd seen it happen before. And this was why what she was about to ask was risky. "I need the month of December off, Ross."

Silence. Darcy stared at the lit windows of the diner. A couple was laughing, framed by Christmas lights. The woman leaned forward to accept a forkful of something from the man. A simple scene. Why couldn't things in her life be simple? How had she gotten so far off track that she'd lost the simple things?

"You're joking." It wasn't a question. "Your account is going to hell and you're asking for a month off?"

They got the week between Christmas and New Year's off anyway, but Darcy wasn't going to point that out. She kept her voice soothing. The best way to deal with Ross was to stay calm. "My family needs me. I wouldn't ask if it wasn't an emergency."

"Your family needs you," he repeated, and laughed. "Darcy, you never talk about your family. I didn't know you had one. It's why you are the perfect employee. You give me—this company—100 percent. Without fail. There's never any drama with you. It's as if you are married to the company."

Tears stung Darcy's eyes because he was right. It wasn't a compliment. She'd given far more of herself than she'd ever get back. And Ross would take as much as she'd give and come back for more. She knew this, had always known this. But she'd managed to convince herself it was a good thing.

"I need the time off, Ross. My uncle had a serious heart attack and I need to run the business."

"What kind of business is that?"

"A Christmas-tree farm."

A pause, then a bark of laughter exploded in her ear. “A Christmas-tree farm? What the hell do they need you for? Are you going to chop trees in a suit and heels?”

Chapter Nine

Darcy was taken aback by this view of her. Clearly, she'd been good at hiding her past, at making herself over—too good. Not that her boss should necessarily be her friend, but the whole idea that he thought it was ridiculous nettled her. "Of course not. That's ridiculous. I grew up here, Ross. I know what I'm doing and they need me to run it." It was more than a business. It was about traditions, for her family and the families that came to the farm every year. "I wouldn't ask if it wasn't important."

She heard the squeak of Ross's desk chair as he dropped into it. It drove all the employees crazy, that squeaky chair. It was the only thing not full-on chic in her boss's office. Hearing it now, she realized he must have been pacing in front of the windows overlooking Michigan Avenue. She'd bet he hadn't noticed any of the Christmas cheer that Chicago put on, or the beauty of the falling snow. She herself hadn't, not for years, and on purpose. "Darcy. I need you here."

"I can manage my team from here," she said, wishing she had room to pace herself, but the wind outside would make conversation difficult. And stomping around in the slushy mess in the parking lot would ruin her shoes. "I've been checking in with them periodically. And really, Mally is perfectly capable of handling this on her own, Ross. You know she is." Darcy had spent much of her professional life putting out fires before they even reached Ross's radar. Mally needed to do that. Darcy was betting that the account wasn't that bad at all. Now he was seeing just how valuable Darcy was—in time for her to step away. She couldn't help wincing. "I've got plenty of time to take off. This isn't a hugely busy time for us."

It took the better part of an hour, but she got Ross to agree to her time off. She called Mally next and filled her in. Thankfully, the woman was calm and unflappable and very good at what she did. She and Darcy made an excellent team. Mally sounded surprised when Darcy told her she was taking an entire month off, but she didn't make a big deal of it. "Good for you, showing him work isn't the only thing you've got in your life. He tends to think that's how it should be. Probably because it is for him."

Darcy didn't want to be like Ross, so tied to his company he couldn't separate out his real life from his work life. But she was well on her way. It made her wonder—for the first time—if something had happened to send him to seek solace in his work. Like what she had done.

She drove back to the house and sat in the driveway for a minute, just looking. The Christmas lights were on, outlining the house and blanketing the bushes. A huge lit wreath glowed on the side of the barn. The tree dazzled in the living room windows. The whole scene was cozy and familiar and Darcy realized how much she'd missed it. Missed being here.

She thought of Mack's house, the charming bungalow that he'd restored so beautifully. But he had no Christmas decorations up, save a small tabletop tree on the dining room table she'd bet he never used…and she'd double down on the bet that the little tree was his mother's doing.

They'd lost so much, at the time of year when families were supposed to be celebrating.

They'd lost everything.

Darcy swallowed and gathered up her stuff. She'd assumed Mack would move on. That he, wrapped in the Lawless name and family, would be able to grieve and let go and start his life over, without the specter of his very short marriage and almost parenthood hanging over him. It was a huge part of why she'd run.

No, not run. Running implied she'd been unable or unwilling to deal with things as they'd been. But they'd been too much of a mess to fix. She'd seen that clearly. Leaving had been her last gift to Mack, the only way she could see to make it all up to him. Setting him free of all of it.

But—maybe she hadn't. And the thought that she'd given up so much for nothing made her feel ill.

Mack knew he was burning the candle at both ends. Which was why he knew it was a waste of time to stop and grab a beer with Chase. Except Chase was insisting on it and Mack had finally given in.

So he parked in the icy gravel lot of Sloan's Bar and got out, noting he'd beaten his brother here. He pushed through the heavy door and headed up to the bar, where they always sat. This late on a Tuesday, the place was fairly empty. He sat and smiled at Sally, the bartender tonight.

"What'll it be, hon?" was Sally's cheerful greeting. She called everyone hon. He ordered from the tap and waited for Chase. She set the glass in front of him. "You alone or are you meeting someone?"

"Chase," he answered drily. "He asked me to come."

"And now he's late." Sally smiled. "Big brothers, huh?"

"Yeah."

He and Sally had graduated together. She had an older brother, too, but he was in and out of jail. Not really the same.

Chase slid next to him then. "Sorry I'm late." He gave Sally his order and dropped his keys on the bar. "Hell of a day."

"Yeah?" Mack was more than happy to listen to someone else's problems. Anything but his own.

Chase explained how he had a supplier that had first sent the wrong kind of shingles, then the correct ones only to realize they had a major defect. Each delay was more of a setback on a project that was running perilously close to being late as well as over budget.

Mack listened sympathetically. Until Chase cut himself off and said, "What's going on with the tree farm?"

"Going on?" If he played a little dumb, maybe Chase would let him off the hook.

Chase gave him a look and Mack nearly groaned. He wasn't off the hook.

"Come on, Mack. You're spending more time there than at your practice."

Mack folded his arms on the bar and fixed his gaze on the hockey game on the TV across the room. How the hell did he know that? "Joe had a heart attack. You know that."

"Yeah. And you told me he'll be okay."

"He will," Mack agreed. "But not in time to finish out the season. So I'm stepping in."

"Stepping in," Chase repeated. "How does Darcy feel about that?"

Mack took a sip of his beer. "She's not thrilled."

"I bet." Chase dug into the bowl of peanuts that Sally had placed in front of them. "How's it going? Is she speaking to you?"

"Fine. And yeah. We're adults, Chase. All that was a long time ago."

"Mmm-hmm. That's why you've been seen with her around town."

Mack opened his mouth, then shut it and shook his head. "That's not your business."

"When it comes to her, yeah, it is." Chase's tone hardened. "She left you. She wrecked your marriage. She wrecked *you*. There's no way you can go through that again. Hell. No way we can watch you go through it."

Mack rubbed his unpeanutty hand on his face. "Chase. Let it go. Please. She did what she needed to do." The words were low in his throat, almost a growl.

"What she needed to do was stick around and see it through." When Mack's head snapped around, Chase held up a hand. "She never gave you a chance to see if you could go on. To grieve together."

No, she hadn't. And that was something that had

bothered Mack for years. Why hadn't she? Why had she shut down and run? He'd never been able to figure out the answer. "Not your business," he ground out, and Chase gave him a hard look, then sighed.

"I know. But after last time—"

"She'll go back after Christmas," Mack said tightly, and Chase gave a hard nod.

They spent the rest of the time talking about nothing and Mack relaxed. When he went home, he went through the ritual with the dogs and headed for bed, for dreams of Darcy, where she came to him willingly.

But he knew that was all it was—a dream.

Darcy spent a good chunk of the next day on the phone with her team. The good thing was, Ross's interpretation of the situation was wrong, which relieved Darcy. Mally had it all well in hand, which she'd already determined from their conversation yesterday. They agreed to stay in touch with emails and calls every other day, unless Mally needed more. Darcy didn't think she would.

Mack's truck, which had been there earlier in the day, was gone when she got back to the farm. No doubt he'd gone to his real job.

She wished she could make him see that she had this under control. That while his help was appreciated, she didn't need him to come every day for ten hours. He didn't have to give anything up for her. For them. For whoever.

He was stubborn. She knew this all too well.

She dropped her laptop off in the house, got her winter stuff on and trudged over to the barn. They didn't open until three on weekdays, so she had a little time.

She checked the wreath orders when she was in there, and started making another one. They had four due to be picked up today, and a few more the next day. This was a part she'd like to expand. The wreath making, the grave blankets, the garlands, all the piney decorations.

Of course, it didn't matter now. This was the end of the road for the tree farm, and thinking of ideas now didn't help. Why hadn't she made the suggestions before now?

Because you hadn't known. You should have known.

And that was a loop that had played in her mind over and over since she came back. It was pointless and frustrating. And maybe wouldn't have made any difference after all. Her aunt and uncle were selling because it was time to move on. Not because of anything she'd done, or not. She couldn't prevent them from aging or retiring.

But the guilt sat heavily in her chest as she went through the motions of making a wreath.

You should have known.

"Darcy." Marla looked up with a smile when she came into the house. Joe sat at the table, still looking pale, but far better than he had been. Recovery was taking a while, but he was getting there.

"How's it going out there?" Joe's question was casual, but the slight tension in his body gave away how much he missed being in the action.

"Just fine," Darcy said. She put the paper with the notes she took in front of him. It had the sales on it and other information he just devoured. It was a kind of unspoken compromise. He'd stay in the house and she'd give him the information he wanted.

Marla held out a carefully packed casserole. "Can

you take this to Mack? I told him I'd be by but—" she glanced at the clock "—I'm not going to get over there before my book club comes over."

Caught, Darcy took the pan. There was no way to say no. "Of course. I'll get right on that."

"Thanks," Marla said gratefully, and untied her apron. "I've got about fifteen minutes."

Darcy was about to ask why she was hosting it, at this time of year, but then she realized of course Marla wasn't going to leave Joe alone. And her friends would understand that.

She went back out the door to her car and drove to Mack's. This time, the porch light was on. She parked on the street and went up the front walk. She knocked and realized that she hadn't asked if Mack knew she was coming.

When he answered the door, his warm smile slipping into clear shock that she was standing there, she had her answer. "Marla couldn't make it," she said, holding out the packages. "She ran out of time. So she sent me instead." This was stating the obvious and she felt a little silly. She was always so off-kilter around him.

He stepped back. "Come on in."

"Oh, I can't stay," she said, and found herself stepping into the warm house anyway.

"I'm sure there's enough for both of us," he said wryly. She wondered if it was what Marla had in mind. Now that she thought about it, she wouldn't put it past her aunt. "Sure," she said, and took off her coat, then followed him into the kitchen. This house was big for a bachelor. Unless—

"Mack, do you have a girlfriend?"

The question was out before she could stop it. He

dropped the silverware he'd just pulled out of the drawer. "What the hell kind of question is that?" He stepped over the pieces on the floor and came over to her, the look on his face completely predatory. "Do you think, if I had a girlfriend, I'd do this with you?" And his mouth came down on hers.

It wasn't a gentle kiss. It was an angry kiss, a punishing kiss. A kiss that shot to her soul and flared to life.

She needed to stop it, to push him away. Instead, she wound her arms around his neck and kissed him back, all the hunger and need she'd felt since she came home—probably well before that—pouring out of her. When he backed her into the fridge, she welcomed the hard press of his body, the way his hands fisted in her hair and his mouth plundered hers.

When he pulled back, the loudest sound in the room was that of their ragged breathing. "Does that answer your question?" His voice was rough, and the sound made shivers skip over her skin.

For a moment, she couldn't recall the question.

"Yes," she managed, when the fog cleared enough for her to think. "It does." But it opened up more questions, the biggest one of which was *why?* Why had he kissed her? Why did he still care? Why did she?

Those weren't questions she could answer. That she *wanted* to answer.

"So I guess I'll leave you to dinner," she said, and edged for the door.

He looked at her, his eyes still smoky with desire and want and need. "Running away?"

She stopped, affronted, but couldn't make herself meet his gaze. "What? No, of course not."

"Are you sure?" He stepped closer. "You were willing to stay until I kissed you."

Caught, she just looked at him, afraid of what he might see, of what she wasn't ready for him to see. Of what she wasn't ready to admit to herself. She tucked her hair behind her ear.

"I'll behave," he said, and the wicked tilt to his mouth made her raise an eyebrow. "Scout's honor."

Now she lifted both eyebrows. "Were you ever a Scout?"

"No," he admitted. "But Chase was."

"All right," she relented, and moved back toward the island. She didn't really want to leave. "Anything I can do?"

He directed her to the glasses and she got out new silverware, placing the pieces that had been on the floor in the sink. It didn't take long to get the simple meal on the table—and Darcy would bet that her aunt had planned this. Book club, dinner, send her out to run the errand—it had Marla's fingerprints all over it.

Darcy couldn't be mad.

They sat at the table, and she refrained from asking him how often he used it. There was a cozy bay window overlooking the backyard, and while it was too dark to really see anything out there, she could tell it had begun to snow. "That's a real tree?" she asked, nodding toward the one on the table.

"It is," he agreed, and took a bite of his dinner.

"Why not have a full-size tree?"

He looked at her as if she'd grown an extra head. "Why would I do that?"

"You work at a Christmas-tree farm," she pointed out. "Surely you could get one there."

He gave her a wry, almost sad, smile. "No need. It's just me. I don't get trees anymore."

Anymore. The implication of that hit her hard. Of course he didn't. When was the last time she'd gotten one? Her last tree, other than a little halfhearted, fake formal tree she did just because she felt she had to, had been here. With Mack.

Oh, no.

"We need to fix that." She couldn't do much to fix the past or her mistakes, but she could give him this. It was a little thing, a small thing, but a start.

"We do? Why?" He sounded truly puzzled.

"Because it's not right. You should have a tree. This house should have a tree."

"Darcy—"

"I happen to know the owner of a tree farm." She offered him a crooked smile. "I think I can get you in."

Damn if he could resist her. "Darce. I don't have any ornaments." That wasn't completely true. He had the boxes of the ones they'd picked out together, all those years ago. His mother had packed them up for him, when he was unable to face anything, much less packing up a Christmas tree. He'd never touched them since. They were in her attic. That wouldn't work.

"That's okay. We can get some. I'm sure there are extras in Marla and Joe's attic."

He carried his plate to the sink and she followed. "When did you want to do this?"

"Now?"

He looked over her head at the microwave clock. "It's eight thirty. The farm's closed."

She shrugged. "That's what flashlights are for."

What the hell? "All right. Let me get my stuff on."

He followed her to the farm. The snow was coming down lightly, a sifting that glittered in the headlights. They both parked by the barn, not the house. She already had on her boots and parka and hat and gloves. She gave him a smile in the light of the big wreath on the front of the barn. “Ready?”

For a guy who hadn’t bothered with Christmas since his wife left him—a wife who was standing in front of him now—he was remarkably ready. “Let’s go.”

He grabbed a saw and she got the flashlight and a cart to haul the tree up to his truck. They walked down the lane, the silence broken by the creak of the wagon wheels, the crunch of their boots on the packed snow and, if they stopped moving, the sound of the snow collecting on the branches around them.

“Spruce?” she asked as they stopped at a fork in the lane. Her breath puffed out in front of her in the cold.

“What else?”

She inclined her head in acknowledgment and turned to the left. She stopped a few feet down and dropped the handle of the wagon. Trying to drag it through the snow would be too much work. “How big?”

He followed her, amused, and still able to pick out the sway of her hips even in the dark. The metallic finish of her blue coat caught the beam of the flashlight. “Six feet or so. Pretty full.”

She aimed the light at him, momentarily blinding him. “Oh, sorry! Are you okay? And have a little faith, okay?”

He’d lost what little faith he had left when she left him. But now wasn’t the time to tell her that. Not when things were going well with them. Whatever *things* were.

It took some time, and he enjoyed stomping around

in the dark with her. She finally settled on a tree that was tall enough and fairly full. "This one okay?"

He took the light from her and flashed it over it. He couldn't resist teasing her a little bit. "Looks good to me. But of course, it's dark out, Darce."

She snatched the light back. "It's fine."

He caught her chin in his hand and pressed a kiss to her cold lips. He couldn't help it. Being out here in the dark and cold, with the sharp scent of pine and the softly sifting snow, made him miss her more. Want her more. When he pulled back, looking in her eyes, even in the dark he could see the desire there. When she breathed his name on puff of peppermint-scented air, he was lost.

This kiss was sweet, bittersweet. He knew they were going down a path that was going to end up in heartbreak for both of them—well, him for sure. Then she dropped the heavy metal flashlight on the top of his foot.

"Sorry," she said sheepishly. "I forgot I had it."

He kissed her forehead. "Good thing my boots are thick. Next time you want me to stop kissing you, just tell me instead of trying to hurt me, okay?"

He was teasing, but only sort of. She fished the light out of the snow and he went over to saw the tree down.

By the time they got it back to his truck, he was cold and wet, but it was worth every minute of her company. "Do you want to come in?" She jerked her head toward the house. "Get something to warm you up?"

Tempting as it was— "No. I'm going to go home and change out of these wet clothes. I'll see you tomorrow."

Disappointment flashed over her face. "All right. Tomorrow we'll get the lights on it."

"Sounds good."

He drove away, seeing her in the red glow of his tail-lights as he went back up the lane to the main road, the tree bouncing in the bed of the truck.

Chapter Ten

Darcy wasn't sure what had come over her the night before. Mack's kisses were seared in her brain, and about all she could come up with was she had somehow fallen back into the past. A time warp of sorts, triggered somehow by being in his presence. For a few minutes it'd almost been as if nothing had happened.

In the early days of their marriage, there'd been no hot kisses like that. Oh, they'd been the ones that had gotten them in trouble. Her pregnancy had meant they'd had to get married. He'd insisted on doing the right thing, and since she couldn't see herself with anyone else—even if she wasn't totally sure she wanted to get married yet—she'd gone along. He'd been happy.

But she hadn't been.

How bad was that? He'd been so sure. She'd allowed him to sweep her off her feet. But then her worst fears had been realized. He only wanted her as long as the baby was in the picture. She, by herself, hadn't been enough. So how had she gotten all caught up in it again?

Her phone rang and Darcy tucked the phone on her shoulder as she answered. "Hi, Corrie."

"Darcy! I miss you, girl. How is it way up there?"

Darcy curled up in the chair and smiled at her best friend's exuberant greeting. "Same as it always is. Cold." Her hands and lips were a little chapped.

"Mmm. How's the ex-husband?"

Just like Corrie to cut right to the heart of the matter. Darcy stared into the flames, which crackled cheerily around the logs she'd added just before the phone rang. "Fine."

"Fine," Corrie repeated. "That tells me nothing."

"That's because there's nothing to tell," Darcy said, trying to keep her voice light. She knew she'd failed when she heard Corrie's sigh.

"Darcy. Come on. Is he hot? Or did he get sloppy?"

"Hot," she answered before she could stop herself.

A long pause. Darcy shut her eyes. She'd stepped in it now.

"Really?" Corrie drew out the word. "That's pretty definitive, Darce. You still have feelings for him."

It wasn't a question, but Darcy chose to treat it as one. "No. No more than nostalgia. We were married, Corrie. That carries some weight, even after all these years." Or so she'd been trying to convince herself. That it was all just based on where they'd been.

"Would it be so bad? If there were feelings between you two? You've shut yourself down pretty tight, Darce. Seems like getting the opportunity to move on would be good for you. Even if it's moving on with him."

She laughed, because if she didn't, she'd cry. "It'd be

awful. I can't stay here. You know that. There's nothing for me here. And Mack—well, he was pretty clear all those years ago it was over. I'm not willing to give it a shot. Plus, there's no time." And thank God for it. She wasn't risking her heart, not with the guy who'd broken it in the first place.

"If you say so," Corrie said softly. "But, Darcy. Promise me you'll keep your options open. Just in case."

Darcy shook her head and pressed her fingers to her lips, even though her friend couldn't see her. "I can't. You of all people know that." Mack hadn't understood then. Why would he now? She wasn't going to risk her heart on that. She'd do what she could to make things right, but she wouldn't give him a chance to steal her heart. It was too risky. She wasn't sure she could take another blow like that.

"You deserve love," Corrie said firmly. "If it's not Mack, well, that's okay. You'd know better than I would. I don't know him. But at some point you need to let *someone* in. You don't want to miss out on the perfect guy for you."

Darcy *did* know the perfect guy for her. But thanks to their past and her choices, they were stuck apart. Mack had kissed her, but how did she know that wasn't based on the old Darcy? The one he'd married? The one he'd made—and lost—a baby with. The one he'd let go.

He didn't know her now. That mattered. And in the three weeks she had left on the farm, there was no real way to get to know him again.

Mack had tried to figure out a way to frame the request. In seven years, he'd never asked about the Christmas ornaments he and Darcy had had on their first—and only—tree together. He wasn't going to go in his mother's house without her knowledge, and he for damn sure wasn't going to ask Chase.

So it looked as though he had to suck it up and face his demons and his mother's questions.

He stopped in on his lunch, which was what he framed the time between leaving his vet practice and getting out to the farm. Mom was there, of course, and she brightened right up when she saw him.

"Mack." She stepped out of the doorway and gestured him in. Little flurries of snow accompanied him and she shut the door quickly. "What's going on? We don't usually see you in the middle of the day."

He dropped a kiss on his mother's head. "Hi, Mom." He raised his voice so his father could hear him over the TV in the den. "Hey, Dad."

His father's reply carried over the noise of the television. Mom rolled her eyes. "This one's about how Sumatrans made their pottery." Mack had to grin despite the nerves in his belly. Dad loved history programs. In the winter, the off-season, he had them on almost nonstop and was enthralled by all of it. Mack had asked once why they just didn't go visit the places he was so interested in, and Dad had just looked at him and said, "I'm an armchair traveler."

Fair enough.

Mom led him into the kitchen, where she had something in the oven that smelled fantastic. "Lasagna," she said with a faint smile as she caught him sniffing the air the way a hound might scent a bird. "There will be extra for you."

"Do you take extras to Chase?" He knew the answer but was trying to stall on his actual request.

"Sometimes. But that boy can cook. He even likes it." She gave him an amused look, then got out a mug. "Coffee?"

"Sure," he murmured, taking in the scene as she poured the mug from the pot that always seemed to be at the ready. He'd always pictured himself in the same kind of marriage his parents had. In terms of the affection, the love, the way they still enjoyed each other's company. He'd thought he'd found that in Darcy. But he'd been wrong.

He accepted the mug she held out. She'd let him sit and stew as long as he needed to spit out what he needed to say. It was a time-honed technique that had worked way too well when he was a kid.

Still worked now as an adult.

They made small talk for a few minutes when he finally blurted out, "I need the Christmas stuff Darcy and I had."

She set her mug on the table and leveled a serious gaze on him. "What are you going to do with it?"

"Put it on a tree," he said, and she nodded, pushed back from the table and started toward the back bedroom. He rose and followed her.

"Do you know what you're doing, Mack?" she asked as she flicked on the light and gestured to the two cardboard boxes sitting on the floor by the bed. Not in the attic? *Mack and Darcy, Christmas* was written in his mother's neat hand in black marker on the lids of both.

I don't have a clue, he wanted to say. *No. Freaking. Clue.* But instead he asked, staring at the boxes, "How did you know?"

She gave him a tiny smile. "Helen's daughter saw you

driving home last night with a big old tree in the bed of your truck. Helen called me as soon as she heard."

Mack opened his mouth, then snapped it shut. There wasn't much to say to that. He should have known his mother would hear about it from one of her friends. Her social network was impressive. He shook his head. "I see. Well. Thanks."

She shrugged. "I hope you know what you're doing, Mack. Not only for your sake, but for hers. Darcy is so fragile."

He almost laughed as he lifted one of the boxes. Darcy was anything but fragile. She was tough, far tougher than she probably knew. "I'll be careful."

She picked up the other box and followed him down the hall lined with family pictures. He was careful not to knock any off with the big box. He put the first one in the truck and came back for the second.

"See that you are," she said quietly, and he didn't even pretend to misunderstand what she meant.

Mack wasn't sure what to do with the boxes, so he put them in his own spare bedroom—not the one he used as a weight room, but the back one he almost never went in. The one that would have been the baby's room. The one that, in the back of the closet, still had a crib in its box. It also had a box of stuff Darcy had left when she split. He wasn't sure why he kept any of it. After several months of no contact, he'd realized she wasn't coming back.

He didn't open the closet.

Apparently, he could have saved himself the trouble of quasi hiding the tree on the back deck and just left it on the front porch. He should have known someone would see and report it to his mother.

He propped his hands on his hips and surveyed the tree. It wasn't bad, considering they'd chopped it down in the dark. There was a fairly sizable hole on one side, but if he angled the tree a little to the left, it was facing the wall.

Better.

He peeled off his gloves and dropped them on the coffee table. Trees like that tore you to pieces if you weren't careful. He poured water in the stand and left the house for the tree farm.

Darcy had spent the better part of the day throwing herself into her work, making wreaths with the team and filling orders. It kept thoughts of Mack at bay. Thoughts of how she had to finish what she'd started with her impulsive Christmas-tree idea.

She mentally kicked herself for the zillionth time. It had been a stupid idea, an uncharacteristically impulsive thing that she never did anymore. Impulsiveness led to mistakes. Mistakes couldn't be undone. She was very careful not to make them, much less ones like this.

She wired the spruce boughs into the large wreath she was making for the wall of the Methodist church. This one would be three feet across, but fairly simple. It would have a huge red bow that'd she make next. It was a good way to stay occupied.

Until her thoughts slipped back to Mack's mouth on hers.

She stabbed herself with the wire and it went through her glove. She pulled the glove off with a muttered curse and Wendy, one of the longtime employees, sent her an amused look.

"Mack on the brain?"

Darcy shut her eyes and then opened them to examine her finger. "No more than usual," she muttered, which could have meant anything.

"He's quite a catch," Wendy said, all seriousness now.

Darcy felt her back go up. "Of course he is."

"But so are you," she said quietly. Darcy could only blink at her as she went on, "I don't know what went wrong, but he sure looks at you like you matter to him."

Like you matter to him. Those words echoed in her brain as they got through the evening, as she sold trees and decorations and poured hot chocolate and made sure the Christmas station was playing at the proper volume.

He hadn't said anything to her about the tree. She had a trunkful of lights at the ready, thinking he might need them. Since it'd been her idea and all and she'd practically forced him to get the tree.

He looked up then, across the cold barn, and his gaze locked right on hers. As if he'd known she was looking at him. The corner of his mouth quirked up in an almost smile. Then someone said something to him and he turned around and disappeared from her vision.

They closed the place down at seven. It didn't take long. Darcy locked the money in the safe and waved to the departing workers.

Except Mack, of course. He was at his truck. Waiting for her.

"So," he said as she approached. "I've got this tree. It needs some love." He arched an eyebrow at her and she suppressed a smile.

"Does it, now?" she said. "I need to eat first and give Uncle Joe a report. I can be at your place in—" she looked at her phone "—less than an hour."

"Sounds good," he said.

She didn't watch him leave. She walked back to the house and it took more willpower than it should have to not look back.

She was at his house, as she'd said, in less than an hour. As she did every night now, she'd delivered her report, her handwritten notes, all the receipts to Uncle Joe so he could pore over them. It made him happy and helped him feel as though he was still a part of everything. She ate a quick dinner, showered and changed, then drove into town.

She pulled the bags with the lights out of her trunk. Their first tree had had multicolor lights on it. She'd bought the same for him.

He opened the door almost as soon as she knocked. "Hey," he said, stepping out of the way.

"Hey," she echoed, surprised to realize she was a little shy. She brushed past him, smelling his soap or shampoo. He smelled yummy enough to make the heat begin to rise in her, just a little.

Even a little was too much.

She gave him her coat when he reached for it and toed off her boots. She saw bags on the coffee table, too. He'd been shopping. Or maybe his mom had.

She mentally winced. What did Mack's mom think of Darcy now? Of her being back in town and even remotely in Mack's life? His mom hadn't been thrilled with the marriage—that had been clear from the start.

It didn't matter. Darcy wasn't staying.

She pushed aside the thoughts and stepped into the living room. He'd lit a fire, she noted. She looked at the tree and then at him, a small smile tugging at her mouth.

"Not too bad for being dark," she said cheerfully, walking over to inspect it. "And you didn't—" She turned around and found him right behind her.

"Didn't what?" His voice was low.

"Trust me," she whispered, and almost closed her eyes, the fragrant tree at her back, the man at her front.

But he stepped back and the moment shattered at her feet like a glass ornament handled carelessly. She swallowed hard and turned back toward the tree.

"It's got a big hole," he said, and his voice was a little rough. So she hadn't imagined the charged moment they'd just shared. "But not too bad for being in the dark."

She smiled and fingered the tip of a branch. If you smoothed the needles right on a spruce tree, they wouldn't draw blood. "I brought lights."

"I got some ornaments." He paused for a moment, a faraway expression on his face. "Nothing fancy."

She shrugged. "It's your tree, Mack."

Not theirs. *His*. Her observation wasn't lost on her, and she tried to ignore the little stab of pain it brought.

He didn't correct her and she started unloading the boxes of lights while he put on the leather gloves and started winding them, tucking them in the branches. The radio played softly in the background from somewhere—the kitchen, maybe—and she found it soothing to work with him like this, companionable. The past seemed to have receded somewhat as she realized she liked Mack. Not as the man she remembered, but as the man he was now.

That was every bit as dangerous as the memories.

She handed him the last string and he hooked it up, then wrapped it around the tree. He stepped back and she leaned over to click off the light on the end table. He peeled the gloves off and nodded as they both took it in. Transformed, it glowed bight and Darcy sighed. "It's beautiful. You did a good job."

"Thanks." He tossed the gloves on the floor and reached for a bag. "Let's see what we've got here."

He'd bought a mishmash of brightly colored ornaments. Nothing real personal. She didn't ask where their stuff was. She wasn't sure she could handle seeing it, even after all this time.

"Plastic," he explained as the smaller dog—Lilly—demonstrated the reason why glass would have been bad. Her tail slapped several on the floor and as they rolled away a calico cat leaped out from under a chair to chase them.

Darcy had to laugh. "Maybe they should go up. Out of tail range," she added doubtfully. "I've seen parents with little kids do that."

Then she froze at her own stupid, thoughtless words. The past came roaring back and sat right down in the living room with them, making itself comfortable in the sharpness of the silence. She opened her mouth again, but for the life of her couldn't think of anything to say that would make it better, so she clamped it shut again.

"Yes," he agreed quietly, and she heard the threads of pain in his tone, even in that one word. "They do. So should pet owners." When she turned to look at him—

Is he really going to let me off that easy?—he gave her a small smile.

He was.

"Want something to drink?" he asked, heading for the kitchen. "I've got beer. No wine, I'm afraid," he said, "but there's some diet Mountain Dew in here, too."

She should go. Before all this became too much and something happened. Something that even now she could feel tugging at her. "Beer's fine."

He held up two different kinds, and she pointed at her choice. He poured them each a glass and handed her one before going back in the living room. Which was far too cozy with the fire crackling, and the lights from the tree sending out a soft light. The dogs were asleep on the hearth, and a wave of longing hit her hard. This was all she'd ever wanted. And someday he'd share it with someone else. She took a drink of her beer and sat down on the couch. He did, too, and she sent him a sideways look as he turned on the TV.

What she should do was go home. There was no reason not to. The night was clear as a bell, if cold. No snow, no ice, no excuses to stay.

He put on a movie, a recent action flick. "Did you see this one?"

She shook her head. She hadn't been to see a movie in ages. "Nope. Missed it."

"Me, too. We can watch it while we decorate."

He got up and went to make popcorn and she tried really hard to make herself leave. Listing all the reasons this was a bad idea. Why it was always a bad idea to get attached.

But when he came back, set the bowl on the table and handed her a paper towel for her fingers, she knew she wasn't fooling even herself anymore. They shared the bowl, sipped beer, hung ornaments and laughed at the antics on-screen.

And Darcy found herself tipping toward him a little more.

Chapter Eleven

This was how it'd always been with them, and there was a time Mack would have given anything for one more night like this.

Be careful what you wish for. He could hear his mother's voice in his head, same as when he was a kid. There was always a price. No doubt. But Darcy was here now, her fingers bumping his in the popcorn bowl, her knee touching his thigh when she tucked her feet under her on the couch after they'd finished the tree. He didn't look at her, or pull away, and neither did she.

Finally, he'd had as much as he could take. The next time their fingers brushed, he twined hers in his. Her head snapped around, her eyes wide and luminous in the soft light of the tree and the TV. He pulled her in and kissed her. Her mouth was a little slick from the butter. He tasted the beer, the saltiness of the popcorn and the sweetness of the butter. She opened to him right away, as though maybe she'd been waiting for this, too.

It felt like a first kiss.

He sank deeper and pulled her in. She turned her body so she folded right into him, her arms around his neck. When he lowered her to the couch, his mouth still on hers, she didn't protest.

He pressed a kiss into her neck, feeling the flutter of her pulse there. It kept pace with his own. She ran her hands down his back and turned her face back to his when he slid a hand under her sweater. Her skin was so soft, so smooth, and he felt her inhale sharply at his touch. He lifted his head and looked her in the eye, seeing the desire and heat there, and the uncertainty, too. "You okay?" he asked, his voice a rasp in his throat. He didn't bother to shift away from her, so he knew she felt the hard length of him pressed into her thigh. Her eyes were molten, and he held still, wanting this so badly.

She lifted up and nipped his bottom lip, but he didn't lower back down. "Darce. I need to hear you say it." He was about to lose his mind, but he'd walk away if he had to, if it was what she needed.

"Yes," she whispered, and there was a small wobble in her voice. She lifted her eyes and met his and he saw the uncertainty was gone. "Yes," she repeated. "I'm okay, Mack." Then she smiled that smile, the one that always made his blood go hot, and he dropped his forehead to hers, relief flooding him, along with something much hotter, and much more intense.

Since he knew where this was heading, he stood up and held out a hand. They'd be better off in his bed than on this slippery leather couch. She took it and walked with him the short steps to his room. There was a slight tremor in her fingers, and when he drew her over to the bed, she laid a hand on his chest. In the faint moonlight that came through the window, he saw the intensity on her face. "What is it, Darce?"

She pleated his shirt in her fingers, then looked back up. "It's been a long time for me, Mack."

"Yeah?" He tugged her sweater up and she lifted her arms for him to slide it off. Her skin was creamy in the pale light. "Me, too, honey."

She seemed to relax then, and reached for the hem of his shirt, which he stripped off and tossed, then pulled her in, feeling the heat of her skin and the raspy lace of her bra on his skin. He closed his eyes, buried his face in her hair and groaned. "Darcy." There were no more words, and yet too many to say. She ran her hands up his arms to his face, which she pulled down to hers, and kissed him. Heat, passion, sweetness, all in one kiss.

He was a goner.

He reached behind her and unhooked the bra, which she shrugged off her shoulders and let it fall. She let out a laughing little "Eep!" when he bent and took those rosy, luscious nipples in his mouth. They were already peaked for him and he played with them both, with his tongue and his fingers, until she was gasping.

He kissed her throat, that sweet little pulse jumping even more now, and reached for the snap of her jeans as she reached for his. It took a little fumbling to get things down—her leg got stuck and she was hopping around trying to kick her pants off until he finally grabbed it and yanked and she went back on the bed with a giggle and a bounce of those glorious breasts. He landed beside her, his own grin so wide he was pretty sure his face was going to split in two. No matter. He'd be a damn happy man.

"Hey," she said softly, and he traced a line with one finger down her chest—a slight detour each way for her nipples—over her smooth belly and the scar there. He stopped there, running his fingers over the roughness of the scar. She reached for his hand and he shook his head.

"Mack—don't—"

"It's part of you, Darcy." It was part of him, too, but he didn't say that. He did lean down and kiss it before slipping farther to the curls at the juncture of her thighs, into the damp heat he found there. She gave a little gasp and he shifted his body. "While I'm here…"

Her legs fell open and he settled in. She grasped his head as he rolled his tongue and fingers around in the sweetness that had always been Darcy.

Darcy was losing her mind. Oh, Mack had always been good at this, so good, so very good. She bucked and he threaded his arms through her legs, resting his hands on her belly, a gentle pressure to hold her in place as he worked his magic. The pressure built like a wave and crashed over her just as fast as she gasped his name. Then his big body was covering hers as he held her through the tremors. She heard the crinkle of the condom package and he was inside her. A shudder racked his body as he held himself still, and pushed up on his forearms.

"Darcy—I'm not going to last long—" he gritted out, and she smiled and started moving against him. Turnabout was fair play and if he was going to make her lose her mind, well, she was going to return the favor.

The joke was on her. She matched him stroke for stroke and held on as he loved her, as the sweet pressure built, and he threw his head back as his whole body strained and shuddered. She followed him right over, the shock and pleasure of the second orgasm floating her gently to the ground.

He lay on her for a minute, breathing hard. "Wow."

She laughed and ran her hands up his sweaty back. "Yeah. Wow." But under all the sweetness was a bit of panic. Nothing had changed. Or rather, it'd gotten better, and it had been fantastic all those years ago. If it had been because they were so in love the first time around, what did that mean now?

She pushed the thoughts away. This might be her only chance to be like this with Mack, when she'd thought it was over for good. This was a gift, even if she'd pay for it later.

He rolled off her, onto his back, and his fingers found hers. They lay in the dark, and Darcy felt the dampness of tears leaking from her eyes.

"Stay," he said quietly, and she wasn't sure if he meant forever, or just tonight.

She wanted to, but her aunt and uncle— "I'm not sure, Mack."

He turned his head to look at her, then shifted and ran his thumb over the moisture at her eyes. "Please." Then, in a lighter tone, he added, "We never actually made it into the bed. We're on the covers." In the dark she saw his grin, and she was lost.

She sat up and scooted back toward the pillows, peeling the covers back, a wicked smile on her gorgeous face. "Well. Can't have that, can we?"

He followed her.

Darcy cracked one eye the next morning. The sky was barely light and Mack was still sleeping, one arm thrown over her like the way he used to sleep. The way they'd slipped into this so easily scared her. She knew why it could never be casual with them, and it made her heart hurt. He didn't stir as she slipped out from under his arm and tiptoed around and gathered up her clothes. She dressed quickly and quietly and let herself out into the cold predawn stillness. She shivered the whole drive home, not so much from the freezing temps but from the loss of the heat she'd shared with Mack. He wouldn't be happy she'd left. But she knew it was for the best. They'd crossed too many lines, and while she couldn't undo that, she could try to draw new ones.

She parked at the house and saw the kitchen light was on. Left on? Or was Marla up?

Darcy rested her head on the steering wheel. She was an adult. No one was going to say anything to her.

She let herself in the side door and saw that it had been left on. It wasn't quite time for Marla to be up yet. Darcy crawled back under the cold blankets of her childhood bed and stared at the ceiling, trying not to relive the night before and finding it impossible.

Marla gave her a knowing smile when she walked in the kitchen a couple of hours later. "So. Did you and Mack have a nice time?"

Darcy's face heated in spite of herself. "Yes. The tree looks nice."

"Mmm-hmm. Took all night to decorate, huh?" There was no censorship in her tone, but Darcy felt slapped down anyway.

"Something like that," she murmured, and grabbed a mug. Thank God there was coffee. She'd had very little sleep, thanks to what had turned out to be a very active night. As if they'd been making up for lost time. But Darcy knew better. There was no way to make it up, to recover what they'd lost. Or to start over and make something new.

Marla laid her hand on Darcy's arm. "Darcy. Be careful. If you're going to leave again, don't set yourself up for heartbreak."

She gave Marla a smile that was more a curving of her lips than a real smile. "I know. I'll be careful. I don't want to go through that again." That was God's honest truth.

As her aunt walked away, Darcy tried to ignore the little voice that told her it was already too late, that she was going to hurt like crazy when she left. That all her hard work, all her careful defenses had been for nothing when the man could strip her bare with just a look. She'd destroyed the last of them herself when she'd fallen apart in his arms last night.

Seemed she'd never learn.

Despite Darcy's predawn exit, Mack was in a good mood the next morning. Oh, he knew this didn't really change anything—no way it really could—but damn. Having her in his bed again was like an early Christmas gift to himself. To both of them.

He hoped this maybe meant they could put the past behind them, where it belonged.

He came into work, actually whistling, and Jennifer narrowed her eyes at him. "You got some, didn't you?"

He did a double take. "What?"

She sighed. "I recognize the signs. The loose walk. The perma-grin. You're whistling, for Pete's sake. Yeah. I'm hoping it was Darcy, otherwise you're a fool."

"Ah." He took a moment to think it through.

"I won't say anything," she added. "You know that. But, Mack… Is it a good idea?"

He rubbed his hand between his eyes. "Doesn't matter now, does it, Jenn?"

She shook her head. "Sure it does. She's leaving. You're taking away her reason to stay."

I should be her reason to stay. But he didn't say that. "What reason is that?"

Jenn looked at him as if he were nuts. "Her farm, dimwit. Why should she stay? Why will she ever come back? You guys are turning it into a subdivision and her family's moving to Arizona. If you think you're going to win her back this way, you're going about it all wrong."

Mack's head spun. "She didn't want the farm."

Jenn smacked his arm. Hard. "You're an idiot, Mack. Really. I expected better from you. You figure it out. I can't tell you what to do. I don't know Darcy. But I do know that if a man wanted me as bad as you want her, he'd damn well better put forth some effort to make me stay."

She was right. Of course she was right.

He was an idiot. And he'd overlooked one very important detail. He wasn't going to get her to stay *for him.* She needed a reason to leave Chicago, something that mattered to her. And Jenn was right—he and Chase were destroying the one place she loved more than anything.

"I don't have a lot of time," he said more to himself than to her. And really, did he want her to stay? Did he want her to be part of his life? Was he ready to go there again?

He wasn't sure.

Jenn had moved on to the end of the row, and the cacophony of hungry dogs and cats allowed him the luxury of no conversation. His thoughts bounced back and forth between his night with Darcy and Jenn's words.

When Mack arrived at the farm, Darcy had hoped that she'd be out on the back forty somewhere, but of course that wasn't the case. He walked right up to her, in front of all the other people that were milling around, and said, very quietly, "Hi."

"Hi," she said back, more of a breath than a vocalization.

There was an awkward moment while they looked at each other, then away. *Crap.* She felt her face burn.

"You okay?"

She looked at him almost shyly. "Yeah."

Then he stepped back and gave her a little smile before heading around back. Darcy took a breath and the cold air burned her lungs. Well. Anyone watching knew exactly what had happened with them. Wonderful. She took a quick look around, but it was hard to tell with so many people moving around who had noticed and who hadn't.

She threw herself into the work, trying not to cue in to him in the most primal way possible. He seemed to be everywhere she was. Or maybe she was just hyperaware of him.

That was probably it.

She smiled at the couple in front of her, and it took her a minute to realize the woman was looking at her with a bemused smile.

Recognition clicked in. "Oh, my gosh. Cheryl?"

The other woman smiled. "I didn't think you recognized me." She laughed.

"No, I—I was distracted, I guess," she admitted, and

came around the table to hug her former friend, whom she hadn't seen in ages. Since before she'd left for good.

"I bet I know why," Cheryl said with a low laugh. "I see Mack here."

"Ah." She darted a quick glance in the direction he'd been, and saw he had his head bent in conversation with a gorgeous black-haired woman. She tore her eyes away and ignored the sharp stab of jealousy. "Yes, well, he's been helping Uncle Joe."

Cheryl raised an eyebrow but didn't say anything else. She gestured to a tall man who was holding a little girl on his hip. She couldn't be more than three, as blond as her mother, wearing an adorable red velvet beret. Darcy couldn't stop her smile.

"Oh, Cheryl. She's gorgeous. She looks just like you!"

"Thanks, Darce. This is my husband, Jake, and daughter, Olivia. We met at college. Been married five years."

Yes, Darcy knew that. Marla had told her, had sent the invite on, and of course Darcy had sent her regrets. "I remember."

Cheryl let it go. "Can I have your number? I'd love to get together for coffee if you've got time."

Darcy's first instinct was to say no, as much as she wanted to reconnect with her old friend. All these connections were like a vine, binding her to this place, holding her back when she knew she had to leave. But at the same time— She pulled out her phone. "Sure. I'd like that."

Mack caught her eye over Cheryl's head as Darcy slid her phone back in her pocket. He'd seen. He'd know what it cost her to connect. He gave her a private little smile and her heart flipped.

She got through the rest of the day and headed up to the house after. It was cold, colder than it'd been yet.

It made the air dry, and the snow was squeaky under her boots. She'd managed to avoid Mack, but she was pretty sure it wouldn't last for long.

He could be determined.

She went in the kitchen and peeled off her layers. She usually just wore a thermal undershirt, a fleece jacket and a vest. Today it'd been cold enough for the full-on parka, even in the shelter of the barn. She unlaced her boots and left them at the door, and peeled out of her wool socks. She had cotton ones on under them, and long underwear under her jeans.

In the kitchen, her aunt and uncle smiled at her, and she pushed down thoughts of Mack and all the stupid feelings he invoked in her.

"Pretty cold," Joe commented, and she plopped into the seat opposite him, handing the papers to him over the cracked and worn linoleum table.

"Yes, but it didn't keep people away," she said simply. "They're just more likely to choose a precut tree rather than go tromping around in the woods."

He grunted. "Mack had extra cut?"

"Of course," she said, getting up to pour a cup of coffee. Decaf, of course, but it smelled good enough she didn't care.

Another grunt, this one of approval. "Smart boy, that one."

In some things, maybe. But Darcy wasn't going to go there. "You trained him, Uncle Joe."

Her uncle laughed, and she smiled back. He was looking better. His color was better, and while still he tired easily, he was coming back pretty good. Marla set a steaming plate in front of her. Chicken, sure, but also mashed potatoes and gravy. Her mouth watered.

Darcy knew if she kept eating like this, she'd need a whole new wardrobe come the first of the year, but she couldn't bring herself to care when she was this hungry.

"How is Mack?" Marla's question was conversational, but Darcy sensed the potential minefield.

"Fine," she said as she dredged a bite of chicken through the potatoes and gravy. "This is excellent, Aunt Marla." She popped the bite in her mouth, hoping her dodge worked.

"Thank you, dear," Marla said. Joe had retired to the living room and his favorite chair and was poring over the records. It appeared he'd pulled out last year's, as well. He was oblivious to the twist in conversation. Marla folded her arms on the table and leaned forward earnestly. "I have to ask. Are you and Mack considering reconciliation?"

Darcy opened her mouth, then shut it again. She pushed a few peas out of the gravy river on her plate. "No. I don't believe we are, Aunt Marla." The words were surprisingly hard to say. Because she wanted it to be true? Or because it hadn't occurred to her?

Who was she kidding? Of course it had occurred to her. How could it not?

Marla sat back. "I will say that's too bad. He's a great guy and you deserve the happiness you had with him."

Darcy shoved her plate away, all appetite gone. No, she didn't. She'd tossed it away as if it didn't matter. Made no difference at this point if it was true or not—he believed it was. "It's a little more complicated than that, Aunt Marla. You, of all people—you know that." She'd been the one to pick up the pieces. Or as many pieces as Darcy had allowed.

Compassion softened her aunt's features. "I do know

that, honey. I know that very well. But a lot of things brought you back here. If there's a chance, an opportunity, why not take it?"

It wasn't too far from what Darcy had been thinking, yet worlds away. She hadn't been thinking in terms of reconciliation. She'd been thinking of apologizing, maybe getting him to understand where she'd been coming from. Somewhere along the line that had changed. And she hadn't even realized it until now.

"Too much time has gone by," she said simply. "We're different people now. That's not a bad thing."

Marla shook her head. "No, it's not, that's true. But you've locked yourself down so tight, you won't let anyone in. How is that a good thing? You're so young."

Darcy gave a little shrug, as she had done when she was a teenager and pinned in the corner by her aunt. She didn't like being cornered. But she wasn't going to explain herself. She didn't think she'd shut herself down that tightly. She was practical, sure, but that wasn't a bad thing. It'd gotten her this far in life.

In her bed that night, she listened to the wind howl. It battered snow against the window—in this kind of temperature, it was little more than hard kernels of snow—and just seemed to underscore her loneliness. She was under the quilt in her old bedroom in her childhood home, instead of in the bed of the man who'd loved her. Who'd married her and done right by her when she got pregnant.

And she'd left him.

She curled onto her side and slipped into dreams of what could have been.

Chapter Twelve

The next couple of days were busy. She and Mack had fallen into a kind of truce. She didn't know what he wanted, but he wasn't pushing her. He was friendly, sometimes flirty, and every time he gave her that slow smile, her insides turned into a total puddle. Was he waiting for her to come to him? That didn't seem likely. Mack wasn't a game player. He was straightforward and solid. But he was clearly holding back. Waiting for her to make the next move?

Racking her brain meant she wasn't paying attention. And not paying attention meant she was recruited to go with Mack out to the far field to check one of the warming stations.

"I can just go," she offered, and saw him cock his eyebrow. "I mean, I'm sure you've got other things to do."

"Let's go," he said, and walked to the ATV. She trotted behind, mentally kicking herself for thinking she could get away from him.

They got in, and while she was grateful for the roar of the engine, she was pressed right up against him in the little vehicle. This was really a one-person ride, not for two, especially when the past of those two people crowded in and seemed to both shove them apart while cementing them together.

She tucked her face in the neck of her zipped-up parka, trying to protect against the stinging wind.

At the station he cut the engine and got out almost before it came to a stop. She hopped after him, feeling resentful and angry and knowing it wasn't his fault.

No, she wanted more and was angry with herself for wanting it.

She restocked while he checked the errant coffeemaker. She loved that he was so handy, had always been, and that didn't appear to have changed at all.

By the time he'd finished she was done. "Why am I here?"

"That's a good question," he said mildly, and all it did was make her madder.

"Mack. You didn't need me out here. And you won't talk to me—"

He was in front of her in about two strides. She gasped and backed up, but the wall was behind her and he'd planted both arms on either side of her, caging her in but not actually touching her. The look in his eyes was molten and she swallowed hard. He didn't say a word, just kept his eyes on hers until the last moment when his mouth came down on hers. Hard. There was no mercy in his kiss. He didn't touch her, but she felt the tension and hardness of his body even without the contact. She fisted her hands at her sides and kissed him back, giving as good as she got. Then she stopped thinking altogether.

He pulled away and the only sound other than the blood roaring in her ears was the rasp of their breathing in the quiet of the cabin. She lifted her fingers to touch her mouth, realized they were shaking and dropped her hand again.

"Damn it, Darcy," he said, but there wasn't any heat in the words. "You've got it all wrong." He stepped back, his eyes still on hers, and she could barely breathe. "All wrong," he repeated, and turned away.

She moved quickly and grabbed his arm. "What? What do I have wrong, Mack?" If he could tell her, if she could know, it would make all this so much easier.

He shook his head. "I just wanted to love you. But you wouldn't let me, then or now. Why is that?"

She stared up at him. It had never been that easy. "Because that's not how it worked for us. And, Mack, come on. We have too much baggage to make anything work. It's better left behind."

"Not a day goes by, Darcy, that I don't think of you. Of the baby. That I don't wonder what if. If we'd stayed together, would we have more? What would they look like?" His voice was so raw tears burned in her eyes and she knew what she had to do.

"I can answer part of that. No. There wouldn't be any more." Her voice was shaky and the words almost stuck in her throat. But it had to be said and it had to be said now.

"Because you didn't want them?" There was bitterness in his tone, and it made her heart ache even more that he'd think that of her, even if it was in anger.

She took a deep breath and looked him in the eye. "No. Because I can't have any more. I can't get pregnant, Mack."

Mack's ears were ringing. Darcy stood in front of him. Her mouth was still forming words, but he wasn't hearing any of them. *Can't get pregnant.* "What do you mean, you can't get pregnant?"

She lifted her chin. "From the damage of the miscarriage and the accident, the odds of me ever conceiving again are nearly zero. I'm more likely to be struck by lightning." Her tone was nearly expressionless.

Shock was reverberating around in him, making her words bounce around in his brain like a bunch of loose Ping-Pong balls. He moved away from her and she stayed where she was.

"Mack. I'm so sorry." Now there was pain in her words, regret and sorrow. She'd known this for how long?

"How long?" The words ripped from his throat. "How long have you known?"

Her eyes widened, but she said nothing. And he knew.

"You've known since you left," he said, almost wonderingly. "And you never said one word. Not one." And hell if he'd ever thought to ask her. He'd said, over and over, they could have another baby. How much he wanted to have a baby with her.

And she'd said nothing. Why not? If she hadn't been able to tell him, why hadn't the doctors told him?

She looked away and he saw her visibly fighting for control of her emotions. Then she looked back at him. "Yes. I knew the possibility was there. And it was confirmed later."

"After you'd already left."

"Mack, the doctor said there was a chance I couldn't get pregnant again! Remember? But you were so dead set on having another one, when I wasn't even out of the hospital yet."

She was already moving toward the door. "I'm walking back up. There's nothing more to say about this. I'm sorry. I really am. But I didn't see any reason to tell you when it was clearly over with us."

It wasn't until she'd left and the swirl of snow she'd let in on her exit had settled that he realized what she'd said.

It'd been a long time since Mack drank enough to, well, get drunk. And he was only half surprised when Chase showed up on his doorstep, grim-faced and tense.

Mack let his brother in and went back and collapsed on the couch. He could still feel, damn it. There wasn't enough alcohol in the world to fill the hole Darcy's words had made in his heart.

"Why are you here?" Or at least that was what he meant to say. It seemed to come out a little slurred.

"Darcy called me. Told me I should check on you." Even in his state, Mack could hear the bitterness in his brother's voice. "What the hell did she do to you?"

He let his head loll back on the couch. Closing his eyes was bad. Things started to spin. Maybe he'd had a little more than he thought. "Nothing."

The crash and clink of glass pierced his mental fog. "All these say otherwise," Chase said as he left the room, the bottles clinking in his hands. "Tell me," he said quietly when he came back in. "It must have been bad if she called me."

Something seemed off about that, but Mack wasn't

quite tracking well enough to get it. Wait. There it was. "Darcy called *you*?" Wow. Cold day in hell, and all that.

"Yeah," he said. "She asked me to check on you. Why?"

"She told me she can't have any more babies," he blurted, then winced. Even in this condition, he didn't want to talk about it. It wasn't Chase's business. He wasn't sure it was even his own. Not anymore.

"Okay," Chase said, his voice level. "But you're not together."

Nope, he wasn't far enough gone to muffle the pain of those words. Damn it. "No."

Chase didn't say anything else. He got up, and when he came back he had a sandwich, which he handed to Mack. "You need this more than another beer."

Mack took it, but he wasn't so sure. What he really needed he was afraid he'd never have again.

His wife back.

The next morning Mack's head pounded. He'd earned the headache. He dragged himself through his day at his vet practice, and while he was perfectly pleasant to his staff, his patients and their owners, his office staff had clearly caught his underlying mood and were handling him with kid gloves.

He went out to the tree farm because it wasn't in his nature to shirk his duties just because it was awkward. He could handle it. Unless it came to his ex-wife, of course. It was becoming crystal clear he had no idea how to handle her.

He didn't see her when he first pulled in. Then he spotted her in her navy fleece jacket and red vest, a bright red hat covering her copper hair. He swallowed hard. She looked up then, spotted him and said something to Wendy, who laughed as she walked away.

Now she was walking toward him, her stride long and purposeful. He didn't move, just shoved his hands in his pockets and let her come, let her make the move. It wasn't in his court. This was all her.

"Can we talk?" Her brown eyes searched his and he saw the shadows on the fine skin under her eyes. She hadn't slept any better than he had.

He was tempted to say no way, but he didn't want to hurt her more. There'd been too much pain between them already. "Sure."

She turned and headed out the door, toward the house. He caught up with her and they walked, wordlessly, through the dark to the house.

Darcy was nervous. Her fingers shook as she unzipped her fleece jacket. She went into the kitchen. "Coffee?"

"Sure," he said, and his voice was quiet and cautious. She didn't blame him. She'd undone everything they'd rebuilt in the space of a few minutes last night. Again. Clearly, this was not meant to work out. Not ever.

She prepared the mugs and handed him one, unable to hide the fact her hands were shaking. The coffee sloshed in the mug but didn't spill. He took it with no comment other than a murmured "Thanks."

The best way out is through. She'd always loved the line from Whitman and it steadied her now. She sat and gestured for him to do the same.

"I'm sorry I sprang that on you like I did last night," she said. This needed to come from the heart, for her sake and his. “And I’m even more sorry I didn’t tell you what the doctor said all those years ago.”

Maybe it would have been easier for him if he’d known they could never be what he wanted so badly. Help him understand why she’d left. Tears burned her eyes. She’d thought she was done crying over this. But the magnitude of their loss hung between them now and she finally saw it differently. She’d held on to it as *hers* for so long she’d forgotten it was really *theirs*.

He sat back, his expression shuttered, his untouched coffee steaming on the table between them. She couldn’t read him, wasn’t sure what was going on in his head. “It was a lot to take in,” she said quietly. “And I handled it all badly.”

He rubbed his hand over his face. “Yeah, we both did.” He sat forward, and rested his arms on the table, gaze on his fingers. She wanted to take his hand in hers, but instead threaded her fingers together tightly in her lap, so tightly it hurt. “Darce. I just wish you’d have told me. Let me carry some of it with you.”

The dark thing, the deepest secret she held, battered against her chest. She wasn’t going to tell him all of it. They had a chance to make a fragile peace. Telling him it had all been her fault wasn’t going to help that, help him. And she owed him the chance to move on. So she said simply, “Me, too.”

Because that was true. If she’d let him take some of it from her, would she have been able to stay? Hard to tell. She’d been a physical and emotional wreck at the time. She’d come back here, to the farm, to recuperate. He’d tried to get her to come home, but she’d refused. And he had eventually stopped arguing with her. Her physical injuries had healed, but her emotional ones ran much deeper. So deep, she didn't think she'd ever get around them. It was an ache she doubted would ever go away.

They sat for another few minutes and Darcy would have given almost anything to know what he was thinking. Then he said, "We need to get back."

Relieved it was over, she pushed back from the table and stood, reaching for his mug. But he caught her hand as he rose from his chair and tugged her around the table toward him. She stood in front of him, inhaling his scent, close but not close enough. She knew it'd never be close enough. Not now. He bent and pressed a soft kiss to her mouth. Then he dropped her hand and stepped back.

She put the mugs in the sink and they walked, wordless, back to the farm. The cheery, noisy bustle of happy families and Christmas music carried down the lane and for a minute Darcy felt suspended between two worlds—the one she had and the one she could have had if she'd stayed.

It was an eerie, unsettling feeling.

They managed to work around each other, but Darcy found the fragile peace they'd forged exhausting. She just wanted to curl up in bed and sleep. Until the day after Christmas, when she could finally go back to Chicago. *Home.*

Or was it?

She missed Chicago, but she'd begun to realize it wasn't quite home. Not the way this place was. Was that because she'd grown up here? Or because she still had some kind of feelings for Mack?

It seemed best to just admit it. That there were clearly lingering feelings, but it was in no way enough to move forward on. If either of them had wanted to. And she did not. There was too much pain in the past that would bleed through to their present.

"It's not enough," she said out loud to the spruce tree in front of her. *There, I said it.* Now all she had to do was hang on to that for the rest of her stay and she could escape mostly unscathed.

Some things just couldn't be fixed, no matter how much you wished otherwise.

The next morning, Darcy disconnected her phone and set it on the table in Java, the coffee shop that had become her closest thing to a home office.

So far, things were moving fairly smoothly in Chicago. Mally had things well in hand, which didn't surprise Darcy. She opened her laptop to check for the file Mally had emailed during their conversation. Perusing her assistant's work, she realized that Mally didn't need Darcy's direction. She knew exactly what she was doing and was in fact fully qualified to take over Darcy's position if she wanted to step down.

She could step right in and Darcy could—what? Leave? And do what? Ross wouldn't give Mally Darcy's job, of course. Not right away. But Ross would move on, fill her position.

Darcy put the thoughts aside. No point in going there when it wasn't going to happen. She'd worked long and hard to get where she was and she wasn't going to throw it all over for—what? Definitely not for something she couldn't even define. That was reckless. And stupid. And so very un-Darcylike.

"Darcy. How are you?"

She looked up at the friendly voice to see Cheryl.

"Hi, Cheryl." She pulled her papers and laptop over so the other woman could sit if she wanted to.

Cheryl hesitated. "Are you sure? I don't want to bother you if you're working."

Darcy closed the laptop and gestured for her to sit down. "I'm completely sure. I could use a break anyway. I'm sorry we haven't been able to get together yet. How are you?"

Cheryl smiled. "Good. Busy. Decided to treat myself to a latte today since we got word that we're being considered as adoptive parents for a teenage mother's baby."

Darcy's heart stuttered. "Wow, Cheryl, that's wonderful. When will you know?"

"Soon. She's about seven months along. She's a good girl, got in a tough situation and wants to give her baby the best life she can. It's not a done deal, but I hope…" She trailed off and took a sip of the latte.

Darcy reached over and touched her hand. "I hope so, too, Cheryl."

"There's something I've been wondering," Cheryl said quietly, her hands closed around her cup. She leveled her gaze at Darcy. "Why did you leave without saying goodbye? And why did you cut off all contact with me?"

Darcy sucked in a breath. There was pain in her old friend's voice, but no censure. She slid her laptop in her bag to give herself a second to regroup. Then she folded her arms on the table and looked right at Cheryl. "I'm not really sure. It hurt too much to be here, and everything was a reminder of what—of what I'd lost. I was just trying to move forward and I know I did a bad job of it." She'd rejected Cheryl's support, everyone's support. How stupid she'd been. "I was just so lost, I guess. In the grief. I'm so sorry I cut you off."

Cheryl nodded. "I figured that was what happened, but I needed to hear it for sure. I would have been there. I wanted to be there, Darce. A lot of people did."

So she was learning. All the bitterness she'd carried like a shield was withering away. She'd erected the shield as a defense to keep herself in, not to protect herself from people who cared. But that was exactly what had ended up happening.

"I wish you'd let me in," Cheryl said quietly now. "And I wish I'd tried harder to reach you. I didn't know what to do and I didn't try as hard as I could have."

Darcy's head came up sharply. "What? No, Cheryl, that's not what happened. You were there. That's all you needed to do, was to *be there*. And you were. I was the one who didn't know how to handle it. Or how to let anyone help me handle it. I just wanted it all to go away."

Cheryl cocked her head. "Did it?"

"No," Darcy admitted now. "Not really. I got good at kind of locking it away. Until I came back here."

A small smile ghosted across Cheryl's mouth. "I bet. There's something I need to tell you."

"What's that?"

"Olivia's middle name is Darcy."

Darcy's breath jammed in her throat. Cheryl couldn't have surprised her more if she'd hit Darcy with a hammer. "You—really? Oh," she said, and the word kind of fell from her lips. "Cheryl—"

"Yes, really." Cheryl's smile was looking decidedly damp around the edges, which was okay because Darcy knew hers was, too. "I just wanted you to know."

The lump in Darcy's throat was almost too big to breathe around. She reached for Cheryl's hand and held on tight, a connection she wished she'd accepted when it was offered all those years ago. "Thank you, Cheryl."

Chapter Thirteen

Mack showed up late at the tree farm. He looked a little ragged, and despite her best intentions to stay away, she went up to him. He gave her a tired smile that didn't reach his eyes. Concerned, she touched his arm. "Are you okay?"

He rubbed his hand over his eyes. "Yeah. No. Rough day."

Which told her nothing, since she could already see that. "We can get by without you tonight if you need to go home, Mack. Don't feel you need to stay."

He dropped his hand. "Thanks, but I need to stay."

Since he wasn't going to confide in her—why would he?—she nodded. "Your call. Let me know if you change your mind, though."

He said nothing as she walked away. Then—

"Darcy."

She stopped and turned. "Yes?"

He drew in a shaky breath. "It was an abuse case. Worst one I've seen yet. Dog beaten within an inch of his life and left out to die in the cold. He was frozen to the ground. I don't know if he'll survive, or if he'll ever be able to go to a new home." His voice was low, and the pain in his words fell heavily on her heart. Horror and anger fired there, too, that someone would treat an animal that way. Any living being.

She walked back toward him. "Oh, Mack. Do they know who did it?"

He shook his head. "No. Not yet. I hope they find the son of a bitch. Because it's more than the dog, Darce. What if this guy's doing this to his family? There's something wrong with a person who can hurt an animal this way."

She gave up and wrapped her arms around him, laid her head on his chest. His jacket was cold under her cheek. He wrapped his around her, too, and they stood there, by the side of his truck, Darcy feeling his warm breath on her hair. This was what they should have had. This was one of those moments that was out of time, from a life she didn't live but could have.

"He's got you," she said finally as she stepped back and looked up to meet his eyes. "And we'll hope the person who did this gets found soon."

"Thanks," he said quietly. "I see a lot in my job. A lot of broken animals, sick ones, too. But almost never something like this. I don't know how he survived as long as he did. I really don't. So I'll cut out early tonight, if it looks like things are under control, to go check on him. Jennifer's with him now."

"It's a Wednesday," Darcy said. "Our slowest day. It'll be fine, whenever you're ready to head out."

They walked to the barn in silence and he gave her hand a quick squeeze before heading the opposite way. Warmth fizzled through her, a little burst of surprise and happiness. He'd never touched her like that in public. She didn't know if anyone had seen.

She kept an eye on him through the evening, and he did leave early. That night, after she'd closed everything down and chatted with her aunt and uncle, she went up to her room and called Mack to check on the dog. She felt a little bit like a teenager as she lay flopped on her back across the bed, knees up. She almost wished for the days when there was a long phone cord to wrap around her finger.

"Hello?"

His voice was just as sexy over the phone as it was in person. Despite the reason for her call, her lady parts gave a little shimmy. She cleared her throat. "Hi. It's Darcy."

He gave what sounded like a pained chuckle. "I know. Everything okay out there?"

"Yeah. I just wanted to see how the dog is. If he's—well, if he's okay."

Mack sighed. "He's not okay, but he's holding. At this point, that's about all I can expect. Still touch-and-go. If he makes it through the night, his chances will be better."

"Poor guy," she said quietly.

"Yeah. I'm going to check him every hour until five, then I'll go home and catch a few hours of sleep while Jenn checks him."

"So you're staying at the clinic?" She knew Jennifer lived above the clinic. Maybe he stayed with her. And it was completely none of her business. Still, an odd twist slipped through her chest.

There was a rustling, as though he was moving around. "Yeah. I keep a cot here. I'll sleep in my office. Grabbed a pillow and blanket from home. I don't have to do it too often."

"That's good," she said.

There was a pause, but it wasn't uncomfortable. They were just quiet. Together.

"Darcy?"

"Yeah?" Why was she whispering?

"Thanks for calling."

"You're welcome."

She disconnected the call and stared up at the dark ceiling, feeling all kinds of fluttery and weird. Truth was, she could have waited until tomorrow to find out about the dog. She'd been concerned, yes, and saddened. But she'd wanted to check on Mack, too, and this had been a convenient excuse.

She rolled over and put the phone on the bedside table. She already missed his voice. Missed him. How sad was that?

"Two weeks until Christmas Eve," Joe announced at breakfast. "This upcoming Saturday will be almost as busy as the day after Thanksgiving. I'm going to meet with you and Mack to discuss a game plan."

Darcy spooned up more oatmeal. She had no idea what her aunt put in it, but it was good. It didn't matter if she didn't need the meeting. Uncle Joe did. "When?"

"Tonight. He'll come to the house when he gets here. We'll have it here, in the kitchen."

"I'll have pie," Marla broke in with a smile.

"Sounds good." If it hadn't been the last season, it would have been a different sort of meeting. Darcy wanted to ask why they'd never branched out into more sales, why they hadn't expanded the tours, why more promotion hadn't been done. Yes, some of that cost money, but they'd have earned it all back and then some. But she wasn't going to ask now. It was too late.

The farm had two weeks left. Then, after the new year, it'd be turned over to Mack and his brother to bulldoze. Appetite gone, she slid her chair back to carry her bowl to the sink. For all Mack still tugged at her heart, he was taking away the one thing that had always been a constant in her life. She needed to remember that.

"I'm so sad this place is closing," one woman said to Darcy later that evening after the meeting with Uncle Joe. "I've come out here since I was a little girl. Now I bring my kids. We look forward to it every year." The kids in question looked to be around five and nine, and happily sucking on the mini–candy canes Darcy had given them from her stash by the register.

"Me, too. We all are. But my aunt and uncle are going to retire. A tree farm is a lot of work." She'd said the same thing many times over the past couple weeks. But now she added, "It's been a wonderful experience, being a part of all these Christmases for all of these years."

The woman handed over the cash for the tree. "So much better than grabbing a tree at a big box store," she agreed. "I wish your aunt and uncle all the best in their retirement. Maybe they'll get lucky and find someone to take it over."

Darcy couldn't bring herself to say it'd been sold and would be parceled off into home lots. "Maybe," she said noncommittally, and smiled as she gave the woman her change.

As she watched them go, Wendy came up to her. "I heard her. Tough, isn't it?"

Darcy sighed. "She's not the only one. I've heard some variation of that several times each week. Some people aren't invested, you know? They'll just get a tree and move on. For others, it's a tradition. I never realized or appreciated how much that matters."

How shameful was that? She'd grown up in a business that catered to people's traditions and she'd still missed the point. Until now.

When it was too late.

Wendy nodded. "It is hard. I've made the same wreaths for a decade for the same people. I know who likes a little more spruce, and who to give the most juniper berries to. Who likes a bigger bow, who prefers flatter. I love to see their faces light up when they come pick them up. It's all part of the package of tradition. I'll miss it." She held out her hands and gave a little laugh. "I won't miss being stabbed fifty times a day by needles, though. Or getting pitch on my clothes."

Darcy smiled and shook her head ruefully. "No. I guess not."

Wendy went outside to check the wreaths and grave blankets—Darcy had sold a few—and it was quiet for a moment in the barn.

Until Mack walked in.

She'd asked him earlier about the dog, whom he'd named Fraser. He'd made it through the night. Mack was cautiously optimistic he'd pull through physically. Emotionally, he couldn't say.

She gave him a little smile. "Hey. Staying warm?"

He walked over and snitched a candy cane from her bowl. "Yep."

She frowned at him and teased, "Hey. Those are for paying customers only."

He arched an eyebrow and the look in his eyes went hot. Oh, my. An answering heat tugged low in her belly. "What's your price?"

Her mind went unhelpfully blank. "Um, well."

"How about I suggest one?" He moved behind the register and the plastic wrapper of the candy cane crinkled loudly as he put his hands on her shoulders. She licked her lips and could say nothing as he lowered his mouth to hers. "This okay?" he whispered, so close but still too far. In response, she pressed her mouth to his.

"Oops," Wendy's voice, and laughter, carried through the little cocoon that had woven around them. "Sorry to interrupt you kids."

He made a hungry sound in his throat and she pulled away, breathing hard, feeling her face flame. He pressed his lips to her forehead and gave a little chuckle.

"What's so funny?" she asked, not seeing anything humorous in the way her body revved and ached for his. For him. Plus, Wendy had caught them, even if she had stepped back out of the room.

"I don't know." He released her and stepped back. "We're just like a couple of teenagers sometimes."

She closed her eyes. "We're at work. This is a family place. When you and I kiss..." She trailed off.

There was a predatory light in his eyes now. "When you and I kiss, what?" he prompted.

She lifted her chin. "It gets out of control, okay? And this isn't the place for that." There. She'd said it.

He caught her chin. "You're right. It's not. Come to my place after we're done here."

He was completely serious. A thrill shivered down her spine. "I don't know."

He leaned down and gave her another quick kiss, and filched another candy cane. "The offer stands," he said, and sauntered out as another family made their way in. He sent her a wink over their heads and Darcy wasn't sure if she wanted to laugh or scream.

Or risk going over to his place. She knew exactly what was being offered there. But she wasn't sure she could spend the time with him and walk away whole when it was time for her to go.

Darcy went home afterward, gave her report to her uncle and headed upstairs to shower. As she stood under the steaming water, she wrestled with herself over Mack's invitation. It wasn't that she didn't want to go. She did. It was that she was afraid she was getting in too deep already.

Maybe it didn't even matter anymore. It was going to hurt when she left either way. This time, though, she could control it. And maybe minimize the regrets.

She turned off the water and toweled off quickly. In the steamy mirror she couldn't see the jagged scar on her abdomen, but she was aware it was there. Mack hadn't been put off by it. In her two sexual encounters in the seven years since her marriage ended, the room had been dark and it had been only one time. Each.

She dressed and dried her hair, combing it into place and securing it with a clip. A little mascara and she was good to go. She took a deep breath. From the time, she knew Uncle Joe and Aunt Marla would have retired to their room. She tossed a few necessities into a small bag she pulled from the closet and headed out before she lost her nerve.

Except Marla was in the kitchen.

Darcy froze, feeling for all the world like a teenager caught sneaking out when Marla's gaze fell to the bag, then up to Darcy's face. She surprised Darcy by laughing.

"Don't look so guilty, honey. No one here is surprised to see this rekindle with you and Mack." Then she sobered. "Is it serious, Darcy?"

Darcy sank down in the chair across from her and let her bag slide to the floor at her feet. "I don't know, Aunt Marla. There are so many reasons why it can't be, and yet..." She left the words unsaid.

"And yet it is anyway," Marla finished softly. Darcy could only nod. "Tell me again why you are fighting this?"

"You mean other than the fact that my life is in Chicago?" Was that her only reason?

Marla nodded. "Where's your heart?" She held up a hand before Darcy could speak, not that she had any answer for that question. "You don't have to tell *me*. You have to be honest with yourself. Go to him. Take some of that pie. And don't come home until morning."

Darcy was pretty sure her face was as red as the flaming red teakettle on the stove. "Yes, ma'am."

Marla drew her in for a hug when they both stood up. "We just want you happy, honey. That's all."

Mack had half expected Darcy not to show up. As it got later, and he looked at the damn clock every two minutes, he tried to convince himself he didn't care.

It wasn't true.

He'd checked on Fraser, who looked to be out of immediate danger but not out of the woods by a long shot. Jenn would check on him a couple more times before morning.

Another look at the clock. The cat sat on the back of the couch and cracked one eye halfway open when Mack leaned forward to check the time on his phone. Again. In case it was different than the time on the wall clock.

It wasn't.

He sat back with a *thump*, which finally dislodged the cat, who stomped over his lap on her way to the floor, where she sauntered off with a baleful flick of her tail.

This was stupid. He stared at the game on TV, not even caring what the score was, and usually he was glued to his alma mater's basketball games.

It didn't mean anything if she didn't come. It meant she didn't come and that was that. He was a big boy and could handle it. He knew she was wavering on the edge and so was he. Just because things had been good in the past didn't mean they'd be good now and all that. After all, they'd never dealt with the things in the past.

He almost had himself convinced she'd done them both a favor by not showing up when there was a knock on the door. He got off the couch as if he were rocket propelled, then forced himself to walk slowly to the door and ignored his stupid racing pulse.

It was Darcy, looking a little nervous as she worried her lower lip between her teeth. A lip he had every intention of kissing in the next few minutes. "Hi," he managed.

"Hi," she said, almost shy. She lifted a container.

"Marla sent pie. She caught me on my way out." Then she blushed.

Mack took the container and Darcy's arm and drew her inside. Something about the way she'd phrased that bothered him. "Caught you?"

The blush deepened as she unzipped her coat. "I went in the kitchen and she was there. I was hoping..." She trailed off and Mack's stomach dropped.

"You were hoping to avoid anyone knowing you are here?"

Her eyes widened. "No. I was hoping to avoid acknowledging what was going to happen when I came here. Even as an adult, it's an awkward thing to share with your relatives."

He pulled her in and kissed her, long and slow and deep. "And what's going to happen now that you're here?"

She plucked the container out of his hand with trembling fingers. "We're going to eat pie, of course."

With a laugh he followed her into the kitchen, watching as she greeted the dogs, who wagged at her as if she were a long-lost friend, before setting the dish down. He came up behind her and slipped his arms around her from behind and buried his face in her hair, like he used to do when they were dating, then married. She wrapped her arms around his and tilted her head so he could kiss her neck.

"Can the pie wait?" he whispered, and pressed against her backside, letting her feel his erection. She made him crazy and hungry and it wasn't for pie. She pressed back, making him groan her name, then turned in his arms.

"Make love to me," she whispered, and he had her

mouth, kissing her as if the whole world depended on it, before she could finish the last word.

They didn't make it very far, just out to the couch by the Christmas tree, and he'd managed to divest them each of their shirts and her bra by the time they got there.

With his hands full of Darcy's glorious breasts, he couldn't get her pants off, but that was okay because right now these needed his attention. He alternated between each sweet nipple with his tongue and his thumb, feeling her rise beneath him as she fumbled for the snap on his jeans. "Mack," she pleaded, and he shifted so she could get where they both wanted her to go.

When she tugged the zipper down and slid her hand into his boxers, closing around him, he groaned. "Darce," he panted.

A wicked smile curved her lips as her hand started to move up and down his length. "What?"

He'd forgotten. "Hell, honey—"

Her hand moved away and she started tugging on his jeans. "Off," she commanded, and he was more than happy to oblige. "Now sit and let me," she whispered. His erection throbbed and jumped and he fisted his hands in her hair as her hot mouth took him to the point the stars exploded around him.

It took him a minute to refocus and when he did, the only thing he saw was Darcy, kneeling between his legs, a smile on her face. Her breasts brushed the inside of his thighs as she leaned forward to get up. He caught her arms. "Your turn."

He had her pants down around her ankles and his mouth on her before she could do much more than gasp. She managed to get one foot out of her jeans and he lifted that leg up on his own thigh so he had better access to her. He wrapped his arm around her rear and held on as she braced her arms on his shoulders. She was so ready for him, so wet and hot, and she tasted like his own personal heaven. Her whimpers turned to cries as she reached her peak, and when she came apart he lowered her into his lap and drove himself home.

"Darcy," he growled, and she wrapped her arms around him, her breasts rubbing on his chest, and all that glorious friction and wetness and heat sent him right over the edge again, and by the contractions around him she was right there with him.

Spent, he lay back on the couch and arranged her next to him. "Wow," she breathed.

He pressed a kiss to her head. "Yeah. Wow." Clearly, they had no problems in the sex department. They never had. But it had never been that—explosive before. And it'd been plenty hot.

Chapter Fourteen

Sometime later, Darcy woke to feel Mack's fingers lightly stroking her flank. She blinked and lifted her head. He chuckled.

"Hey, sleepyhead."

She started to sit up and his hand came up to cup her breast. "Did I doze off?"

"We both did." He pulled her on top of him and took a nipple in his mouth, giving it a slow, lazy circle with his tongue. The tip of his erection pressed against her thigh. She adjusted so she could slide right down and take him all in. His hips rose to meet her and he let out a low groan.

This time they moved slow and sweet, and when the climax broke over her, he followed her over and held her while they floated back down, their bodies still joined. This wasn't sex. This was intimacy. That meant there were feelings involved.

Her stomach growled and he laughed. She lifted her head off his chest and managed a grin. "I guess it's time for pie."

It was a wonderful evening. They ate pie naked and talked—not about the past—and made love one last time, in his bed, before falling asleep. Her last thought, before she drifted off, was this was how it was supposed to be, all those years ago.

In the morning when she woke, Mack was gone, but she smelled coffee. Her clothes were neatly folded on top of the dresser, and her bag was on the floor in front of it. She stretched and couldn't help smiling at the slight soreness. They'd been busy and she'd loved every minute of it.

She got out of bed, took a quick shower, dressed and went in search of the coffee. There was a note on the counter.

Good morning, sexy. Had to go check on Fraser. See you soon.

Not a lot, but it made her smile.

She poured the coffee into the mug he'd left out for her and patted the dogs, who seemed quizzical as to why she was still there. "It's okay, girls. I'll be on my way soon."

That was true in more ways than one, she knew. She'd be out of Holden's Crossing in a couple of weeks. And this would all be a wonderful memory. Much better than her last memories of her and Mack. They both deserved better.

It still meant she had to leave.

* * *

"Did you have a nice time, dear?" was all Marla asked when Darcy walked in the kitchen.

She held out the pie plate, trying not to picture her and Mack eating from it naked, feeding each other straight from the dish. Seemed very inappropriate here in her aunt's kitchen. "Yes."

"That's good." Marla turned to the chicken she was preparing. "Joe's going to go out to the barn tonight with you guys for a bit. Will you help me make sure he stays put and doesn't wander off to overdo it? You know your uncle. He'll want to 'check'—" here she used air quotes "—everything."

Darcy smiled, grateful the topic of her and Mack had been dropped. "Oh, yes. He will. Of course. We'll find a way to keep him busy." Her phone rang. A local number, but not one she knew. "Hello?" she said as she left the kitchen.

"It's Cheryl. Are you free for lunch today? I know it's short notice."

"I'd love that. When and where?"

Cheryl named a new café Darcy wasn't familiar with and they agreed to meet just before noon. That would give Darcy enough time to do some catching up with work emails and then be back in time for the evening's shift at the farm.

"So nice that you and Cheryl are reconnecting," Marla commented when Darcy told her her plans. "I was always so sad you let all those friendships go. Wasn't healthy for you to be so alone."

Darcy stood in the kitchen, her briefcase in one hand and her phone in the other. A stab of regret hit her hard. "I know. I just—couldn't do it. Be reminded." She'd had to bury her son and her marriage, too. It had been too much to hold. She'd been afraid that someone would tell her how Mack was doing and she'd never been sure what she'd been more worried about—that he'd be fine, or that he wouldn't be. Either one made no sense.

Marta laid her knife on the counter and wiped her hands on the dishrag. "I know. But you never allowed yourself to heal, Darcy. You closed it all off, but never let yourself work through the pain. It was too much for one person."

She didn't want to do this. Not now, not ever. "I'm fine."

Marla sighed and nodded. "I won't push. But let yourself feel, Darcy. You deserve to be happy. So does Mack."

Darcy slipped on her boots and walked out into the falling snow. Of course he did. They both did. But the only way she'd ever been able to really make him happy had been in bed. That hadn't changed, clearly, as they were combustible together. But didn't that mean they hadn't changed in other ways—and she hadn't been enough for him then. Why would now be any different?

Darcy pulled into the café's parking lot with five minutes to spare. She was looking forward to this, but a little nervous, too. She didn't want to blow it. She'd love to leave here with her friendship with Cheryl back on track.

Of course, she might have to come back sometimes for visits. But she wouldn't let that stop her. She could probably manage to avoid Mack, if it came to that.

They placed their orders with the cheerful girl behind the counter once Cheryl came in and greeted Darcy with a hug, as if they hadn't been apart for years. They chatted for a few minutes while waiting for their food, and once they were seated Cheryl asked the question that Darcy had been trying to figure out if she was going to bring up. “So. Tell me about Mack. Are you back together with him?”

“Ah.” Darcy gave a little laugh and set her sandwich down. She hadn’t even managed a bite. “No. Not really.”

“*Not really* isn’t an answer,” Cheryl said slowly. Her expression was sympathetic. “What’s going on, Darce? You don’t have to tell me,” she added quickly. “I understand.”

Darcy gave up and filled her in, sparing no details except those of their actual lovemaking and ending with, “I’m not sure what to do. This isn’t what I thought.”

“No?”

She shook her head. “No. It’s different this time. Not like, ‘Oh, okay, we shared a past,’ but more like—” She stopped, unsure of exactly what she wanted to say. Of what it meant.

“More like you share a future?” Cheryl said softly.

Darcy pressed her free hand to her eyes. “Yes.” The word was a whisper.

“Oh, Darcy.” There was a world of sympathy in Cheryl’s voice. “What are you going to do about it? How can you make it work?”

Darcy thought of her job, her life in Chicago. That promotion was poised to take her to the next level, one she’d been working toward since she got there. How could she give that up? What would she do for income? She had savings, sure, but not enough to make that kind of life change. Did she even want to? “I don’t know how. Or if it can be done.”

“You love him.” It wasn’t a question.

"Yes." There was no point in denying it. "But what if it's left over from before, when we were married? How can I know it's real?" It felt real enough. But she just couldn't be sure.

"You know," Cheryl said simply. "You know you do. Trust yourself."

"There's one more thing," Darcy said quietly. "I didn't want to get married the first time. I was pregnant and he insisted. Not in a bad way or a mean way, just he really wanted to be married and start a family and all that. And I wasn't ready. I know it was too late to not be ready, cart before the horse and all that, but, Cheryl, I wasn't happy. I was freaking out and he thought it all was fine and wonderful." Now the tears were flowing, right there in the café, but she couldn't stop the words. "I didn't want any of it. Now, when I can't have any of it, I want it so badly it's tearing me up inside."

"Oh, honey," Cheryl said. She reached over and took Darcy's hand. "Did you tell him? Does he know that's how you felt, either then or now?"

"No," Darcy whispered. "I couldn't. He was so sure. I thought maybe there was something wrong with me, that I didn't want it, you know?" Mack hadn't known. He'd never guessed. Probably foolishly, she'd hid the truth from him instead of giving him the chance to help her. And he would have. He'd have moved heaven and earth for her if she'd allowed him the chance. But she hadn't.

"You need to tell him," Cheryl said firmly. "He needs to know, because that's a big part of why you left, correct? You have to set him straight because that's the only way you can really move on and start over. You both deserve the chance to know the truth and decide where to go from there. Don't make this decision for him, Darcy. It's not fair."

Even though her friend's words were spoken in a gentle tone, they still stung, because Cheryl was right. She'd made that decision for him, for them, once. She couldn't do it again.

She took a deep breath. "Okay. You're right. I will. Soon."

"Saw Darcy's car in front of your place yesterday," Chase said, and Mack rolled his eyes. "I'm not going to tell what I'm supposed to ask you. But I will ask—have you lost your mind?"

"No," Mack said, taking the phone off speaker. This wasn't going to be a good conversation for his staff to overhear. "I haven't." But he had had his mind blown several times last night with the incredible sex he'd shared with Darcy. That wasn't a detail he planned to share with anybody, especially not his big brother.

Chase blew out a breath. "You are a glutton for punishment, little bro. I can't save you from yourself."

"No, you can't," Mack agreed. "So back off and don't try. Let me do this."

"She'll hurt you."

No doubt. "I can handle myself, Chase. I know she's leaving. She does, too. It's fine." But deep down he knew that wasn't quite true. It wasn't that easy. It never had been easy with Darcy, and it hadn't changed. There was too much history between them, history they hadn't touched, to be anything more than temporary. Because then they'd have to really examine the past and frankly, Mack couldn't see that going anywhere good.

He also knew it'd have to be dealt with sometime.

He owed her a lot, and as much as he wanted her in his bed, he didn't want to be destroyed by her all over again.

He hung up after promising he'd meet Chase for lunch tomorrow and exacted a promise from Chase that he'd drop this thing with Mack and Darcy. It had been grudgingly given, and had taken some minor threats, but his brother had agreed.

He didn't want to be reminded it would end again. That she'd leave again. He knew this, felt the time slipping past him like water in a fast-moving stream and every bit as impossible to hold on to. But it made it awfully hard to stay in denial—his current happy place, though he wasn't stupid, knew he'd have to deal with it sooner rather than later—when people kept waving her leaving in front of his face.

Even though their intentions were good.

He couldn't help but hope that somehow they'd be wrong. And that was why this was so dangerous.

On impulse, Darcy stopped at the vet clinic after her lunch with Cheryl. She wanted to check on Fraser and frankly, see Mack. She called him from the parking lot, hoping she'd caught him at a good time.

"Hello?"

"Hi, Mack, it's Darcy."

"I know." There was a smile in his voice and she heard barking in the background. "What's up?"

"Are you on lunch? I was wondering if I could see Fraser. If it's no trouble." She held her breath. If he said no and saw her car out here, she'd feel silly.

"Sure. I don't really take a lunch, but I've got a few minutes. Are you close?"

"Yeah," she said. "I'll be there in a couple minutes."

When she walked in, he was behind the counter. Her heart gave a jump and she felt a bit of a blush as their night together flashed before her eyes. He wore jeans and a light blue button-down and she just wanted to melt into him.

This was bad. Even knowing what she did—that she loved him, still—it scared her.

He gave her a smile and she was glad there was no one in the waiting area to see her blush. “Hey,” he said, and came around the end to drop a kiss on her mouth. Brief, but hot and way too public.

“Hey,” she said back. She loved the kisses, darn it.

A tall blond-haired woman strode in from the back, looking at some papers in her hand. “Mack, are we out of the purple packages of the dog flea treatments? I thought— Oh,” she said as she looked up, drawing out the word, her gaze flying to Mack, then settling on Darcy. “Hello.”

“Jenn, this is Darcy. Darcy, Jenn. She’s the other vet here. And yes, we’re out of that for now. Sherry said they called this morning and are back-ordered. They can deliver Monday, I think it was. The notes are on the desk there.”

Jennifer came forward, hand extended, papers tucked under her opposite arm. “Good to know. Thanks. So nice to finally meet you, Darcy. Mack talks about you a lot. Or as much as a guy will talk.”

Darcy couldn’t help smiling as Mack shifted uncomfortably beside her. “Jennifer.”

She looked at him innocently. “What?”

He just shook his head.

“It’s nice to meet you, too,” Darcy said, and meant it.

Mack rested his hand on the small of her back and

steered her toward a door. "We're going to check on Fraser."

"All right. He told you about that?" Jenn said to Darcy, and she nodded. "It was awful. Just—awful."

"You told her about me?" Darcy asked once he'd closed the door behind them.

His jaw tightened. "She'd heard some rumors. She made some guesses."

She stopped and laid a hand on his arm. His muscles flexed under her touch and she slid her hand down to grab his hand. "Mack. Is that okay?"

He paused at another set of doors. "Yeah. I just don't want you to think I go around talking about you. Or us. Or our past. It's private."

"I know," she said. "I wasn't worried or mad." But he seemed embarrassed. A light went off in her head. "Did you date her, Mack?"

He pushed open the door. "No. Not really. We'd hang out, I guess you could say, but it was never a date situation."

She followed him through the doors. The light was dimmer here and the smell was defiantly hospital-like. She swallowed hard. He stopped at a cage where a big dog lay under a blanket.

Even in this light, and when it was clear the animal was asleep, she gasped. She could see the scars and cuts and what looked like burns on his head. Tears burned her throat. "Oh, Mack."

His face was grim. "You should see the rest of him. He's in bad shape. He's going to lose a front leg. I was hopeful, but it's not going to heal right. But I couldn't do it at the first round of surgery."

She touched the cage quietly, not sure if she'd wake

him if she made too much noise. He was sleeping, breathing even. Mack noticed. "You won't wake him. He's under right now. Helps with the healing and the pain."

"Who pays for his care?"

"There's a fund that people donate to for situations like this, when an animal needs serious help or when an owner can't pay the bill. Same with Minnie. We do fund-raisers to keep it going. That will cover some of it."

And he'd pay the rest. He didn't say it, but he didn't have to. She knew. She tucked herself into his side and wrapped her arms around his waist. He slid an arm around her and squeezed. She could hear the steady beat of his heart under her cheek and felt the warmth of his skin through his shirt. "You're a good man, Mack."

He went still. "Anyone would help out, Darce."

No, they wouldn't. But she let it go. And she knew now what she'd given up when she walked away. She'd been so, so shortsighted. Stupid. So she held on while she could, knowing she'd have to leave again, and they stood there, in the dimness, and watched Fraser sleep.

A *clang* from inside the clinic broke the spell. She stepped away and he let her go. She cleared her throat. "Well. I guess I'll let you get back to work. I'd like to see him when he's awake, if you think that'd be okay."

He slid his hands in his pockets and started walking toward the door. "Should be. Starting tomorrow, I'll keep him on pain meds, but not keep him under. I'll let you know."

"Thanks." Darcy hitched the strap of her purse up, but before she could take a step, he turned her to face him and kissed her. A real kiss, hot and deep. He pulled away.

"That's the greeting I wanted to give you," he whispered.

She blinked at him. “Well, hello, then.”

A slow, sexy grin spread over his face. “Hi.”

“Thanks for the coffee this morning, by the way.”

“You’re welcome. Last night was amazing. Hands down the hottest night I’ve ever had.”

Darcy was pretty sure her blush had spread to her toes. She swallowed hard. “Yeah. Me, too.”

He kissed her again, a gentle one this time. “Thank you.”

“For what?”

“For taking the chance to come over. I know it wasn’t easy for you.”

His gaze was gentle and saw too much. She wasn’t ready to face that, to let him all the way in. So she just smiled back and followed him out of the ward and back into the clinic, where an older man sat with a cat carrier. The occupant was yowling with displeasure.

“Ah, Doc,” the man said with a wry smile. “Yoda is awfully excited to see you.” He winked at Darcy and she couldn’t help smiling.

“I can hear that,” Mack said drily. “I’ll be ready for him a few.”

“No problem. We’re early.” The man went back to his magazine.

Mindful of all the ears that were suddenly around them—she’d seen Jenn in one of the offices when they came back out, and voices came from somewhere she couldn’t see—she turned to Mack and gave him a quick smile. “Thanks for letting me see him.”

“You’re welcome. See you at the farm later.”

Darcy nodded and walked out into the bright sun, which reflected off the snow and made her sneeze. He’d always teased her about her sneezing in the sun.

Chapter Fifteen

Jenn was waiting for him when he went back to his office to grab a fast bite to eat. Mr. Franklin was early, and while Mack would get to him as soon as possible, he needed three minutes to wolf down a sandwich.

"Not now," he said as he pulled the sandwich from the bag he'd retrieved from the office fridge. "Please."

Jenn shook her head and ignored him as he'd known she would. "Mack. It's serious, isn't it." Not a question. A statement.

He chewed his ham sandwich, not tasting it. He swallowed and reached for the water bottle on his desk. "Just a lot of history."

She shook her head. "More than that. Lots of people have history. You've got chemistry and clearly the two of you still have feelings for each other."

Now he choked on the bread. "You got all that from a one-minute introduction?"

She looked at him straight on. "Yes. It's obvious, Mack. Not only from seeing you together, but the way you talk about her. Do something about it, even if it's just settle the past so you can move on. You're not over her."

"I'm over her." The denial was quick and sure. He was. He had to be. It'd been a long time. "But what happened was really awful, Jenn. For both of us."

"It must have been," she said quietly. "I know you lost a child."

So she did know. His child and his wife. His family. His future. He wasn't interested in replacing them. He couldn't. He threw the last of the sandwich away, his appetite gone. Jenn was right. Things from the past needed to be settled before Darcy left again.

He finished out the afternoon at the clinic, ran home to take care of his pets and change his clothes as well as grab another bite to eat. He drove out to the tree farm, anticipation building in his chest. Jenn wasn't too far off. He'd fallen right back into this. It had been way too easy.

Sure enough, Darcy was there. She turned when he came in and gave him a smile. Things were growing there, no doubt about it. What they were exactly was a whole nother story.

"Mack." Joe's voice caught him off guard and he looked over to see the older man sitting on a stool behind the register, Marla smiling behind him.

"Joe. Good to see you out here. Feeling better?"

"Yep. I can be out here for a while. Can't do the heavy lifting, though. Doc won't let me, and my girls are keeping a close eye on me." The words were grumpy, but there was a twinkle in his eye.

Marla patted his shoulder. "That's 'cause we want you around for a good long time, dear."

Mack chatted with them for a couple more minutes, then excused himself to go outside, pulling his gloves on as he went. He wanted to talk to Darcy, but didn't think she'd want him hunting her down under the watchful eyes of her aunt and uncle. Not that they weren't adults. But he knew she was a little nervous about all this, and bringing them into it wasn't going to help matters.

Marla caught Darcy as she was walking past the register. "As soon as Mack came in, he looked for you." Marla's voice was gentle. "As soon as he saw you, he relaxed. Darcy, that man is in love with you. What are you going to do about it?"

Her heart pinged painfully in her chest. What was she going to do? She was going to leave because there was no other option. "It's been a long time, Aunt Marla. Too long. And we never talked about our past."

"Then, you need to do that. Work it out and see where it goes."

Darcy shut her eyes. She already knew she had to do that. Her conversation with Cheryl had driven that home. "I know we need to talk. But there's nowhere it can really actually go."

Marla reached for the box of mini–candy canes. She scooped a handful into the bowl that sat next to the register. "That's just an excuse, honey. You can make this work if you want it to. So I guess the question is, do you want it to?" She held up a hand. "You don't have to tell me the answer. It's between you and him. I'm just trying to make sure you don't make a big mistake you'll regret."

Another big mistake, Darcy amended silently. She'd made a lot in a short time, and no matter how casual she'd kept it, or tried to, the fact was it was going to hurt when she left. But was it a mistake to leave? That was what she wasn't sure of.

"I'll keep it in mind," she said finally. "I understand and appreciate your concerns. I really do." She stopped short of saying she knew what she was doing, because frankly, it wasn't true. The whole thing had gotten away from her as soon as Mack kissed her the first time.

Marla gave her a quick one-armed hug, the bowl of candy canes in her other hand. "We love you. We want you to be happy. That's all."

Darcy managed a smile as Marla hurried away to get Uncle Joe back to the house. She put the box of candy away and took a couple of deep breaths, trying to get her bearings. *That man is in love with you.*

She shook off the thrill the words gave her. No, he was in love with who she'd been years ago. He didn't really know her now. She'd changed. *So has he.* They were getting to know each other now, too, but how could it be enough? Could she be sure?

He was buying this farm. Once she left it, there was no coming back to it. Not like this. Marla and Joe were heading to warmer pastures. There'd be nothing here for her, nothing but memories. The physical places would be gone. That meant there was no reason to come back, to be here.

If she walked away from Mack, it would be for good. She wasn't foolish enough to think they could stay in touch. The contact would open old wounds each time. She knew that for a fact. But after she talked to him, would he want to be with her?

* * *

Darcy went out and filled in in one of the warming sheds. She kept the fire going, and the coffee and hot cocoa ready. She answered questions about trees, and directed people to the proper areas for the type of tree they were looking for. At the end of the evening she banked the fire, cleaned the pots, swept the little cabin and set everything up to go the next day.

It was snowing pretty good when she came out, the kind that had been sifting for a few hours and had piled up about three inches. Then Mack came around the curve. He stopped in front of her and cocked an eyebrow. "Want a ride?"

"Sure." She walked around and climbed onto the ATV, and he executed a three-point turn to head back in. The rough ride jostled them together and she couldn't even pretend she didn't mind the press of his arm on hers, even if she couldn't feel his heat.

"Your aunt and uncle went back to the house already," Mack said. "He looked happy, Darce. It was a good thing for him to be out here."

"That's good." She brushed the snow off her arms and looked up as Mack pulled her in for a kiss.

"I've been waiting for that all evening," he said, resting his head on hers. She leaned into him, even knowing it wasn't a good idea. She just couldn't help it.

"Me, too," she admitted.

"Come home with me tonight," he said, then the corner of his mouth quirked up. "I can't cook you dinner, but I can spring for takeout."

She should say no. There were so many reasons why this was a bad idea. Too bad she couldn't remember them at the moment. "That sounds wonderful."

But the truth was she couldn't bring herself to stay away. One more night wouldn't hurt, right? One more night before she had to tell him the truth.

"Excellent. Will you ride with me or bring your car?"

She hesitated, but only for a second. "I'll follow you."

They went up to the house and Darcy went to pack a bag while Mack talked to Marla and Joe. She tried not to dwell on the weirdness of it all, but failed. She threw in a change of clothes and her toothbrush, then sat on the bed and took a deep breath.

Things had shifted. How, exactly, she wasn't sure. But she had the feeling she'd finally reached the point where she couldn't go back.

And that scared her.

The snow had picked up and the plows hadn't been out yet—four inches or so wasn't much in terms of a northern snowfall—but it was coming down pretty hard and the wind had picked up. She kept her eyes on the taillights of Mack's truck and both hands on the wheel.

The trip took twenty minutes instead of the usual ten, but she gave a sigh of relief when they parked at his house.

He got out and came over to her. "We can ride together to the diner," he said.

"Okay." She gathered her keys and purse and left her bag on the backseat.

His truck was warm and smelled spicy, like him. Wonderful, like him. She buckled in and pulled her gloves off. He put it in Reverse and they drove the few minutes to the diner in silence. The lot was nearly empty, and they hurried in, the snow falling fast and hard.

"What can I get you?" The waitress wasn't the same one they'd had before. She was older, but friendly.

"Looking to place a take-out order," Mack said while Darcy scanned the menu quickly.

"Are you closing early?" she asked.

The waitress, whose name tag said Denise, nodded. "Night like this, we don't get much business."

They placed their orders and waited for the food. It didn't take long. Even in the fifteen minutes they'd been inside, there was significant snow to brush off the truck.

He pulled in the driveway next to her car, since with the plows it wasn't a good idea to park in the street. She opened the back door, got a bunch of snow dumped on her for her efforts and pulled out her bag. Inside she stomped off her feet and laughed. "Wow. It's quite a night out there."

He kissed her, a hungry openmouthed kiss that had her dropping her purse on the floor to hang on to him. "Yeah. Hopefully, in here, too."

She gave him a smile, her body tingling all over.

He built a fire and she set the food out on plates she found in the kitchen. They sat on the couch and ate, the dogs looking on hopefully.

"Wow, I didn't realize how hungry I was until I started eating," she admitted, reaching for the ketchup for her fries, a treat she almost never had. And the ones from the Town Line Diner were still the best.

"I knew I was starving," he said cheerfully as he polished off another bite of his burger.

"Your mom not cook for you lately?" she teased, and took another fry. Heaven.

"It's all good," he said. "She brought a potpie the

other day. It's in the freezer. It makes her happy and saves me time. Win-win for both of us."

Darcy didn't remember her own mother. She'd left not long after Darcy was born and died a few years after that. She'd been raised by her father, and her aunt and uncle. She didn't think her mother would have been the type to fill her freezer with leftovers. But Marla was. So she didn't feel left out. But there was the occasional pang of sadness that she'd never know the woman who gave birth to her.

"I can see that" was all she said, and took a bite of her own burger, another splurge. "Mmm. So good. It'll be so hard—" She stopped, as she'd been about to say *when I go back.* But she could tell from the way Mack stiffened that he knew what she hadn't said.

"Hard to what?" His attention was on her now, not on the food.

So he wasn't going to let her off easy. "To go back to Chicago."

"Then, why are you going?"

She stared at her burger, so good a moment ago. "Because it's where my life is." That was true. But she was starting to worry it wasn't where her heart was. How did she reconcile those things? Could she?

"Is it?" he murmured. "Darcy. Why did you leave?"

She froze. "You know why I left. After—after everything it was pretty clear we weren't going to make it." Which was true, and had played a big role in her leaving. But it wasn't all of it.

"You didn't give us a chance," he said quietly, but there was a hard note in his voice.

She slapped her hand on her chest. "I didn't?" Then

she pointed at him. "You didn't, Mack. You went to your family and left me alone."

"You wouldn't let me in," he said. "You wouldn't talk to me or let me see you. You shut me right down."

She shook her head. "That's not what I did, Mack. It's not."

He looked at her over the plates and stood up. He walked away, down the hall, and she heard him open a door. Should she leave? A glance out the patio doors showed the snow still coming down pretty hard.

Mack came back out in the living room with two boxes stacked in his arms. Darcy put her wineglass down and stood. "What are those?" She asked the question, but she knew the answer already. *Mack and Darcy, Christmas* was written on the tops in his mother's neat script.

He set them down carefully and looked at her solemnly. "My mom kept these. She packed it all up. After—after everything." Her heart started up as he opened the first one. "Look."

She set the glass down and the liquid sloshed around because her hand was so unsteady. She came over near him and saw ornaments from their first tree. Her breath caught. "Oh. Oh, Mack."

She touched the glass balls on top. The memories hit her hard, ones she'd tried so hard to keep at bay. She and Mack choosing these ornaments—none of them particularly special or expensive, but they'd had fun picking them out. That trip had, of course, ended in the bedroom and they'd wound up decorating the little tree in their apartment nearly naked, with Mack constantly touching her pregnant belly. She'd been six months along and had enough of a bump she'd just started wearing maternity clothes. He'd loved her pregnant body.

He'd loved her.

She swallowed. "What do you want to do with them?"

"We can put them on the tree," he said quietly. "Or we can divide them up and you can take them home."

Tears blurred her vision. That had been such a magical time. Not that they could ever really re-create it, but maybe they could use it as a new start. For something.

"Let's put them on the tree," she said when she found her voice. "They should be used."

He put on a Christmas station, and the festive tunes helped alleviate the pain she held in her heart. This would be fun, but bittersweet. Because he'd have to take them off the tree. Alone. After she'd gone. Like he'd had to the first time she'd left.

She pushed the thoughts aside and lifted out the first box. These were four chili peppers, because he loved spicy salsa. She couldn't hide her smile. "Remember these?"

He looked up from the other box and smiled. "Yeah."

It was easier than Darcy had thought to go through the boxes. Mack kept her laughing and sometimes he kissed her. But she caught him looking at her in that way, the way he used to, back when he loved her.

Marla's words echoed in her head. *That man's still in love with you.*

It wasn't possible. Was it? How could that be, after all this time?

She picked up a glass ball, hand-painted with the words *Darcy and Mack, First Christmas* with a heart and the year of their marriage. She froze, and held it in her hand. Did this go on the tree? Or did she try to bury it in the box?

She sent a furtive glance at Mack. He was looking in the other box, not paying attention. She could just tuck it in the tree, where it wouldn't be visible. She slipped it around the side and hung it deep in the branches, where it couldn't be seen if you were just walking by or sitting on the couch. When she came back over, he'd returned from the other side of the tree.

Mack's phone rang and he answered it with an apologetic look at Darcy. She smiled at him to let him know it was okay, and wandered over to check out the snow. The wind was howling now, banging against the windows. Peeking out the door, Darcy could see by the porch light the snow was really piling up. Several inches were on the porch, and her car was a white lump. She clearly wasn't leaving tonight. Not that she'd planned to, but it was always in the back of her mind. An escape plan in case things got to be too much, she supposed.

She went back to the tree and sat on the couch, just looking at it, now that it held their ornaments. It made the tree more theirs. She could hear Mack's voice in the kitchen. The dogs snored in front of the fire. The cat was asleep on the couch, too. It was cozy. Comfy. And she was content. This could have been her life. So different from her life in Chicago.

Mack came back and sank down next to her. "Sorry about that. Jenn was checking in. Normally, we don't do that unless there's a patient we are watching closely. In this case, Fraser."

"And how is he?" She didn't protest when Mack took her feet, one at a time, and pulled them into his lap.

"Making progress. He's got a long way to go, but

he is healing. Barring a serious infection, I think he'll make it. And I'm doing my damnedest to keep infection at bay. He doesn't deserve any less."

"I agree," she said softly. "What will you do with him when he's healed?"

He started to massage her foot. She scooted down a little closer. "When he's well enough he'll go to the shelter. They'll take care of him and see if he's adoptable. There's a list of people who will take him, but if any of them are suitable or if he's going to be able to be adopted is another matter."

"If he's not?"

Mack sighed. "I'll take him. Or find a home. He's terrified of people, thinks we're going to hurt him."

Her heart caught. "Of course he is. Poor guy. Any luck on finding who did it?"

"Actually, yeah. There's a promising tip that came in they are checking out. Hopefully, it pans out and they can make an arrest." He tugged her socks off and dropped them on the floor. She flexed her toes and propped a pillow under her head. They said nothing for a long while as they sat there in the light of the tree and listened to the crackling of the fire. Darcy found herself dozing. She couldn't shake the feeling that she was home.

Chapter Sixteen

When Darcy nodded off, Mack just sat and watched her for a few minutes. He wanted her, to be sure. But right now what he felt was more tender. He just wanted to keep her here, in this house he'd bought for them, in the little cocoon they'd spun tonight. Sure, it wasn't reality and he knew that all too well. But damn if she hadn't slipped right back in his life, as if she'd never been gone.

She stirred and he squeezed her leg. "Hey, sexy. Let's go to bed."

She sat up, sleepy eyed, and gave a big yawn. "Okay."

She got her bag and he heard her in the bathroom, as he banked the fire and unplugged the tree. It looked right now, with their ornaments on it. Then he went into the bedroom as she came out of the bathroom. Flannel bottoms, a long-sleeve T-shirt. No bra, as he could see her breasts sway gently as she moved. He gave her a slow smile. "Flannel? I'll keep you warm."

Her nipples peaked against the shirt and he took that as a yes. "Unless you're too tired."

She shook her head and he kissed her, long and slow. He was in no hurry. None at all.

It didn't take long to get her out of her pajamas—she was bare under the bottoms, too—and he took his sweet time with her body before finally sinking into her. They moved slowly and he never took his eyes off hers, even when her eyes blurred and she rose with her climax. When he followed her and collapsed on top of her, he knew this had been different. Something had changed. He rolled off her, then tucked her against him. She kissed his arm and he buried his nose in her hair as he pulled the blankets over them both.

Something had changed, all right. He was afraid he knew exactly what it was.

They made love once more in the night, and in the morning before he went to the clinic. Mack figured it was a great way to spend the night and start the day. In fact, he'd happily do it every day.

The snow hadn't stopped, but it had tapered off. There was a good foot of new stuff on the ground. Their vehicles were just white mounds. He went out through the garage and shoveled quickly—it was light and fluffy, so it didn't take too long to get it out of the way. Then he brushed off both his truck and her car and got in. This was why he had a four-wheel drive truck, he thought as he plowed his way down the street. They were last in line for the plows, being a residential neighborhood, so if he wanted to get anywhere on days like this, it was four-wheel drive and a steady hand.

It took him nearly three times as long as usual to

make the trip to the clinic, but he got there. He figured there'd be plenty of canceled appointments today.

Jenn was in the back when he walked in. "You made it" was her greeting.

"Ha. Yeah. No school today, I take it."

"Not according to the news, no. Do we want to call off any of the techs for today?"

Mack hesitated. "No, but tell them there's no rush. If they can't get here safely, then tell them not to risk it. We'll be okay today."

"All right." She gave him the report on the animals and went to call the techs while he went to see Fraser.

He looked at the big dog in the cage, who looked back at him with pain and fear and suspicion. He talked to him quietly. Jenn had already done the morning's meds. He'd change the bandages later when the meds had a chance to take effect. He made a point of talking to him quietly several times a day to try to win the dog's trust, or at least let him know Mack wasn't going to hurt him. He was very careful to avoid sudden moves and loud noises, as well.

It'd take time.

He went back up front as Jenn was hanging up the phone. "All done. They both said they'll try it but promised not to take chances. I don't think either of them will be here before ten."

"That's fine." He wondered when Darcy would attempt to go home. Would she stay? He hadn't asked her to, but not because he didn't want her to. It was because he wondered what she'd say.

Plus, asking her to stay sounded needy. He wanted her to do it—or not—because it was what she wanted.

Sure enough, almost all of the patients canceled. But

they still had a couple discharges to do today, and those people came in for their animals. Jenn went home for lunch and Mack sat behind the desk, looking over supply orders. This was the techs' job and they did it well, but since they weren't here, he figured he'd do it. When the bell on the door jingled, he looked up.

It was Darcy.

He rose as she plopped a huge bag of cat food on the floor at her feet and slapped one of the tags from his tree on the counter. Then she smiled. "Here you go."

He came around the counter and pulled her into his arms, allowing himself a deep kiss, which she happily gave. "Thanks," he said.

She stood there for a minute in his embrace. "I've got lunch, too. Let me go get it."

"You didn't have to—"

"It's not fancy," she laughed. "Hold on."

He transferred the cat food bag to the room he kept that stuff in. They made regular runs to the shelter and dropped items off. She came back in, a whirl of snow coming with her, and held up a bag. "Where do you want this?"

"Let's go in my office." He led the way and she followed. When she opened the bag, she pulled out sandwiches and fruit and chips. From another bag she took out two pops and offered him one.

"This is a nice surprise," he said. It was. It was wonderful to see her in his space, spending time with him. Just being together.

She gave a little shrug. "I just thought it'd be nice to have lunch together."

They chatted and finished. Then he asked her if she wanted to see Fraser and she said yes.

The dog gave a thump of his tail when he saw them, which was the first time he'd done that. She gave a little inhale. This time there was no blanket covering him. All his cuts and scars were out in the open. "Oh, Mack. Oh. You poor thing," she said to the dog, who shut his eyes and gave a little huff. She turned to look at Mack. "He looks awful."

"He's had it rough," he agreed, and that was an understatement.

"Are the circles cigarette burns?" she asked, and there was anger in her tone.

Fraser whimpered.

"Easy," Mack said to both of them. "Watch your tone. He's really sensitive to tone." No surprise given the abuse.

"Of course. Sorry, puppy," she said to the dog, who relaxed again, apparently not sensing any danger from them. "Heartbreaking. Sickening, too," she said to Mack, who nodded.

"That pretty much sums it up." He just hoped they'd find who did it, and soon. Fraser deserved nothing less than justice and a good home. A lot of animals in his situation got neither.

Darcy left for her aunt and uncle's after promising she'd be careful.

"I drive in snow," she pointed out. "We get our fair share in Chicago."

He knew that. But the accident still lingered with him after all these years. He'd never forget seeing her, banged up and bleeding and broken in that hospital. Ever. It was the moment his heart had stopped. "Just be careful. Please."

She gave him a kiss as Jenn walked into the room. With a quick greeting to Jenn, she was out the door.

"You have to tell her if you haven't already, Mack," Jenn said quietly. "She deserves to know."

"Tell her what?" Mack wasn't keeping anything from her.

"That you love her."

Mack shook his head, but he was afraid Jenn was right. "Jenn."

"Mack. You let her go once. Are you going to do it again? Because she's going to leave without knowing. How can you do that?"

Easy. If she left without knowing how he felt about her, he didn't have to run the risk of having his heart punted back at him. Again. The first time had been hard enough. He wasn't going to risk it again.

So he said nothing and Jenn sighed. "Mack. Don't be stupid."

"I'm not," he said. "I'm smart enough to know how this ends."

"Do you?" Her voice was quiet. "How can you be sure, if you haven't asked her?"

I don't have to ask her. No, she'd left once. That was enough for him. If she wanted to stay, she would. She'd find a way. But he couldn't risk rejection anymore. This time would kill him for sure. He just shook his head.

She sighed but left it alone. For that he was grateful.

Darcy made it to the farm. It took a while, but she got there, snow and all. The main roads had been plowed but were still tricky. The lane to the farm had been plowed as well, but the packed snow was still slippery. Her SUV was designed for this. Probably why she'd bought it, even in Chicago where she relied mostly on mass transit—she'd gotten so used to vehicles with four-wheel drive that it hadn't occurred her not to purchase one for herself.

Ironic that back here was where she needed it the most.

She parked and hauled her bag out of the backseat. Joe had a checkup with the heart doctor today, so her aunt and uncle weren't there. Luckily, they didn't have to drive far for it. She was kind of relieved that she didn't have to come in with her bag after an overnight at Mack's.

But last night had been different.

She was trying not to dwell on it, but something had shifted. What that was, she couldn't quite pinpoint. She did know she needed to tell him what had really happened, and she needed to tell him tonight.

The nerves wouldn't quit.

The farm was open, even in the snow, and Mack was everywhere. Darcy was jumpy and distracted all evening. Marla kept giving her strange looks, but she managed to stave off any questions because they were so busy. She kept rehearsing what she wanted to say in her head. Running through it over and over.

It didn't help.

Finally, when it was all said and done, she went up to Mack, whom she'd been somewhat avoiding all evening, torn up by guilt and nerves. "Do you have time to talk?"

Clearly, he'd picked up on her tension, because he looked at her closely. "Darcy. Are you okay?"

She hesitated, then nodded. "But we need to talk," she repeated.

"All right. Can we go back to my place? I need to check on the dog." He was looking at her with concern.

It took about fifteen more minutes to close down, say good-night and get everyone out the door. Darcy's nerves had taken the form of huge angry butterflies in her stomach. She followed him to the clinic, where she stayed in her car, then to the house. By the time they got there, she was ready to explode. Was it the right thing? To tell him, after all these years? Did it matter anymore?

Yes. It did matter.

"What's going on?" His voice was quiet once they got in the house and the dogs were wagging around them. She saw the concern in his eyes, but he didn't reach for her. Clearly she was giving off stand-back vibes. "Darcy."

She took a deep breath and looked at him, at this man she loved so much. Always had and, she suspected, always would. "I wasn't ready to get married," she blurted. "I wasn't ready for any of it." She put her hands over her eyes. That was the easy part of the truth.

He moved closer but still didn't touch her. "What do you mean?"

It was so important she make him see. "You were so sure. *So sure*, Mack. Of yourself. Of us. Of everything. And I went along because I wanted to be sure, too."

"Why didn't you say anything?" He sounded shocked, as if it had never occurred to him. Maybe he hadn't noticed the change in their relationship after they'd gotten married. She'd tried so hard to hide it.

She laughed, but it was more of a sharp bark than a joyful sound. "I was pregnant, remember? We had to get married. I thought maybe some of your optimism would rub off on me, too."

He just looked at her, his face unreadable. She forged on. "And again, you are so damn sure you know what's best here, too. Buying the farm, making it into something you know I'd never want it to be."

She drew a shaky breath. “I loved you then, Mack. So much. But you didn’t feel the same, after all that sureness. You let me walk away.”

“Come with me.” He didn’t offer her a hand, but stalked off down the hall, and she followed after a moment. He went into the room that usually had the door shut. It had some boxes stacked up. Clearly, he used this one for storage. He opened the closet door and took out a couple of boxes labeled—

Oh, God.

Labeled *Baby.*

She wanted to back away, but couldn’t make herself move, much less look away. “Where have those been?”

“My mom held on to them.”

Of course she had. If she’d held on to the ornaments, she’d hold on to the baby stuff. Behind him, in the closet, she saw a long box. Her heart stopped. “Mack. What is that?”

He moved out of the way, his jaw set, his arms crossed over his chest. “Look. Look at all of it, Darcy.”

It was the crib. They’d bought it two days before the accident. Had never had the chance to open it, much less set it up. He didn’t move when she pressed her hand to her mouth and laid the other on the box. She couldn’t speak.

“Look in the others,” he said, his voice rough.

She did. She moved from the crib, her hands shaking so badly she almost couldn’t open the next box. But she managed and couldn’t stop the tears. More baby stuff. Things they’d picked out together. Blankets, onesies, the changing table. Crib bedding, printed with trains. Not to mention their wedding china and other assorted gifts that he’d never used. All of it, he’d held on to for all these years. She finally sank to the floor and sobbed. All of it, the pain, the regrets, the truth spilled free. And then Mack was behind her, pulling her in and she felt his own tears on her hair. She wrapped around him and burrowed in, the sobs shaking them both. He stroked her hair and finally her sobs reduced to hiccups.

He just rested his head on hers and held on. He didn't ask if she felt better, which was good because no, she didn't. She really, really didn't. She felt worse. She'd assumed he'd gotten rid of all this stuff. Let it all go, the pieces of their old life that never really got started. But here it was, their old life, real and tangible and oh-so-painful.

"Mack," she whispered finally, and he said, "What?"

She pulled away and looked at him. His eyes were red rimmed and her heart ached because she wasn't done delivering the blows. "I'm so sorry. For all of it. For causing the accident—"

"It was an accident, Darce. You didn't do anything."

She lifted her chin. It was time he knew. "I did. I turned left instead of right because I was delaying coming home." At his confused look she faltered, her stomach twisting in knots, then forced herself to continue. He deserved to know the truth. "I can't stress this enough. You were so sure, Mack. So sure of us, of the baby, of our future. Everything. But I wasn't. We got married because of the baby. And then it was gone and with it, the whole reason for our marriage."

He sat there, stunned, and stared at her tearstained face. "What do you mean, the whole reason for our marriage?"

"I wasn't ready to get married, much less be a parent. I thought maybe it'd get better. I knew I was going to have to figure out parenting. But the marriage…" She trailed off, looking lost.

"But the marriage, what?" His voice didn't sound like his own. It seemed to come from far away.

She swallowed hard. "I was going to see if we could separate."

Her words couldn't have hit him any harder if she'd shot him. He gaped at her. "Separate? You wanted to leave me? While you were pregnant?" What the hell was this? How had he missed it?

Her face was ghostly pale and her eyes were full of pain. And guilt. "Yes. I wasn't thinking straight and it was an impulsive decision. So I turned left and—" Her voice caught, and then she continued, "And the other car was there. I didn't see it because I was trying to make the light."

Which had been yellow and she'd broken no laws. The other car had run the light and hit her broadside. He wasn't fully tracking here. She'd wanted to leave him. That had been her plan all along.

Then it hit him. "You had no intention of ever staying," he said slowly. "Not then. Not now. All this was just for, what? Show? Pity?" Anger filled him, white hot, and that was better than the equally strong pain that was trying to push through.

She touched his leg and he pulled back. He couldn't have her touch him. She affected him in ways—still—that wouldn't help him get over her. "Mack. Please understand. We were so young and I was scared and confused." There was a plea in her voice. He couldn't understand.

He looked away. She couldn't have talked to him about it? Was he that awful? Had he been that bad a husband? He didn't remember their marriage being awful. Yeah, she'd been a little nervous, but weren't all new parents-to-be? Clearly, he hadn't known her as well as he'd thought.

"And now?" He waited for her answer, knowing he wouldn't like it.

There was a long pause and he heard her breathing, which seemed so loud in the quiet room, almost as loud as the blood rushing in his ears. "Now I know better," she said finally, her voice sad and low.

He couldn't move. She'd left him once, and it had nearly killed him. And here she was, leaving again, without giving their future any thought.

He hadn't learned. All these years, and he hadn't freaking *learned.*

After a moment, she stood up and left the room without a word. He was pretty sure there was nothing left to say. He heard the front door close shortly after that. It was pretty clear—she'd never felt for him what he had for her. He remembered his mother's words—she hadn't been ready. He'd waved her off, but it seemed she'd been right after all. Darcy would never be ready. Not for what he had to offer.

He got up off the floor and left the room and pulled the door shut, not bothering to close the boxes that were open and all over the floor. They didn't matter now. They were part of a life that hadn't ever really existed, apparently.

What a fool he'd been.

Chapter Seventeen

Mack moved through the next day in a fog. Jenn gave him worried looks, but didn't ask any questions. He didn't go out to the tree farm. He wasn't sure he had it in him to act as if everything was okay. So when his brother showed up to take him to grab a beer, he didn't have the energy to turn him down.

Chase booted up his laptop once they were seated. "Been making plans for the new sub. Want to see?"

He really didn't want to see it, or have anything to do with anything Darcy related right now. Mack stared at the screen when Chase turned it to face him. "This is Darcy's farm?"

"No," Chase said slowly. "Darcy left. This is Joe and Marla's farm. That they are going to sell to us after the holidays. Remember?" He looked at Mack. "Ah, shoot. You did it, didn't you?" He swore.

"Did what?" Mack asked, his gaze back on the computer screen. Chase had left a lot of trees and had carved out large home sites. It'd be gorgeous. Darcy would hate it. The thought gave him no pleasure.

"You fell in love with her."

His gaze flew to Chase's. Actually, it was more accurate to say he'd never stopped loving her. "She's out of here in a few days." She'd been crystal clear there was no hope of a future. She hadn't wanted one back then. She didn't want one now. Then again, he hadn't asked her, had he? He'd been more than happy to have her company, both in bed and out of it. He'd been afraid if he'd asked for more, she'd bolt.

Of course, as it turned out, she was going to bolt anyway, so it wasn't as if he'd saved himself any grief, now, had he?

"Clearly, that doesn't matter." Chase took the laptop back and closed it, slipping it into his bag. "I noticed you didn't deny it. So. What are you going to do now?"

"Nothing. Like I said, she's leaving." The words were bitter in his mouth. He took a deep draw of his beer to try to erase the picture of her tearstained face.

"You're a coward," Chase said flatly.

Mack's head snapped up and he barked out a laugh. "What? Why? You've been telling me all along to let her go. To not get involved." He could not win.

"And you did neither of those things," Chase pointed out. "You *can't* let her go and you *are* involved and not in the kind of way that will allow her to walk away from you without ripping out your heart. So." He leaned on the table, looked Mack in the eye and threw down the gauntlet. "I repeat. You're a coward. What the hell are you gonna do about it?"

Mack opened his mouth, then shut it again. "You're an ass. You know that, right?"

"Yeah, thanks. But it doesn't solve your problem."

Chase was right. Mack didn't really want to acknowledge it to his brother, much less himself. Still, denial hadn't served him so well. He let out a breath. "I'm not being a coward if I let her go. She wants to go. Why would I fight that?"

"But you want her to stay," Chase pointed out quietly. "And you're going to let her walk. That's gonna suck for you. So why not try? At this point, what do you have to lose?"

A lot, actually. If he took a stand and she left anyway, it'd be too damn hard. Chase was right. He wasn't willing to risk the pain. "She's going to leave anyway."

Chase shook his head. "How do you know? Have you given her a reason to stay? No," he answered himself. "You haven't. I don't get this. I understand not wanting to get hurt, because that sucks. But you've got a second chance with the woman you love and you are letting her go without a fight."

Mack hadn't been enough the first time around. Why would now be any different?

He rubbed his hand over his face. "I can't explain it, okay? She hasn't given me any hint she's willing to give it another shot."

"No? She's in your bed, am I right? You rearranged your whole schedule to be out at the farm more. She looks at you the same way you look at her, with that sappiness couples in love have. It's all there, Mack. If I can see it, you damn well should be able to." Chase leaned forward. "Go. Talk to her. Fix this, Mack. For both of your sakes."

Mack just stared at his brother. He wasn't sure what to say. Chase had been so adamant that he stay away from Darcy. Not that Chase had any control over Mack's life, but he knew how bad it had been for Mack in the aftermath and had been trying to keep that from happening again. "Why are you doing this?"

Chase rose from the table and picked up his laptop bag. He put money on the table to cover his bill. "Because you should be happy. Think about it," he said, and slapped Mack on the shoulder as he went past him.

Happy. Darcy had made him very happy, until she'd left him. But he hadn't made her happy. Was Chase right? He hadn't tried hard enough to see what she was feeling? She'd lost so much—they both had. He didn't even care if she was infertile. There were lots of ways to make a family. In retrospect he could see that he hadn't handled everything so well. All he'd wanted was for them to be happy. In trying to give her space, he'd pushed her away.

They'd both made mistakes. But the question was—was it too late to fix them?

Marla called up the stairs, "There's someone here to see you, Darcy."

Darcy frowned at the laundry she was folding. "Be right down," she called back. If it'd been Mack, Marla would have said so. But it wouldn't be him, not now. Not since she'd told him the ugly truth. She'd handled it poorly, to be sure. She'd run when she should have tried to make him see. The look on his face when he'd shut down—she shivered at the memory. He'd never looked at her like that. As if she were a stranger.

She came downstairs and stared at the man in the

kitchen. Chase. She hadn't been expecting to see him, either.

Marla folded the dish towel and hung it over the stove handle. "Nice to see you again, Chase." She gave Darcy's arm a little squeeze as she left the room.

"Um, hi," she managed. Chase had been decidedly unfriendly to her over the past weeks, clear in his anger over her treatment of Mack all those years ago. She'd never blamed him, had accepted it as her due. "Have a seat," she suggested, and started toward the table. Chase shook his head.

"No, thanks. This will only take a minute." He looked at her, and she could see his mistrust of her hadn't abated, but there was resignation in there, too.

"Okay," she said slowly, curiosity almost getting the better of her. But she waited for him to speak.

"Are you leaving?"

"Yes," she said slowly.

He nodded. "Mack is in love with you. Still. Hell, he'd kill me if he knew I was here. I don't know what you feel for him, if you ever loved him. You left him behind awfully easily."

"It wasn't easy," she shot back. It'd been so hard. So. Hard.

"You left him," Chase repeated. "Is this time going to be different?"

"What do you mean?" His words were starting to sink in. *Mack is in love with you.* Chase would probably know that. More than anyone else. He and Mack had always been close. Her heart gave a little flutter.

He looked her in the eye. "You know what I mean," he said quietly.

She lifted her chin. "That's my business."

"I disagree. It's Mack's, too. Fix this for both of you or he'll be the wreck he was when you left the first time."

"Wreck?" He hadn't tried to contact her after the divorce. They'd communicated only through lawyers. It had only served, at the time, to reinforce she'd done the right thing.

"Yes. A wreck. Now you're going to walk away. Again. And leave him to pick up all the pieces. Why?" He turned to go. "I'm not the one who needs the answer to that question. But if you love my brother, you'd better figure this out quick. I don't think you'll get a third chance."

She didn't want a third chance. She hadn't been sure she should have a second chance. She stood for a moment, heard the door close, then an engine start.

Chase was right. She had to do something, something to fix this.

She hurried out into the living room, where her aunt and uncle were watching a Christmas movie on TV and Marla was knitting. "I'm going into town."

Marla frowned in concern. "Now? It's so late."

"I know. It's important." More important than anything.

"All right," Marla said. "Are you going to see Mack?"

She didn't hesitate. "Yes. Yes, I am."

Her aunt and uncle exchanged smiles. "Good for you," Marla said at the same time Joe said, "'Bout time."

Darcy took the stairs two at a time, grabbing her purse and keys and running back down. She didn't know what kind of reception she'd get. Or if he'd even be home, actually.

She knew exactly what she was going to do. It was all so clear, and felt completely right.

* * *

She drove as fast as the conditions allowed, but once she got there and parked in front of the house, she sat for a moment. She'd been trying to rehearse what to say to him, but nothing really stuck. Now, in front of the house, seeing the dark shape of the tree they'd picked out and decorated, her heart squeezed.

She'd been so wrong. So afraid. And she'd taken it out on him.

She got out of her car and took a deep lungful of the cold, still air. All around were houses all decked out for the holidays—trees in windows, twinkle lights on trees and houses and bushes. But this one—this one was dark.

She walked up the drive to the front door and knocked.

After a moment the door opened. Mack stood there, silhouetted against the frame. She linked her fingers to keep them from shaking. "Can I come in?"

In answer, he stepped out of the way and she came in, closing the door behind her. He went and sat back on the couch, arms crossed. So he wasn't going to make this easy. That was okay. It shouldn't be easy.

She perched opposite him on a chair, her back to the tree and the window. She unzipped her coat but didn't take it off. He muted the TV and gave her his full attention, but she couldn't read his expression. She took a deep breath. "Mack. I'm so sorry. I really handled this wrong." It was an understatement and didn't really cover the depth of her feelings.

He leaned forward and rested his forearms on his knees. He was wearing gym shorts despite the cold temperature outside. "Me, too."

That stopped her in her tracks. She frowned. "You? How did you?"

"I didn't pay close enough attention, then or now. You weren't wrong. I was pretty sure of myself. Of us. Too sure." He gave her a pained grin. "I didn't mean to be overbearing, Darce. I just thought—I just thought it'd all kind of work out on its own."

That little flutter of hope grew into a flare. She took a chance and moved next to him on the couch. He didn't move away. "I should have talked to you, told you what I was feeling, instead of hiding it from you. And I should have come home long before now to apologize." Of all of it, that was what she regretted the most. She'd let so much go—not just Mack, but her friendships here in town, and let her aunt and uncle down, too. All because she'd been unable to face her feelings.

"Darce." There was a tenderness in his voice now that made her eyes burn. He ran his hand along her jaw and she turned her face into his palm. The heat of his touch made her want to burrow into him and never let go. Ever. "No apologies. We both screwed up. If I could go back, I'd ask you what was wrong and pester you until you told me. I won't make that mistake again."

She opened her eyes and looked at him, almost afraid to breathe. "What are you saying?"

"I love you. That's what I'm saying. I never stopped. I was going to ask you to stay, but I realized that's not fair. Jenn can run this practice with one hand tied behind her back. I can find a place in Chicago—"

"Wait." Her heart leaped with joy. In all that was one important point she needed to hear again. "You love me? Really?"

"Really." He pressed a kiss to her mouth.

"I love you, too," she whispered, and kissed him back, trying to pour all she felt into the kiss so he would know she'd never leave again. Just as his hands came up under her shirt, she eased back. "But. There's one thing you should know."

He eased back but kept his arms around her. "What's that?"

She took a deep breath. "I'm not leaving. I'm not going back to Chicago. Well, not for long anyway. I'm going to quit my job and move up here to run the tree farm."

Mack stared at her. "You what? You are?"

She nodded. "I haven't been happy there since I left here. Coming back here was coming home. You're here. My roots are here. And I want to make all that work." It had taken losing him—again—to make her see it and realize it.

He sat back. "Wow. Do your aunt and uncle know?"

She shook her head. "No. Not yet. I just decided. I know you guys wanted to buy it—"

"I think your aunt and uncle will be thrilled to sell it to you. I think that's part of why they wouldn't finalize the sale until after you left. They were hoping you'd take it over."

Sneaky of them, too. "I don't know how it all will work. You've got this adorable little house. I'd hate to move you out to the farm—I mean, if this is going anywhere..." She faltered. Was she getting ahead of herself? He pulled her in for another kiss.

"Oh, it's going, sweetheart. As soon as you're willing, I'm ready. I bought this house for us. Well, I found it and before I could tell you about it, the accident happened. But this is where I wanted to raise our son, and any brothers and sisters he might have had. After you left, I went ahead and finalized the sale and remodeled it. It's what saved my sanity."

Darcy stared at him, her jaw on the floor. She hadn't known he'd bought a house at that time. Or even that he'd been looking. She'd shut down at any mention of Mack and her aunt had eventually stopped bringing him up. It had been too hard.

"I— Wow. Mack. You bought this house for us?" Was that why it'd felt so homey to her? Tears gathered in her eyes, but this time they were happy tears. "Then, let's stay here."

"No rush to figure it out," he whispered against her neck. She laid a hand on his chest. He stopped and looked up at her, heat and exasperation in his gaze. "We're still talking?"

She had to laugh. "Yes. We are still talking. There's one more thing."

He sighed and trailed his hand up her side, over her breast, clearly with something else on his mind. "Okay. What's that?"

She hesitated. "I know you wanted more kids. And you know I most likely can't have them."

"Yeah."

"And?" She held her breath.

"And what?" He sat up and looked at her steadily. "There are lots of ways to make a family, Darce. We can adopt. Try fertility treatments if you want. Be foster parents. I'm open to anything."

The love she felt for him rose and nearly swamped her. She couldn't say anything, so she just nodded.

He kissed her again and pulled her in close. "Now are we done talking?" The words were a playful growl.

She laughed and wrapped her arms around his neck as he scooped her off the couch and started toward his bedroom. She pressed her face into his shoulder, closed her eyes and held on tight.

Oh, yes. She was definitely home.

* * * * *